Twin Soul Omnibus

Winner Twins
and
Todd McCaffrey

Books 11-15

OPHIDIAN'S TEARS Copyright © 2019 by Brianna Winner, Brittany Winner, and Todd J. McCaffrey. First Edition.

CLOUD WAR Copyright © 2019 by Brianna Winner, Brittany Winner, and Todd J. McCaffrey. First Edition.

STEEL WATERS Copyright © 2020 by Brianna Winner, Brittany Winner, and Todd J. McCaffrey. First Edition.

CURSED MAGE Copyright © 2020 by Brianna Winner, Brittany Winner, and Todd J. McCaffrey. First Edition.

WYVERN'S CREED Copyright © 2020 by Brianna Winner, Brittany Winner, and Todd J. McCaffrey. First Edition.

TWIN SOUL SERIES OMNIBUS 3: BOOKS 11-15 Copyright © 2020 by Brianna Winner, Brittany Winner, and Todd J. McCaffrey. First Edition.

All Rights Reserved. No parts of this publication may be reproduced, or stored in a retrieval system, transmitted in any form or by any means, electronic, mechanical, photocopying, recording or otherwise without prior written permission of the publisher.
Cover art by Jeff Winner

Books by The Winner Twins and Todd McCaffrey

Nonfiction:

The Write Path: World Building

Books by McCaffrey-Winner

Twin Soul Series:

TS1 - *Winter Wyvern*

TS2 - *Cloud Conqueror*

TS3 - *Frozen Sky*

TS4 - *Wyvern's Fate*

TS5 - *Wyvern's Wrath*

TS6 - *Ophidian's Oath*

TS7 - *Snow Serpent*

TS8 - *Iron Air*

TS9 - *Ophidian's Honor*

TS10 - *Healing Fire*

TS11 - *Ophidian's Tears*

TS12 - *Cloud War*

TS13 - *Steel Waters*

TS14 - *Cursed Mage*

TS15 - *Wyvern's Creed*

TS16 - *King's Challenge*

TS17 - *King's Conquest*

TS18 - *King's Treasure*

TS19 - *Wyvern Rider*

Books by The Winner Twins

Nonfiction:

The Write Path: Navigating Storytelling

Science Fiction:

The Strand Prophecy

Extinction's Embrace

PCT: Perfect Compatibility Test

Poetry Books by Brianna Winner

Millennial Madness

Books by Todd McCaffrey

Science fiction

Ellay

The Jupiter Game

The Steam Walker

Collections

The One Tree of Luna (And Other Stories)

Dragonriders of Pern® Series

Dragon's Kin

Dragon's Fire

Dragon Harper

Dragonsblood

Dragonheart

Dragongirl

Dragon's Time

Sky Dragons

Non-fiction

Dragonholder: The Life And Times of Anne McCaffrey

Dragonwriter: A tribute to Anne McCaffrey and Pern

Map

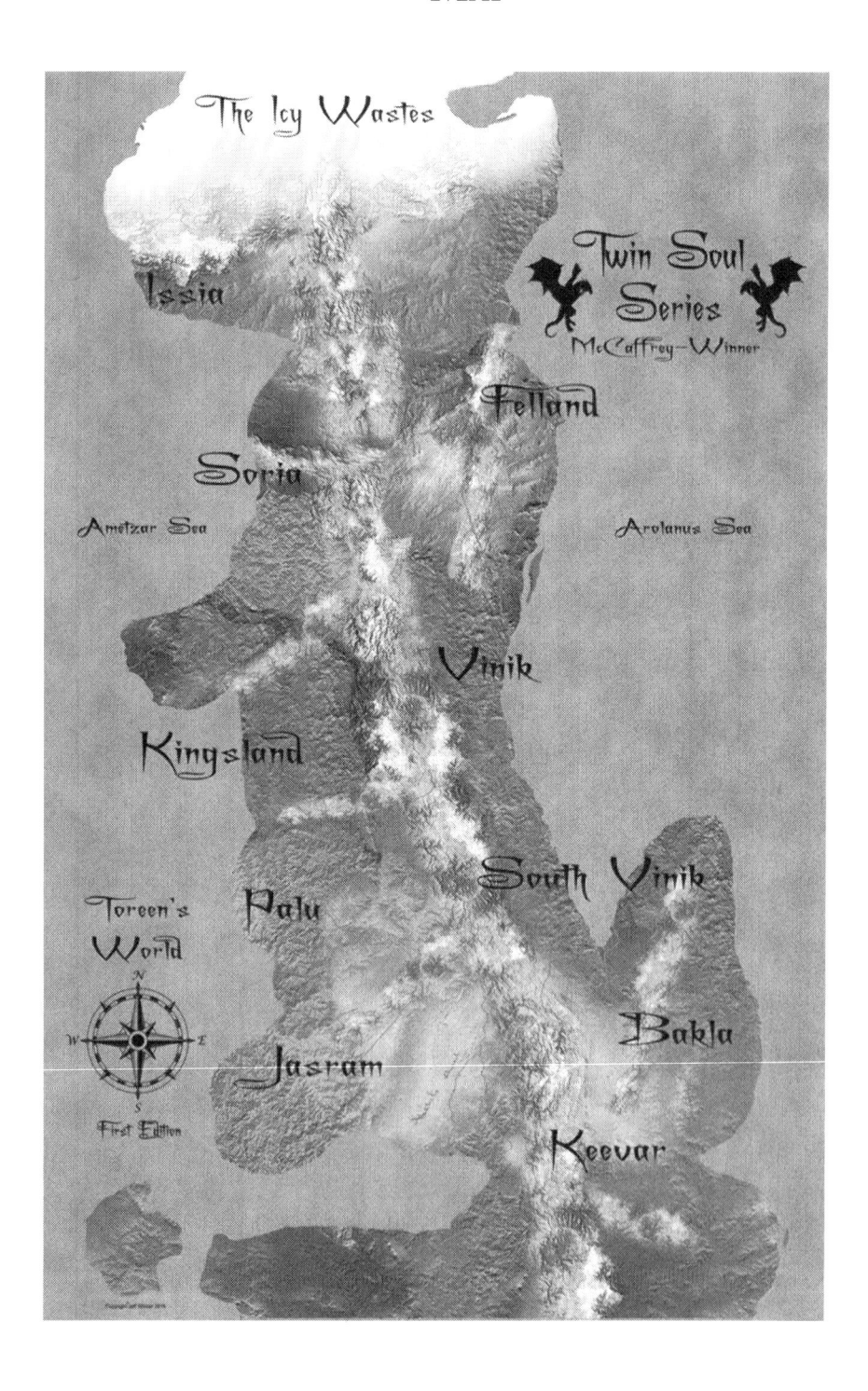

Contents

Twin Soul Series Omnibus 3   1

Map   6

Ophidian's Tears   9

Prolog   10
Chapter One   12
Chapter Two   20
Chapter Three   27
Chapter Four   37
Chapter Five   45

Cloud War   48

Chapter One   49
Chapter Two   54
Chapter Three   59
Chapter Four   64
Chapter Five   70
Chapter Six   77
Chapter Seven   84
Epilog   92

Steel Waters   93

Chapter One   94
Chapter Two   97
Chapter Three   105

Chapter Four	113
Chapter Five	119

Cursed Mage   129

Chapter One	130
Chapter Two	135
Chapter Three	139
Chapter Four	144
Chapter Five	150
Chapter Six	156
Chapter Seven	164
Chapter Eight	170
Chapter Nine	175

Wyvern's Creed   184

Chapter One	185
Chapter Two	195
Chapter Three	202
Chapter Four	209
Chapter Five	216
Chapter Six	222
Acknowledgements	227
About the Authors	228

Ophidian's Tears

Book 11

Twin Soul series

Prolog

"Mannevy, who *are* these people?" King Markel demanded testily as two ill-dressed dirty men who brought into his presence. It had been over a week since the last of the troops had been sent to their positions, waiting only on news from the north before starting their attack on the southern sea pass.

"Mage Tirpin and Captain Martel, at your service," the older of the two said immediately, bowing deeply.

"Nevins said you were dead," the king said, looking at them with renewed interest. "And what of your airship and your crew?"

"Destroyed, mostly dead," Mage Tirpin said sourly. "We came back to the capital to bring you the news."

"You're too late, I have it already," the king replied. He glanced at the captain. "I suppose you want an airship again, do you?"

"If it pleases your majesty," Captain Martel said with another bow.

"Your majesty," Mannevy said suavely, "I was wondering if perhaps we could use these gentlemen to dispatch an airship to join up with Colonel Walpish and his troops."

"Troops?" the king repeated, puzzled. He frowned. "Whatever for?"

"The airship could locate the cavalry, sire, and report to General Gergen, letting him know when to begin the assault," Mannevy suggested. The king's frown deepened. "We could send a messenger to the general by the train, telling him of this change of plans."

"An airship could cow the enemy's troops from the sky," Mage Tirpin added temptingly.

"Scare the piss out of them, I'm sure!" King Markel said, chuckling. He nodded firmly to Mannevy. "Do it. Give them something small —"

Mage Tirpin looked up in alarm.

"— small and fast," the king continued, waving a hand toward his first minister.

"We have a brig working up, sire," Mannevy said with a firm nod. He turned to Captain Martel, adding, "She's the *Wasp* and just awaiting the last of her crew."

"We'll take her," Mage Tirpin declared firmly, slapping a hand on his comrade's shoulder and jerking him toward the exit. He turned back to bow to the king, adding, "If it pleases you, sire."

"Yes, yes, get on it," king Markel said, waving them out. When they'd left, he turned to Mannevy. "First minister?"

"Sire?"

"Why is it you must always present me with unbathed subjects?" the king demanded. Before the minister could he reply, he continued, "From now on, have them washed."

"Of course, sire," Mannevy said.

"Bad enough to get bad news, worse to get news that *smells*," the king muttered, leaning back in his throne wearily.

"She's a fast ship, even without proper engines," Mage Tirpin allowed as *Wasp* returned from her maiden flight. Beside him, still stomping around with one leg in a cast, Captain Martel nodded in agreement.

"Yes, she is," Martel agreed, wincing in pain as he settled his injured leg. Sourly, he added, "She's a perfect first command for a *lieutenant.*"

"It *is* a step down from your previous command," Tirpin agreed diplomatically, "but it is at least not encumbered with the failings of that last command."

"And you'll be able to lift her?" Martel demanded. Mage Tirpin nodded readily. "Higher than a *fort?*"

"Of course," Tirpin replied. "I know what that fool, Borkin, did and I can better it."

Martel grunted sourly. Mage Tiripin, of vaunted ability, had had to stoop to vaguely questioning the *rejects* of Borkin's hastily-created school for shiplifters in order to learn the other man's spells.

"And I can get the *drop* on him whenever I want," Tirpin added with an evil grin.

This time, Martel's grunt was one of agreement. "The keel's ready."

"And won't they be surprised," Tirpin agreed. "They'll come back with their gold or their steel and we'll get the drop on them — and in the ruins we'll find proof for this king."

"Proof enough to get our reward," Martel agreed. Even a percentage of all the riches they suspected Nevins was planning to steal would make the two of them very wealthy. And, with Nevins and Borkin destroyed, they'd be the only two experts in airships — King Markel would have to deal with them alone.

"First, we should show 'King' Wendel the error of his ways," Tirpin said.

Captain Martel nodded firmly.

"So, we're ready to leave in the morning?" he asked.

"Yes, sir," Tirpin said. "Although I wish you had more crew."

"Or better," Martel agreed with a grimace. *Wasp* was small enough that, aside from idlers, she really needed no proper seamen… or *air*men if one insisted. It was just as well, *Wasp* was crewed by the worst of the Navy's castoffs, combined with a few grim-looking fellows who had escaped the hangman's noose to serve "at the king's pleasure." The ship had only four pop-gun four pounders — canons hardly worthy of the name. But the saw-cut metal band Martel had ordered bolted onto her keel made her a ship with very sharp teeth. Sharp teeth, indeed.

Chapter One

"He saved my life," Hamo Beck said, looking toward the crumpled mass that was all that remained of Ibb, the mechanical man. They were in the infirmary in the underground kingdom of the zwergs. Hamo lay in a cot, one of many that had filled the halls of the infirmary since the battle the day before. He glanced toward Rabel. "Can you save him?"

Rabel clenched his jaw and shook his head. "I don't know," he said. "I've never seen him damaged like this."

"It's my fault," Ellen said miserably.

"That he's *here*," Rabel corrected her forcefully. "That he's even got a chance."

"He is sturdier than you can imagine," Ophidian said from beside Jarin Reedis' bed. The twin soul dragon was in human form, resting soundly. He looked to Rabel. "What do you plan?"

"First, I'm going to get his caravan," Rabel said. "I'm sure I can find the workshop in it and maybe the library."

"Oh, I love libraries!" Ellen exclaimed. The others gave her a startled look. In a quieter voice, she explained, "My parents were teachers. I knew how to read by the time I was three."

"That's rare," Annabelle said, reaching forward and grabbing Ellen into her arms. After a startled squeak, Ellen let the witch hug her. "I learned about the same time, so I know what you mean."

"Is there something special with girls?" Ophidian asked the room.

"Doting fathers, mostly," Rabel said with a fond glance toward Ellen who had startled giggling when tickled by the older witch. "And the ability to sit still."

"For a good book?" Annabelle said. "Always."

"I read everything I could," Ellen said. "Until…"

"Until your parents died," Ophidian finished for her. She looked up at him and nodded.

"They caught the cold that never let go," Ellen said with a sniffle. "I got it but got better, after…"

"What happened?" Annabelle asked in a soft voice.

"I ran away," Ellen said in a voice barely a whisper. "We used to sleep together to keep warm." She took a long, slow breath and closed her eyes. "I couldn't wake them one morning. Not momma, nor poppa." She opened her eyes and glanced toward Rabel. "My father told me that I had to get away if anything happened to them. That otherwise I'd go to the poorhouse and wouldn't have a chance. So I ran."

"How old were you?"

"Five, nearly six," Ellen said. "I found my way into a gang and things were good until the watch went after us."

"What happened to the others?" Imay asked, her eyes wide with alarm.

"The boys went to the ships or the army," Ellen said. "And the girls…" her eyes grew dark "… some went to the Inn, others to the poorhouse."

There was an uncomfortable silence until Annabelle cleared her throat. She ran her fingers over Ellen's ribs, tickling her. "Well, you're here now —"

"And under *my* protection," Ophidian said firmly.

"What about the others?" Ellen said, pulling away from Annabelle and moving to stand in front of the dragon-god, her arms on her hips. "Why weren't they under your protection?"

Ophidian gave her a look of shame and sighed. "I cannot be everywhere," he told her. "I can only help those who ask for it —"

"And they wouldn't," Ellen said with a glum look, eyes downcast. "They didn't even know about you, only Ametza."

"They don't know about Geros or Granna?" Imay asked in astonishment. When no one answered, she persisted, "How could that be?"

"Ametza is a jealous god," Rabel said with a frown. "She doesn't like competition and deterred it in her kingdom."

"And now, she's trying to take over Soria, isn't she?" Annabelle guessed. Rabel gave her a surprised look. "That's why you're here, isn't it?"

"Is it?" Rabel asked, looking to Ophidian for an answer.

"Ametza has not always been this way," Ophidian replied evasively. "But she's got King Markel determined to make war." His lips turned down. "It's a habit some gods permit themselves."

"Back to the matter at hand," Rabel said firmly, turning to catch Ellen's eyes. "You melted Ibb, correct?"

"*Melted* him?" Annabelle repeated in astonishment.

"Only his back," Ellen said. "He was crushed under the stones of the fort, keeping it from killing the humans underneath him."

Annabelle pursed her lips, eyes wide with astonishment. "So you melted him so that…"

"The zwerg built a scaffolding to support the stone above him," Rabel explained. "Ellen melted him enough that they could pull him out."

Annabelle turned toward where the metal man lay in a cot. She knelt down and ran a hand over the deformed head, frowned at the crushed back of his shoulders and arms. She glanced up to Rabel, "And you can fix him?"

"I can try," Rabel said. "First, we need to get his caravan and find his library."

"His library tells us how to fix him?" Ellen asked hopefully.

"Some of how," Rabel said with a nervous glance toward Ophidian. Imay caught his nervous expression.

"My god Ophidian," she said with a bow, "you remember my oath?"

The dragon-god turned toward her, raised an eyebrow in surprise and, slowly, as enlightenment dawned, smiled. "Yes," he told her. He turned to Ibb. "Imay dragon-sworn promised to take care of Ibb, among others."

"Does her oath, then, extend to the rest of us?" Rabel asked hopefully.

"No," Ophidian said, shaking his head. "But I will allow any sworn to me to aid her in fulfilling her oath."

"Fair enough," Rabel agreed.

"So we must find the caravan," Imay said, grinning at Rabel, "and how do we do that?"

"We have to go back to the village of Korin's Pass," Rabel said. Imay's brows rose in surprise. "That's where we left it."

"To do that," Hamo Beck spoke up unexpectedly, "you'll need me."

"By now, the king's men have seized the village," Diam said, shaking her head. "They'll be looking for you, wanting to get your parole to bind the rest of the village to them."

"You're in no shape to move," Rabel said, gesturing for the man to stay in his cot. "You need to rest and recover." He saw the guard captain stir, preparing to speak and snapped, "You're no better."

"I could go," a small voice piped up from near the captain's cot. A small boy stood up from where he'd been crouching, holding his father's hand. "I know the village."

"You're going to stay here," Diam ordered. "Your father will want to see you when he wakes."

"What's your name, child?" Ophidian asked, moving gracefully toward the small human, who shrank back down beside his father's bed fearfully. Ophidian paused, then crouched down to get to the boy's level. "I'm Ophidian, god of changes, fire, and tricks."

"I am Myles Berold," the boy said.

"That's a good name," Ophidian agreed sagely.

"I don't know about changes or fire," Myles admitted.

"But I bet you're just full of tricks," Ophidian allowed.

The boy flushed started to shake his head and then, in shame, nodded slowly. "A few."

"Well, Myles Berold of few tricks," Ophidian said, "how about you stay here with your father? So when he wakes you can tell him that a god gave you orders."

"You did?" Myles asked in surprise. "I — I have to stay here?"

Ophidian leaned in close to the boy's ear and shook his head. He whispered, "No. It's a trick."

Myles' eyes popped wide open in surprise and he snorted in amusement. Ophidian nodded to him and took a step back, rising to his full height.

He turned to Rabel. "So who's going to the village?"

"Hamo Beck," Annabelle said, looking to the injured man, her lips quirking upwards, "in the spirit of Ophidian's trick, are you married?"

"Married?" Hamo repeated blankly. He shook his head. "No."

"So, how about I pretend to be your wife?" Annabelle asked, smirking.

"The village is too close-knit for that," Hamo said. "They'd be furious with me for marrying without inviting them to the wedding." His eyes lit as he continued, "But you *could* be my mistress."

"Maybe when you get better," Annabelle told him with a wink.

"Actually… that's not a bad idea," Granno said slowly. Annabelle shot him a dirty look. The older zwerg shrugged it off, continuing, "Particularly if you came back from the fort."

"I was looking for him?" Annabelle guessed. Granno nodded. "And didn't find him?"

"But how does that get us the wagon?" Rabel asked. He turned to Hamo. "You remember where you hid it, right?"

Hamo's face fell and the others groaned. "I put it someplace safe," he said slowly. "Someplace where no one could find it."

"It's still snowing," Rabel said, "if it's out in the weather, someone will notice."

"I put it someplace safe," Hamo repeated with renewed confidence. "I put it — I put it… someplace safe." He gave the others a hangdog look. "That's all I remember."

"Well, if you give us a list of places you usually put things, we'll look," Annabelle said firmly. She nodded to Rabel. "Get a bucketful of snow and start throwing snowballs inside wherever Hamo suggests."

"That will have to do," Rabel agreed.

"In which case, all three of us should go," Ellen said firmly. Rabel pursed his lips in thought, then nodded. He looked to Imay. "Can you keep an eye on them?" His wave included Reedis' form, Hamo Beck, the fort's captain, his son, and all the others still recovering from their burns.

"I will stay here, also," Ophidian declared. Rabel nodded but the dragon-god felt compelled to explain to the others, "In case Jarin or Reedis or Ibb have need of me."

"It shall be our honor to see to your friends," Diam said carefully. Beside her, Granno nodded in agreement and approval of her form.

"We should eat before we go," Rabel suggested.

"I'll have food brought to our council chamber," Diam said, waving them off. With a bow, Rabel left, followed by Annabelle who grabbed up Ellen and threw her over her shoulders. The little girl giggled with delight, playfully banging her fists against Annabelle's back.

#

"You were the one who made my demons, weren't you?" Ellen asked Annabelle while they were eating a quick lunch in the council chamber.

"The ones Captain Ford had me make?" Annabelle guessed. Ellen nodded. "That was you?" Ellen nodded again shyly pulling one of the blue-white demons out from her top. Annabelle spread out her hands and Ellen carefully slid the demon into them. Annabelle brought the demon up to her eyes and smiled at it before passing it back to the young girl. "You keep it, it has attached itself to you."

"I loaned the other two to Imay and Lissy," Ellen said with a worried frown.

"That was a great idea!" Annabelle's words wiped the girl's worry away. Her tone changed, as she continued, "Although, you know, I didn't really *make* the demons."

Ellen gave her a quizzical look.

"I summoned them and asked them to serve me," Annabelle said.

"I thought so," Rabel said. "Queen Diam and the zwerg were upset to find them in Ellen's care."

"Demons often work for the zwerg," Annabelle said. "In fact, these were a gift to me."

"A gift?" Ellen said.

Annabelle nodded. "I did something for the zwerg of the Shredded Hills and they introduced me to their demons."

"What, may I ask?" Rabel said. Annabelle gave him a look, so he expanded, "The zwerg don't give their treasures lightly."

"No, they don't," Annabelle agreed. Her expression grew pensive, distant. Finally, Ellen touched her arm. Annabelle looked down at her hand.

"You don't have to tell us," the little girl told her solemnly.

"Actually," Annabelle said in a small voice, raising her head to meet Rabel's eyes, and leaning back in her chair, "I think I do."

She took a breath and began, "I was in the South of Palu, near the border of Jasram at the edge of the Shredded Hills." She saw Ellen's glazed look and added, "Palu is the land below Kingsland and Jasram is the kingdom south of that." Ellen gave her a quick nod of understanding. Annabelle smiled at Ellen, a sour smile, a sad smile. "My mother was a witch."

"A witch?" Ellen said.

Annabelle nodded. "She made herbs and mixed roots to create healing brews and teas," Annabelle said. With a frown, she added, "I never knew her but I think she was self-taught." Annabelle's eyes glittered with unshed tears. "S-she laughed all the time and we'd cavort among the flowers —"

"What sort of flowers?" Ellen asked, glancing toward Rabel thoughtfully.

"All sorts," Annabelle said. "Yellow and white, mostly."

"Not wyvern flowers," Ellen remarked to Rabel. She smiled at Annabelle encouragingly.

Annabelle accepted the encouragement with a dip of her chin and then continued, "We lived at the edge of the hills, away from the village." She made a face. "I didn't see many other children growing up. The villagers would come sometimes to cut the trees for firewood." Her lips twisted. "I got the feeling that mother didn't like that but she didn't protest." She shrugged, dismissing some past concern. She took another breath to continue, "One day, the villagers came to us. We were out gathering berries and roots, so we found them waiting inside —" her expression twisted on that word "— for us." Annabelle put her hands on the long table and Ellen noticed that she was playing nervously with her fingers. Ellen reached over and put a hand over the older woman's. Annabelle smiled at her, took a breath and continued, "Th-they said that there was a sickness in the village. They said that children were ill, some had died already. They begged her to help. They say that they'd brought one of the sick children with them. That she was in my bed, and could my mother help them?"

"She was in your bed?" Rabel asked anxiously. Annabelle turned her head to him, almost as if she'd forgotten he was there, and nodded jerkily. Rabel tightened his lips in a frown, nodding for her to continue.

"If she was sick, why did they put her in your bed?" Ellen protested. "What if she left the illness in your sheets?"

"That's what they planned," Annabelle said bitterly. "They hoped to force my mother to find the cure by infecting me." Ellen gasped in outrage. Annabelle accepted the sympathy with a smile. "My mother told me to put the roots in our root cellar and to get back out to collecting berries. To the villagers, she explained that I was behind in my chores."

"She was lying," Ellen guessed. Annabelle's lips twisted upwards for a moment in agreement.

"I was little — younger than you —" Annabelle said, dipping her head toward Ellen "— but I knew that wasn't normal. I didn't argue — with my mother there was never any reason to argue with her, she was so sweet-natured. I did what she said, while listening as much as I could to what was happening in our home." She paused, pained by the past. "After a while they left. I ran back to the house but mother met me at the doorway and told me that I couldn't come in." Annabelle's hands rose from under Ellen's and she spread them helplessly. "I cried and cried and told her that I would be good but she was steadfast. She told me that I could camp in the trees where we'd built our fort." Annabelle's lips twisted again, sadly. "After a while, I gave in. She didn't touch me but she led me where she meant and showed me.

"We'd climbed those trees before and there many broad branches. We'd started to make a fort the year before and even had some old blankets stored against the tree. Mother pretended that I was a great adventurer, traveling to distant lands." Her lips twisted upwards as she added, "She told me, 'Why you might even go to Soria someday!'"

"What happened?" Ellen asked, darting a glance toward Rabel who seemed way ahead of her. "The plague in the village?"

Annabelle nodded, her eyes forlorn. "Mother had caught it, of course. That's why she sent me away. For a week I lived up in the tree, coming down with the dawn to be met by my mother. Every day she grew weaker and weaker. Then, one night, after dark, I was woken by a commotion.

"The villagers had come," Annabelle said after a heavy pause. "They came with torches. My mother met them, I could hear her voice. But the villagers said that it was her fault the children and the women were dying. That she was a witch and that her child — me — was a witch and they were going to cleanse the valley."

"Mother pleaded with them, begged them, cried to them," Annabelle's voice grew raw with emotion. She shook her head. "They didn't listen to her. Wh-when they killed her —" her voice broke and Ellen jumped out of her chair, rushing over to hug the older woman tightly around her neck and muttering soothing noises. Annabelle gestured feebly at Ellen's arms, nodded in gratitude, and pushed the little girl back into her chair. "I'm better now," she said to Ellen. She turned to Rabel, unwilling to meet the little girl's watery eyes. Annabelle calmed herself and continued in a cold, hard, dispassionate voice that had had all emotion ruthlessly forced out of it, "When they killed her, they tore up the rest of our house, looking for me." Annabelle shuddered. "I remember shivering up in the tree, squeezing tight against the trunk as their torches passed nearby. Finally someone decided to torch our house and they went searching again, with the extra light. They never thought to look up, so they never found me." Annabelle shuddered again and Ellen put a hand on her shoulder soothingly. Annabelle turned toward it and smiled at Ellen. "The ashes and the smoke kept me up all night. But the villagers were gone. I went back to the embers but there was nothing. Only ash and… bones."

"Oh, Annabelle!" Ellen cried, unable to control herself, leaping out of her chair again and wrapping the seated woman in her arms. "I'm so sorry!"

Annabelle patted her feebly and the two cried together for some moments before Annabelle leaned back enough to wipe the tears from her eyes.

"Thank you," Annabelle said to Ellen. Gently, she pushed Ellen back to her chair. "After that, I wandered back to the hills, away from the village." Her lips twisted viciously. "I didn't want to see people. Ever again.

"I ate the berries that I knew were safe, and there were some leaves that could be chewed to make a tea in my mouth," Annabelle said. "But I was growing weaker and weaker each day." She glanced toward Ellen. "I was dying. I knew it and I didn't care."

"What happened?" Ellen asked.

"I fell asleep in a cave one night because I'd spotted someone riding in the distance," Annabelle said. "I was afraid it was the villagers." Her lips twisted again. "I was too young to realize that they were unlikely to be still searching for me."

She continued, "But I woke the next morning shivering. I realized that I was going to die and I almost welcomed it. But then I heard a noise. It was a girl, crying."

Ellen's gasp of surprise caused Annabelle to nod her head.

"At first I thought it was just echoes from my crying," Annabelle said. "But then I got to listening and realized that it was not. The sound was coming from deeper in the cave —"

"You found a zwerg girl!" Ellen burst out. "And she was crying because —"

"Because she had a broken leg," Annabelle said. "She was afraid of me and wouldn't talk at first. But I knew enough about splints — it was the sort of thing mother would quiz me on when we were walking — that I got some branches and used some of her dress and some of my top to bind the pieces around her leg.

"'We've got to get you back to your people,' I told her because I could tell that she wasn't human — she was smaller than me but older and she didn't look a thing like the villagers.

"Her name was Alva," Annabelle said. Rabel gasped in surprise and Annabelle nodded toward him. "You've heard of her."

"I've *met* her," Rabel said. "We've had dealings in the past."

"Of course," Annabelle said, her expression clearing. "She became queen —"

"She became queen when their new chambers collapsed," Rabel interjected with a dark look in his eyes. "The chambers trapped half their people, her father, and all their gold."

"Yes," Annabelle said in a small voice. "King Alanior took me in and raised me as his own daughter."

"You lived with the zwerg?" Ellen asked.

"For seven years," Annabelle said. "Until the day when they agreed that they had to mine the collapse to get the gold. The day Alva became queen."

"What happened then?" Ellen asked.

Annabelle dipped her head for a moment and looked up again with a more devilish expression. "Then I figured out how to steal five ships full of gold and replenish their treasury."

"Five ships?" Ellen squeaked in awe.

Annabelle nodded firmly. "Five."

"I heard about that," Rabel said. "That was some years back. Captain Ford and his men were livid."

"They cursed the gold," Annabelle said by way of agreement. "I got it to my people —"

"To the zwerg of Shredded Hills?" Ellen asked. Annabelle nodded.

"I got it to them and Alva cried with joy," Annabelle's lips twisted in memory. "They were going to work themselves to death trying to shift all the fallen rock." She bit her lip. "They would have died trying to free that gold."

"They would have died without it," Rabel said quietly. Annabelle shot him a sharp look but Rabel waved it aside with one hand. With the same hand, he gestured for her to continue.

"The curse struck," Annabelle said. Again, her lips twisted, this time into something resembling a smile. "Or maybe I was in love?"

"With Captain Ford?" Ellen asked breathlessly. When Annabelle's eyes answered her, she continued, "So what happened?"

"It took awhile to find him," Annabelle said with a sorrowful look. "And he was not happy to see me." Her gaze fell toward her lap. "And then we went after the serpent and… he died."

"I'm sorry," Rabel said. Annabelle looked up, meeting his eyes. "Captain Ford was always a… troubled soul but I'm glad to hear that he had your heart."

Annabelle sniffed and wiped her nose with her sleeve.

"We should go find Ibb," Ellen said into the silence.

"Ibb was how I got the gold," Annabelle said. She met Rabel's surprised look with a smile, "That's what I wanted to tell you." She continued, "He helped me when I needed it most, so I will help him."

"Very good," Rabel said, rising from his chair. "I think soonest would be best."

Annabelle nodded but held out her hands, urging him to wait. Rabel raised an eyebrow in surprise. He said, "What?"

"I once met Ibb in the rainy season," Annabelle said slowly. Rabel motioned for her to continue. "He was out in the rain. I worried that he'd rust —"

"He doesn't rust," Rabel assured her quickly.

"So I learned," Annabelle said. "But it was violent storm. There was lightning —"

"It struck Ibb," Rabel cut across her, his voice growing warm with memory. "And his body absorbed it."

"It was like he was feeding on the lightning," Annabelle agreed in a voice full of wonder.

"I think he was," Rabel said. He met her eyes and nodded. "I think that lightning is one of the ways that Ibb feeds himself."

"I just wanted to say it," Annabelle said, "because maybe the lightning will help revive him."

"I'm sure it will help," Rabel said.

"But it's winter!" Ellen protested. The others looked at her. "It doesn't lightning in winter, does it?"

"Ah," Rabel said with a gleam in his eyes, "it does if you can get a *god* to help!" He rose and gestured for the others to follow him. "First, we have to find Ibb's caravan."

As the other two moved to follow him, Ellen snuck her hand into Annabelle's and squeezed the outside with her fingers. Annabelle squeezed back.

Chapter Two

"So, tell me again, how high are the mountains?" Mage Tirpin asked Captain Martel nervously as the airship *Wasp* neared the growing darkness that marked the line of the Silver Earth mountains which separated Kingsland from Soria.

"No more than four thousand feet," Martel said, lowering his telescope and turning to stare at the mage. "You can handle that, can't you?" Before the mage could reply, Martel waved a hand toward the nervous apprentices just out of earshot. "Or perhaps of these gentle folk, trained by Mage Borkin, could oblige?"

Tirpin drew himself up to his full height in suppressed rage. "No one can manage four thousand feet!" He waved a hand dismissively toward the apprentices. "*They* barely got *Wasp* into the air."

"I recall," Captain Martel said drolly. He waited a moment before continuing, "But four thousand feet is the highest the mountains go and that happens nearer where they join Cuiyivals." Tirpin grunted. "We should be able to find a pass at two thousand feet."

"I shall have no trouble getting us to that height," Mage Tirpin allowed, "if you can guarantee that we'll need to go no higher."

"I can't guarantee that," Martel snapped. "No one's ever flown an airship over mountains before, as you might know, mage."

"I suspect Ford and his man might have done it," Tirpin said academically.

"No one that we *know* of," Martel amended sourly.

Tirpin shrugged in agreement. "And once we're through the mountains?"

"We turn west, find the cavalry and guide them onto the enemy's rear," Captain Martel replied.

"And after that?" Tirpin asked. Captain Martel smiled at him evilly.

#

"And one *other* advantage of an airship," Captain Nevins observed happily to mage Borkis, "is that we can use it to provide us with a great deal of illumination at night."

Borkis pursed his lips in a frown. "I'm afraid we owe that more to mage Bromley than to our airship, sir."

"Be that as it may," Nevins returned with a dismissive wave of his hand, "our friends on *Pace* are doing splendid work even in the middle of the night."

Indeed, the small crew of the second airship had already extracted two of the twelve long slabs of dragon steel from the ruins of the Sorian fort and were on schedule to have the rest removed by morning.

"I'm worried that they might be too heavy to lift, when all that steel is aboard," mage Borkis said nervously.

"I'm sure your apprentices will manage," Nevins said negligently. Honestly, he cared not one *jot* if the king got his steel. He gestured toward the other groups of men wandering on the ground. "What matters more is our business."

"We were lucky in finding those survivors, sir," Borkis added sagaciously.

"Luck had nothing to do with it!" Nevins snorted. "We were *looking*, Borkis, because I expected to find them."

"And… what they said?"

"Said?"

"About the dragon, sir," Borkis finished nervously.

"Do you see a dragon?" Nevins said, waving his hand at the gloom below them. "I'm sure it has long since departed with whatever gold it managed to collect."

"But if it took the gold —"

"Borkis, my man!" Nevins said chidingly. "Whatever makes you think that a dragon could carry all the zwerg's gold?"

Borkis frowned. "I suppose that's so…"

"We'll know soon enough," Nevins said, waving his hand back to the search parties beneath them. "Especially if your mages —"

"Apprentices, sir," Borkis corrected with a sniff.

"Mages if they manage," Nevins said. "Anyway, the honor will be short-lived." He lowered his head toward the mage. "You *have* been feeding them, haven't you?"

"Of course," Borkis said. "But only the ones on our ship." He added hastily, "As you ordered, sir."

"Good," Nevins said with a quick jerky nod.

#

"The hoists are all manned, we're ready to lift the third one aboard, sir," first mate Evans said to Captain Walters with a smart salute.

"Good," Walters said, turning toward the stern of his airship and raising his telescope toward *Harbinger* behind him.

"Sir?" Evans asked, moving to the captain's side.

"I was just wondering what Captain Nevins was up to," Pace told him. "He was quite upset when I suggested he add his work parties to ours."

"Didn't he say he had his men searching, sir?" Jeremiah Evans asked his captain. He pursed his lips, adding wisely, "I'm sure he knows what he's about. He was in the battle with that fort."

"And there *are* those strange excavations…" Walters said in agreement. He turned to face Evans directly. "Do you suppose it's true? That are cave-dwellers nearby?"

"You mean the zwerg, sir?" Evans asked. When Walters nodded, he continued, "I wouldn't rightly call them cave-dwellers from all I've heard, sir. Rumors are that they build whole underground cities —"

Walters cut him off with a derisive snort. "Tales to frighten children! Old wives with nothing better to do, stories to convince men to dig up the ground in search of piles of gold!" He waved a hand in irritation. "Nothing an educated man should consider."

"Aye sir," Evans said diplomatically. He waved a hand at *Harbinger*. "Still, it's a shame they won't let us borrow some of their men."

"Honestly, Evans, I think their men are worse than ours," Captain Walters confessed in a low voice to his first mate. Walters drew a scented handkerchief to his nose, adding, "Honestly, Evans, I think some of them have *never* bathed!"

A shout from one of the search parties distracted him and he lifted his telescope, searching in that direction. "Hmm, well it seems they've found something. Or someone."

#

"How is he?" Rabel asked as he entered the infirmary, nodding toward Jarin Reedis in his cot.

"He has not stirred," healer Molle said as she moved up along the line of beds. From the other side of the infirmary quick steps alerted them to the presence of queen Diam and princess Imay. The heavier steps of Granno followed behind them.

"Ophidian has healed all those he could," Diam said.

"And Hamo? Has he recalled anything more?" Annabelle asked with a polite curtsy.

"No," Diam said. She pulled a piece of paper from her waist. "He has recalled all his possessions, lands, houses, and warehouses that he has."

Rabel took the paper and examined it quickly. "He has stables, too?"

Diam nodded, pointing toward the bottom of the paper. "There," she said. "Although that would seem too obvious."

"Only to those who know to look for an invisible wagon," Annabelle said. She made a face. "I hope he knew enough to hide the tracks."

Ellen moved away from the others to stand by the battered form of the metal man. She raised her hand and stroked the metal skin softly, looking up to the mechanical's face. With a gasp, she turned back to the others, "We'd better hurry."

Rabel raised an eyebrow in question.

"His eyes," she said, pointing. "They're getting dimmer."

"Let's go then," Rabel said, turning decisively and waving the others after him. He paused long enough to look back at Imay invitingly. "Would you like to learn the mysteries of the mechanicals, princess?"

"Could I?" Imay asked.

"Yes," Rabel said, turning back and adding over his shoulder, "You've taken Ophidian's Oath, after all."

#

They took a cart from the infirmary to the northwest gate, the same one they had first entered so many weeks before. Imay was careful to identify all of them to the guards on duty and warned them to pass the information on to their reliefs.

"I'm not sure we'll be able to get the caravan through this gate," Ellen said as they entered the anteroom before the final door. She spread her arms. "I think Ibb's vehicle is too long."

"We'll get Ibb to it," Rabel promised. Adding, "Once we find the caravan, we'll bring it somewhere nearby."

Outside, Ellen gasped as the cold winter air hit them. "It wasn't this cold down by the fort!"

"That's because the mountains are holding winter at bay for a while," Rabel said. He pursed his lips. "I imagine they'll start seeing the next snows down there any day now."

"But it was snowing in Kingsland when we left!" Ellen protested.

Rabel smiled at her. "That was early snow," he said. "It came, it went and now it's probably come back again with a proper winter."

"Oh," Ellen said.

"We don't worry much about the weather," Imay said primly. "Being underground most of the time."

"Of course," Ellen said. She jerked a thumb toward Annabelle. "Annabelle knows all about that."

"She does?" Imay said, her eyes cutting toward the older woman. "How?"

"She lived with the zwerg when she was a child," Ellen said in a babble. "When their cave collapsed she left them and stole five ships full of gold to repay their kindness."

Imay gasped, eyes going wide. "You're Annabelle Alva?"

"Alva?" Annabelle repeated, brows furrowing. "No, I —"

"Queen Alva named you so," Imay interrupted. She nodded her head toward Annabelle. "She made you Duchess, in her kingdom. Duchess Alva, inheriting her own dukedom."

"What?" Annabelle said, flustered. "She's still alive, isn't she?"

"Very much so," Imay assured her quickly. A thought crossed her face and she patted her dress, drawing out her blue-light demon. "This is yours?"

"Yes," Annabelle said, nodding slowly. "Duchess?"

Imay laughed. "She has more lands, she ceded them to you. I'm surprised you didn't know, my lady."

Annabelle let out a peal of laughter. "Duchess? I'm a duchess?" Imay nodded solemnly. Annabelle turned to Ellen. "I'm royalty!"

"I like you all the same," Ellen said, grabbing Annabelle's hand.

"We need to move more quietly," Rabel told the group reprovingly.

"Duchess," Annabelle whispered to herself in wonder.

Ahead of them stretched the cold, darkening night and snow-covered ground.

#

"We've found something, sir," a grizzled seaman reported to Nevins by knuckling his forehead in salute. Nevins met him at the bottom of the ladder that descended from the side of *Harbinger* and ended a few feet before the ground, billowing slightly in the evening breeze.

"And?" Nevins demanded.

"It looks like a cave-in," another man reported. Nevins shot him a look. He was one of the miners that Nevins had signed aboard. "Like it was done on purpose, sir."

"Where does it lead?" Nevins asked. The man gave him a questioning look and Nevins suppressed a groan. "Toward the fort or away?"

"Away, sir," the man said. He worked his lips, then added, "And it looks new-built, too."

"Newly built?"

"In the last month or so, maybe less," the miner allowed.

"Can you follow it?"

"Probably best to dig it out," the miner suggested.

"How about if we blast it out instead?" Nevins said, pointing back up toward the ship loaded with gunpowder. Nevins wondered idly if the mage who was so good with light might also be able to create a better explosion, as well.

"Might work," the miner allowed.

Nevins nodded and jerked a thumb toward the sailor. "Climb back up. Have the first mate send down two barrels of gunpowder."

"Two barrels, sir?" the miner asked with a gulp.

"Not enough?" Nevins asked mildly.

"No, sir!" the miner responded quickly. "Not at all!"

#

"Your majesty!" a guard called anxiously as he rushed into the infirmary, clutching a stitch in his side. "There are humans working at the fort!"

"Taking the steel, no doubt," Diam said soothingly. She identified the guard as Xinian and gave him an appreciative nod and added, "We expected as much."

"There are others, too," Xinian continued anxiously. Granno moved closer to the queen, listening attentively with a worried expression on his face.

"Others?" Diam asked. "And what are they doing?"

"They're probing our cave-in," Xinian said. "We can hear picks and axes, so we think they've got human miners with them."

"That's trouble," Granno swore sourly. He shot a troubled look toward his queen. "Should I alert the guard?"

Diam made a face, raising her hand to gesture toward the long rows of injured men. She stopped mid-gesture, a smile growing on her lips as she spied one particular person.

"Jarin?" she said, moving toward the sleeping figure. "Would you feel like stretching your wings?"

#

Jenthen Barros made sure to sit with the fire to his back, scanning the horizon carefully with his magically enhanced sight. Dusk and dawn were the worst times to see anything, he knew.

Up here on his mountain, the snow fell steadily but he paid it no mind. In another ten minutes, he'd finish his scan and turn back to the fire and the stew heating in a pot above it.

There! Something was different. He raised the magical telescope to his eye and peered through it. Shapes moving in the snow. Heading north but coming from close to the mountains. No danger yet.

They were heading for the village, Korin's Pass, that much was obvious. What he couldn't figure was where they had come from? He rose from his cross-leg crouch and moved to the edge of the mountain, peering down as far as he could with his telescope. Nothing.

The people — seemed like two adults and two children — had come from nowhere. And that meant magic.

Jenthen Barros made a note of their path and moved back to his camp. He smiled. He would need his bow soon.

#

"I'm impressed, I must say so myself," mage Tirpin preened as he peered down at the mountain beneath them. "Easily three thousand feet, perhaps more."

"Yes," Captain Martel agreed. "You did well." He did not look at the two exhausted apprentices who lay near the warmth of the boiler nearby. He had had more than enough time to come to an understanding of how Tirpin thought and what he thought of — himself. He nodded toward the hatchway leading below. "Get some rest," he told the mage. "Tomorrow we'll find the cavalry and lead them to victory."

"Good," Tirpin agreed, stretching to relieve his muscles before turning away from the captain and heading to his cabin. He did not, captain Martel noted with a grimace, bother to salute.

When the mage was gone, Martel moved to the exhausted apprentices, gesturing for his first officer to attend him.

"Have the cook bring them something hot and then let's get them below," Martel said. He looked at the glow of the fire feeding the boiler. "And have someone relieve the stokers and engineer. We'll want them fresh in the morning."

"Should we stoke the fires, sir?"

"No," Martel said after a moment's thought. "We'll continue at one third power until dawn." He turned to the helmsman. "Note it in the log, if you please."

"Aye sir," the voice of the helmsman replied from the darkness near the stern.

"And double the watch on top," Martel said with a thoughtful frown. "We must keep vigilance."

"Aye, sir."

#

"Sir, the second division reports all accounted for!"

General Gergen looked up at the officer standing at the entrance to his tent and returned the crisp salute. He beckoned the officer to enter. "Well done, Ivar, this calls for a toat!"

General Ivar Gideon, the commander of Kingsland's second division nodded and entered, noting in passing that General Ambrose, the third division's commander, was already present. So was the wizened old mage who sat wearily in a chair near the folding table that held the army's disposition map.

Margen, that was the man's name, Gideon recalled. *He looks like one good breeze would carry him away!*

"You're on the left flank, what's the situation there?" Margen asked the general in a high, peevish voice.

General Gideon cut a questioning look toward his commander. General Gergen's lips twitched but he waved a hand toward the mage, indicating that he should answer.

"I'm a bit concerned about the marshes on our left flank," Gideon admitted, "but aside from that, I think we'll have no trouble."

Margen snorted. "If you stick to the plan, my mages will protect you."

Mages? General Gideon thought with a mental sniff. Two of them seemed older and feebler than Margen himself while the other two still had pimples and voices that cracked when excited. He did not like the notion of trusting his 'protection' to such a feeble force.

"Let's go over the plan, shall we?" General Gergen said affably, motioning the others to the table.

"We can do nothing until we know where your cavalry is," Margen croaked.

"I know," Gergen said, reaching to the table to pick up a folded piece of paper. "My latest news from the king is that he has sent the airship *Wasp* over the mountains —"

"Over the mountains?" Margen interrupted. The others looked at him and he returned their gaze with widening eyes, surprised to be the center of attention. "It's just that — well, these *airlifters* — they're not proper mages, after all." Three pairs of confused eyes met his declaration. "I mean, how can we know they can lift a ship *that* high? What is the point of sending the ship out if it can't do the job?"

"I'm sure that his majesty would have thought of that, mage," General Gergen replied frostily. He waved the dispatch again, adding, "Our orders are clear: we're to wait until we get a signal from either the cavalry — that would be that yellow fire signal you gave them, mage — or we spy the airship coming toward the town."

"And then the enemy will wet their pants in surprise!" General Ambrose chortled happily.

"Or, at least, attempt to retreat," General Gergen allowed mildly.

"Sir, what if they decide to accept a siege?" General Gideon asked.

General Gergen smiled and nodded toward mage Margen. "In that case, our mage will discourage them of that notion."

"Their walls will not resist my magic, you can be certain," Margen said raspily.

"In the meantime," General Gergen said, "we should ensure that our troops are alert but rested." He allowed himself a small smile. "Afterwards, we shall enjoy the destruction of the Sorian army."

"And after, sir?" General Gideon asked.

"With no army, their king will either surrender when we send our demands or we'll send the cavalry up to the capital and he can surrender there," General Gergen assured him.

Chapter Three

"The door's locked!" Annabelle said when they reached the entrance to Hamo Beck's mayoral office.

"Please, let me," Rabel said, motioning her aside and kneeling before the locked door. He turned back to Ellen, saying, "Watch carefully."

He produced two thin, sturdy lengths of steel and put them into the lock. He carefully twisted them until there was a *click* and the door opened.

"Ibb's caravan can't be here, surely," Annabelle protested as the four of them snuck quickly inside. She turned and closed the door as a precaution although, with the evening and the snow, she very much doubted that anyone would notice them. And, if they did, she would merely tell them the tale of her searching for Hamo.

"I'm pretty certain it's not," Rabel agreed, moving toward the door to the Hamo's office. The door wasn't locked and he opened it, saying over his shoulder, "But the keys to all his other places are probably here."

Ellen, unbidden, brought a spot of light from the tip of her finger and, skirting past Rabel, prowled around the office. Imay, not to be outdone, burst a flame from the end of her finger only to gasp in alarm at its brightness. Ellen turned and smiled. "It's okay," she said, "it takes a while to learn to make small flames."

"It's different from pulling burns out of people," Imay confessed, trying again and coming much closer to matching Ellen's small point of light.

"You can pull burns from people?" Annabelle asked, looking first to Ellen, then Imay, and finally Rabel for confirmation.

"It's one of Ophidian's gifts," Rabel said. "As a smith, I found it quite useful on a number of occasions."

Annabelle nodded in appreciation, then said, "I usually use a salve, myself."

"This is better," Imay said. She gave Annabelle a nervous look as she added, "I pulled the burns out of many of my people, some had burns all over their bodies."

Rabel, meanwhile had moved around to the far side of Hamo's desk and sat in the plush chair, frowning as he examined the drawer under the wide desktop. "Ellen, Imay, could you bring your light here, please?"

The two moved, one on either side of him. Frowning, Rabel knelt down to examine the drawer more carefully. After a moment he sighed. "This is spelled."

Annabelle moved to join them, brows furrowed. "What does it do?"

"I don't know," Rabel said. "But if I were a cautious person, I'd set a spell that would either make it impossible to open this drawer or would set the contents on fire if it were opened."

"That's not good," Annabelle said. "But would Hamo really put his keys in his drawer?" She moved back to the door and pushed it closed. Frowning, she gestured, saying, "Ellen, would you come here?"

With a nod of permission from Rabel, the young girl complied. She stood behind Annabelle and raised her finger up to illuminate the backside of the door.

"Move your finger a bit," Annabelle said, moving closer to the door and peering at it closely. Ellen moved her finger. "Stop, keep it there." With one hand, Annabelle moved toward the door and stopped when her hand hit something invisible, which tinkled. With a smile, she snatched at the invisible bulk and pulled it down. She turned with a triumphant look back Rabel. "I believe I've found your keys."

"That must be Ibb's work," Rabel said, moving to the door and eyeing the ring of keys in Annabelle's hand.

"He's good at making things invisible," Ellen explained to Imay.

Rabel motioned for Annabelle to give him the large ring of keys. He frowned at it. "This is going to make things more difficult."

"I'll say," Annabelle chimed in. "There must be twenty keys there. We'll be looking all night, just to find the right key to fit in the first door we find."

"We could just pick the lock," Ellen suggested.

"Actually, I think not," Imay said. The others looked at her in question. "Well, these keys were hidden, protected. What's to say that all other places aren't protected, like the drawer? And if we don't open them right, what happens to what's inside?"

"But we opened the front door!" Ellen protested. "There was no alarm."

"Actually," Rabel said with a grimace, "there quite well may have been."

"What?" Ellen demanded. "We got in, didn't we?"

"But maybe if we'd used the right key, *these* keys wouldn't have been hidden," Rabel said, jangling the ring of keys in his hand. Ellen accepted that with a thoughtful nod. "I think our best chance is the stables," he said at last, raising the keys. "I wouldn't be at all surprised if Hamo has a special key for some of his stalls, so he could have easily hidden the caravan in plain sight."

"Well, except that no one can see it," Ellen reminded him primly.

"And there's probably an invisibility spell on whatever the door contains," Rabel added in half-agreement. "But it's one thing to find a locked door. It's quite another to bump into something that you can't see." He nodded firmly. "We'll try the stables first."

"And after?" Annabelle prompted.

"If it's not there, we'll consider our options," Rabel told her. He gestured for her and Ellen to step back as he opened the door and stepped back into the anteroom, heading toward the door back to the outside. The others followed quickly, Ellen pointedly extinguishing her light and glancing toward Imay to do the same before they returned to the silent, night and the white snow blanketing the village.

#

Crown Prince Sarsal heaved a sigh of relief as the last of his attendants left his bedchambers and he could allow himself to drift into sleep.

The event of the day, his hasty execution of the all-too-clever spymaster, Vitel, had taken a huge toll on him emotionally. His step-father had been much distraught and his mother the queen had fled to her chambers in tears after consoling Sarsal on his near escape from death.

Immediately after there had been a hasty purge of all those who had previously worked with the spymaster and were now considered unreliable. Fortunately, Sarsal had a replacement already picked — Matilda Gregory.

"She comes by her arts naturally," Sarsal had said when defending his choice. "I've been watching her for some time and consider her abilities superlative."

Tilly — Matilda — had answered all the questions asked of her and Sarsal himself used his 'remorse' to lean heavily on his mother for backing. King Wendel had very little choice in the matter when all was said. Tilly, as soon as she was appointed, took care of all the 'unreliables' — men and women whom Sarsal had no reason to keep near his person — and presently the entire espionage organization of the kingdom was under his control.

Sarsal smiled, rolled over in his bed and snuggled against his bed warmer, saying, "It's been a good day, Tilly."

Matilda Gregory smiled in agreement and, presently, encouraged the prince to his slumbers.

#

"Sire?" Spymaster Hewlitt said as he glanced up from his desk later that night in surprise at finding the king before him.

"Don't rise," King Markel told him amiably, waving the spymaster back to his chair.

"I thought you had retired," Hewlitt said by way of apology. Actually, he *knew* that the king had retired and would have words with his men — and women — later. Belatedly he noticed the head of his man on duty peering woefully around the corner of his door.

"I couldn't sleep," King Markel replied testily, unconscious of the man behind him. He looked around and added in a grumble, "And I don't think much of your men if I can get to you undetected."

"A lapse which I assure you will be corrected," Hewlitt replied smoothly, sparing a glare for the unfortunate spy. "However, I believe that as you are in your own home and you have plenty of guards on duty at the walls, the chances of harm befalling you are, accordingly, much lowered."

"Yes, yes," the king agreed with sour sniff.

"You said you could not sleep?" Hewlitt said. "Your presence here indicates that this is related to my duties." He gestured to the chair in front of his desk and the king sat, even as Hewlitt glanced pointedly to the man at his door. "How may I help you? Some herbal tea, perhaps?"

"I was not aware that your duties included royal cook," the king grumbled.

"Indeed not," Hewlitt replied in a tone that indicated he thought the king was jesting, "but I do have connections in that area."

"Looking for poisons and all that," King Markel muttered sourly. "No doubt you do."

"Indeed, your majesty, I concern myself with all things related to your reign," Hewlitt said suavely. "And, again, how may I help you, sire?"

"The death of that woman, the one who ran the Inn of the Broken Sun," the king said. "How could that have happened here in the castle?"

"I see," Hewlitt said, assembling his thoughts quickly. "I think I understand your concern, sire." The king glanced at him expectantly. "If someone could gain access to the castle so readily as to murder madame Parkes, you may ask, how can we be certain of your safety?"

"Actually," the king said testily, "I was wondering if we couldn't arrange the same fate for the queen." Hewlitt's brows furrowed and he opened his mouth for a response but the king's raised hand forestalled him. "I know that we've got plans already," the king assured him quickly, "but I was thinking that perhaps we should consider a *backup* plan."

"I see," Hewlitt said, leaning back in his chair in relief. After a moment he leaned forward again, decisively. "I imagine we could easily create such a backup plan, your majesty but I wonder if perhaps it might not be a waste of resources."

"Just in case this war goes wrong," the king said.

"You're worried about the war?" Hewlitt asked in surprise.

"Our airships were supposed to be invincible in the skies," Markel said bitterly. "Arivik herself assured me and I received no warning omens from Ametza, either."

"Yes?"

"And now we've lost *three* of them!" the king wailed, rubbing his hands together nervously in his lap. "The treasury is nearly empty and the war isn't properly started!"

"I imagine when King Wendel hears of the loss of his fort in Korin's Pass, the war will be unavoidable," Hewlitt replied. King Markel glared at him. Hastily, Hewlitt added, "But he'll be so busy concentrating *there* that our rout of his forces at the South Pass will be a complete surprise."

"How can you be sure?" the king demanded.

"No one can be sure, sire," Hewlitt said reasonably. "We plan carefully, arrange our forces as best we can and then we launch them."

"You're the spymaster, what do your spies say?"

"Unfortunately, sire, my supply of spies is not as great as I'd like," Hewlitt said apologetically. Before king Markel's red face could explode on him, Hewlitt added, "The treasury, as you have noted, sire, is not bottomless." He shrugged. "So I work with the number of spies I can afford."

"Surely now that you've got madame Parkes' establishment, you can afford more."

"In time, sire, in time," Hewlitt agreed spreading his hands placatingly. "As it is, I must spend money on that endeavor to re-establish order in the house."

"Order?"

"Some of madame's people took her death… unhelpfully," Hewlitt said, choosing his words carefully. He felt that telling the king that nearly half of the women of the establishment had fled the city would not calm the king's concerns. "I find myself having to expend efforts to reassure them."

"I see," Markel said. He shrugged one shoulder. "Well, talk with Mannevy. He has a lot of experience in matters of that kind."

"Indeed he does, sire," Hewlitt agreed. "But, given your original question: my spies to the north have not reported in quite a while."

"They haven't?" Markel barked in surprise.

"I am not yet concerned, sire," Hewlitt said quickly. "They were only to report if they heard anything untoward. Their silence may mean merely that everything is working according to plan."

"Or that all your spies have been revealed," Markel grumbled sourly.

"I consider that a low probability as I have arranged a redundancy of spies," Hewlitt replied. "Some of my least spies — the lowest paid — are engaged merely to report if they hear of anything happening to a… list of people of interest to our realm."

"People of interest?"

"A mix of our spies and other notables, suitably lengthy to make guessing our true concerns difficult," Hewlitt said. "And I have several different groups of small spies assigned to this task."

"Hmm," the king said thoughtfully.

"From all that we can ascertain, then, sire, all our schemes are currently running to plan," Hewlitt assured him.

"The trains broke down, *two* of them!" Markel grumbled. "That delayed Gergen and Tashigg both! And then there's that issue with the fort and the dragons —"

"Actually, sire, I am not convinced that there were dragons involved," Hewlitt said. The king raised an eyebrow, demanding explanation. "I have spoken to some of the survivors that have trickled in and I believe that there may have been only one dragon."

"One dragon?" the king muttered. "But it destroyed two airships!"

"No, sire," Hewlitt said, "all reports agree that the floating fort destroyed *Vengeance*. The dragon is only responsible for the destruction of *Warrior* and that after it had already sustained damage in its encounter with the fort."

"Hmmph," king Markel said. "I suppose that's so." Even so, he was not mollified. "But that still doesn't explain the loss of *three* airships. Three!"

"*Warrior* and *Vengeance* were unexpected, sire," Hewlitt agreed. "But I understand that *Spite* is still on her mission and might return to us."

"I hope not," Markel growled. Hewlitt gave him a look. "My son is on that ship."

"And she has been gone a long time," Hewlitt added quickly. "Perhaps she's suffered a mischance."

"And how come your spies don't know?" King Markel demanded.

"My spies are concentrated around Soria and the coming campaign, sire," Hewlitt replied. "All that they know is that no one in Soria spotted *Spite* heading north." He shrugged. "Beyond that, I know nothing." The king scowled, so he added smoothly, "I could see about collecting more information on the matter, sire but that would require more men."

"And they don't know at your Inn?" the king asked with a smirk.

"I assure you, sire, if any of my people at the late madame Parkes inn had heard any rumors, I would be in possession of them immediately," Hewlitt replied. He spread his hands once more. "Unfortunately, there has been nothing to report."

"Hmmph," the king snorted in disappointment.

"Actually, sire, that is good news," Hewlitt told him gently. The king raised an eyebrow at him again. "From what I can understand, the gossip at the Inn is mostly concerned with the tragic demise of madame —"

"She deserved it!"

"— and how much she deserved it," Hewlitt finished with a small grin.

King Markel allowed a smile to touch his lips and then yawned, mightily. He rose from his chair and turned toward the door, finally spotting the waiting guard as he peered around the doorway. He turned back to Hewlitt to acknowledge the security, then said, "Very well. I think I shall return to my slumbers now, spymaster."

"I wish you pleasant dreams, sire," Hewlitt said, rising from his chair and bowing from his waist.

King Markel grunted and waved his words aside, turning back and stomping out the door.

#

The caravan was *not* in the stables, despite Rabel's logic. It took them over an hour to confirm that fact, at the end of which, Annabelle was practically fuming with impatience and Ellen was little better, clearly tired and worried.

Only Imay remained upbeat. "As you say, it was the logical place." She looked around the village as they closed the door to the stable, the cold air and the lessening snowfall seeming to sap their strength every moment. "Where is the most illogical place, I wonder?"

"It could be anywhere," Annabelle grumbled. "We might search all night and not find it."

"The longer the search, the more likely someone will notice," Rabel admitted. "So we must work as carefully as we can."

"What places does he have?" Imay asked.

"He's got a warehouse, a home, his offices, and an old forge," Annabelle rattled off. She had memorized the list the first time Rabel had showed it to her, 'Just in case.'

"He's the mayor of the town," Imay said. "And he's a friend of the zwerg."

"He's half-zwerg," Ellen corrected.

Imay frowned at her, whispering, "That's a secret we'd like to keep."

Ellen gave her an apologetic look. Imay smiled and patted her to assure her that the zwerg princess wasn't angry.

"Wouldn't he have some way of trading with the zwerg, then?" Annabelle asked. "Some place the humans wouldn't know? Not close to the village but not so far away that his absence would be noted."

"Of course!" Imay said. She turned toward the edge of the village, back the way they'd come, gesturing for the others to follow her. "I know where it is!"

Rabel stood his ground, a hand upraised. "How far is it?"

"About ten minutes walk, half the way back to our entrance," Imay said. She caught his look and added, "Why?"

"Well, we've just found that one logical place was wrong, why can you be certain that this next logical place is right?" Rabel asked.

"And how would he get the caravan moved?" Annabelle asked.

"He didn't," Imay said. "Master Ibb would have seen to it himself."

"So," Rabel mused, "Hamo would have made suggestions but it would have been *Ibb* who made the final choice."

"Yes," Imay agreed. "That seems so."

Rabel nodded. "In that case, princess, I believe you are correct." He gave her a quick box. "Please lead the way."

"Of course, if we're wrong," Annabelle muttered, trudging at the rear of the small group, "we'll have wasted a lot more time."

#

They were not wrong. Ten minutes later, Ellen's fourth snowball smacked against something unseen, three feet off the ground in a small dell nestled against the rising Silver Earth mountains. Attracted by her joyful cry, Rabel and the others soon felt out the dimensions and the front of the caravan. Rabel then led them to the rear and felt for the steps. When he found the handle, he clasped it, saying, "I am Rabel Zebala, a friend of Ibb's. He is in great need. Please let us four in."

The door clicked open and Rabel disappeared inside. Imay and Ellen followed quickly after, leaving Annabelle to glance around the empty dell to assure herself that they were unseen, then ducked through the doorway.

Inside, she gasped in surprise.

"It's bigger on the inside," Ellen told her with a grin.

"I was never inside before," Annabelle said. Her expression changed and she drew in a sharp breath, looking to Rabel. "Are you sure this is safe?"

"Why?"

"Back —" she found that she could not say the name "— back where Reedis and I were, we found another caravan."

"The one Ibb sent to collect my daughter," Rabel said, raising an eyebrow for confirmation. Annabelle nodded. "What about it?"

"It collapsed on itself and disappeared," Annabelle said, glancing nervously around the large room. It was fitted with a long comfortable table surrounded on two sides by long benches and headed up by a large comfortable chair. To the rear of the table, off to one side, was a compact galley kitchen. Light diffused from the eaves of the roof, a soft warm yellow that wasn't quite sunshine.

"It collapsed?" Imay repeated. "Was there anyone inside?"

"They got out," Annabelle said. "I warned them."

"You warned them?" Rabel said. "What alerted you?"

"Something felt… off," Annabelle said, taking her memory and quickly applying it to the room they were in. She felt nothing wrong. There was a pot on the stove behind her, warming slowly from the heat of a hot rock. She could smell fresh bread as well. It was like the caravan was welcoming them. She met Rabel's gaze. "I don't feel anything wrong with this caravan."

"Good," Rabel said. "Because neither do I." Annabelle gave him a look. "I have known Ibb for quite a while. I know that he protects his treasures carefully."

"So we are safe?" Imay asked, glancing around the room. Rabel nodded. Imay let out a sigh of relief, then asked, "But how does this —" she waved a hand around the room "— help Ibb?"

"This isn't the only room," Rabel and Annabelle answered in unison. Imay and Ellen both gave them amused looks which the older two ignored, staring at each other instead.

"Captain Ford and Angus entered the other caravan from different ends," Annabelle explained. "And each entered a different room."

"I never tried that," Rabel said. His brows furrowed. "Angus? Angus Franck?"

"Yes," Annabelle said. "I thought we told you."

"He worked with the caravan?"

"The caravan collapsed and tried to kill him," Annabelle explained. "But he learned lifting magic from Reedis." With a quirk of her lips, she added, "As did I."

"Really?" Rabel said, sounding both surprised and pleased. A moment, his brows furrowed and he asked, "And why was that?"

"We had to help Ophidian," Annabelle said. Thoughtfully, she added, "I was dying and I traded him a week's worth of service for my life."

"A week?" Rabel asked. "And he took it?"

"He only wanted three days," Annabelle said. "If I'd known, I would have bargained harder."

Rabel snorted in amusement. "And how much of your week is left?"

"About a day," Annabelle replied, surprised at the notion. She shrugged. "Maybe less."

"We've got to worry about *Ibb*," Ellen interrupted testily. Imay looked at her and nodded, moving carefully from the rear to the front of the room and back again. Ellen glowered at her. "What are you doing?"

"Measuring," Imay told her. She glanced to Rabel. "The caravan's too long for our entrance."

"I'd thought so," Rabel said. "So we'll have to bring Ibb to the caravan." He pursed his lips in concentration, turning to Imay. "How many zwerg would it take to lift him?"

"About five, if I remember correctly," Ellen said. Rabel darted his eyes toward her. "Remember, I was in the ruins when they pulled him out."

"That was brave of you," Annabelle told the young girl.

Ellen turned red as she admitted, "I was the one who melted him."

"But not before he'd been crushed by the weight of the fort," Rabel reminded her. "Don't chide yourself so."

"He's right," Imay added stoutly. "You did the best you could. Ibb's alive because of you."

"He's dying," Ellen said with a sob. She raised her head to glare at the adults. "We need to get moving!"

"Of course," Rabel said. He waved towards the bench and the chairs. "If you'll just wait here, I'll get us moving." He moved to the top of the room, pushing aside a set of curtains set in the plush fabric walls of the caravan.

"I'll come with you," Annabelle volunteered, moving after him.

She was surprised when she pushed through the thick curtains and out into the cold, snowy air of the evening. There was a bench seat just beyond the curtains and Rabel had already climbed into it. Annabelle settled herself beside him as he reached down and pulled up two leather reins, snapping them swiftly and releasing the long wooden brake at his side.

"There's a blanket," Rabel muttered as he turned the caravan slowly around and snapped the reins again for more speed.

"Where are the horses?" Annabelle asked, glancing in front of them. "Are they invisible?"

"There are no horses," Rabel told her with a laugh. "This is Ibb's caravan. A long time ago he told me 'I am a mechanical, why would I not have mechanical horses?'"

"I don't see them either," Annabelle said.

"He was lying, of course," Rabel assured her, stomping a foot on the wood of the caravan. "The 'horses' are built into the caravan."

"There was a steam room in the other caravan," Annabelle recalled thoughtfully.

"And there might be in this one as well," Rabel allowed. He stopped their turn and snapped the reins again to increase their speed. Then he let the reins go and turned to Annabelle. "When I learned about his 'horses,' I asked him about making steam engines."

"You did?"

Rabel nodded. "And that began our invention of the locomotives." He frowned in thought. "Ibb said to me when I mentioned it, 'Yes, I think it is time.'"

Annabelle sat in silence for a while, thinking. Finally, she asked, "How old is Ibb?"

"Thousands of years, at least," Rabel replied with a shrug. "Ophidian might know."

"But he might not tell us."

"When we fix Ibb, we can ask him," Ellen's voice piped up, causing the others to turn and realize that she'd come through the curtains. Behind her, they could make out the form of Imay.

"I suppose you had to see," Rabel said in a resigned tone. He moved out of his seat and gestured for Ellen and Imay to replace him. "Come inside when you're cold."

"We should get to the entrance soon," Imay allowed.

"After which we'll be busy," Rabel said, continuing through the curtains. "I'm sure that water is boiling. I'm going to get some tea, some of that excellent bread I smell and probably I'll find butter and jam to go on it."

"You can bring us some," Ellen said. Rabel turned back to face her, eyebrows raised demandingly. The little girl sighed and added, "Please."

Up in his tree hideout, Janthen Barros stirred. Something was wrong, something was different. He strained his ears in the still of the night, listening over the light breeze that promised dawn was still distant, ignoring the soft sounds of snow falling and the chill of the air.

There! His ears confirmed the noise. A distant, rumbling, soft noise. Something heavy was moving on the ground in the valley below him.

Janthen Barros moved slowly, carefully shifting his limbs one at a time until he was upright. He scanned the ground beneath him, repeated his scan twice to ensure that his sleepy eyes had not fooled him and then, satisfied, began a slow, silent descent from the tree to the ground below.

When his feet touched the earth, he stopped, hands ready to draw his bow or his dirk as needed. He paused, glanced around and closed his eyes to concentrate his hearing.

The noise was still there. With a silent grunt, he moved back toward his long-hidden campfire and his roost over the valley below.

There was work to do.

#

Rabel noticed when the caravan stopped. He moved forward through the curtains to the front and peered out. Imay saw him and said, "We're close enough." Rabel gave her a look of surprise, so she explained, "We can't get too near or someone might follow the wagon tracks to our entrance."

Rabel accepted this with a nod and gestured for the others to come with him, saying, "We leave through the back."

Outside, Imay bit her lip as she glanced at the long line of tracks left by the caravan's heavy wheels. "It'll be hours before they disappear in the snow."

"We could send someone to brush over them," Annabelle suggested.

"If we have time," Rabel said. "And if we have need."

Imay agreed, shrugging. "We are about five minutes away." She pursed her lips in a frown. "It's closer than I'd like, honestly."

"Perhaps Ibb will know something to help," Ellen suggested hopefully. "But I'm glad we're not too far from the entrance. We're still a long way from the infirmary."

Imay agreed with a nod and started trudging back toward the hidden zwerg entrance.

#

"They say that the zwerg like the night and hate the day, their eyes being so used to the underground," Aldis Dalton said to captain Nevins as they stood where the grunting sailors were offloading the two barrels of gunpowder. The ship's engineer — stolen by Nevins when he'd left *Pace* for *Harbinger* — had come down the rope ladder to report on the boilers and had stayed to take in the adventure playing out on the ground.

"Do 'they'?" Nevins returned levelly.

"I'm thinking that if that's right, captain, it might be a good idea to wait until dawn before you set off your explosions," the engineer allowed. "I imagine a sleeping man — or zwerg — is a lot easier to kill."

"Hmm," Nevins murmured. "There is something to what you say." He moved quickly, like a snake, and clapped the startled engineer on the back. "Very good, Dalton. I shall take your suggestion. When the explosives are placed, we can all take a rest. A good nap until dawn, eh?"

Dalton nodded jerkily, his heart still racing from surprise at the captain's unexpected display of admiration.

#

"Mother," Imay said as she saw queen Diam napping in one of the chairs beside Reedis' still form. Diam's eyes snapped open and she sat up, stretching quickly before accepting her daughter's acknowledgement with a jerk of her head. "We found Ibb's caravan. We're ready to bring him there." She glanced around, saw Granno lying nearby on an unused cot but no other guards. "Can we get some help?"

"I'm afraid you might have to wait," Queen Diam said, nodding sadly toward Rabel, Ellen, and Annabelle as they strained to catch her words. "There are humans above, near the fort and the old cave."

"Humans?" Imay repeated, aghast.

"Yes," Diam said. "And I don't want to spare any men until I'm sure the kingdom's safe."

"But… Ibb!" Ellen said, pointing to the metal man anxiously.

"Perhaps I can help," a voice spoke up from nowhere. Ophidian appeared as he spoke the last word. He moved toward the shattered metal man and glanced at the body appreciatively. He turned to queen Diam. "I understand that you wish to use my son as amulet against possible hostilities?"

Diam pursed her lips and nodded.

"You helped him in need," Ophidian said after a moment. "I see no reason he can't return the favor."

"Thank you," Diam said, closing her eyes wearily.

Ophidian turned to Rabel. "Shall we go?"

Rabel gave the god a quizzical look.

"We may have need of your friend here," Ophidian said, wrapping both arms around Ibb's body and easily lifting him off the floor, cradling him in both arms like a long spear and moving carefully toward the doorway.

"Mother?" Imay said, glancing toward the metal man and the dragon god carrying him.

"Go," Diam said waving her daughter away. "You should learn what you can."

"Your majesty," Rabel said, bowing toward her gratefully.

"You have children," Diam said in response, "you know what to do."

Rabel's lips twisted in agreement and he motioned Ellen to precede him. Annabelle, with a nod toward the zwerg queen, turned and brought up the rear once more.

Chapter Four

Janthen Barros nodded grimly to himself as he spotted two long lines in the snow. Something large had been moved. Something he couldn't see — the tracks just seemed to end. Their beginnings were already filled in by drifting snow and in another twenty minutes they would all be obliterated. He was lucky — no, he was good.

Even so, there was nothing he could spot with his telescope beyond the tracks. But something had come, something that had moved with a noise that had woken him.

Janthen Barros was patient. He turned back to his campsite, brushed away the hidden ring of his old fire and placed a bundle of kindling in its remains. He sprinkled the magic fire powder over it, clicked the fire rocks together and sparked a new fire into life. Janthen smiled to himself, thrilled at the gift of the mages.

Today he would kill. It was always a good day when he could say that.

#

They made it back to the caravan in ten minutes, Ophidian handling the broken, bent metal man like he was only a small child. The dragon god smiled as he leaned Ibb's silent form on the ground beside him and waited for Rabel and the others to catch up.

"Perhaps I should have made you even younger," Ophidian said to Rabel as the smith wheezed to a stop beside him.

"Perhaps you should recall that not all of us are gods," Rabel replied between gasps. Ophidian acknowledged the jibe with a small smile and waited for Rabel and the others to recover from their walk — almost a trot. Ellen alone of the four was unwinded and stood beside Ophidian, eyeing the space where the invisible caravan loomed with a frown. Ophidian's eyes glittered with amusement. The dragon god said nothing.

"What do we do now?" Imay asked, eyeing the shape of the caravan suspiciously.

Rabel gave her a look which showed that he had no idea. He turned toward the rear entrance to the caravan and walked up the invisible steps and put his hand on the door knob.

"We have Ibb," he said. "He is injured and needs help. Can you show us what to do?" Nothing happened. Then the door clicked open. Rabel turned back to the others, glancing at Ophidian who still held Ibb outstretched in his arms like a parent carrying a sick child. "Can you bring him in?"

"You want me to enter a palace of the immortals?" Ophidian asked in amusement.

"A palace?" Rabel repeated, surprised. He shook his head. "This should just be Ibb's workshop. Or maybe the library."

"It is a palace, a special place," Ophidian said. "A place where gods are most *specifically* not welcome."

"A palace won't help," Rabel said. He frowned. "Perhaps it is a workshop?"

"It could be," Ophidian admitted after a moment. He nodded toward the door. "You want me to enter?"

Rabel nodded. Ophidian sighed, motioned for the human to move aside and walked up the invisible steps to the doorway. Rabel pushed the door open and Ophidian disappeared inside. Rabel, with a backwards glance to the others, shoved himself in after.

Ellen would have been next but Annabelle stopped her, grabbing her hand. Imay looked at the two of them and moved in front, quickly disappearing inside.

"Are you ready for this?" Annabelle asked the little girl.

"I am," Ellen said. "I saw all the injured zwerg and I was with Jarin when he was in the treasury." She took a quick breath and gave Annabelle a nod, leading the way up the stairs.

"It might get messy," Annabelle warned.

Ellen snorted. "I used to live by the slaughterhouse."

"Messier," Annabelle said reprovingly. Ellen paid her no heed, pushing through the doorway and inside.

#

High up in his watchful eyrie, Jenthen Barros' eyes were blinded by a harsh light. He turned quickly toward the talisman hidden in his pack. He pulled it out. Already it was dimming.

"This will let you know if magic is nearby," the mage, Vistos, had said when he'd reluctantly presented it to Jenthen after he'd completed his training.

"How?" Barros had asked.

"The brighter it shines, the greater the magic, the nearer to you," Vistos said. He made a face. "It is a small magic, it will fade after a while." He paused, as he often did, as thought lost in thought, before adding, "Although it recharges off the magic it detects and you'll have magic arrows with you." He tilted his head toward Barros' quiver. "It could well last out your mission."

"Perhaps I should hide it, if it shines so brightly," Barros had said, frowning at the small gem wrapped in thin lines of silver.

"Oh, it would never shine brighter than a candle, even near great magic," Vistos had said with a dismissive wave of his hand. He had scoffed at the assassin's fears.

And now the gem shown like a beacon.

Barros shoved it deep into the bottom of his sack, rolled the sack up and turned it upside down. Even so, he could still see a gleam of light reflected in the snow surrounding his pack. He narrowed his eyes even as a thrill of fear pumped through his body. Then, just as abruptly, the light went out.

Jenthen Barros turned from his campfire and moved quickly and silently to the ledge which looked into the valley below. What magic could be so great?

#

"*This* is not here!" Ophidian exclaimed as he moved further into the large void that greeted them.

"What do you mean?" Annabelle asked.

"Feel the magic," Rabel said.

"We're not near home," Imay said with a whimper. She clutched tighter onto Annabelle's hand. "We're not anywhere near home."

"We may not be anywhere," Ophidian said as he moved forward into the large cavernous space. He turned to Imay, his eyes glowing a dim red. "Are we underground?"

"Inside," Imay said hesitantly. A moment later, her voice stronger, she declared, "But not under."

"That was my feeling, too," Ophidian agreed. He turned to Rabel and raised an eyebrow.

"I think you put him down," Rabel said.

"Didn't the mechanical give you instructions?" Ophidian asked frostily.

"He said that if ever I was unsure, I was to put him down, facing away from the door," Rabel said with a shrug. The dragon god, with a shrug, slowly put the metal man on the ground, leaving him standing. "And move away."

Ophidian gave Rabel a look and moved to join the others, standing at the front. Nothing happened.

Rabel made a noise and moved in front of the dragon god, closer to the inert metal man. "I am Rabel, a friend of Ibb's —"

Before he could continue, Ellen and Imay moved to stand on either side of them, saying almost in unison: "I am Ellen, a friend of Ibb's." "I am Imay, princess of the zwerg, and a friend of Ibb's."

The two girls could hardly see Rabel's expression but they could feel his surprise and concern. In the far distance of the vast chamber, dim lights came on. It made the sheer enormity of the expanse apparent. Fog or haze shrouded objects in the distance.

"I am Annabelle and I am a friend of Ibb's," Annabelle said as she stepped forward to stand between Ophidian and Ellen. More lights flicked on and they could hear, dimly the sounds of motion — of metal gears and steam hissing, echoing throughout the chambers. Behind them dim lights flicked on and continued until they found themselves ringed in by small flickers of light in the floor and high up above them.

Ellen cleared her throat and peered up at the dragon god challengingly.

Ophidian glared back at her for a moment. She gave him a demanding gesture and opened her mouth in silent pantomime. Ophidian gave her one final affectionate glare and looked up, speaking clearly.

"I am Ophidian, the dragon god," he said in a clear, resounding voice that echoed through the chamber. "Ibb is one of my acquaintances." When nothing changed, Ellen moved closer to Ophidian and nudged him with her elbow. The dragon god raised an eyebrow in surprise but turned back again, adding in the same echoing tones, "I should regret his demise."

Behind them the ground rumbled and they turned in surprise at the sound.

"Sit down," a voice echoed from above them.

Ophidian glanced up to the heights above them. The others followed his gaze as a number of lights flicked on, some red, some blue, some green. The lights flickered and moved, their motion betrayed by the sounds of large metal mechanisms beginning to move ponderously.

"It's a couch," Ellen said as she took in the object behind them. She moved to it and sat. It was covered in a marvelous red velvet cloth and looked new. The others joined her.

"We're seated," Rabel called to the darkness.

"Watch and learn," the voice replied.

"Is that Ibb?" Imay asked. Rabel considered the question and shook his head.

"There is more than one immortal," Ophidian said, allowing his gaze to travel throughout the huge cavern appreciatively. "And they have roamed the world many thousands of years."

A brilliant light burst forth with a loud sound and bathed the ruined form of Ibb. Another, and another, and another light burst on with the same loud sound until all that they could see clearly was the ruined form of the metal man.

"The damage is extensive," the voice called out.

"You can fix him, can't you?" Ellen asked in quavering tones. Her words burst forth. "He was injured when the fort fell but he saved three lives and I had to —" She let out a sob "— I had to melt him so that we could —"

"What is your name?" the voice cut across her.

"Ellen," the girl said. "Ellen Ford."

"One moment," the voice replied. From the floor beside Ibb a metal hatch clanged open and a long, thick tentacle shot out and up, landing on Ibb's head and clutching it firmly.

"Don't hurt him!" Imay cried, leaping from her seat only to be grabbed by Ophidian and pulled back.

"Accessing data," the voice said. A moment later it added, "Ellen Ford confirmed. Fond memories." The tentacle seemed to grasp Ibb's head and turn it forcibly. His dimly glowing eyes turned toward them. "Rabel Zebala. Annabelle Ford. Princess Imay and —" the voice faltered.

"Ophidian, the dragon god," Ophidian said amiably. "Perhaps you've heard of me?"

Silence. Ibb's eyes dimmed and it seemed like everything in the entire chamber stopped.

Imay growled and shrugged herself out of Ophidian's grasp, rushing forward to stand by the broken metal man and shout to the ceiling above. "He is here by my request! I swore an oath to him to protect Ibb —"

"You swore an oath to the dragon god?" the voice returned, emotion coloring its tone for the first time.

"Ophidian carried Ibb here," Rabel said, standing and moving next to Imay.

Silence.

"If you won't help him, we'll find another way to fix him," Annabelle said, moving to stand beside Rabel.

"No god has ever looked upon this," the voice said.

"So I gathered," Ophidian said with a chuckle. "Is that a problem?"

"Imay," the voice replied, "you swore an oath?"

"Yes."

"And tied the others neatly in their oath to me," Ophidian added. "Ibb is under their protection."

"Is Ibb under your protection?"

"We've worked together in the past," Ophidian said, dodging the question.

It seemed enough for the voice. "Return to your seat," it said. "Repairs will commence thereafter."

The three humans, zwerg princess, and dragon god needed no further prompting, returning to the red velvet couch.

"All will be well," the voice warned as another light flared on. It was red and thin. It moved toward the ruined metal man. When it met his metal skin, the skin flared and melted.

"You're hurting him," Ellen cried, "stop it!"

"Repairs require inspection," the voice replied.

"They're helping him, Ellen, no worries," Annabelle said soothingly to the girl even as she moved forward in her seat and propped her head on her arms to get closer to the operation.

"His gears and inner workings will have been damaged," Rabel added. "They'll probably have to replace them."

With a loud *clang* that startled them all and caused Ellen to squeak in fright, the back half of Ibb's metal body crashed to the ground. The ruins of his back were visible in the bright lights that engulfed him.

"Are those gears?" Annabelle asked as she took in the sight presented to them.

"They're all smashed," Ellen said miserably.

"Repairs are in process," the voice assured them. Suddenly the floor behind Ibb's back transformed into a maze of moving tentacles. From the distance a rumbling sound heralded the arrival of a large cart from the back of the cavern.

"Analysis," the voice said as the tentacles rose and slipped up and into the voids in Ibb's bare back. Lights at the ends of the tentacles flickered and flared. Ibb seemed to be engulfed in a maze of tentacles that sprouted finger-like extensions.

#

Captain Nevins couldn't sleep. It was often a problem for him, being on land. Even airmen, he noted ruefully, had *sea* legs. With a grumble he rose from the blankets he'd wrapped himself in — pity there was no place to throw a hammock — and moved to the edge of the camp.

The sentry turned at the sound of his approach, identified him and nodded before turning back to scan the horizon around them.

"All quiet, sir," the man reported. "The miners say the barrels are all placed, fuses ready to be lit."

"Yes," Nevins agreed. He'd known that before he'd gone to sleep, the guard was just being chatty. Careful.

"Sun'll be up in another hour or two," the man added, clearly nervous at Nevin's presence.

Probably wondering what he did wrong, Nevins thought to himself.

"I'll take a look around," Nevins said.

"Shout if you need, sir."

With a negligent wave, Nevins moved off, first toward the miners' excavation to check on it and then toward the ruins of the fort. On the way there, he entertained the notion of perhaps digging down to the fort's powder magazine. With a shudder, he rejected the notion — what if it were set off by the digging?

#

Jenthen Barros pulled the gem out of his backpack and eyed it carefully. It was dull, no sign that it had ever shone with the brilliant light that had startled him before. He thrust it deep into the pocket of his trousers, picked up his bow and moved back to his vantage point over the valley. *Something* had caused the gem to flare — if it came again, he'd be ready.

#

Ellen's jaw dropped as the tentacles moved back and the cart in the distance rumbled up. The tentacles moved to the cart, crawled over it.

"Central timer," the voice said as a tentacle hefted a large, brilliant metal gear into the air. Another tentacle grabbed another gear. "Repeating gear." And suddenly the voice became of torrent of words as different tentacles flashed in the light and waved various parts — gears, pulleys, frames, housings — into the brilliant lights surrounding Ibb's still form.

Annabelle let out a squeal of delight at the parade of sound and light. Ellen looked at her and the older woman said, "It's a dance! It's a healing dance."

"It is," Imay said, eyes alight with wonder.

Rabel said nothing, trying to absorb every movement and word as the tentacles flew and grabbed parts.

"Commencing replacements," the voice declared as all the tentacles stopped their movement. Suddenly one of the brilliant lights shifted and flooded them with light. Two more lights swiveled around and the three bracketed Rabel, bathing him in a brilliant glare. "Can you affect replacements?"

"What?" Rabel grunted in surprise.

"Stores are being used," the voice explained. "They must be replaced. Can you make the replacements?"

"If you give me the plans, certainly," Rabel replied. "And the metal."

"Acceptable," the voice replied.

"Same terms as last time," Rabel added with an apologetic glance toward Ophidian. "Only the Silver Earth zwerg are added."

There was a moment's silence, then the voice said. "Is that acceptable, Princess Imay?"

"Pardon?" Imay said, turning in her seat to shoot an anxious glance toward Rabel.

"We'll make new gears and return them with Ibb," Rabel told her. She started to protest but he held up a forestalling hand. "It will be to your profit."

"'The last time'?" Ophidian repeated to Rabel quietly.

Rabel waved him off. "I'll explain later."

"I eagerly await this explanation," Ophidian replied.

"Princess?" the voice repeated.

"Uh, accepted," Imay said. "On my behalf and the others here. I cannot bargain for my queen."

"Very well," the voice replied. "Repairing." And suddenly the brilliant lights swiveled back toward Ibb but Ibb was not there. Instead an army of tentacles were swarming over the outline of his body with flashes of metal at their tips.

"Removing inoperative components," the voice said. "Main gear. Central timer. Repeating gear —" and the voice continued faster and faster as the tentacles moved quicker and quicker until they were a blur and the voice a high-pitched buzz of information.

Suddenly the voice stopped. The tentacles slid to the ground. Ibb's back was bare, his chest empty.

Ellen gasped in terror.

"Replacing and rigging," the voice said. And another wave of tentacles surrounded Ibb's back and more gleaming pieces flowed into the metal man's empty chest. The voice went faster and faster until, once again, its words were a blur, a song of construction.

And finally, it stopped.

"Repairs complete," the voice said. "Re-assembling main components."

Another cart glided into view. It was loaded with a long metal piece that was polished and new. Ibb's back.

Tentacles reached for it and placed it upright, moving it carefully to align with the front half of the metal man.

"Avert your eyes," the voice said.

"Pardon?" Annabelle said.

"The light will be too bright and can cause damage to your function," the voice explain. "It is best to turn your head, put your arm over your light sensors and close them firmly."

"Got it," Annabelle said.

"Please confirm that all life-forms have complied," the voice said.

"Confirmed," Ophidian said after scowling Ellen into submission.

"You too," the voice said in a tone that brooked no argument.

With a sigh, Ophidian did as asked, muttering, "I'm a god."

"Extensive testing has not shown that light sensors of gods are not affected," the voice said by way of explanation. "Commencing weld."

The air hissed with the sound of super-heated metal and, even through his shielded eyes, Rabel could see brilliance leaking through.

The sound of welding ceased and there was silence.

"You may open your eyes," the voice said. "Repairs have been affected. Replacements will be designated and raw materials provided."

Ellen jumped out of her seat and rushed over to Ibb, peering down at the now seamless floor that had just recently erupted in tentacles. She went around to his front and looked up.

"What's wrong?" Ellen demanded, glaring up to the ceiling. "Why isn't he moving?"

"A restart is required," the voice reported.

"Restart?" Ellen repeated, frowning at the unfamiliar word.

"His power levels are dangerously low," the voice said.

"He needs energy?" Ellen asked as the others approached her.

"Of course," the voice said. "Rabel, you are aware of the requirement, are you not?"

"Ibb likes to stand in the rain," Rabel said in response to Ophidian's inquiring look.

"Lightning?" the dragon god guessed.

"Exit is required," the voice said. "Restart is required. Upon completion, data will be relayed."

"We're supposed to leave," Ophidian guessed. He sighed and picked up the repaired but still inert metal man. He waved the others to precede him and started toward where the door now appeared In the distance, sounds were fading. The brilliant overhead lights whooshed off, more distant twinkling lights were extinguished. Ophidian turned around once. "You do good work," he said. He added, "How do I address you?"

"I am Fixer," the voice said. "It was enjoyable analyzing your reactions."

And then the voice was gone and all the remaining lights winked out as one.

Ophidian snorted in amusement and turned to follow the others back out of the caravan and the strange place it had accessed.

#

Jenthen Barros' pocket suddenly flared with the brightness of the gem. He swore and then glanced down to the valley below. With one hand, he pulled the gem from his pocket and buried it beneath him, sitting on it so that its light did not blind him and with the other he raised the magic telescope to his eye, scanning the valley below.

There! Right where the strange tracks had ended. They'd been hidden by the snow long since but Jenthen knew where to look. Something was moving.

People. They seemed to appear from nowhere. He narrowed his eyes as he realized — from just where the tracks had ended. The brilliant light of the buried gem flared again and Jenthen bit back a curse as another form appeared. It was small. There was another. A bigger person was in front and another big person was just behind. Zwerg? And humans? And then some other, darker form appeared. A glint of metal flashed into the eyepiece of his telescope. The form was carrying something, something metal, cradled in its arms.

Jenthen Barros dropped the telescope from his eye, leaned forward to mark the target in his sight and reached back for his bow.

Six targets. He had seven arrows. It was going to be a good day.

#

"How long have we been gone?" Annabelle asked, peering around and sniffing at the air.

"Dawn in less than an hour," Rabel said, with a frown. "Does that mean three or four hours?"

"Yes," Ophidian said. "The repairs were extensive." He stood the metal man down on the ground. He glanced to Rabel. "Lightning?"

"He has other sources of power," Rabel said. "But lightning is the surest."

"Except that we're in the middle of winter," Annabelle grumbled. She turned toward Rabel. "How often have you seen lightning in a winter storm?"

"Perhaps we should ask for help from the gods," Rabel said with a nod toward Ophidian.

"For a price," Ophidian allowed. He glanced around. He saw that Ellen was moving around, looking around her worriedly. "What is it?"

"Something's wrong," Ellen said.

#

Jenthen Barros knocked his best arrow first. It was a special one, he'd held it back just for this instance.

"A wizard or mage will be able to find your magic," mage Vistos had warned as he'd presented Barros with the arrow. "*This* will kill him."

"I've got plenty of arrows for that," Jenthen had said, nodding toward the pile of poisoned arrows.

"Against magic you need a special arrow," Vistos had told him. "An arrow that a mage can't destroy." He nodded toward the arrow again. "An arrow that will always hit the strongest mage."

Jenthen Barros smiled as he drew back his bowstring and let the arrow fly. He had six more but he knew better than to leave the mage alive. He would kill the strongest first, then the rest.

The arrow flew straight and fast.

Chapter Five

"What is it?" Annabelle asked, sensing Ellen's alarm and seeing the way Ophidian was looking.

"There's something —" Ellen said. She shook her head, glancing around. "There!"

From above them, nearly lost in the last flakes of the evening's snow, a dark shape flew down toward them, its flight unerring. Its target locked.

"Ellen!" Annabelle shouted, throwing herself toward the young girl as her eyes spotted the merest shadow of movement.

"Ugh!" Ellen cried as the woman grabbed her by the shoulders and the two of them went flying toward the ground, Annabelle twisting protectively around the young girl.

#

"What?" the word was torn out of Jenthen Barros as he realized where the arrow was heading. "How?"

Could the mage have been wrong? The arrow's target was the smallest of the group. The little girl. The woman rushed toward her, grappled her and —

#

"Ah!" Annabelle cried as the arrow hit in her left shoulder. She fell to the ground, Ellen still in her arms.

Ophidian let out a roar that shook the valley. He rushed over, joined by Rabel and Imay.

Ellen's eyes bulged as she landed on top of Annabelle and found herself surrounded. Rabel gave her an appalled look and Ellen rolled to the side, turning to kneel beside Annabelle.

"Annabelle?" Ellen said in a small voice. Her hands went to the arrow sticking out of Annabelle's shoulder but Rabel's hand blocked her.

Annabelle's eyes were stuck open, her skin a blotched sickly blue.

"Annabelle?" Ellen repeated.

"That arrow is poisoned," Rabel said.

"It was magic," Ophidian said. He turned his eyes to Ellen. "It targeted magic."

"Annabelle?" Ellen wondered, turning to the large woman. She turned her eyes to Ophidian. "Can you help her?"

"The poison… she's dead," Ophidian said in a small voice that none had ever heard before. He shook his head, his hand going toward Ellen. "Her heart has stopped."

"No," Ellen said, tears filling her eyes. "She saved me. She — that arrow was meant for me!"

"I know," Ophidian said, giving Ellen a strange look.

Ellen brushed his words aside, reaching inside her blouse to pull out one of her demons. She pushed it over toward the arrow that stuck out of Annabelle's body. Pushed the demon into her still form. "Here," Ellen said. "Take it. Use it."

Imay moved beside her, pulling her loaned demon out of her waistband and passing it to Ellen wordlessly.

45

"Ellen —" Rabel began but she ignored him, taking the demon and shoving it around the arrow and into Annabelle's unresisting body.

"We have to get the arrow out," Ellen declared, glaring up toward Rabel. When he said nothing, she repeated, "We have to get it out!"

Rabel sighed, pulled his knife from his side and cut the arrow halfway. "We're going to need to push it through, it's probably barbed." He knelt and began to roll the still form on her side. Ophidian moved to aide him, giving the smith an imploring look. Rabel met it with a shake of his head. He took the flat of his knife blade and used it to push the arrow out, sickly, through Annabelle's shoulder. He took a rag from his pocket and carefully pulled the head and broken shaft out of the woman's lifeless body. With a nod, he and Ophidian rolled the body back to the ground.

"The arrow's out," Ellen said, leaning forward to whisper into Annabelle's ear. She wrapped her arms around Annabelle's neck and squeezed. "You can wake up now. Your demons. They should help." Ellen raised her head, looking at Annabelle's nostrils. "You saved my life. You can't die." She turned her head up to Ophidian. "You can save her?"

"That is not a gift I have," Ophidian told her softly, shaking his head.

Ellen burst into sobs, burying her head against Annabelle's still form.

"Ellen," Imay said quietly, moving to place her hand on the girl's shoulders. Ellen shrugged the arms off angrily.

Ellen raised her head again to glare at the dragon god. "You're a god! You have to save her!"

"I *can't*," Ophidian cried. "She's not one of my children, I can't save her!"

"She's not —" Ellen stopped and her expression brightened. "Your tears!" Ophidian gave her an uncomprehending look. "The wyverns! They're your tears!"

"What are you saying?" Ophidian asked slowly.

"Cry on her!" Ellen said. "Make her one of yours!"

"That's not — that's not how it works," Ophidian said.

"How do you know?" Ellen challenged. "How do you know if you don't try?"

"Ellen," Ophidian said in a small voice, "I can't cry. I can't make tears." His lips twitched in sorrow and he shook his head. "I haven't been able to for thousands of years."

Ellen's hope collapsed and tears streamed down her face, matched by Imay and Rabel. She buried her head against Annabelle's still form. "I'm sorry," Ellen said. "I'm sorry. All I can give you is tears and —" she broke off. "Ophidian!" the god looked at her. "Use *my* tears!"

"What? I can't —"

"Try!" Ellen said. Pleadingly, she added, "Please?" Before the dragon god could react, she leaned back up, grabbed his nearest hand and drew it to her face. She brushed her tears on his finger, soaking it and then she moved it away, to hover over Annbelle's lifeless blue cheek. Ophidian drew in a breath to speak but Ellen stopped him, wrapping her hand over his. "Please?"

Ophidian looked at her, sighed, and lowered his tear-soaked finger to touch Annabelle's cheek. He drew it back again as if stung and pushed Rabel behind him with an outstretched arm.

"Ellen, Imay, get away!" Ophidian ordered. The two girls struggled back on the other side of Annabelle's body as her dead cheek turned a brilliant white. Ophidian glared at Ellen. "I told you —"

"Look!" Ellen said.

The flaming white in Annabelle's dead cheek flared and flowed across her face, down her neck and throughout her body.

"Stand back!" Ophidian shouted. "Now!"

His warning was not a moment too soon as the body of Annabelle flared with a brilliant blue-white light and disappeared, flashing into the sky above them.

Brilliant, gossamer-thin translucent glowing wings carried the blue-white wyvern high into the sky and away from them, up into the clouds.

Ophidian stared after it and then back to Ellen, eyes amazed, jaw agape. "What did you —?"

Ellen silenced him with a raised hand, palm out. She strode past Imay toward the departing wyvern and shouted up to the skies. "Come back right now!" In a lower voice, she added, "I'm not done with you."

The wyvern's wings flared in the night sky, faltered and turned reluctantly back toward them.

"Ellen —" Ophidian called in warning as the wyvern's glaring eyes grew visible on its long sinuous head.

"I know," she said softly, turning her head to bestow a quick smile on the dragon god. The wyvern landed in front of her, its nostrils flared with heavy breathing, its wings flapping lightly up and down as its heaving chest drew in air. She turned back, raising a hand up toward the wyvern's snout.

"It's time," she said as her fingers hovered above the quivering nostrils. She smiled up at the glowing eyes. "We're going to be friends, never fear." The wyvern drew its head back in alarm but Ellen shook her head, saying soothingly, "I know what I'm doing. Trust me."

Hesitantly, the wyvern that had been Annabelle lowered her head again and took a deep breath just above Ellen's outstretched arm. Ellen turned back to smile at Rabel and grin at Imay, saying, "Watch this!"

She turned back to the wyvern and nodded. The wyvern inhaled deeply — and Ellen's body shivered and stretched into a clear smoke that entered the wyvern's lungs.

"Ellen!" Rabel shouted, moving forward.

But the girl was gone.

"It's all right," Ophidian said, with awe in his voice. He turned to Rabel. "It's more than all right." He moved toward the wyvern, his smile becoming warmer as he stood before her, arms outstretched. "My daughter, I welcome you!"

The newest wyvern roared in pleasure, turned, and leapt into the air.

A moment later, the dragon god followed her, his great wings flapping lazily in the cold morning air.

As Rabel and Imay watched in awe, the blue-white wyvern and the jet black dragon circled and danced in the sky.

A lightning bolt rained down between them and struck the still form of Ibb squarely in the chest.

Rabel and Imay turned as the huge thunderbolt lit the valley around them.

"Rabel, princess," the deep voice of the metal man rumbled, "to what do I owe this pleasure?"

Cloud War

Book 12

Twin Soul series

Chapter One

The arrow! Jenthen Barros groaned as the arrow flew toward the little girl in the valley far below. It was supposed to hit only the *strongest* magic! How could it — the woman leapt in front of the girl, snaring the arrow in her shoulder. The shaft buried itself in her. The woman fell to the ground; the girl clutched in her already dead, lifeless arms.

Jenthen grunted in anguish and surprise. He was a killer. He was always a killer. But to kill a little girl…!

But the girl was alive. The arrow hadn't hit her. It had hit the woman. Maybe *she* was the most magical.

He let his bow go limp in his hands as he drew his telescope and put it to his eye. What was happening? He could barely make out the shapes in the far distance. He saw the little girl, saw the body, saw the others move.

They were trying to save the woman. The men were — what were they doing?

Removing the arrow, rolling her on her side. One of the men was smart, he pushed the arrow through the corpse's shoulder. Jenthen's lips tightened: with the arrow head the man might be able to detect the magic and poison. He might be able to trace them back here.

Jenthen moved from the ledge, his speed increasing as he went. He stopped as brilliant light burst in front of him. What? He looked down. The stone, the mage stone. It flared brilliantly. Did that mean that the person with the most magic *wasn't* dead?

Hastily, he grabbed the stone, stuffed it in his pack along with the telescope, slung his bow, and rushed back to his fire. He kicked snow over the glowing embers, dousing it quickly and moved off.

He was going to get away. Far away.

He only hoped it was far enough.

#

"Are the men ready?" Captain Nevins asked, glancing around anxiously at the small camp which had been created in the shadow of his airship, *Harbinger*. The sky was growing lighter. The zwerg would be sleepy, it was the perfect time to blow open an entrance into their kingdom — and their treasures.

"Yes sir," Mage Borkis reported crisply. "They're ready when you are."

"Very well," Nevins said. "Send the signal to *Pace* and let's go get our gold."

Borkis nodded and smiled. "With pleasure!"

#

"Sir, sir!" the lookout called. "Movement below!"

"What sort?" Captain Martel called back to the lookout at the top of the balloon that kept the airship *Wasp* aloft. "Cavalry or soldiers?"

"There are horses," the lookout called back in confusion. "Don't know if they're — no some men are mounting them now."

"Mage Tirpin, bring us down!" Captain Martel shouted forward. "And well done!"

The sky was brightening and soon the sun would rise on the horizon. The timing was perfect. Captain Martel would meet up with the cavalry commander, give him his orders and lead the advance to trap the Sorians in their South Pass village. Once the troops there were encircled and destroyed, it would be but a moment's work to conquer the rest of the country. And King Markel, his treasury bulging with plunder, would remember those who had brought him this victory.

#

Colonel Walpish was not used to receiving orders wrapped in lead ballast. Nor was the unfortunate trooper who had first received it — directly on his head. It snapped his neck and now Walpish was short one trained cavalryman. But the airship was still hovering over them, with its strange and menacing bright steel teeth running the length of its keel from stem to stern.

The flag, barely visible from the hillside to which Walpish had sent one of his smarter scouts, declared it to be a warship of Kingsland. Given that Walpish had heard of no other nation possessing airships, he had little reason to suspect that this *Wasp* was not working for the King — even if he entertained the wish that he could exact revenge for his ballast-murdered man.

On the other hand, the accidental death of his man was a poignant reminder of the power of these flying ships, one that Walpish would not readily forget.

Ensign Berry rode up beside him, saluted and reported, "All troops report ready, sir."

Walpish nodded, noting idly to himself that in this case the word 'troop' referred to the four troops that made up his cavalry squadron — each the size of an infantry company — rather than an individual member of his armed force. The plodding infantry sometimes liked to refer to an individual as a 'troop' — perhaps to bolster their spirits or simply to confuse the enemy.

"And the burial detail?" Walpish asked.

"They've returned and are in formation," Berry reported.

Walpish made a face, pulled forth the piece of paper which contained his previously airborne orders and read them once more:

Upon receipt of this order you are to coordinate with the royal airship Wasp *in the pursuit of your duties, to whit: to take the enemy forces encamped at the South Sea Pass in their rear and affect a rout. Upon which you are further ordered to engage in the pursuit and destruction of said forces, ensuring that no single enemy soldier evades capture.*

There was also a second sheet of paper detailing the signals he could expect to receive from above and those that he could send in return.

He turned back to his command. They had done much. He wished that he hadn't had to leave the detachment back in the village of Korin's Pass but the dratted infantry was so *slow*. He hoped that Mitchener would catch up quickly but he feared that he would continue the war short one rather decent platoon of troops. *There, he'd said it!*

"The squadron will advance at the walk," Walpish ordered loudly, turning toward his bugler and nodding. The bugler dutifully blew the command. Walpish started moving forward at the walk, ensuring that his small detachment of bugler and color-bearer were keeping pace. He turned to the color bearer, "Dip the colors twice, Tavis."

Trooper Tavis did as ordered. Walpish swiveled in his saddle to scan the low hills where his scout was located. He spotted a flash of light — the trooper had seen *Wasp* did her colors in acknowledgement. Walpish sighed resignedly, annoyed with himself as he craned his neck back and spotted the airship, its large white pinwheels — 'propeller' was such an awkward and inaccurate word — circling faster as the steam engine *propelled* the airship in a lazy turn and straightened it on a course directly for the east end of the town of the South Sea Pass.

The war, *finally*, had begun.

#

Ensign Mitchener kept half of his platoon behind in the village, a squad in reserve, and rode forth boldly at the head of the remaining squad toward the approaching troops, shouting, "Halt, in the King's name!"

The soldiers, marching four abreast continued forward while the man in the lead — a captain by his dress — lengthened his stride and turned toward the mounted ensign. "And who might you be, sir?"

"What is the password?" Ensign Mitchener challenge, reining his mount in and signalling for his men to be ready. He spotted another formation behind the first, and another dimly in the distance on the road through Korin's Pass.

"'By air assured'," the captain replied correctly.

"Advance to be recognized," Ensign Mitchener said, even as he mentally conceded that the captain — and his soldiers — were very clearly visible.

"I cannot stay long," the captain said as he moved toward the horseman. Mitchener spurred his horse to pull alongside the captain and saluted down to him.

"Ensign Mitchener, sir, of the King's cavalry," he said, waiting until the captain returned his salute.

"Captain Welless, first division," the captain replied. He gestured toward the town. "Your people have possession?"

"Colonel Walpish left my platoon to guard it," Mitchener said in broad agreement. Welless gave him a look. Mitchener leaned forward in his saddle. "There's a lot more of these villagers than there are of my men, sir."

"I understand," Welless said. "Lieutenant Martin! Take your platoon and secure the village."

A smart lieutenant saluted sharply and presently his platoon split off from the rest of the march, heading toward the town center.

"Corporal Mattingly!" Ensign Mitchener called out. "Detail an escort for the lieutenant and his men!" He turned back to the captain. "I shall return to my troops and prepare for their departure."

"You'll wait until Captain Baker gives you leave," Captain Welless told him sternly. At the ensign's confused look, Welless relented and explained, "Captain Baker commands the battalion."

"Very well," Ensign Mitchener replied, confusion written across his face.

"There was a battle," Welless explained, "And General Filbert was killed, along with a large number of this battalion."

"Terrible," Ensign Mitchener said, shaking his head in commiseration.

Welless made a face and gestured the ensign closer, leaning up to whisper, "The general was after the gold."

"Gold?" Ensign Mitchener repeated blankly.

"Zwerg gold," Welless said.

Mitchener's eyes widened. "And that did not go well?"

Welless snorted derisively. "Lost half the battalion." He glanced around nervously, pulled back from the ensign's horse and said loudly, "Very well. You have your orders, ensign."

Ensign Mitchener nodded in affirmation, turned his horse and spurred it into a trot, signaling his squad to fall in line behind him.

#

The sun was over the horizon, warming the new-fallen snow as Jenthen Barros reached the clearing he'd picked weeks back as his safety camp. He scrambled down the difficult rocky cliff that brought him down to this new level, and turned to scan the small dell before him.

There was a fire. Barros stiffened in shock. Someone had lit a fire in his oldest fire pit, one that he'd sworn no one could have discovered.

"I have stew," a voice called from beyond the fire. "It's quite tasty." A girl. She looked up and with a start, Barros realized it was the little girl from the valley below. The little girl he'd shot with the magic arrow. His heart beat heavily in his chest. Impossible.

"You may as well eat," the girl said, waving him genially toward the opposite side of the fire and scooping a ladle into a clay bowl — one of his hidden horde. "After all," she said, her voice hardening, "it's customary to offer the condemned a final meal."

#

"Fire in the hole!" one of the miners shouted in warning and suddenly the whole earth shuddered.

Captain Nevins, from his little camp below *Harbinger*, sipped at the morning tea the cook had provided from his special stores. He glanced toward mage Borkis and the two exchanged gleeful looks.

Stones and pebbles flew in the air, raising a cloud of dust in the distance. Nevins waited patiently, finishing his tea before inquiring of Borkis, "And the men, have they been fed?"

"Aye, sir," Borkis replied, dipping his head slightly.

Nevins nodded and passed his cup back to the sailor who stood at the ready. He turned toward the explosion and said to Borkis, "Then I suppose we should get moving."

#

Queen Diam stirred, yawned, and stretched as the tremor of the explosion rocked the infirmary. She glanced toward Granno.

"Kavim had the men pulled back, the area is prepared," Granno told her.

"So we've only to spill the oil and light the fire," Diam said with a small smile. She nodded toward the sleeping form of Jarin Reedis. "I suppose he's rested enough." She leaned forward and said, "Dear dragon, how would you like to play?"

Jarin Reedis opened his eyes and glanced up at the small zwerg queen in confusion. "Play?"

"With airships," Diam said. "Remember the last time? When you and Ellen destroyed the two that attacked our fort?"

"Really," Reedis said in surprise, sitting himself up. "Jarin did that?"

"You don't remember?" Diam asked with a note of worry entering her voice. "The Kingsland airships attacked our East Pass Fort and your friends destroyed them."

"Destroyed two airships?" Reedis asked in surprise. "However did they manage that?"

"Don't you remember?"

Reedis' expression slacked as he grew thoughtful. After a moment his eyes popped open wide. "They made the fort *float!*" He gasped in amazement. "I would have loved to have been there — well, I suppose *part* of me was." He turned his head to one side, recalling

Jarin's memories intently. "I — Jarin *flamed* the second ship! Amazing! I'd always wondered —" he cut himself off and turned back to the queen. "You want me to attack *two* airships?" Jarin said angrily, using Reedis' mouth. "Do you want us to die?" A moment later his expression changed and Reedis said, "No, wait. I've got a better idea."

"Reedis?" Diam asked, unfamiliar with this new person that was half-dragon Jarin, whom she knew, and half-mage Reedis, whom she had hardly met at all.

The man nodded. "Indeed," he affirmed. "I was just reminding my... colleague... that *I* am a mage of hot and cold."

Queen Diam gave him a puzzled look.

"I was the mage for the first airship, *Spite*, until its tragic demise," Reedis told her. "In fact," he continued in a more animated tone, "I was the *first* mage to lift an airship."

"And?" Granno asked, glancing between the dragon mage and his queen.

Reedis smiled. "And I was just informing my friend that we have more options when it comes to things that fly."

#

Skara Ningan grimaced as she knelt down and retrieved the quarrel-shot bird from the snowy clearing. Her tongue stuck out from her mouth in her expression of disgust as she soiled her hands with the bird's blood while struggling to remove the small paper tightly-wrapped around its leg.

Why Vistos had demanded that she shoot even birds she identified positively as his was beyond her... although she suspected that the mage did it just out of cruelty.

She unrolled the spiralled message and read it quickly, knowing that the paranoid mage would have enspelled it to wither in the sunlight. Her scowl grew sharper as she absorbed the words: she *hated* when plans changed.

A sharp smile twisted her lips and she dropped the dead bird and the yellowing message, shuffling loose snow over the two until they were invisible. Ensuring that her crossbow was cocked and the safety lock on, she slung it upside over her shoulder. Then she turned and trotted off toward her usual eyrie. Let mage Vistos wait for her return message, she decided, finding her hiding spot and pulling out the magical telescope. Rather than ensnare and ensorcel another small bird for the mage's delight, she'd give him the *signal* just as ordered.

She scanned the valley back along the mountains, took her eye off the telescope to rest it, and scanned again. *By all the gods!* There it was. She looked away and looked back again to be sure but the smudge was getting bigger and clearer — a ship floating hundreds of feet above the ground, suspended by a large balloon.

Vistos would be pleased. Skara collapsed the telescope, rose carefully from her position and backed away, pocketing the 'scope as she moved gracefully back toward the landing below.

Five minutes later, Skara pulled out her crossbow notched her quarrel and, frowning, attached the strange bulbous tip to it. She aimed up high, over the village of the South Sea Pass and fired.

She crouched back down immediately, so as to present less of a target but she couldn't keep herself from following the thin quarrel's arching flight and smiled as a black puff of explosive blossomed into a large blue cloud.

There! She thought to herself. *Vistos has his message.*

Chapter Two

Captain Nevins stood at the edge of the pit the explosion had created, watching as the miners and his engineer, Dalton — who professed an interest in such things — charged through into the darkness.

"Signal *Pace* to begin lifting," Nevins ordered the mage, Tortis Borkin. He smiled as the mage turned and waved his hands to create a small burst of red brilliance above him. An answering green ball of light from *Pace* confirmed that the message had been seen and understood. Nevins watched with idle interest as *Pace*'s crew startled scuttling back aboard the airship and the balloon above grew taught as the ship's mage prepared to lift them skyward.

He glanced toward the cart waiting near and frowned. It was too small, they'd require several trips to get all the gold out. He turned to Borkis. "Perhaps we should bring *Harbinger* over the opening?"

Tortin Borkis shot him a questioning look, so Nevins expanded, "We could use cargo nets and lift the gold up directly."

Borkis considered this and nodded slowly. "But we'd need the engineer —"

His words were cut off as a roar of flame illuminated the pit below and screams filled the air.

"What the —?" Borkis exclaimed.

"Get back to the ship!" Nevins shouted, grabbing at the mage's sleeve and tugging him away.

"But the men!"

"That was fire, you fool!" Nevins swore, tugging harder. "They're dead or dying and, either way, we want to be where they *aren't*."

#

Ophidian turned back from the sight of the rapidly diminishing blue-white wyvern as it soared into toward the mountain heights and speared Rabel, Imay, and metal Ibb with a fierce scowl.

"I should kill you all now," he growled, his eyes glowing with a fierce yellow flame. The air around him trembled with waves of heat and the ground shook.

"Why?" Rabel asked, carefully lowering his arms to his sides. "And what would you say to my daughter?"

"If I must end my days," Ibb began casually, "I would feel relieved if I were to know the reason."

"The 'reason' is why I have to kill you," Ophidian said, the fire in his eyes dimming.

"Even so," Ibb replied. "I come back into my senses — and thank you for that lightning bolt, by the way — to discover you cavorting with a wyvern I've never seen before and my friends looking fatigued, distraught, and tear-stained." He glanced around. "Where is little Ellen?"

"Her tears," Imay said, hugging herself and looking at Ophidian in wonder.

"You didn't know you could do that!" Rabel exclaimed, nodding toward Ophidian. "She taught you something new, didn't she?"

Ophidian glowered at him and raised a hand. A ball of fire appeared in it. "I truly regret this," he told them miserably. "But no one must ever know."

"I cannot help but think that there are better ways to keep a secret," Ibb said, "than to incinerate one's friends and oathsworn."

Rabel nodded and turned toward Ibb, putting his back to the dragon god. "I agree," he said, gesturing for Imay to come to him. "Ibb, Ophidian has discovered that our Ellen can raise the dead by using his tears to create a wyvern —"

"The wyvern?" Ibb said, glancing around toward where the wyvern had vanished. "Who was the dead?"

"What do you remember?" Rabel asked.

"Many things, dimly," Ibb replied. "My last clear thought was of the fort falling and the people around me." He paused. "Did they survive?"

"The captain, the son, and Hamo Beck are in the infirmary," Imay said, moving to grab Rabel's hand and leaning against him when he wrapped an arm around her shoulder and tugged her closer. She glanced up at the mechanical man, smiling. "They will live because of you."

"I remember little Ellen crying," Ibb said. "She was sad because… she had to hurt me?"

"She melted you," Rabel said. "It was the only way we could get you out from the ruins of the fort."

"Obviously, it was quite efficacious," the metal man replied, "considering our current situation." He jerked his head quickly in the direction of Ophidian, then back again. "Which seems quite fraught with peril."

"Did you meet Annabelle?"

"Annabelle?" Ibb repeated in surprise. "You mean the one who stole all the gold?"

"The very same," Imay said. "She gave the gold to zwerg who saved her life."

"I helped," Ibb recalled. "She made a most compelling argument." He dropped his chin toward Imay. "Is she here, then?"

Imay pointed up over his shoulder to the mountains behind them. "She's the wyvern."

"The wyvern?" Ibb repeated, confused.

"When we came back from the cavern," Rabel said, "out of your caravan —"

"Your Fixer is quite an interesting character," Ophidian said, pacing over toward them. "I have never had its acquaintance before."

"Fixer prefers to be female and she," Ibb said, nodding toward the dragon god. "You took me to Fixer?"

Rabel nodded. "You were quite broken."

"I took severe damage," Ibb agreed. "Although I recall that little Ellen —" he stopped abruptly. Gears whirled and his eyes flashed rapidly. He turned abruptly toward Ophidian. "Am I to understand that Ellen is now a twin soul wyvern?"

Ophidian dipped his head fractionally.

Ibb was silent for a long moment. Finally, he said, "I see." He took a step toward Ophidian and stretched out his arms in surrender. "I understand now why you consider our permanent termination to be of paramount importance," the metal man told the dragon god solemnly. "You may proceed."

"Well, I don't," Rabel snapped sourly, turning to glare at his oath sworn god. "Explain to me."

"If I may," Ibb interrupted in his deep bass voice, nodding toward Ophidian. When the dragon god did not react, he took it as permission and continued. "Rabel, Imay, we three — and Ellen Annabelle —"

"What a preposterous name," Ophidian muttered under his breath.

"Will you kill her, too?" Imay asked, sliding out from under Rabel's protective embrace and turning to face the dragon god squarely, her arms on her hips. "Will you kill your own daughter?"

#

Jenthen Barros moved in a blur. He drew his bow from his shoulder, notched an arrow and fired before the girl could finish speaking.

The girl glanced up, waved a hand and the arrow disappeared, engulfed in a flame that turned it to ash just before her nose.

Jenthen fired again. And again.

"It won't work," the girl said, turning arrow after arrow to ash. "You may as well come and eat, you know."

Jenthen fired his last arrow and charged the campfire, drawing his dirk as he flung his now useless bow to the ground. This girl would die.

The girl rose from behind the campfire, stepped through it and stood before him, her arms at her sides.

Jenthen Barros paused just a moment to recognize how small the girl was, how young. She couldn't be yet seven. But he never wavered as he struck with his knife.

The girl staggered back, dropped into the fire with a yelp of surprise.

Jenthen Barros stood back and glared down at the girl. "The blade's poisoned," he told her. "You'll die soon enough."

The girl scrambled back up and out of the fire. She glared at him, pulling the knife from her chest and glowering at the blood that flowed.

"That hurt," she said. She dropped the knife to the ground.

Jenthen Barros' eyes widened in surprise.

"But it hurt a lot less than your arrow," she told him. Her expression changed, hardened. "It was poisoned too, wasn't it?"

Jenthen Barros said nothing, eyeing the girl and his surroundings warily. A hiss and a crackle from the fire distracted him, he tore his eyes away from the girl long enough to catch sight of the upturned pot and saw a bit of burnt stew hiss and steam into the early morning air.

"I know it was poisoned," the girl continued, her tone and demeanor changing, becoming more threatening, more potent… older. She touched her chest where the blood flowed and a light flared from her fingertip. The blood hissed and steamed, burnt away by the flame of her finger. When she moved her hand again, the wound was gone. She glared up into Barros' eyes. "I can feel it with every breath." Her expression changed and she seemed once again like a little girl as she continued, "Annabelle can." She shrugged. "After all, that's how you killed her. Poison." Sorrow filled her eyes. "She feels it all the time. The poison's in her blood, it burns." She clenched her jaw. "It burns in me, too."

"What are you?" Barros asked in horror.

"What am I?" the girl repeated. "I am what you made me," she said, her chin rising her, eyes defiant. "I was Ellen Ford and she — the woman you killed — was Annabelle."

"I work for the king," Barros growled. "I was only doing my duty."

"I shall remember that," the girl replied. She turned back toward the far side of the campfire. "I'm afraid your stew was spilled when you shot me."

Jenthen needed no other chance. The moment her eyes lift his, he turned and bolted. Just a few more —

Something dark, heavy, and small darted by him and pierced the ground in front of his feet. The snow hissed where it landed.

"I wouldn't, if I were you," the girl said. Jenthen eyed the ground carefully and turned back to the girl. "After all, the dart is poisoned."

"Poisoned?" Jenthen said, fighting for time. He darted his eyes over the girl, trying to find where she'd kept her weapon. Some sort of projectile device, he guessed.

"Yes," the girl said. "Poisoned, just like your arrow." She made a face and her expression changed again, grew older. "It hurt unbearably, actually. I was almost glad to die." Her eyes turned a luminous purple as she glared at him. "I imagine you will be, too."

"You're bluffing," Jenthen said, starting back toward the girl. "You're nothing but a little mage with some special magic. Vistos and Margen are better than you. And I work for them."

"Good to know," the girl agreed. "And what were you paid?"

"Paid?" Jenthen Barros snorted. "I didn't do this for the money, girlie!" He leered at her. "I did it for the pain."

"Then you won't mind at all," the girl said. Jenthen had just a moment to realize that she'd changed, that she was no longer a girl but a brilliant blue-white beast. *A wyvern.* And then the wyvern spat. Six small darts shot at Jenthen Barros and pierced him before he could react.

Squirming, writhing in agony, he fell to the ground.

"I told you it would hurt," the little girl said a moment later. Jenthen forced his eyes to open even as his legs spasmed and cramped in agony. She crouched down beside him and peered at him intently. "It won't last long," she told him academically. And then her expression changed and she seemed much older. "But I guarantee it'll *hurt*."

#

Wings fluttering in the distance, rapidly approaching, distracted Ophidian and the others from their impasse.

Rabel glanced up, eyes alight with amazement until he caught of an ugly gash on the left side of the wyvern's chest and then he cried out with alarm.

The blue-white wyvern — no, more purple-white, Rabel realized with surprise, landed and turned back into the shape of a small girl.

Ellen strode briskly over to Ophidian. "He is dead," she told him. Her expression twisted as she added, "He took a very long time to die. It was quite painful."

Rabel grunted as her words struck at him but before he could react further, Ophidian lunged down, his hand swinging across her face in a resounding *slap* which was repeated on his backswing.

Ellen burst into tears.

"Ophidian!" Rabel bellowed, rushing forward to grab the girl from behind, even as Imay moved to kneel beside her.

"You cannot do it," Ophidian roared at his newest daughter.

Ellen whimpered and twirled to clutch Rabel around the neck.

"You cannot learn to like killing," Ophidian said to her back. "It may have to be done but it should *never* be enjoyed."

"But he killed me," Ellen's voice wailed into Rabel's breast.

"Even so," Ophidian growled. "If you let it, it will consume you."

"This has happened before?" Ibb said, moving up to stand opposite the dragon god. "One of yours was consumed?"

Ophidian turned his head away sharply.

"What happened?" Rabel asked, still working to comfort the injured girl.

Ophidian looked down to meet Rabel's eyes. "I should kill you."

"But you won't," Ibb said firmly. The dragon god turned his eyes to the metal man. "There is much going on, much I don't understand," Ibb confessed. "But I begin to see a pattern. A pattern I hadn't considered until now."

"Yes?" Ophidian said in a dangerously encouraging tone.

Ellen turned in Rabel's arms and glanced up to the dragon god. "You are right," she said with Annabelle's tone, "it is wrong to enjoy it."

Ophidian's eyes dipped to hers and he gave her a small nod. He pointed to her chest and she glanced down.

"Oh, that!" she said, her lips twitching. "He stuck his poisoned knife in me."

"And yet here you are," Ophidian said, his tone thoughtful. She smiled up at him, tentatively, and the dragon god smiled back. He raised his eyes toward Ibb. "You are right," he said to the metal man. "One of my children became consumed by evil."

"And?" Rabel asked softly, even as he felt Imay's hand work its way nervously in his left hand. He squeezed it gently, comforting the zwerg princess as best he could.

"He is no more," Ophidian said, his eyes glancing down to Ellen. "That is why I don't want you to learn the ways of hate."

"I understand," Annabelle said with Ellen's voice. "I see what you mean. And you are right." She raised her hand to brush against her reddened cheeks and rubbed the pain away ruefully.

"It hurt you," Ibb said, his voice, strangely, full of compassion. He pointed to Ophidian to make his intention clear. "When you destroyed your child, it hurt you."

Ophidian turned toward the metal man, arms raised as if ready to destroy but he lowered them again, the fierce glow in his eyes dimming as he nodded.

"Father," Ellen said, glancing up to meet his eyes sadly. "Who is trying to kill you?"

Chapter Three

General Gergen was surprised by the appearance of the mage — he was rarely available this early in the morning.

"The signal, General!" Mage Vistos declared. "My man's given the signal. You may proceed."

"How very kind of you," General Gergen said frostily. "But my troops must be alerted, the cannon prepared, and I've no wish to send my men to certain death."

"General," Vistos replied tightly, "you may be assured that all is ready. My spy reports the airship is in sight."

"Ah?" General Gergen allowed. "And just where is it?" He stood from his camp stool and moved toward the tent flap. "Can you point it out to me?"

"Of course not!" Vistos said. "It's on the way, not visible now."

"I see," Gergen said, turning back to his stool. Vistos fumed and fluttered his hands anxiously. Gergen took in the mage's exasperation with delight before relenting enough to say, "Mage Vistos, you have made your report." He nodded to the old man. "I shall prepare the troops forthwith."

Vistos huffed in irritation, turned so sharply that his robes twirled around him and rushed out of the tent, chin held high, expression haughty.

Gergen waited until he was certain the mage was out of earshot, then waved a hand beckoningly, not even glancing up when the ensign on duty snapped to attention beside him. Gergen dashed off two quick messages, folded them over, addressed and signed them before passing off to the waiting man.

"Have these delivered to the second and third divisions immediately," Gergen said. He stood and returned the ensign's snappy salute. He followed the ensign through the tent flaps and out in the morning air, drawing in a deep breath.

It was going to be a *good* day.

#

Rabel stood, keeping his grip on Ellen and drawing Imay next to him with his left hand.

Ibb glanced down to the young girl and nodded slowly. "I believe you are correct, Ellen Annabelle."

"That's an absurd name," Ophidian muttered.

"It is my proper name," Ellen Annabelle told him. "My wyvern half was Annabelle Ford, so one could argue that I should be Ellen Ford. Again. Still." She smiled. "But Ellen Annabelle I am. It is my name, I name myself so."

"Ellen Annabelle," Ophidian repeated, tasting the sound on his tongue. He nodded to the girl. "Very well," he conceded. "You are right, though how you know the ancient laws —"

"I grew up with the zwerg, in the south," Annabelle reminded him with Ellen's piping voice. "I learned from my king and later my step-sister, the queen."

"*And* you're a Duchess," Imay added stoutly. The others looked at her. "Queen Alva declared her thus."

"Duchess Ellen Annabelle," Ibb said, bowing toward her. "I am delighted to make your acquaintance."

"Just call me Ellen," little Ellen said. A moment later, Annabelle added with Ellen's voice, "Or Annabelle."

Ibb accepted this with a nod, then turned his attention to the dragon god. "So, great Ophidian, what do you know? And are you still committed in our demise?"

"What?" Ellen said. She glared up at the god, her father, then turned back to Rabel. "What is going on?"

Rabel looked down at her and then back up to the dragon god. "Ophidian has learned something new this morning," he said. "He has learned that he can make new wyverns." He smiled down at Ellen. "*You* taught him."

"And you can bring the dead back to life," Imay added in a voice that quavered just a little. "Don't forget that."

"The poison," Annabelle said with Ellen's voice. The others looked at her. "Poison heals," she explained. She pointed to the hole in her blouse and the unwounded flesh. She glanced up to Ophidian. "That's right, isn't it?"

"I do not know," Ophidian said. "None of my children have your power."

\#

"Sir, sir!" a messenger ran into General Alvin Dartan's quarters, shouting urgently. "Sir, the enemy are approaching!"

"Well, it's about time," General Dartan declared, rolling out of his bed and rubbing his eyes blearily. His white hair was ruffled, a quick movement of his hands fixed that. He stroked his beard to settle it, too. He waved the messenger away. "Go! I'll be up presently."

The messenger needed no urging and hurried off.

"And send my man with coffee!" Dartan bellowed at his fleeting form. He rose and dressed quickly, leaving his quarters just as his man brought him a mug of steaming coffee. "About time," Dartan muttered without rancor, taking the mug and draining it quickly.

He walked purposefully down the stairs and entered the bright room that had been assigned for his headquarters, opened the door and called the assembled officers, "So, gentlemen, what is that idiot doing?"

"Lookouts reported something in the sky from the east," General Adkins said, proffering a small sheet of paper.

General Dartan took the paper and eyed it quickly, thrusting it back when he was done. "So?"

As if in answer, the ground shook and the air rumbled with an explosion. It was followed immediately by many more.

"Get my horse," Dartan snapped. He turned to general Adkins, "Have your men close the gates to the east and send the bulk of them to join us at the western gates." He pursed his lips in restrained fury. "We'll show King Markel how we can *bleed* his army."

The room became of blur of bodies in motion, gathering papers, donning swords, marshalling equipment, and departing with haste.

Dartan was first down the wide ornate steps to the courtyard, pulling himself up into the saddle of his best stallion with an ease that belied his years.

\#

"Watch and learn," General Gergen said to ensign Fetter, the aide standing at his side, as they stood on a hill overlooking the battle.

He pointed toward the troops on the right, on either side of the road leading into the South Sea Pass. The town of the same name was a burgeoning port which had twice expanded beyond its walls in the past fifty years or more. Each time the Sorians had built new walls, unintentionally giving the town three lines of defence. The main road from Kingsland to Soria pierced the walls under a huge pair of guard towers. The road crossed the ditch surrounding the walls by a drawbridge which had already been raised up.

Beyond that, the entrance to the town was blocked by not one but two portcullises, giving the town the ability to trap and hold any enemy troops so brave as to make it across the ditch under the drawbridge and crawl back up onto the road. "Impenetrable, right?"

The aide, safely prompted, dutifully nodded.

"Our pimply-faced friend," he nodded toward one of Vistos' apprentices, "is going to prove this wrong."

"Sir?" Ensign Fetter said, glancing in surprise first at the apprentice mage and second at his commander. He glanced back again to the pimply-faced mage. "How can that be?"

"And who is our god?" General Gergen asked with a smile.

"Ametza," Tobias Fetter replied hesitantly. His eyes widened and he turned in surprise to the young mage. "Master Halston is going to call forth a flood?"

Gergen snorted derisively. "Master Halston, according our great mage Vistos, is going to provide a distraction only." He pointed to the left, where the second division was moving forward. "My opposite number is a feeble old soldier who's done nothing more adventurous than kiss his mistress in secret," Gergen said, his eyes lidding with humor. "General Adkins — Piers Adkins — has been at his post for the better part of twenty years, odiously climbing his way higher and higher rank without doing anything more than knuckling his head and turning out foppish displays of his troops for whichever king Soria has at the moment." Gergen snorted. "He must have wet his pants the moment he saw us, and he's certain to have sent for reinforcements." Gergen pointed to the peak at this end of the Silver Mountains and smiled. "He doesn't know that he's not going to get any, although I'm sure he's wondering by now."

"We've got someone up there, sir?" Ensign Fetters asked, glancing up with a hand to shield his eyes from the brilliant early morning sun.

"Yes," the general told him. "That was that blue ball of smoke we saw earlier."

"But sir," Ensign Fetters said nervously. General Gergen gave the young man a look. "Isn't it always a bad idea to attack into the sun?"

"Always," General Gergen agreed. He smiled, and nodded toward the pimply-faced mage. "Unless you have a god on your side."

"Ametza can turn off the sun, sir?" Fetters asked, paling with fright.

"Nothing so drastic," Gergen said.

The apprentice mage, Halston, moved to the edge of the hill, raised his arms, closed his eyes and intoned deeply. His voice grew smoother, steadier even as his arms seemed to sink under some invisible weight and his knees to buckle under an unknown strain.

"This starts it all," Gergen said. He added, "And the nice things is, if it doesn't work, we won't lose a man at all."

#

Skara Ningan snapped open her leather roll and arrayed it on the ground in front of her, tugging on the far end to create a small arc around the ground where she knelt. She pulled the first quarrel from the farthest part of the roll, knowing that reaching too far would slow her down when she needed speed most.

She placed the quarrel at the end of her crossbow and smiled as the magic pushed it back against the taut steel bowstring, cocking the crossbow for her. The quarrels were magic, too, spelled to have greater speed, range, and penetration — as well as having poisoned tips to make them more deadly.

Skara carefully laid the cocked crossbow on her legs and pulled her telescope to her eye. She scanned the east watch towers, brilliantly lit by the early morning sun. The officers were easy to spot by their dress. Some even still wore the old feathered bronze helmets, relics from the days before the magic of gunpowder.

She was ready. All that was needed was the signal.

#

"If your newest daughter has the gift of healing, it would seem quite wasteful to destroy her," Ibb rumbled, pointing a hand toward Ellen Annabelle.

"How can anyone kill a god?" Rabel asked, returning to Ellen's disturbing question.

"I believe it has been tried before," Ibb said. "And gods have been trapped, powerless for long periods of time."

"What did you learn when you destroyed your son?" Ellen asked Ophidian. He lowered his eyes toward her. "It was you, wasn't it?"

Ophidian nodded, his eyes filled with sorrow.

"The wyverns are your tears, the dragons, your blood," Imay said thoughtfully. "When you hurt them, it hurts you?"

"And it weakens me," Ophidian admitted.

"Hmm," Ibb rumbled, deep in thought, his red eyes glowing brightly. "It is reasonable to assume that every new wyvern, every new dragon, increases your power."

"Except that I cannot make new wyverns, not since my son, Eravar," Ophidian admitted.

"Because you can't cry," Ellen guessed. Ophidian jerked his head in the merest hint of a nod.

"What you need, my friend," Ibb said slowly, "is to be certain that we won't betray you." He shook his head. "As our deaths will be noticed by too many others, you must either begin a war you know you cannot win… or learn to trust us."

"Ellen Annabelle is a new wyvern," Ophidian said. "Dragons, and wyverns will know this." Bitterly, he added, "So will the gods."

"The gods did not record every tear, every drop of blood shed," Ibb said. "If they had, they would have known about Jarin."

Ophidian grunted at that logic, then shrugged. "There are two who know without doubt, among the gods." He glanced at Rabel. "Your daughter has met them."

"But outside the confines of their domain, they guard their names," Annabelle said with Ellen's mouth. "Which is why I do not say them."

Ophidian's lips twisted as he agreed wryly, "They appreciate their privacy."

"So they would be unlikely to reveal this knowledge," Imay guessed.

"And their daughter would probably protect me," Annabelle said again through Ellen. Ophidian glanced at the twin-souled girl and nodded slowly.

"So there remains the dragons and wyverns," Rabel said, pursing his lips thoughtfully. He raised an eyebrow at the dragon god. "Do they not have to know of Jarin Reedis?"

"Why not introduce the two at once, and leave the impression that both came from the frozen wastes, blood and tear together?" Ibb suggested.

Ophidian shook his head. "Too many would know of Annabelle."

"But not of me," Ellen said with certainty. Ophidian glanced down at her. "I was an orphan, an urchin and no one cared about me at all." She paused, sad. "Until Captain Ford."

"He was an orphan, himself," Ibb told her.

"So you would have us call you Annabelle Ellen?" Ophidian asked. "Because the wyvern name is always last."

"Jarin Reedis is going to change that, why not have it be the same with me?" Ellen asked. "In fact, why not say that Jarin and I were siblings, born at the same time?"

Ophidian's expression grew thoughtful. Slowly he nodded. "It could work."

"So, at least for the moment, dragon god, will you refrain from plotting our demise?" Ibb asked politely.

Ophidian gave the metal man a sour look and said, "I could melt *you* and no one would mind."

"I'd mind," Imay said. "I swore an oath to protect him."

Ophidian hissed in defeat and threw up his arms. "Ibb, you are the only one not sworn to me, the only one I cannot trust by that bond. Will you give me your allegiance?"

"No," Ibb said quickly. "You know why. I do not believe in the gods. And you know why that is so." A moment later he extended his hand to the dragon god. "But I do believe that we are working toward the same goal —"

"Whatever *that* is," Ophidian growled.

"— and I am willing to swear that I will keep your secret," Ibb said. "I understand how much this could affect everything."

Ophidian glowered at the metal man for a long moment, before taking his hand and shaking it solemnly. "I accept."

"You carried me when I could not walk," Ibb said. "We had made oaths to each other. You could have left me lifeless." The metal man nodded his head, his eyes glowing a warm yellow. "I would like us to be friends, if that is possible."

"I should like that, too," Ophidian said.

"Good, now that that's all settled," Ellen said, stretching to her full height, however little that was, "where's Jarin?"

"We need to find him," Ophidian agreed. "As soon as we can, we are going to the Dragon Council."

"All of us?" Ibb asked in surprise.

"I would appreciate your presence," Ophidian said. "And I know that your people live on our island."

"And you've figured out how to ensure our silence," Ibb said. Ophidian inclined his head in question. "Do you not maintain a very hidden castle that is the seat of your power on that island?"

Ophidian chuckled. "Oh, immortal man, you are *always* a delight!"

"And you never said who is trying to kill you," Ibb replied.

"That's because I don't truly know," the dragon god admitted with a shudder.

Chapter Four

Tiko Ashumi dragged an annoying lock of her yellow hair from the side of her face and quickly returned her attention to her drawing. The flying thing was still far off but she could make out the large balloon and the ship's body beneath. With deft strokes she captured the image and flipped the page on her sketchbook, ready for the next drawing. The yellow hair was scratchy and it annoyed her. She was certain it would annoy her more as the sun rose and heated it and the tight cap she wore to hide her coarse black, short-cropped hair.

Tiko pulled one of her special colored pens from her roll and quickly sketched the billowing smoke cloud that was slowly dissipating in the morning breeze. She had drawn it earlier, when she'd first spotted it.

All her pencils were spelled to record the time they were applied to the paper, so she could later recall exactly how long it took the magic blue smoke to disappear, just as she could use her next drawing of the flying ship to determine its speed.

Tiko Ashumi, though just barely a woman, was quite skilled at her job. It was a great honor and she would be well-rewarded when she returned to her home. Besides, it was fun to spy on the round-eyes. And they were so smug in their conviction that only *they* could make their special toys.

She shut her pad, slid it and her pencils into her messenger bag, and climbed back down from the rooftop where she'd hidden herself long enough to make these sets of drawings.

A loud noise distracted her and she turned in time to see a huge cloud forming and spreading with unbelievable speed at the east edge of the town. The hairs on her arm stood up in tension. Magic.

She raced down the rest of the way to the street below and moved quickly to blend in with the crowd. With seeming aimless motion, she made her way toward the forming cloud. She found shelter in a doorway, pulled out her sketch pad, picked blue, gray, and black pencils, and began a quick sketch of what she saw.

The cloud was the water god's work, she was certain. Ametza.

#

The alarm from Captain Nevins had startled Captain Walter when he heard it — then he spotted the ball of fire rising from the ground. Seeing that, Captain Walter shouted at his men, sent a pleading look to his mage, and shouted, "All hands, all hands, lift ship!"

"I'm trying, sir!" Martin, the apprentice mage called back in despair. "It's just too heavy."

"Bannos, Grestin!" Walter shouted. "Get over there and add your spells to Martin's."

"How, sir?" Edon Grestin asked. "A spell's for one person."

"Lift a part of the balloon, then," Walter said, shaking his head in fury. "Just *do* something!"

Pace, carrying three of the large dragon steel slabs was only inching its way skyward. A moment later, it lurched and seemed to tremble as the other two apprentice mages added their spells to Martin's and the airship's timbers groaned with the strain. But it moved upwards, faster.

"Engineer, deploy the propellers!" Walter bellowed. "Full steam ahead!" He glanced ahead, realized that they were heading toward the ruins of the fort and hastily added, "Right full rudder!"

"Full ahead, aye!" the engineer shouted back in acknowledgement.

"Hands to the fire!" Walter shouted. More men scurried back to the boiler and grabbed shovels, filling the flaming grate with coal.

"Don't choke the flames!" the engineer shouted in warning. "Steady, lads! Ease up a bit, let the fires catch first."

"Right full rudder, aye," the helmsman called just as Walter could see the bow of the ship sliding past the foreboding rubble of the fort. He let out a breath he didn't know he was holding and turned back to see what Captain Nevins was doing aboard *Harbinger*.

What he saw dismayed him. *Harbinger* was still on the ground, men scrambling up the ropes. He saw the smoke from a hastily lit fire obscuring the stern and realized that Captain Nevins had lost a large part of his crew, rendering his ship half-manned. But *Harbinger's* balloon grew taught as mage Borkin cast his spell and the airship started inching slowly up into the morning light and the cold air.

#

"Are we too late?" Granno asked as he, the queen, and Jarin Reedis opened the camouflaged sortie portal near the old west entrance. No other unblocked entrance remained closer to the old fort. He saw the two airships a half mile in the distance, the dark oil-soaked smoke of the underground explosion spreading up to the sky and frowned as he saw that both airships were trying to escape.

"Is there nothing you can do?" Queen Diam anxiously asked Jarin Reedis. "I know that two airships, even half-armed is a threat to your life but —"

"Your majesty, I'm the mage who taught airships to fly," Reedis informed her smugly. "Might I beg the indulgence of your attention?"

Queen Diam blinked at Reedis' courtly speech and then nodded. "You may," she said with a languid wave of her hand, "I shall great you such an indulgence."

Beside her, Granno snorted and shook his head at the young man. "You spent too much time with that king!"

"I spent more time with his queen," Reedis replied with a smirk. He caught Diam's look and hastily added, "Not that I ever slighted her royalty."

Diam gave him a probing look and murmured, "I shall not question you on the matter further." She pointed to the rising airships. "Now, what of them?"

Reedis moved into the clearing beyond the sortie port and rose to his full height, inviting the queen and her chief to join him. When they did, he raised his hands, took a theatrical breath and said, "Observe!"

For a moment, nothing happened. And then, in the distance, they could see the highest airship halt its upwards movement. A moment later, it plummeted to the ground, hitting hard with a dull, booming sound as it broke its hull on the hard stone below and was shattered by the rigid dragon steel slabs crushing it from above.

Queen Diam leaped to her toes and clapped with joy. "Excellent, excellent!" she cried, turning to Jarin Reedis with a huge smile. She pointed to the remaining airship. "And the other?"

Jarin met her question with a smile.

General Gergen turned to his ensign as the clouds rolled overhead, blocking the sun. "Do you think our troops will have any trouble now?"

Ensign Fetter shook his head, his jaw agape.

"That's just the opening move," Gergen said, pointing toward the left of his army. "Can you guess what comes next?"

Ensign Fetter shut his mouth with an audible snap. He glanced at the left flank, then back to the right where the clouds had wrapped themselves around the two guard towers that protected the enemy's gate.

"A diversion on the left and an assault on the towers, sir?" Ensign Fetter replied hesitantly.

General Gergen smiled even as he shook his head. "That's what that dodderer Adkins will no doubt think." He nodded toward the enemy's walls. "So we use his thinking against him and let his mistakes be our gain."

"We attack on the left, sir?" Ensign Fetter asked in surprise. "But isn't that through the marshes? Won't our men get bogged down?" He gestured to the long wall that ringed the town. "And there's still the walls, sir."

"All true," Gergen agreed. "But mage Vistos reminds us that waters can flow and that a river can carve through mountains."

"Sir?" Ensign Fetter said, with a confused frown. "But doesn't that it a long time to carve through mountains? Or walls?"

"Unless Ametza helps," Gergen agreed. "Of course, she probably won't."

"She won't?"

"Which is why we're not going to try asking her," Gergen said. He smiled at the imposing walls surrounding his enemy's town. "But they don't know that, do they?"

"No, they don't," the ensign admitted. "So we're going to trick them, sir?"

"Indeed," Gergen agreed. "We're going to get them to open the gates for us, and we'll march in and accept their surrender."

"Yes sir," Ensign Fetter said with the resignation of one who realized he would never be able to guess the general's plans.

#

Skara Ningan had selected all her shots with care. And she had hit every target. Now she was down to her final three bolts. She reloaded her crossbow, a grim smile on her face.

She turned as a noise distracted her. The flying ship was now level with her position. It turned just beside her and four cannon roared, showering the town with shot. It fired twice and then turned again toward the town.

Skara Nangin took careful aim with her crossbow, sighted her target and loosed the first of her special bolts. She waited patiently as the magic bolt tore through the distance from the mountain to the gate.

She saw the explosion long before she heard it but by then she'd already shot her second bolt. Even as the echoes of the first shot reached her ears, she saw the plume of the second shot as it hit the hinge at the top of the right-hand gate. The top of the left-hand gate was already shifting, its hinge destroyed. She fired her last bolt and grabbed her gear and started away without looking to see if it hit.

She was already a hundred feet down from her eyrie when she heard the crash of the gates falling to the ground.

In the distance the cavalry trumpeted — *charge*.

Captain Nevins looked in horror at the wreckage that had been the airship *Pace* and turned fearfully toward Tortin Borkis. "What happened?"

"I don't know," Borkis said, shaken. "It's like their magic failed."

"Lower the ropes, prepare to hoist survivors!" Nevins shouted to his men. To his helmsman he said, "Steer toward the wreck."

Borkis gave him a questioning look and Nevins shrugged. "We need crew."

The mage accepted this with a sigh, turning his attention back to the balloon that was lifting them slowly into the sky.

"First mate!" Nevins shouted. No response. He glanced around irritably and realized that the mate had died in the fire below. "Second mate!"

"Crippens, sir," a man said, scuttling back from the bow and knuckling his head. "Midshipman."

"Really," Nevins said without enthusiasm. From his uniform and bearing, the boy was one of the transfers from the navy. "Form up a party and jettison the guns."

"Sir?" the young man asked in surprise.

"We need to get high and move quickly," Nevins explained. "The guns are the heaviest and the easiest to move."

"Blow them overboard?" Tortin Borkis called from where he stood under the balloons. "Like last time?"

Captain Nevins allowed himself a pained sigh and nodded in agreement, calling back, "Excellent idea, mage! We'll make a seaman of you yet!"

"Got to have water, first, sir," Mage Borkis called back with a grim laugh.

"You heard him," Nevins said to Crippens. "Bring up some powder, cut the lashings, and blow the cannon overboard."

"Aye, sir!" Crippens said with obvious reluctance. He nodded toward two men and gestured for them to follow him as he went below to the powder room.

"Just like old times," Tortis Borkin called back to the captain.

"Be quiet, mage," Nevins said quellingly. "And tend to your work."

#

"Those men are trying to climb up to the other ship," Granno said as he spotted the distant silhouettes crossing from the wreckage.

A gust of smoke erupted from the ship and moments later they heard the *boom* of a cannon, followed by another billow of smoke and another *boom*.

"What are they firing at?" Queen Diam asked, craning her neck toward the distant scene.

"They're not," Reedis said. "They're firing their guns off the ship to lighten it." He smiled evilly. "I think we should help them."

"What do you mean?"

Reedis drew a spell in the air with his arms and, with a smug look at the queen, pushed it on the distant airship. A moment later the ship lurched rapidly upwards, its ropes pulling through the hands of the few men who'd grabbed them from the ground.

The ship seemed to be leaning to one side as it streaked upwards.

"They've fired off their port side and now they're heavy on the starboard side," Reedis said with a chortle. Academically, he mused, "I wonder if they'll fire or just release the other guns?"

"They're getting away," Diam said with a worried glance toward the mage dragon.

"No, your majesty," Reedis corrected happily, "they're getting *higher*."

\#

"By the gods, man, what did you do?" Nevins bellowed at Borkin as he lurched from the stern to the mast amidships where the mage was holding on for dear life. "We're going up too fast!" He jabbed a finger toward the hull and the ground below. "We'll never get those men onboard!"

Before Borkin could reply, Nevins spied the midshipman laboring up to the deck with more powder. "Belay that!" he shouted. "Just cut the lashing and the let the starboard cannon *fall!*"

Crippen accepted this change in orders with a stricken look, dropping the bag ashamedly and going for his dirk even as he motioned his two seamen to do the same. This was a mistake. One of the seamen stumbled and Crippen only had time to open his mouth to shout before the seaman's dirk cut through the bag of gunpowder that Crippen had dropped to the deck.

The three men all had a horrified moment to realize what was going to happen — and then the punctured bag exploded, throwing them up high in the air and away from the blast.

Nevins saw the disaster as it was happening, grabbed Borkin tightly with one hand and the rigging with the other. When the bag of gunpowder exploded, they were buffeted but unharmed.

Nevins took in the devastation, saw the way the survivors tried to crawl back to their feet, saw the horror on the faces of his remaining crew and turned to Borkin.

"We must strike."

"What?" Borkin said.

"We must surrender," Nevins said. The mage's eyes widened.

"To whom?" Borkin asked.

\#

"There's someone climbing up the balloon," Reedis said. "At least I think that's what that is."

He had shouted with joy when he'd seen the explosion, wondering if perhaps the airship would destroy itself and then, with Diam and Granno, had watched in growing confusion at the continued antics on the ship which still listed to starboard, unbalanced by the weight of the cannon on that side.

"They're short of crew, they're scared, they're doomed, and they know it," Queen Diam said without rancor.

"It is nothing more than they deserve," Granno said.

"Indeed," Queen Diam agreed.

"What?" Reedis shouted, pointing to the airship. "I don't believe it!" He turned back to the queen. "They've struck their colors!"

"What?" Diam said.

"They've surrendered, your majesty," Jarin Reedis said bowing to her. "The airship has surrendered."

"To whom?" Granno wondered.

"Us, if we want it," Reedis replied. He waved a hand toward the distant, limping ship hanging from its balloon. "What say you, your majesty? How would you like your own royal airship?"

Granno grunted in surprise and then groaned in shock as he took in Diam's growing delight. "You can't be serious!"

"Jarin Reedis, I believe that my kingdom would be *delighted* to take this prize."

Chapter Five

"What did you *do?*" Tortin Borkis shouted as he saw captain Nevins descending from the rigging.

"I surrendered the ship," Nevins told him loftily.

"To whom?" Tortin demanded, gesturing around the empty sky around them and stopping abruptly, his jaw agape as large black shape raced toward them.

"I suppose to the dragon," Nevins said. He peered closer. "Or those that are riding on it."

"Isn't that the same dragon that flamed *Warrior* from below?" Tortin quailed. "What makes you think it won't burn us in the sky?"

"Nothing," Nevins said. He turned to the mage. "But consider: there are people riding on it. If it wanted to flame us out of the sky, it would not need or want to carry passengers."

Borkis frowned at the logic. Then his eyes narrowed as the dragon grew closer and he could make out the shapes riding on it. "Those are zwerg."

"Zwerg, Sorians, it doesn't matter," Nevins said. "We've killed both and they've no reason to be merciful."

"So why did you surrender?"

"Because I have no chances once the Ferryman takes me," Nevins said with a shrug. He nodded toward Borkis. "Does that make sense?"

The mage frowned. "I suppose so."

"Besides," Nevins added stoically, "they probably need a mage. They might not kill you."

Tortin Borkis could only shrug in agreement.

Nevins squinted at the approaching dragon. "There's something different."

"The other dragon was black with bits of red," Borkis observed. "This one is black with purple."

"Well, it's just as big," Nevins said with a wave of his hand.

"How are they going to get aboard?" Borkis wondered.

His question was answered as the dragon approached the stern quarter and matched height with the airship, its neck angling inwards. Three armed zwerg rushed up the neck and jumped overboard to land heavily on the ship's wooden deck. The three fanned out, drew crossbows and stood ready to shoot anyone who threatened them. Captain Nevins moved toward them, hands upraised and palms out in the universal sign of surrender. A fourth zwerg jumped into the middle of the group. He turned back and stretched out a hand to the dragon's right claw — and the dragon disappeared. The zwerg pulled the man that had replaced it onto the ship.

"You!" Captain Nevins swore in surprise as he caught sight of the man.

"Captain Nevins?" Reedis replied.

"I can't believe I'm doing this," Colonel Thomas Walpish muttered as he finished hooking himself into the harness. He glanced toward the airship captain, the Sorian, Martel. "Are you sure this is safe?"

Martel shrugged. "We're testing it now."

Walpish swore under his breath and shook his head. His squad was close by and he knew to keep his spirits up so that they wouldn't worry.

"Excellent!" Walpish said loud enough for his troopers to hear. He caught one glancing at another and winking. "We're going to be the first of a new force of arms, men! The King will surely heap us with honors!"

"Never mind the honor, I want the plunder," one grizzled veteran, Oswald, growled to the delight of the others.

Walpish nodded to the captain and moved to the opening in the ship's rail. To his men, he declared, "We're going to be the first ones to walk the plank into battle!"

The twelve men roared approval.

A shout from above caught Colonel Walpish's attention and the captain nodded at him, gesturing at the gangplank.

"We're over the rooftop, you need to jump now," Martel told him.

"When we're down, you'll haul off and start shelling?"

"Yes," Martel agreed with a sigh. "We'll raise dust and smoke behind you in the city and mask your cavalry's charge."

Walpish nodded jerkily. "I'm counting on you, captain," the colonel said sternly.

"Indeed," Martel replied, waving his hand to the gangplank.

"Now trust me and get off my ship."

Walpish's jaw tightened but he turned, grabbing hold of the rope overhead and guiding it along with him as he walked out of the gangplank.

"Ready?" the captain said as Walpish got to the end. The colonel nodded. "We've got your slack. Jump."

Colonel Walpish jumped into the thin air over the south guardtower's roof.

#

Tiko Ashumi raced to the docks. The gates both east and west had already been ordered shut. The port would be next. But there was always one boat ready to flee at the last moment — there!

"Ahoy!" Tiko called, "where are you headed?"

"Anywhere but here," the grizzled seaman at the helm shouted back. His eyes narrowed as he examined her. "And what business is it of yours?"

In response, Tiko finished a large gold coin from her pocket and waved it over her head.

"You'd need a lot more than *one*," the seaman grumbled, waving her to come closer.

As she got to the jetty, she got a clearer sight of the seaman, the crew, and the boat. The boat was nearly a wreck, her sails old, threadbare and unpatched. The crew matched the ship.

"I need passage," Tiko said. She turned back the way she came and saw a crowd rushing up behind her — others seeking to flee the city. "And you need someone to get you away or they'll swamp your boat."

"And you can do that?" the seaman asked gruffly. "A little girl with straw for hair?"

"I can do many tricks," Tiko said, pulling another two gold coins from her pockets.

"Get aboard," the seaman said gesturing for her to jump. The boat was near the end of the jetty, soon it would be too late.

Tiko tensed, grit her teeth and ran. She jumped — and her feet scrambled to kick off the boat's railing and land her in a heap on the deck.

The seaman rumbled in delight at her crash landing. She shot him a look and he glared at her then turned to look back to the jetty.

"Best get us moving, girlie, unless you want company," the seaman told her.

Tiko Ashumi pulled herself back to her feet, pulled her backpack off her shoulders, reached into a pocket and pulled a small ball from it.

"What's that going to do?" the seaman guffawed.

"Watch," Tiko replied, throwing the ball. It landed in the rushing crowd and burst into a ball of smoke. A moment later the crowd had halted, turned and broke up into small knots of people all retching violently.

"Hmm," the seaman allowed. He turned to the breakwater that marked the harbor's entrance. "Where to?"

"Wherever you're going," Tiko replied.

"That'll cost you five pieces of gold," the seaman replied.

"Four," Tiko said, adding another coin to the three she already held.

"Five, if you want to eat."

Tiko pulled out another coin and passed them to seaman.

"What's your name, girlie?" the seaman asked.

Tiko reached to her head, tore off the hat and fake hair and threw them overboard. With her other hand, she reached into her blouse and pulled out a necklace with a bright yellow stone hanging at its end. She drew herself up regally, and said, "I am the princess Yuri Moko of the Westward Kingdom and you shall bow before me." She spun the yellow gem slowly, catching the light of the sun and reflecting into the seaman's eyes.

"Princess," the seaman said, his eyes suddenly vacant as he bowed deeply. "What do you wish?"

"Van, you old pirate!" a voice called up from the cabin below. A head popped out. "What are you doing looking like that? We've got a course to steer and —" he broke off as he spotted Tiko. "By the gods, who are you?"

"I'm your new captain," Tiko Ashumi told her with a grim look. She turned the gem to shine at him. The man's angry scowl faltered, then disappeared.

"What are your orders, captain?"

Tiko Ashumi moved over to the bowing seaman, dug into his pockets and retrieved her gold. She might need it later.

"Set a course due west," she said. "And then have someone bring me the rest of the crew. And food, I'm hungry."

"Aye, captain."

Ten minutes later, the cook was woodenly serving her some hot noodles, and the rest of the crew were trimming the sails. All called her 'captain' now. She didn't bother to learn their names. The crew would need those no longer than she needed them, so learning their names would be a tedious waste of her time.

#

"Have the men form up and prepare to attack," General Gergen said to General Ambrose as he rode up to the third division's command post.

"I saw the clouds," General Ambrose said with a grin. "The men are ready."

"Good," Gergen said. "Make it look real but let's not lose anyone we don't have to?"

"You're worried about the men?" General Ambrose asked in surprise. Soldiers could be replaced, that's why the kingdom had plenty of serfs.

"I want to save them for later," General Gergen told him reprovingly. "New ones take training and don't fight as well when they're worried about being uselessly sacrificed." General Ambrose dipped his head in acceptance... but not agreement, as Gergen knew all too sadly from years of experience. Ambrose was tough but he was a blunt instrument — he'd follow his orders and keep attacking until his division was nothing but blood and bodies regardless of the ground gained. Fortunately, General Gideon was cut from a different mold.

Speaking of which, General Gergen turned to his aide, the ensign whose mount had managed to keep pace with Gergen's stallion. "Send the signal."

"Yes, sir," the ensign saluted, reaching into his messenger bag and pulling out a long paper stick: a signal rocket.

"Best get off your horse, first," Gergen advised. "Unless you want to be delivering your message in person."

Red-faced the ensign dismounted, briskly moved a few paces away and lit the rocket which whistled into the air and burst with in a brilliant red cloud hundreds of feet above. Gergen glanced northwards, toward the sea, waiting for the response from his left wing. He got it a moment later: an answering red flare.

Second division would begin their 'attack' immediately.

"Get going, general," Gergen said, nodding to his aide as he remounted. "We're heading back to my tent."

"Yes, sir!" General Ambrose said, saluting sharply. When Gergen returned it, he dropped his hand and turned gestured for his officers, ready to send them to battle.

#

"That idiot Gergen is going to get his army ruined," General Dartan muttered happily to himself as he saw the Kingsland third division start to move slowly up toward the town's walls.

"But with the clouds, they'll be able to see our men," General Adkins remarked.

"They'll be able to see our *walls*," Dartan corrected him. He waved towards the battlements and the soldiers crouching behind them. "We'll be able to see his *army*." Dartan frowned as the enemy soldiers began their steady march toward certain death. Something wasn't right. He put his telescope to one eye and peered to his right, far down the wall toward where it curved at the sea.

A red flare burst above them. A moment later it was answered by a red flare on the right.

General Dartan lowered his telescope and snapped it shut with a curse.

"Sir?" Adkins asked.

"This is a feint," General Dartan swore. "Send the reserves to the north, they're attacking on our right!"

"Through the marshes?" General Adkins asked in surprise.

General Dartan waved a hand toward the clouds overhead. "Their god is Ametza. If she can make clouds here, what can she do to the marshes by the sea?"

Color drained from Adkins' face. "They say that the last king took the capital when the goddess flooded the river."

"Exactly," Dartan agreed grimly. He waved the other general away. "Get those men moving!"

"Sir!" Adkins said, saluting sharply and rushing down the stairs to the courtyard below, shouting for his aide to join him.

#

Captain Martel glanced behind him to see Colonel Walpish wave his hat from the top of the guard tower at the gate. Captain Martel waved back and turned to his first lieutenant, saying, "Have the crew man the port side guns, and bring the ship to starboard."

"Sir!"

"We're going to give the Sorian on those walls something to let us know we're here," Martel said, pointing to the walls to the west of them.

"What about these walls here, sir?" Lieutenant Eccleston asked, pointing to the walls just behind him.

"The cavalry won't appreciate our interference," Martel said mildly. "Besides, we want the soldiers over there —" he pointed west "— to be distracted."

"Very well, sir," Eccleston replied, saluting sharply and turning back to the deck. He started shouting orders and in a few minutes the guns were loaded and run out. "Port side battery ready to fire, sir!"

"Ship heading due north, sir," the helmsman reported. *Wasp* was pointing toward the sea, with guns bearing on the walls surrounding the town.

"Mechanic, bring us to a halt," Captain Martel ordered.

"Engines stop!" the mechanic shouted to his men.

"Lieutenant, your target is the guard towers of the west wall," Captain Martel called.

"Aye, sir," Eccleston replied crisply. "All gunners, sight your target." He waited until the guns were shifted before reporting, "Target acquired, sir!"

"Fire when ready," Captain Martel said. "And keep firing until they surrender."

"Surrender, sir?"

"You'll see," Captain Martel said with a grin.

#

"However did you get command of an airship, sir?" Mage Reedis asked Captain Nevins in outrage. "Surely the king —" Reedis broke off in surprise.

Nevins gave him an evil smile.

"King Markel gave *you* an airship?"

"Two airships, actually," Nevins told him. "The first you destroyed when we fought your fort."

"Not me," Reedis said.

"Some other black dragon, then?" Nevins wondered.

"Ah," Jarin said with Reedis' mouth. "Yes, that would be me."

"You?" Nevins said, confused. "Didn't you just say —"

"Different person, same mouth," Reedis told him.

"Sir, who is this?" Mage Borkin demanded anxiously.

"Tortis Borkin, may I make you known to Sir Reedis, formerly mage aboard the King's airship, *Spite*," Nevins said, waving a hand between the two men. His eyes narrowed. "And how is your captain, these days?"

"Dead," Reedis said in an icy voice.

"Good," Nevins said. "I hope he died horribly."

"I believe so," Reedis replied.

"And are we," he waved a hand at his crew, "now also to die horribly?"

"Do you surrender?" Reedis asked.

"Why should we surrender?" Tortis Borkin asked. "He's just one man and these zwerg people — there are only four of them."

"And the dragon, don't forget," Nevins reminded him easily. "Also, did I mention that Sir Reedis is the first mage of the airships?"

Borkin gave Reedis a sharp look and bit his lip. "*Spite*, that was the one with ten balloons?"

"Harder to destroy than the one," Reedis said, raising a finger and pointed it toward the balloon straining above them. Borkin gulped as Reedis created a small, bright flame at the end of his fingertip.

"So, mage, do we surrender?" Nevins asked Borkin mildly. He didn't wait for a reply before returning his attention to Jarin Reedis and the zwerg surrounding him. "Do I surrender to you or them?"

"You'll surrender to me," Reedis said.

"Very well, I surrender my men and this airship, *Harbinger*, unto you," Nevins said mildly. "May the gods bless this day."

"Now what?" Tortin Borkis asked.

"Bring the ship around and over the crater there," Reedis said, pointing toward the broken circle which had once been the base of the East Pass Fort. There were still several large dragon steel slabs lying there.

"Very well," Nevins said. He turned to the helmsman and the mechanic. "You heard the man, helm about and power to the propellers." He turned back to Jarin Reedis. "May I offer your men something to drink? Tea? Coffee? Poison?"

"No thank you," Reedis said, gesturing to the zwerg leader and moving to the far railing. "We're going to see after our prisoners."

"Prisoners?" Borkin said in surprise. "But we're your prisoners."

"Only some of them," Reedis replied. He gave Nevins a hard look. "You've surrendered your ship, sir. Don't think to abuse our kindness." He jumped over the railing. Tortin Borkis cried in surprise which turned to awe when he saw the black dragon rise where the man had been. The four zwerg quickly jumped the railing and onto the dragon's back. It spiraled away and down to the broken ground below.

Nevins moved to railing and followed the dragon's descent. Mage Borkin joined him. "Why don't we run, sir?"

"Two reasons, Tortis," Nevins told him easily. Tortis Borkin raised an eyebrow. "Firstly, that's a dragon," he said, raising one finger. "It could flame us out of the sky in an instant."

"And?"

"Second," Nevins raised another finger. "That's the mage who knows how to make airships fly —"

"But I know how to do that!"

"— and leap into the sky even when another mage is controlling it," Nevins continued implacably.

"*He* did that to us?" Borkin exclaimed. He glanced down to the ground below. The black dragon had discharged his passengers and had leaped back into the sky, moving to corral the few sailors who were able and trying to escape. Borkin moved closer to Captain Nevin and said, "We're going to run out of food soon."

"They'll give us some, I'm certain," Nevins replied. "Unless they want us to starve, of course."

"The food for the sailors, sir," Borkis said urgently. "When it runs out —"

"I'm looking forward to that," Nevins replied with an evil glint in his eyes. "I expect it things will get quite interesting then."

"Oh," Borkis said. Then his eyes grew wide. "*Oh!*" He grinned. "Is that why you offered them food?"

"I figured only the best for our captors," Nevins replied smoothly.

"And when they were out of our special food?"

"I imagine that even with just our men, things will get interesting," Captain Nevins said. "Maybe *quite* interesting.

"Yes, I suppose they will," Tortin Borkis agreed, a smile coming to his lips as he deciphered the captain's plan. "Perhaps even interesting enough to let us escape."

"We can hope," Nevins agreed easily.

Chapter Six

"If you don't know, we must be very very careful," Rabel said to Ophidian when the dragon god revealed his greatest secret.

"It is difficult to kill a god," Ophidian said.

"But not so difficult that it can't be done," Ellen Annabelle said, glancing up to the dragon god, "right?"

Ophidian dipped his chin in acknowledgement.

"But I can help," Ellen said.

"I think so," Ophidian agreed. "We won't know until we get a chance to try again." He grimaced. "And, of course, we have to live long enough to be presented with the opportunity."

A loud *clunk* came from inside Ibb's caravan, followed moments later by more sounds.

"The pieces," Ibb said, as if that were explanation.

"Pieces?" Imay asked, jumping as a particularly loud 'piece' *clunked* inside Ibb's caravan.

"You," Ibb said with a slight inclination toward the princess, "may find this most interesting." He turned to Rabel. "You've seen this before."

"And have the scars to prove it," Rabel added ruefully, holding up his hands. He shot a glance toward Ophidian, "I meant to ask, is there a reason that you kept my old scars?"

"So that you wouldn't forget how you got them," Ophidian told him, sounding surprised that the answer wasn't obvious. He nodded at the metal man. "I would be very much interested in your loud *clunking* objects."

"It would be a trade of secrets," Ibb warned holding up a cautioning hand.

"No doubt," Ophidian agreed. "But you remember my last war."

"I do," Ibb agreed. He waved toward Ellen Annabelle. "She may find some of this boring."

"No, I won't!" Ellen protested reflexively. She stomped a foot on the ground for emphasis. "I like learning new spells."

"This is less about spells and more about metalworking," Rabel told her.

"Do I get to make fire?" Ellen asked. When the smith nodded, she smiled at him. "Then that will be learning enough."

"Indeed," Ibb agreed, gesturing toward the caravan. "If that is your decision, then we should retire inside." He glanced toward Ophidian. "May I have your word on this, dragon god?"

"On what?"

"That what you see and what you learn will not be disclosed to others as knowledge owned by us," Ibb told him solemnly. "You saw much when we were in Fixer's cavern, you will learn more."

"Does this have anything to do with the many rooms we saw in the other caravan?" Annabelle asked with Ellen's voice.

"Very much so," Ibb agreed.

"Then I would be *very* interested," Annabelle said. "There were things about the *smell* of that caravan which worried me."

"By all means, let us see what you now *smell* in my caravan," Ibb allowed, moving toward the hidden steps leading up to the invisible doorway.

#

The room they entered was not one Imay or Ellen Annabelle had ever seen before. It was very obviously larger than the outside of the caravan but not as unimaginably immense as Fixer's cavern. There was a forge at the back end of the room on the right. There was worktable before it and stocks of metal and fuel stacked on one side. On the other side —

"Is that a library?" Imay said, eyes going wide as she rushed to the left of the room and stood in awe of the rows and rows of books stacked floor to ceiling.

"It is but a minor part of the whole," Ibb allowed. Ophidian's eyes glittered as he glanced at the metal man in amusement — he could hear the barely hidden pride in the metal immortal's voice. Ibb gestured to the right, just inside the door where a jumble of metal pieces lay spilled all over themselves including what seemed one incredibly large gear which was bent in half. "I see that Fixer has not lost her sense of humor."

"That was never inside you," Rabel said as he followed Ibb's gaze and spied the huge, bent gear.

"It is a joke and a responsibility," Ibb said. "Fixer is testing me. It causes her joy, so I will not object."

Ellen Annabelle moved over to the pile of pieces and crouched eyeing it from a safe distance. Rabel stood behind her. Imay turned from the library and walked over to join them.

"All this must be repaired?" she asked Ibb.

"Or replaced," the metal man said.

"That's three weeks worth of work for a good crew," Imay said judiciously.

"We shall work faster than that," Rabel told her. "In fact, princess, I believe that you will find Ibb a great teacher."

"Ibb?"

"He cannot cast spells," Rabel said in response to her surprise but added, "but he has had centuries instructing those who can."

Ibb's innards whirred in a noise that might have meant agreement.

Imay glanced over to the newly-gleaming metal man and back to the pile. Gingerly she lifted one particularly mangled gear, eyeing it dubiously, and said, "How do we even know what this was supposed to be when it wasn't broken?"

"Fixer has sent drawings," Ibb said, pointing to a table. Imay saw that there were papers on top of it and a rack of dowels beneath on which they could be draped. He moved toward the table, gesturing for Imay to follow.

"It's the molds that will take the most time," Rabel said with a frown.

"That," Ibb said, turning to smile at him, "is why we have apprentices."

"Apprentices?" Ellen Annabelle asked, glancing around nervously. "Like Lyric?"

"Like you," Rabel told her with a twist of his lips. He moved to a closet, opened it and pulled out several work coats. He put one on — Ellen was surprised to see that it had his name embroidered over the breast pocket — and passed the others around.

"I am a god," Ophidian said when Rabel tried to hand him one.

"You're going to enjoy this," Rabel promised. "And you'll want the extra pockets." Ophidian eyed the bottom of the proffered coat critically and noted that in addition to a tool-laden belt, there were many large pockets and some thick fabric loops for hammers and other such instruments. Ophidian did not look happy. Rabel smiled at him, adding, "You'll get to hit things."

"Hard," Imay added, belting her coat tight and pulling out a large hammer with a look of glee. "Ibb, what needs hammering first?"

"In here you'll put on the goggles you'll find in the pockets and then the hearing protectors hanging on your side," Ibb told her. "These walls echo and I will not have you go deaf."

"I'm a zwerg!" Imay protested. "We're used to loud sounds."

"You will do as I ask," Ibb said. "It is my forge, you'll follow my rules."

Ophidian, the dragon god, snorted in amusement. But he put on the goggles and the hearing protectors.

"And the work gloves," Ibb added as the others all complied.

#

Of the crew of thirty, Jarin Reedis had only found twelve alive. Two were suffering so much from their injuries that he doubted they'd last the night.

"War is stupid," Reedis said aloud to Jarin. The dragon was silent, thoughtful. Reedis understood.

None of the crew had protested when Jarin Reedis had declared them prisoners and had placed them under the zwerg guard.

Harbinger had followed his orders and was coming into position just above the crater that had been created when the ruined flown had floated up into the sky so many days past.

With a smile, Reedis pointed up to the airship and said a simple spell.

What did you do? Jarin thought to him.

"I am mage of hot and cold," Reedis said aloud in answer. "The air in the balloon is now cold enough that it cannot support the airship at its height and is now seeking a lower level."

I see. Jarin sounded intrigued, almost impressed. *Of course, we could just turn the whole balloon to ash. That'd do the job quicker.*

"But the airship would not survive," Reedis told his dragon twin.

An airship killed Annora, Jarin thought heatedly.

"I was on that airship," Reedis confessed. "And I've met Krea Wymarc. She accepted my apology."

"Did she?" Jarin now used Reedis' voice to ask this question and seemed rather happy with the effect it had on the mage.

"In fact, I pledged my life to her," Reedis said, suddenly full of wonder at what that now might mean.

"Good," Jarin said, surprising his mage twin soul. "If I hadn't been such a fool, Annora might still be alive."

"Possibly," Reedis agreed. "Nestor apologized to her, too."

"And who is he?"

"The one who ordered us to shoot you out of the sky," Reedis said in a small voice.

"Then I shall look forward to vengeance," Jarin said happily.

"That might be… a bit difficult," Reedis said cautiously.

"Why?"

"Because he's joined souls with Pallas," Reedis said. "And I think Ophidian wouldn't be happy if you tried to hurt them."

"Pallas?" Jarin repeated in surprise. "What is a 'Pallas'?"

"Pallas is the snow serpent that the sea god Arolan kept trapped in the bitter north for the last two hundred years," Reedis explained.

"Well… a sea god," Jarin said dismissively.

"We stopped Pallas before she could get back to the sea and freeze the whole world," Reedis said in warning.

"She's that powerful?"

"So your father told us," Reedis said.

"Your father, too, now," Jarin reminded him. He mulled this news over and shrugged. "Very well, until we have a chance to talk with Krea Wymarc and this Nestor Pallas, I shall not plot their demise."

"Not much of a concession," Reedis muttered. After a moment, he said, "That little girl, why does she mean so much to you?"

"She was my friend when no one else thought to be," Jarin said. "And she's a good person who needs friends."

"I see," Reedis said. He was silent for a long moment before he felt a tickling in my head. "What are you doing?" he demanded of the dragon.

"Catching up," Jarin said. "If you try, I'm sure you can find my memories, too."

"Can I, now?" Reedis said, intrigued.

#

Ophidian was surprised to discover how restful it could be to work with others. He'd known Rabel for a long time and had occasionally helped the man at his forge, particularly when he'd taught him the secret of dragon steel. But the dragon god found working with the young zwerg woman a marvel. Imay was skilled and learned quickly. Her delight at discovering that she could create the dragon's flame necessary to create dragon steel was sheer joy to the dragon god — after all he had fought a war with the other gods just to give humans, zwergs, and all the intelligent creatures of the world the ability to work with fire. He recalled with a sardonic grin how Vorg and Veva had first opposed his 'radical' scheme so many thousands of years ago and were now his firmest supporters. His expression faded as that thought reminded him yet again that his existence was once again under threat. He moved the gear he was working on over to another table and commenced to hammer it most happily.

It took him a long while before he realized that all the others had stopped and were watching him worriedly.

"What?" Ophidian said, pausing in his hammering.

"I was just observing your obvious delight in reshaping that metal," Ibb said drolly. The two girls sniggered. Rabel smiled and shook his head. Ibb waved a hand. "Pray, continue in your endeavors."

Ophidian, momentarily abashed, returned to working at a more sedate and restrained pace. It did not last.

In fact, the dragon god managed to reshape and fix more than half of the damaged pieces. They finished in record time, mostly because of him.

"Ophidian, if you ever wish to work in my forge again," Ibb told him solemnly, "I shall be delighted to have you."

Annabelle grinned through Ellen's eyes at the dragon god. Imay nodded in agreement, saying, "My mother would say the same, any time you wish, great god."

"It is not an operation I often engage in," Ophidian allowed. "I have more important matters to attend, usually."

"Naturally," Ibb agreed. "But, all the same, the offers stands."

Ophidian inclined his head.

Ibb turned to the others. "Princess, Ellen Annabelle, I would extend the same offer to you. It was… pleasurable working in your company. And we were most productive."

"May I instruct my people on the techniques I have learned here?" Imay asked the metal man hopefully.

"Anything to do with the making of metal or the creation of gears I will be happy to have you share," Ibb said.

"Sometime soon I would appreciate an understanding of how your 'rooms' work," Ophidian warned the metal man quietly.

"For that, dragon god, I would be willing to barter," Ibb said with a slight inclination of his metal head. He turned to the others. "In fact, I imagine you require sustenance," Ibb said. "If you would follow me out of this room, I can arrange for a more appropriate setting."

"What does that mean?" Ellen asked impulsively.

"He's going to bring out his kitchen," Rabel said, moving toward the locker and motioning the others to follow, carefully placing his hearing protectors and goggles back in his work coat before placing it back on the hanger. The others followed suit. Ophidian examined his coat with a certain reluctance as he placed it back in the locker.

"I can arrange for one to be reserved for you," Ibb offered the dragon god. Ophidian turned sharply toward the metal man then more slowly back to the locker.

"I think I would like that," the dragon god allowed.

#

Colonel Walpish scrambled down the stairs from the now empty guard tower as his ensign waited below, leading Walpish's mount behind him. The other troopers with him were handed their horses and Walpish waved them forward at the trot.

"What are we going to do?" Ensign Mitchener asked, over the sharp booms of the airship's guns and the roar of the cavalry tearing through the town in front of them.

"We're going to accept General Adkins' surrender," Colonel Walpish said, gesturing to the far side of the town and the distant guard towers. He turned to his remaining troop commander, "Barricade the gates, turn the guns down the street, and disarm all prisoners."

"What will we do with them?" Captain Lewis asked, eyeing the small group of enemy survivors.

"Send them out the gates and have them make camp," Walpish said. "Tell them that the airship will have them under its guns, should they think to go further."

"Yes, sir!" Captain Lewis responded with a cheerful salute.

Walpish reined his horse, turned it down the road and spurred it into a quick trot. The detached platoon followed after him jauntily.

#

General Ambrose eyed the enemy soldiers on the battlements above their wall with amusement. The clouds overhead were dispersing but the sun was high enough that it would not blind his troops in their attack. Of course they *weren't* going to attack, but Adkins didn't know that.

Ambrose pulled out his telescope and scanned the battlements, picking out the gold-covered cockade hat of a general. He smiled. General Ambrose. Then the gold-covered cockade turned and Ambrose saw *another* gold-plate cockade hat.

"Messenger," Ambrose snapped, "get to General Gergen and tell him that there are *two* generals on the tower walls."

If one was Adkins, then the other had to be — General Ambrose grimaced — General Dartan. Dartan was an entirely different general than aged, infirm Adkins. A man like Dartan would not be easily fooled.

#

"Sir, General Ambrose has returned!" an officer said to General Dartan as he paced the battlements, projecting calm and assurance to all those around him. Dartan turned and saw the general puffing his way up the steps. Dartan waited until the general had recovered enough to salute and then returned the salute smartly.

"The troops are deployed, sir," General Ambrose reported. "The northern marshes are safe." A loud *boom* arrested their attention and they turned just in time to see the first broadside rain down on them from the airship floating smack in the middle of the town.

"Steady men, steady!" General Ambrose shouted. "Their guns can't —"

A crash and explosion erupted not ten feet away as soldiers and stone were both shattered by cannon shot.

General Dartan turned away so that no one could see him wince. When he recovered he turned back, calling, "Form up! Form up! They're only trying to scare us, men!"

Of course, they are succeeding, Dartan thought sourly to himself as another broadside roared out from on high.

"General Ambrose, see if you can train our guns on that… thing," Dartan said, projecting languid boredom over his fears.

"I could, sir," Ambrose replied, eyeing the airship unfavorably. "But I'm afraid any shot would fall on the town."

"And we'd be doing their work for them," Dartan allowed with a sour look. "Very well, get your best sharpshooters up in the tower —" He pointed to the left and above but before he could finish his sentence a cannon ball burst on the roof and shattered it. "Get some men to fire back," he amended ruefully.

Ambrose snapped to attention and saluted crisply. "At once, sir!" He turned and raised his arms to cup mouth as he shouted, "Sharpshooters, return fire!"

Startled soldiers turned at his command, looked up, saw the airship and dubiously brought their long muskets up to take aim.

"Of course," Dartan mused to himself, "the spent bullets will fall back into the town as well."

The men commenced firing anyway. Dartan allowed himself a grunt of satisfaction even while grimly acknowledging that the airship could pound his walls into submission at its leisure.

But that was not to be. An explosion burst above them and a ball of blue smoke fell. It was answered by cannon firing from Ambrose's men outside the walls.

"To the battlements!" General Adkins cried valiantly. "Cannons, return fire!"

General Dartan gave the aged Adkins a sour look but said nothing. Of course Ambrose would fire at them. The were trapped between the guns of the airship inside the town and the guns of the enemy at the gates. It was only a matter of time before he would be forced to surrender.

He waved a hand toward one of his messengers. "Get to the mages, have them send word to King Wendel."

"Sir?"

Dartan gestured the man closer and said lowly in his ear, "Tell them that we will have to surrender the city."

"Sir!"

"Just go!" Dartan snapped, his eyes flashing in anger. The poor messenger snapped to attention and spun on his heels, moving smartly to carry out his orders. Dartan followed him with his eyes as the man brushed his way through the trickle of troops climbing upwards.

As such he was looking just down the road as a squadron of horsemen trotted into view. Dartan's heart leaped when he spotted them. Someone had sent reinforcements. He could order the cavalry to sortie — a suicide mission, certainly — but one which would give him a chance to throw Ambrose off his guard, perhaps long enough to evacuate his army from the town.

One squad reined up, jumped off their mounts and took cover. Crossbows were drawn and fired off, their ends looking odd.

Dartan had just enough time to frown as the crossbow bolts hit the gates and exploded. The hinges disintegrated and the gates groaned heavily as they began to tilt away then fell outwards with sickening speed. A bugle bellowed from the cavalry opposite the walls. It was answered by a distant trumpet from Ambrose's troops.

Dartan didn't need to turn around to know that Ambrose's division was marching toward the now-ruined gates.

From in front of him, from the cavalry, the *enemy* cavalry, a magically amplified voice called out, "Surrender in the name of King Markel!"

Chapter Seven

"You are the mayor of this town?" Captain Welless asked he and his squad marched into the well-appointed office.

"Hamo Beck, at your service," the man replied, nodding. "Please forgive me for not rising, it's not out of respect for you, captain…?"

"Welless," the captain said, frowning at the short bearded man seated opposite him. "First Brigade, First Division, Kingsland Army."

"Yes," Hamo agreed with a nod. "I recognized the uniform."

Captain Welless shot the man a critical look: was he making fun of his uniform? He hadn't been able to change since he'd been detached and he knew that he was filthy.

"I meant no disrespect," Hamo said swiftly. "As I said, I can't rise. I fell off my horse when it bolted and it has left me with a broken leg." He patted the white cast heartily in evidence.

"I see," Welless allowed, thawing a little. "I am here on the orders of General Tashigg."

"Indeed," Hamo said. "He was the fine gentleman who marched through here northwards with his unit."

"I am charged with maintaining order in this town, in the name of King Markel," Welless explained.

"You will get no trouble from us," Hamo assured him. "We are a peaceable folk." He spread his hands. "How may I help you in your task?"

"I'd like to set up my office here, in your front room," Welless said. "I need to meet with all the town leaders and get their loyalty."

Hamo nodded, reached behind him and pulled a bell cord. "Of course," he said. "I'll get my man to collect them."

Welless hid his surprise. He could easily imagine, after the destruction of the East Pass Fort, that the villagers would have felt betrayed and angry — some of those who had died certainly had relatives and loved ones here. The villagers might not openly oppose his force but they could make life difficult: be unwilling to trade or charge too much for their goods — lots of little things that could make an officer's life difficult, perhaps even miserable.

"Your cooperation is welcome," the captain found himself saying sincerely.

"I hope your men and my people can live together amicably," Hamo Beck replied, nodding as his man entered the room, eyeing the soldiers nervously.

#

"Now that you've been suitably recharged," Ibb said as the others leaned back from the table groaning under the remains of their hearty lunch, "I believe we are ready to proceed." He gestured them toward the door. "I must change rooms, return the goods to Fixer and then we will be able to depart."

"Can I say farewell to my mother?" Imay asked Ophidian fearfully.

"Certainly," Ophidian replied. Imay gave him a grateful and surprised look. "After all, I have to retrieve my son," he turned an eye toward Ibb as he added, "the mage."

"This is a first for you," Rabel guessed.

"No," Ophidian said. "But it *has* been a long time since."

"I remember," Ibb said. He opened the back door and politely waved the others through before following. He turned back at the bottom of the steps and said to the caravan, "Fixer, the work is complete."

From inside caravan came a very strange series of noises — like large metal pieces un-*clanging* from where they'd been carefully stacked. The sound was not as loud as when the pieces had been delivered and it was not unpleasant — just odd.

When the sound stopped, Ibb leaned forward, grabbed the invisible handle, turned to the others and said mildly, "Please step far back."

"Why?" Ophidian asked even as he pulled the others away.

"I do not want you to get hit," Ibb replied, taking a step back, leaning forward and pulling *hard* on the invisible handle. The air grew tense and then imploded with a loud noise. Ibb seemed to heave the invisible handle up and around his back, resting it on the far side of his shoulder as though it were now the strap of a small pack. It clanged heavily as it landed on his metal backside and settled with a few strange tinkling metal sounds. Ibb staggered slightly as though adjusting to a great weight and turned around again to face the others.

"It's not often that I find the need to carry my home," Ibb said, bestowing a bemused look on the others. He nodded to Imay. "Princess, if you're ready?"

Imay's eyes flashed in delight and she turned south, leading the others toward the hidden entrance to the zwerg kingdom.

"You absolutely *must* show me how you did that," Ophidian said to the metal man as they brought up the rear of their party.

Ibb rumbled in amusement and waved a hand in acknowledgement.

#

Tiko had her men lower the sails and stream an anchor so that she could draw the battle. The airship seemed key to her. Its untouchable guns distracted and dismayed the soldiers on the ground and battlements below. From somewhere out of her sight some other commotion occurred and she noted with interest when the flag over the battlement — and then over the town hall — were lowered and the colors of Kingsland raised in their place.

South Sea Pass had fallen to King Markel.

Tiko turned the page on her pad and quickly drew an outline of Soria. She drew quick arrows from South Sea Pass — one following the coastline and the other darting by the best roads toward the capital. She frowned and added another line from Kingsland through Korin's Pass. It might be the smaller force but it would probably already be thrusting toward the capital. It would, at the very least, distract the Sorian Army while the other force fell on its flank — a repeat of the tactic used to take South Sea Pass.

She wrote at the bottom of the sketch: *One month. Maybe less. Certainly not more than two.*

The whole continent of Cuiyeval would be in an uproar by next summer. She allowed herself a smile. Her master would be pleased.

She turned to the seamen. "I've seen enough," she said. "Let's get moving."

The blank-faced men heard her and moved to fulfill her desires.

#

"General Dartan," General Gergen said as he halted his horse and looked down at the sorry party of disarmed Sorians, "what a surprise." He nodded toward General Adkins who acknowledged him with a glum look.

"I commend you on your tactics, General Gergen," Dartan said, bowing his head before the conquering general. He glanced up then to the airship, adding, "I had only heard rumors of their existence before you attacked."

"I find that surprise is a valuable tool," General Gergen said with a small smile. He gestured toward General Ambrose who moved up to his right side. "General Ambrose will discuss the surrender and deployment of your troops." General Dartan nodded to the third division commander. "We shall be happy to oblige." He turned his head to ask Gergen, "I request, however, that my troops not be required to march in your victory parade."

"That will be for King Markel to decide," Gergen replied. "I will not be here." He had already ordered general Gideon to form up the second division: they would move out in the evening. With the South Sea Pass secured and his news from Colonel Walpish that Korin's Pass had been taken, Gergen wanted to move his men through the snow-covered winter plains and up to the Sorian capital, Sarskar, before King Wendel could form a defense. If all went to plan, they'd take the capital in the next three weeks — four if the snows were too heavy. Of course, that depended on the new rail line being laid through Korin's Pass. Gergen imagined that it would be more difficult in the winter snows but the King's mages and first minister had assured him that those problems would easily be surmounted.

"You will not?" General Dartan inquired in surprise. He made a face. "I had hoped to discuss your strategies and tactics over a meal, perhaps even this evening."

"I'm afraid that won't be possible," General Gergen said with a half nod. "Perhaps some other day."

General Dartan sniffed in reply.

#

"Did you send the message?" Mage Vistos asked the girl waspishly. Margaret Waters nodded dutifully. The mage didn't like her or didn't like girls — she couldn't tell which — but she'd learned to be silent in his presence. It would never do for him to learn that she was a better mage than he. She took care to ensure that no one knew her full strength. Certainly Minnor and Halston were convinced she was next to useless. She hid a smile. They would learn when the time came — spymaster Hewlitt had promised.

"*We* sent it," Minnor said, waggling a finger between himself and Halston. With a smirk he added, "Mage Waters suffered a mischance."

"Hmmph," Mage Vistos noted sourly. He waved them away. "We must prepare." He waved a hand toward the girl, saying, "You may disarm the wards by the sea."

Margaret Waters nodded in acknowledgement, turned and left the tent.

"I shall have words with the King," Vistos said when the girl had departed. The two young mage apprentices exchanged satisfied looks. "Clearly, magic is too much for a woman's tender sensibilities."

#

"You captured an airship?" Annabelle said with Ellen's child's voice as they came out through the sortie door near crater which housed the dragon steel slabs.

"Actually, it was Jarin Reedis who did," Diam admitted. She led them down a winding path and into the clearing that had been the underground cavern until Rabel, Ellen, and Jarin had raised the fort into the night sky so many days ago.

Rabel's eyes widened as he took in the tight knot of sailors — airmen, he guessed — lounging uncomfortably under a watchful zwerg guard.

"We got their captain, their engineer, and their mages," Diam continued gleefully. She waved at the ship which was leaning over on its side. "Jarin Reedis has some notions on what we can do with it."

The dragon mage heard his name, turned and caught sight of the others. He raced over, beaming until he got close enough to examine the group.

"Where's Annabelle?" He asked, his expression changing to worry.

Ellen started to answer but Ophidian cut her off with a raised hand. "She'll meet us later."

"Ibb!" Jarin Reedis said, seeing the metal man among them. He trotted over and clapped the metal man on the shoulder. "You're fixed!"

"Indeed I am," Ibb agreed. "We are all together again —"

"Except Annabelle," Diam noted, glancing toward her daughter with a thoughtful frown.

"Where's Lissy?" Ellen asked, glancing around.

"Sleeping," Diam said tartly. She turned to Imay. "Just like her sister should be." Her expression widened to take them all in. "In fact, I believe that a rest is in order for all of you, now that we've got things back under control."

Ellen's eyes had not stopped moving. When she spotted Captain Nevins, her eyes narrowed and she drew in a deep breath. With an anxious look she turned to Ophidian and peremptorily beckoned for him to lower his ear to her mouth. She spoke quickly, quietly. When she was done, he put a comforting hand on her shoulder and turned to the others.

"Queen Diam," Ophidian said to the zwerg queen solemnly, "I must ask you and your people to withdraw from here for a moment."

"What?" Diam demanded. She glanced at Imay. "Why?"

Imay looked wretched and shook her head. Finally, she said to her mother, "Remember when Lissy wouldn't let us in the treasury?"

Diam's eyes widened in surprise and then narrowed as she considered her eldest daughter's words. "I do."

"This is like that," Imay told her. "Please, do as the dragon god asks." Diam looked doubtful. "I'll stay here with him, for the zwerg."

"How far must we go?" Diam asked, her tone making it quite clear how reluctant she was to accede in this matter, even to the dragon god.

"Go where you cannot hear," Ophidian said. He glanced to Jarin Reedis. "And Jarin will make sure that you cannot see."

"What?" Mage Reedis barked in surprise. "Why should I —?"

"If you cannot," Rabel interrupted, "I believe that I can."

Diam frowned for a moment. "A mist spell?"

Rabel nodded. Diam muttered something angrily under her breath, gestured to Granno and turned back the way she'd come. Granno barked an order and the rest of the zwerg joined them.

"How are you going to guard those men?" Granno asked as he turned to follow his queen.

Ophidian smiled at him and waited until the zwerg officer remembered to whom he was talking.

"Oh," Granno said at last. "Yes, I suppose a god will get them to behave." With one final hard glance at the prisoners and the others, Granno tramped after the other zwerg.

Ophidian waited calmly until they were gone then turned to Jarin Reedis. "Can you make a mist, or should I ask Rabel?"

"It is an artefact of hot and cold," Mage Reedis said with an audible sniff. He turned back to the prisoners in estimation, then back to the cavern where the zwerg had departed. He smiled at Ophidian, raised his hands and made a series of gestures rising from the ground on high and again from the ground and up high.

From the ground just in front of the zwerg's exit rose a steady, thick fog. Reedis repeated his incantation and movements one more time and turned back to Ophidian, raising an eyebrow in expectation.

"Not bad," Ophidian allowed. "But others eyes might be watching." Ophidian turned to Rabel who glared back, sighed, and waved his arms overhead. A thin bluish-white haze gathered over the dell, enclosing it in a fog almost like a domed ceiling.

"If you'd told me you'd wanted that, I could have done it," Reedis told Ophidian with a hurt look.

"No matter," Ophidian said, turning to Ellen. "What do you propose?"

"I'm just a silly girl," Ellen said. She gestured to Rabel. "And he's just an old man." She nodded toward Imay. "And I'm showing the princess how well I can cook."

"Cook?" Reedis said, brows furrowing in thought.

"Very well," Ophidian said, waving the three away. "Go. We'll remain." He gestured for Ibb and Reedis to come closer then his eyes flared with bright anger. When they cleared again, he said. "No one can hear us now."

Reedis frowned. "What happened to Annabelle?"

"She died," Ibb said. Reedis gasped. "A poisoned arrow, not even Ophidian could save her."

"What?" Reedis cried, turning on the dragon god. "What —" and his tone changed as Jarin spoke, "Father, was there nothing you could do?"

Ophidian gestured toward the three others making their way toward the prisoners and the cooking fire. "Watch."

#

Tortin Borkis stopped mid-sentence and turned, saying to a perplexed Nevins, "Magic."

Captain Nevins turned away from the cooking fire and glanced around. He saw the fog hanging above them, saw the deeper fog where the zwerg had disappeared and turned back to the mage in annoyance. "You pointed this out already."

Borkis shook his head, pointing toward the three people approaching. "*They're* magic," he said. He shivered and Nevins shot him a worried look. "One of them is very powerful."

"There's a god over there, too," Nevins reminded him tartly.

"It's not the god," Borkis said. "Only close."

The little girl broke away from the group and skipped over to the fire, calling over her shoulder, "They've got food!"

The others trotted to her. "Ellen, you don't —" the man said. But the little girl giggled and pointed over to Nevins. "Are you the captain?"

Nevins turned and moved toward her as she continued, "They said there was a captain here."

"I'm Captain Nevins," he told her as he and Borkis approached. The other sailors gathered a knot nearby — a mixture of despair and cunning. The man glanced toward the men and gave them an appraising look. Nevins felt their despair growing.

There were only three: two girls, one a zwerg, and a man not much older than Borkis.

Ellen picked up a bowl near the bubbling pot, emptied it and shook it out before dipping it in the cook pot and ladling a hearty bowl of stew.

Borkis drew in a sharp gasp and gave Nevins a look but the captain jerked his head, silencing the mage's protests. At this response, mage Borkis grew still, thoughtful.

Ellen cheerfully cleaned off a spoon from among those salvaged from *Harbinger's* galley and dipped it in the stew, glancing toward Nevins expectantly. Captain Nevins returned her look without a word.

"Miss," one of the knot of sailors called out, "that's *our* food."

"The captain had it made for us himself," another added. He glanced toward Nevins. "I don't know if there's enough to go around."

Ellen ignored him and swallowed her mouthful. Nevins felt Borkis relax beside him. The captain's smile only shone through his eyes.

Ellen looked at the bowl of soup and said to the disgruntled sailors, "It's tasty. Not much. I could do better."

"I'm sure, miss," one of the sailors replied dryly. "You've had years to perfect your craft."

"Well," Annabelle said with Ellen's child voice, "at least I do a better job of hiding the taste of poison."

Nevins felt Borkis tense beside him, raising his hands for a quick spell.

#

"Annabelle has just told them that the soup is poisoned," Ibb told the others. Jarin Reedis glanced his way and the metal man explained, "I have very good hearing."

"And he can read lips," Ophidian added, giving the metal man a sidelong look as if trying to decide whether Ibb had tried to be humorous or was deliberating hiding all his skills.

"Annabelle?" Reedis said, brows going up in surprise. He turned to Ophidian. "You said she was dead."

"I said she'd died," Ophidian corrected. Reedis spluttered in protest but Ophidian silenced him with a hand, gesturing toward the campfire. "Watch."

#

Rabel nodded to Imay: he was ready. The zwerg princess' lips drew up in a feral grin and she moved her hands quickly.

"Ow!" Borkin cried in alarm, raising his hands to his unbelieving eyes. "I've been burned."

"One should be careful about playing with fire," Rabel said dangerously.

"Or poison," Annabelle added sweetly in Ellen's voice. She turned to Nevins. "Why did you poison your crew? What were you going to do when they were dead?" She turned toward the knot of crewmen, some of who were now turning their gaze to their former captain.

"The gold," one of the men growled, moving toward Nevins and Borkin angrily.

"The gold," Ellen Annabelle said. She raised an eyebrow toward Nevins. "You were going to kill your men so you could have more gold?"

The growl from the men was all the warning Nevins needed. He dropped down in a crouch, reached into his boot, pulled his stiletto and threw it at the girl in one quick motion.

It didn't reach her. The zwerg princess turned her eyes on him with a satisfied look as Nevins saw the stiletto turn bright red mid-flight, falling as a blob of molten metal feet from the little girl.

"Queen Diam might show mercy to those who are willing to swear to her service," Rabel said to the men. He nodded to Ellen. "My friend here can cure your poison."

"We were only following orders," one man said, pushing forward through the crowd. He was little more than a boy and wore a tattered, dirty uniform. He walked with a limp which caused him to wince with each step. "You cannot kill us for that."

"He could," Ellen Annabelle said, pointing to Nevins. "And the zwerg prefer to keep their secrets to themselves."

"Particularly when it comes to gold," Imay agreed darkly.

"Don't sailors always say that dead men tell no tales?" Ellen Annabelle asked sweetly.

The young man — little more than a boy — dropped to one knee and nodded toward the princess. "I swear to you that I will serve you with my life," he said, turning back to wave a hand at the men behind him. "Only don't let these men die."

"What's your name?" Imay asked haughtily.

"Midshipman Abner Crippens, your highness," the young man replied.

"Your oath is your own to give," Rabel said, moving to stand before him. "But you cannot swear for the others. They must make their own choices."

Slowly the others moved forward, arraying themselves behind Crippens and bent their knee.

Imay walked from each to each, accepting their oath with a nod and a pat on their head. She motioned for them to rise and move toward the still simmering pot of stew.

"Good," Ellen Annabelle said. "My father doesn't want me to kill without cause." She closed her eyes, waved her hand over the pot, and sighed. A purple haze steamed up from the stew, turned a sickly green and dissipated into the air as she waved it aside. She leaned forward over the pot, sniffed deeply and smiled. "There! The killing is gone, the curing is in the stew." She opened her eyes and frowned when she saw the confusion in the sailor's eyes. With a sigh, she waved at them. "Get some soup and get cured."

There was a rush of feet which halted at Imay's disapproving growl. Midshipman Crippens rose, hobbled over to the front of the men, and sent them one by one toward the pot.

"Leave enough for everyone," he told them. Ellen Annabelle nodded in agreement, serving up a spoonful to each.

"It's good!" the first man to try it cried in delight. Soon the others were adding their praise in growing volume.

"Your leg," Ellen Annablle said, gesturing to Crippens.

"There was an explosion on our ship and I was thrown into the air. I landed hard," Crippens said, clenched his jaw to hide his pain.

"Yes, I can see," Ellen Annabelle said. She motioned for him to come closer. When he reached her, she said, "Stand right there." Nervously, midshipman Crippens stood. Elllen reached over, putting one hand on the front and back of his knee. She glanced up at him sympathetically. "This is going to hurt," she said as she jerked against his knee.

Crippens shouted in pain. And then he cried in delight, "My leg! It's fixed!"

"Of course," Ellen Annabelle agreed. She glanced over to Imay, then to Rabel who nodded in acceptance of her unspoken plan. Ellen Annabelle rose to her feet, turned to Nevins and Borkin and said, "There's only one more thing to fix."

Nevins said nothing, raising an eyebrow in sardonic defiance.

"Do you know about wyverns?" Ellen Annabelle asked the captain.

"Ford was sent to kill one," Nevins said. "I imagine he bungled it but he was always a bungler."

"He was my friend," Annabelle said through Ellen's lips, her expression hardening. "He learned the wyvern's wrath." She smiled at him. "Now it's your turn."

Ellen Annabelle took a step forward, leaped up, turned into her wyvern form and spat two neat, quick poisonous darts — one, two. Even before the two bodies fell to the ground, their eyes bulging in shocked horror, Ellen Annabelle was a little girl again. She turned her eyes to the stunned sailors. "And *that* —" she gestured at the two purpling bodies "— is why it's never a good idea to underestimate children."

#

"Did she just condemn those men to death?" Ibb asked, turning to the dragon god.

"Why?" Jarin Reedis said, glancing at the dead bodies in the distance. He had seen the girl turn into the wyvern and had grunted in surprise. "What does it matter that Ellen's a wyvern?"

"Not just Ellen," Ibb said.

"Not just —?" Reedis stopped. He turned to Ophidian. "You said that Annabelle died."

"She did," Ophidian agreed. He gestured toward the small girl in the distance. "Ellen saved her."

"*Ellen?* How?"

"She gave him her tears," Ibb said. Jarin Reedis threw up in his hands in frustration. Ibb explained, "Your father cannot cry. If he could, he could make wyverns —"

"You made Annabelle into the wyvern?" Reedis cried in amazement. He looked back toward Ellen then back to Ophidian. "And Ellen twinned with her?"

"And he can make more wyverns," Ibb said. He glanced back to Ophidian, his expression sad. "Which is why those men can never tell this secret."

"Oh," Ophidian said with a lazy smile. "I'm not worried about them."

"Why?" Ibb said. "Surely they will remember!"

Beside him, Reedis startled chuckling — a deep, full-throated sound. The metal man drew his brows down in question. Still laughing, Reedis pointed to Ellen's child form in the distance. "Oh, no! Not with Annabelle's cooking! They won't remember anything except how good the food was!"

Epilog

Tiko Amushi looked up at the sound of wings flapping above her in the darkness. She craned her neck up to the night sky and saw three huge shapes blot out the stars overhead. One seemed to be streaked with white, another with purple, and the third — Tiko shivered in awe — the third was jet black. She thought she saw metal gleaming on its back and dimly heard a woman's cry of delight from the purple one — a wyvern.

"Turn the ship," Tiko told the men. She pointed toward the shadows. "Follow the dragon."

Steel Waters

Book 13

Twin Soul series

Chapter One

Margaret Waters waited, head downcast, hood covering her face, as the last of the passengers disembarked from the train just arrived in triumph from the capital of Kingsland, transporting the king and his retinue for the victory march through the Sorian — formerly Sorian — town of South Sea Pass. She kept to the shadows as the King's men fought to retrieve the king's destrier from its stall on one of the rear cars. Fought and failed. They brought out a much more docile mare and hastily switched the gear. Margaret smiled sourly at that — the stallion was sick from the train ride but the mare was ready to do her duty.

A hand touched her shoulder and she collapsed to the ground, drawing her dagger in her left hand and her wand at the same time, pointing them up at the ready to her assailant.

"Good, you are alert," Peter Hewlitt said in a soft voice. He smiled down at her as she flicked her wand to pull aside any concealment spells, only sheathing her dagger when she detected none. "Are you ready?"

"I have been dismissed in disgrace," Margaret told him, her expression veiled. "Mage Vistos called me, 'Nothing but a useless shrill. Not a drop of talent, not one!'"

Hewllitt's smile broadened. "Sounds just like him." He cocked his head toward the waiting train. The engine at the front was steaming, ready for the return journey. "You did well."

"He suspects nothing," Margaret agreed.

"And your father, is he well?" Hewlitt asked, gesturing for Margaret to rise. "People are looking, you know."

"So toss me a copper," Margaret said, "and they'll think I'm just a beggar."

Hewlitt chuckled and fished a coin out of his pocket, tossing it to her. "You know what to do when you get back to the capital," he told her.

"And the orders?" Margaret asked. "Are they ready?"

Hewlitt nodded and pulled a roll of parchment from the inside of his coat. He passed it to her. "When you return, you will report to the trainmaster as Matthew Wayfarer."

Margaret took the roll with a nod. "And this Wayfarer, does he exist?"

Hewlitt shook his head. "Not any more."

A whistle from the engine at the front of the train distracted them and they both turned to see the king's party draw together and start off for their triumph.

"I must go," Hewlitt said.

"You're in the party?" Margaret asked with surprise.

Hewlitt shook his head. "Never," he told her. She looked disgusted on his behalf so he added, "I learn more from the shadows, as you should well know."

Margaret nodded. And turned toward the train, before turning her head back, "One more thing."

Hewlitt gestured for her to speak.

"This Wayfarer, how old was he?" Margaret asked.

"He was in his late teens," Hewlitt said. "That's not a stretch for you, is it?"

"Five years?" Margaret scoffed. "Nothing at all."

"I had figured as much," Hewlitt said, waving her away and raising his voice. "Now be off with you! You've got your copper, you'll get not a penny more!"

Margaret took on the expression of a beaten-down beggar and ducked and nodded her obeisance, slowly backing away to the train station and becoming lost in the crowd and the darkness.

Hewlitt moved on without a backward glance. He knew his people. She would get on the train before it left. She would do her job.

The kingdom was counting on it.

#

"All well?" King Markel asked Colonel Walpish as the cavalry formed up in front of the cavalcade.

"Perfect, sire," Thomas Walpish replied, bowing deep in his saddle.

Markel waved at Walpish's escorts. "Are these the men?"

"Hand-picked for their valor, sire," Walpish replied. He did not add, out loud, *and for their discretion* but he trusted the king to understand.

Judging by the king's smile, he did. "I shall be delighted to receive them. Later."

"We are all ready, sire," General Ambrose said, gesturing to his buglers. "Sound the advance!"

The three buglemen blew the royal attention signalling the presence of the king and then the advance.

Ahead, Walpish's cavalry spurred their mounts into a slow walk. Walpish eyed them critically, waiting until the last of the front rank was in motion before dipping his hat to the king and urging his horse to join them.

It was a marvelous procession.

#

"Alain, I'm tired! How much longer?" Lisette whined as they rolled to their feet that morning, hidden from the harsh wind in the remnants of some long-abandoned shack.

"At least a week, sister," Alain Casman wearily replied. "But then! Father will be overjoyed! And we'll have *decent* food and proper clothes!"

"It's been so long," Lisette whined.

"Months," Alain, once known as 'Little Britches' and 'No Britches' before he acquired a special jeweled locket that erased the effects of Queen Arivik's magical 'tea', replied with feeling.

"I miss the house," Lisette said.

"Sister of mine, we have no house, only a castle," Alain reminded her.

"The House of the Broken Sun," Lisette corrected. "I was warm and they loved me there." She made a face. "Father…"

"Perhaps he will have changed his mind," Alain said. "We've been gone for months, perhaps he'll understand now that you are not ready to be married."

"No," Lisette replied firmly, "he won't."

"It is the only home we have, sister," Alain told her.

Lisette turned back toward the north and Kingsland. "I could have had a home there."

Alain swore and then swallowed his ire when he caught the alarm in his little sister's eyes. It wasn't her fault that Lisette was so young, so uneducated in the ways of the world. Alain had been like that, too. Oh, he'd known that there was something wrong with Madame but it wasn't until he was delivered into the queen's clutches that he even began to understand what the Madame of the House of the Broken Sun had planned for his poor little sister. And, shortly after drinking the queen's tea, he hadn't been able to understand much at all. Except for —

With another curse, he cut the thought out of his head.

"Come on, we should be moving," Alain said, gesturing toward her. "Maybe we'll find a town and we can barter for some food —"

"With what?" Lisette challenged. They had spent the last of their small coins days back and were rightly fearful of revealing any of the large stash of gold they had hidden on themselves and their mounts.

"We'll figure something," Alain said out loud. *I'll steal.* "Come on."

#

Skara Ningan loved a challenge. The mage, Vistos, had only growled at her when she'd reported in, the day before, passing her eight special quarrels.

"You're to shoot when it's dark, at the darkest jackets. They'll be new, and there should be seven of them," the mage had told her.

"What's the eighth for?"

"In case you miss," Vistos said. Skara started to argue but the mage merely scowled at her. "I've already sent one useless girl back home, I see no reason not to make it *two*."

Wordlessly, Skara took all the quarrels.

"Come back when you're done and you'll be properly rewarded," Vistos told her.

"Yes sir," Skara said, eyes downcast. Vistos had threatened her early on with the withdrawal of his magical gifts if she did not behave 'properly.' She recalled the first time they'd met — when she'd beat out fifteen boys and men to prove herself the best with a crossbow — the mage had glared at her.

But the *magic!* Skara loved the magic, loved what it did for her accuracy, her distance, her killing.

"With your permission," Skara now said, eyes still on the floor.

"Go!" Vistos said with an airy wave of his hand. "And next time, bathe beforehand!"

Skara backed away, fleeing as soon as she exited the room. She made her way cautiously through the bustling town and only heaved a sigh of relief when she left it and entered the quiet of the outlying hills. She climbed quickly back up to her base camp and curled up in a fur to rest for the evening.

Chapter Two

"Guards, guards!" Peter Hewlitt shouted in the dark of night. "Come quick, the queen!"

The sound of rushing armored men brought a smile to Hewlitt's eyes that he quickly crushed. He waved them toward the room. "The king," he bellowed, "send some men to see to his safety!"

The guard captain nodded and detailed three men who took off in a sprint. The captain followed his remaining men inside the queen's chambers, hastily selected earlier that day. He blanched as he caught sight of the blood all over the sheets, framing the dead queen as though she were in a rose garden — and then rushed to the window as he caught sight of the wind-swept curtains. A shout to the men outside brought no reply. Angrily, with a jerk of his thumb, he sent some of his men through to the outside even as the rush of feet from the doorway caused him to turn around in time to catch one of the men sent to the king returning.

"The king is safe!" the man declared, pausing to rub out a stitch in his side.

"Get back to him," the captain ordered. "I'll have more men sent presently."

"Whoever did this —" Hewlitt began and then stopped as he saw something lying on the ground. He knelt and picked it up, turning to display it to the guard captain.

"That is the crest of Soria," the captain declared immediately. Hewlitt nodded and placed the crest in the man's hand, rising and moving his eyes carefully over the horrid sight of the dead queen.

"Her throat was slit," Hewlitt said professionally as he examined the body. "Ah! But she did not die in vain!" He pulled a fragment of cloth from one of her dead hands.

"That's the cravat of Dartan's division!" the guard captain declared.

"And here's something better," Hewlitt said, retrieving another object from the queen's other hand and displaying it to the captain.

"That's a colonel's crest!" the guard captain said. He glanced to Hewlitt. "How many Sorian colonels are there still free?"

"Send one of your men to the prisoners," Hewlitt ordered. "I'd say some escaped. And committed murder. Murder most foul."

The captain paled, selected a soldier and sent him off. But before the man got far, a clatter of hoofbeats alerted them and they saw Colonel Walpish and a squad canter into the courtyard in the back.

"We found them!" Walpish shouted as he spotted Hewlitt. He gestured to the dead body draped over the horse's rear and pointed to the rest of his troop whose mounts were all similarly adorned. "Seven! And one of them a colonel!"

"They killed my wife!" King Markel wailed as he stormed into the room, shaking off determined guards in his rage. Markel rushed the bed, saw all the blood and grabbed the dead queen in his arms, disregarding the flow of blood as he clamped her lifeless form to his breast. He turned to the others. "I shall have vengeance!"

"As is your right, sire," Peter Hewlitt said with a low bow. All in all, he thought, things had worked out perfectly.

#

"No! You must take these as a symbol of my regard," King Markel insisted as Colonel Walpish and his hand-picked men met the king early the next day. He gestured to the gorgeously decorated hand-sewn crimson leather jackets that he'd ordered specially for these most trusted men.

"Your majesty is too kind," Walpish said, bowing deeply as he gestured for his men to precede him in receiving the special leather jackets.

"It is the least I can do," the king said. He nodded to Walpish who moved forward to receive the last jacket. "You know she was a traitor," he told the colonel in a low voice as he passed him the jacket.

Walpish nodded and bowed as he stepped backward, his new-won prize firm in his hands.

"Your Majesty, it is time," Peter Hewlitt, who had stood close by the king throughout the meeting, intoned solemnly.

"Of course," King Markel said, turning back to his colonel. "My minister here tells me that I must not delay you in your next mission."

Colonel Walpish rose from his bow and raised an eyebrow towards the king's spymaster.

"We'll need you on the road, to take the van in front of General Gergen," Hewlitt told him.

Walpish jerked his head in a quick nod. He turned his gaze back to the king. "Your majesty, with your permission?"

The king smiled at him and leaned forward in his makeshift thrown, presenting his lordly ring to the cavalry commander. So honored, Walpish moved forward on bended knee and brushed his lips in acceptance of this royal honor.

"Go with all speed," King Markel told him, retrieving his hand and waving to the cavalry beyond. "I look forward with great fervor to our next meeting."

Walpish bowed once more and quickly departed.

After they had left, King Markel turned his head to gaze at his spymaster.

"That is all we needed, sire," Hewlitt promised. "The orders have already been sent."

King Markel nodded and turned his head forward once more.

#

"It is quite an honor, sir," Trooper Tavis said when he spotted the new jackets. "It's not often that the king recognizes a trooper for valor."

Walpish eyed his color bearer sourly. "It's not as warm as my jacket," he grumbled. "And leather's going to take forever to break in."

Tavis started to say something but Walpish forestalled him, heaving off the crimson leather jacket and passing it to the trooper. "You wear it."

"Sir?" Tavis said in shock. Walpish glared at him and gestured peremptorily for the man to put the jacket on. Tavis struggled out of his white jacket, looked around for someplace to stow it and was surprised when Walpish prompted him to pass it over. It was nearing dark, replenishing their supplies and resting the troops had consumed the day.

"Pew!" Walpish swore as he sniffed the coat. "Man, don't you ever bathe?"

"Haven't had time, sir," Tavis said diffidently. Walpish growled at him as he wrestled his arms into the white trooper's jacket. When Tavis offered him back the new jacket, Walpish glared at him. "Just put it on, man!"

Tavis pulled on the leather jacket.

"It looks good on you," Walpish growled. He sniffed, made a face at the jacket he now wore and said, "I suppose this will do until we make camp." He turned toward his aide. "Prepare to move out."

The aide nodded and spurred his horse in a tight circle before charging back to alert the rest of the squadron.

"Bugler! Sound the assembly," Walpish snapped. He nodded toward Tavis. "Take the colors forward."

Tavis gaped at him like a fish until Walpish waved him ahead.

"And pass me the colors!" Walpish bellowed. Tavis turned back to him, eyes wide in surprise. "Well, man, if we're going to switch places, may as well do it all the way!"

"But you've not the cup in stirrup, sir!" Tavis protested, turning back to pass the squadron's small guidon to his colonel.

"I'll manage," Walpish growled, placing the butt of the long wooden stake at the top of his boot. It promptly slid forward but Walpish caught it and placed it more firmly on his boot. He looked up to see the colors trailing down beside and smiled. "There! We'll make me a proper trooper yet!"

Tavis couldn't help smiling at his commander's jest.

"Buglers," Walpish bellowed, "Sound walk." He dipped the colors as required and moved up beside his color bearer. "Be careful, Tavis, or I'll have your job!"

"As the colonel says, sir," Tavis replied, spurring his mount forward.

Slowly the cavalry squadron passed through the broken east gates of South Sea Pass and out into the dark night, bearing north.

#

Skara Ningan allowed her lips to curve upwards in a smile as she spotted her targets in the distance. She had her quarrels laid out before her, with one already loaded and her crossbow sitting in her lap at the ready. The distance was impossibly far for a normal crossbow bolt or a normal crossbow.

Skara raised her weapon with both hands, pointed it at the furthest target, aimed, and pressed the trigger. She reloaded her weapon without bothering to see if the first bolt had hit its target. She fired again. And again. And four more times until all the dark targets were down — leaving only those dressed in the white of the King's Cavalry behind. The color-bearer reined in his horse and turned back, jumping down to the first of the victims.

Skara backed away from the ledge, into the surrounding snow and the dark night, her mission accomplished.

#

"They're all dead," Thomas Walpish confirmed as captain Lewis dismounted beside him.

"And they're all wearing the new jackets," Sam Lewis observed grimly.

Walpish pursed his lips tightly and nodded. "I noticed." He pointed to the hills behind them, rising from the edge of the South Sea Pass. "The shots came from there."

Lewis grimaced. "We could send a troop, but I doubt they'll find anything."

"I'm going," Walpish said. The captain gave him a sharp look. "You take the men on, keep on the trail and meet up with Gergen." He smiled at the captain. "I'll brevet you to major."

"Sir!" Lewis exclaimed. "I— I —"

"Get moving," Walpish said. "There's no telling what's afoot and I don't doubt that Gergen will need your eyes to guard his men." When Lewis made ready to protest, Walpish added, "That's an order, major."

Sam Lewis met his commander's eyes firmly, drew himself to attention and saluted smartly. "As you say, sir."

"I do so say," Walpish retorted. He turned and turned back again, passing the colors to the newly-made major. "Here, you'll need these." He paused, glancing at the seven dark-jacketed bodies. "See that they are buried promptly," he ordered Lewis. "I don't want them found."

Before Lewis could react, he raced to his horse, drew himself up and spurred the mare into a canter back across the snow-filled plains.

#

"All the quarrels were fired, save the spare," mage Vistos said as he bent down beside King Markel to speak in his ear alone.

"Good," Markel said in the same quiet voice. "And shooter?"

"The last quarrel is for her," Vistos said with a small smile. King Markel turned to him and blinked. "She is only a girl, not even worth breeding."

Markel nodded slowly in response. A moment later, he added, "Be sure to tell me when the deed is done." Vistos nodded in acknowledgement. "I want no loose ends."

Vistos straightened and said, louder, for those listening nearby, "As you majesty desires."

#

"We can either go west, to the coast," Alain said, waving with his arm, "or continue south through the Shredded Hills."

"It's awfully hard going through the hills," Lisette complained, staring south at the smudge of hills rising in the distance. "And there are supposed to be… things there."

Alain grunted in agreement. "Going to the sea could add weeks to our journey."

"Do we even want to go home?" Lisette asked, turning her head to the north with a look of longing. "Weren't we happier back in Kingsland?"

They had crossed into the kingdom of Palu through Midpass — the pass in the Callat Mountains that was furthest south and east in Kingsland. Alain had chosen that path, certain that the closer Masjar Pass would be full of king's men determined to capture them.

"It's death for me if I go back," Alain told her. "And you would not be happy for long, either way."

"Alain!" Lisette wailed, taking his last comment for criticism of her temperament.

Alain chuckled at her discomfiture, shaking his head, "No, little 'Sette, I meant that there would be those who would treat you ill."

"Oh," Lisette replied, huffing out her distress. She turned her head back to the south pass. "How much food do we have?"

"Enough," Alain replied firmly.

"And if we go to the sea?"

"Not enough."

"Then we should take the Shattered Hills and hope for the best," Lisette said, turning her mare southwards and spurring it into a slow walk. Alain snorted in amusement and set his horse after hers.

#

Thomas Walpish eyed the clearing in front of him carefully. It had been over two hours since his men were murdered and the sky was dark. Snow on the ground reflected a little and his eyes — well, his eyes were doing quite well in the dark. Thomas smiled. It always paid to be careful and prepared.

Thomas Walpish had been prepared since the time long ago when his rich father had first purchased his commission in the cavalry. Walpish's father had little use for him — a bastard unclaimed but not completely forgotten — so sending him into the military had been a convenient way for the Duke of Callat to rid himself of an embarrassment while at the same time pleasing his lady wife and enriching his grateful king.

In the decade since, Walpish had risen steadily in rank through his efforts — and his ability to think strategically. He had found the use of magic items to be of much benefit to his profession and had been the first to encourage General Gergen to arm the soldiers with magical muskets and enchanted weaponry of all varieties.

The goggles he now wore over his eyes were one such example. As was the pendant on the necklace he wore hidden under his tunic. One let him see in the night, the other let him find magic.

He had felt the tug in the pendant when the king had presented him with the marvelous leather jackets and had — foolishly — thought nothing of it. It was right and proper that the king would give his trusted soldier a magical gift. It was only when he saw the bolts sticking out of the backs of his equally 'honored' men that Thomas Walpish realized that he'd been betrayed.

He was willing to bet that the murderer would also be betrayed — it was now apparent that King Markel wished no witnesses. His brows furrowed as he noticed light indentations in the snow on the clearing in front of him. Someone had covered their tracks. But wind and time had revealed them again — just barely — to someone equipped to look for them. Thomas had grown up a hill-man in the mountains of his father's domain, unluckily for his would-be murderer. The tracks led… to a cliff, white and perfect. Too perfect.

He slowly circled away, climbing up the hill overlooking the cliff. He crouched down and took in a slow, steady lungful of air. *There!* The scent of a long-unwashed person came up to him from below. Thomas smiled to himself. Slowly, he turned to scan the ground behind him, felt for and dug out a large rock. He turned back again and waited once more. *All quarry is skittish, lad.* Thomas recalled the voice of his long-dead teacher from the distant mountains. Thomas took careful aim and launched the rock so that it fell on the whitest part of the cliff — pulling away the fabric covering that guarded a cave.

Two shots raced out of the hole in rapid succession, Thomas saw the flash of the crossbow bolts as they flew into the distance. He held his breath and waited, listening.

It was ten minutes before he heard movement from inside the cave. He waited longer, expecting a ruse.

When the figure finally crept toward the entrance, clothed in white as Thomas had guessed, it did not loiter long. For one moment the assassin waited and then, decisively, stepped out of the cave's mouth.

Thomas dropped on top of it, his knife drawn as he fell, his aim going true and cutting through the leather strap that held the quiver on the assassin's back. The assassin twisted like a snake and was on him with bared teeth and a long blade in an instant.

Thomas hit the face full on and then punched with his other hand for the throat, determined to make an end of it. But he pulled his punch to the left, away from the killing blow to the larynx at the last minute as he heard a grunt from his victim at the pain of having her nose broken.

"You're a girl!" Thomas exclaimed as he used his weight to bear the two of them into the snow-covered clearing. The girl — woman — he wasn't sure which did not offer to confirm his observation, rolling under him in an attempt to rise to her knees and scurry away from him. Thomas was not so much of a gentleman that he let her get away with it. He rose with her, leaped to one side and kicked her hard in the back of the head. The girl gave one grunt of pain and collapsed. He raised his boot to kick her again — a killing blow — but stopped himself just in time. *Answers before vengeance.* Still breathing hard, he reached down and grabbed one of her feet, dragging her back into the cave. He was not gentle about it but twisted her over onto her back before they entered the stone-covered cavern.

#

It was nearing midnight when the train finally left the siding. Engineers were hard at work expanding the line to the edge of the South Sea Pass and Margaret could see where they were ready to blow the walls of the city on the new path for the rail line. Soon the line would run right into the center of the city with a new line constructed leading out. King Markel and his first minister had plans.

Margaret slipped into the shadows at the station before she unrolled her orders. As expected there was a piece of skin inside it. She smiled and, touching the skin, began the magic that would activate the spell. She stopped when her voice suddenly lowered into male tones and she felt the spell grip her. She felt the shape of her nose and was not surprised to find it different. The bristles of hair on her cheeks were more annoying. The eyebrows were not hers, not the thick hair growing from her head. She was not a chesty girl and doubtless was now less so — the magic of transformation was insistent in that way.

Until she said the counter-charm, Margaret Waters was no more. Matthew Wayfarer stood in her place. Margaret rolled the piece of skin back into the parchment, stuck it into her coat pocket and moved out of the shadows to join the others thronging toward the train.

Her boots still felt comfortable but she was aware that her clothes could do with improvement. She generally wore clothing that was nondescript but she decided to augment that with a few additions, probably switching her top for a man's shirt. There was a knot of young men just in front of her; one of them would doubtless suffice.

Moments later, suitably attired, Matthew Wayfarer pushed his way forward to the steam engine.

"I need a ride," he said in a deep voice to the driver, pulling forth his parchment and letting one corner show. "King's business."

The engineer took one look at the royal crest on the paper and beckoned for 'Matthew' to climb aboard.

#

Skara Ningan groaned in pain as she returned to her senses. She tried to stretch but found her arms bound behind her back. Her legs were trussed. She was still in her jacket. There was a fire.

Someone was going through her things. It was the man who'd tackled her. Dimly the memory came back. Her throat was raw, she could taste blood. Her nose throbbed in agony. And her left foot was cold.

"You're right-handed," the man spoke up from out of her sight. She heard a rustle of fabric as the man moved. She could hear him grunt as he touched something and threw it on the fire. The fire brightened as it consumed the latest offering and a greenish light flared for a moment before dying down while the air above the fire flashed with smoke and a cloying, acrid scent wafted up.

"Why the extra quarrel?" the man asked.

"In case I missed," Skara said in a low, sore voice.

"You were the one who blew open the hinge on the gates," the man declared in a strange tone. He was silent for a moment, regarding the fire and the remains of the crossbow bolt. "You don't miss," he said to himself. He turned toward her, still just out of her sight. "Are you so stupid as to not realize that was meant for you?"

"How —? What —?" the words were startled out of her before she could control herself. The pain in her head flared. "I am your prisoner. Kill me now."

In response the man chuckled sourly. He moved into view at last. Before Skara could get a good look at his face, he rose and strode quickly to crouch back down at the end of her legs.

"You killed seven of my troopers," the man replied. "Good men, all." His face twisted in anger. "I want to know why."

"I had my orders," Skara said.

"As had I," the man said. He reached forward and pulled off her right boot, using his dagger to cut through the laces. He was not gentle about it. Skara's ankle added its pain to the rest of the complaints of her body. He pulled off her sock, exposing her foot and toes to the cold winter air.

Skara tried to jerk her foot away as she felt the prick of cold steel on her littlest toe.

"Seven men," the man said, moving the knife to prick each toe in succession, "only five toes." He shook his head. "That doesn't seem fair, does it?"

Skara didn't answer.

"So we'll take half the foot for soldier number six," the man said. "And I'll have the rest for my color-bearer, trooper Tavis." He paused. "A good man who liked the look of the leather." He moved his knife and slid it lightly over her base of her heel. "Do you think your employer will still want you when you're a cripple with only one foot?"

"I serve King Markel," Skara declared proudly. "I will gladly die for him."

The man snatched his knife away and sat on his haunches. "Funny, so do I." Skara fought to keep her surprise from showing on her face. The man noticed and nodded toward her. "Colonel Thomas Walpish of the First Cavalry," he introduced himself. "And you are?"

Skara clenched her lips tightly. Walpish caught her expression and nodded to himself.

"Let me tell you a story," Walpish said. "A story of kings and treachery." He shook his head sadly. "King Markel approached me a long time ago, telling me that his queen had betrayed him. That she had done unthinkable things — that she was plotting his assassination and planning to elevate her son, Crown Prince Nestor, to the throne." He cocked his head at her. "Does any of this sound familiar?" When she didn't reply, he continued, "So the King had a plan. He was going to war with Soria to the north, the goddess Ametza at his side — just as she had helped his father gain the throne years before, she was now prepared to grant him larger lands." Idly, he tapped her smallest toe with his knife. "When the king took South Sea Pass — which he did with no small amount of help from myself, my troops and... you, am I right?"

Skara did not respond.

"I think so," Walpish said after a moment's silence. "Your skill, even magic-aided, is quite unique." He paused. "Although you are not alone in that." Skara said nothing but her breathing changed. "Yes, there was another man, an archer, assigned to Korin's Pass."

He cocked his head at her. "Did you know him?" He waited for her response but Skara said nothing. He shrugged. "Apparently not, then. But he had magic enchanted arrows, not unlike your crossbow bolts, and an amazing range." He sniffed and added, "He also seemed to have your aversion to water, or at least, cleanliness."

Skara's eyes narrowed in anger. Surely he should know that it was impossible to be squirreled away and still *bathe* regularly?

"So, anyway," Walpish continued, "we had our orders." He nodded to her. "We, to take South Sea Pass and then to arrange for the queen's murder." His lips tightened as he continued, "And, apparently, you were to ensure that none of us lived to tell the tale." He pointed to the fire. "That bolt, so nicely enchanted, was meant for you." He paused for a long moment, lost in thought. When he moved it was to put her sock back on her foot and push her boot over it.

"What are you doing?" Skara asked in astonishment.

"Do you like your life?" Walpish asked in reply.

Skara blinked at him.

"Do you think it wise to ally yourself with those who plot to kill you at their earliest convenience?"

"They — they took me in," Skara said hesitantly.

"And now they are done with you," Walpish said. He moved, his knife flashing as it tore through the ropes binding her. He stood up and turned away. "As am I."

"Wait!" Skara called after him as she rolled over and stumbled to her feet.

Walpish turned at the entrance, his knife still in his hand.

Skara turned around and gestured. "My hands, can you untie them?"

"And then what?" Walpish replied. He shook his head, turned and walked away.

"Please!" Skara called after him, her head aching and vision swirling. Slowly she toppled down to the ground, leaning over as her stomach heaved in protest. She fell face first, just avoiding the small steaming pile of vomit, to lie on the cold dark ground with her arms tied behind her, her knees supporting her.

Footsteps approached her and a hand touched her forehead. "You're burning up!" Thomas Walpish swore in surprise. "Did that ass poison you?"

Her world swirled into darkness and the last thing Skara could feel was her stomach heaving feebly in protest.

Chapter Three

Alain stared up into the dark night sky, the point of a sword — his sword — pressing against his throat. *I was stupid,* he berated himself. He'd made the mistake of looking too long into the fire when the bandits attacked. Lisette had had one chance to shriek and then was silenced — quite likely by a hand wrapped around her mouth. Alain had been thrown backwards away from the fire and against the cold hard ground.

"He has a sword," a voice called near his ear. Alain did not move when his belt was cut and his scabbard pulled away from him. He could hear the sound of his rapier being pulled from its sheath.

"It's been used," another voice — near his scabbard — declared. There was a hiss as the voice added, "It killed a woman."

Alain felt the blade bite into his neck. "Who did you kill?"

"Someone who earned it," Alain replied harshly. "She will not be missed."

"And who are you to be her judge and executioner?" the voice near his neck demanded.

"No one," Alain said, his blood running cold, his heart beating slowly. *So this is what death must feel like,* he thought to himself.

"He is ready to die," the other voice declared, the one near his blade.

"Please," Alain pleaded, "my sister. She did no harm. Please let her be."

Lisette whimpered in the distance and Alain was surprised to hear her squirm for her freedom.

"She's feisty," a voice came from Lisette's location. "She's got spirit." The voice suddenly shouted and grunted. "She bit me!" A moment later it added, "Catch her, she's getting away!"madame

"Run, Lisette!" Alain dared shout.

"Run to your death," the voice above him replied. "You'll not last the night out here, girl."

"Run, for your honor!" Alain shouted. The blade on his throat bit harder.

"Honor?" the voice above him demanded. "What is this, then? Maro, come smell!"

"She'll get away," the voice that had been nearest Lisette replied. Maro. The voice was a woman's, or a girl's.

"Not far," the voice above Alain replied. The pressure against his throat eased. "There was a woman's blood on your weapon."

"Yes," Alain said. "Madame Parkes. Madame of the —"

"The House of the Broken Sun," the voice above him growled. The blade on his throat waggled as the speaker continued, "Did you kill her?"

"There's gold!" Maro's voice called out as she approached. "The horses are carrying gold!"

"So you are a common thief?" Alain's captor growled at him.

"There's something more!" Maro shouted, rushing closer. Suddenly a face appeared just above Alain. He was right — she was a woman. Only tiny. Broad faced, curly hair — Maro's hand reached under his tunic and pulled at the necklace around his neck. With a cry of triumph Maro snapped the chain even as Alain cried in protest.

"Oh, this is choice, this is!" Maro crowed as she smelled the glowing blood-red jewel encased in the gold locket.

105

"Don't keep us in suspense," the voice above Alain said in a warning tone.

"Of course not, your majesty!" Maro replied. She sniffed again then said, "It has many properties, Alva —" she grunted as a figure darted out of the darkness and shoved her away.

"Get off my brother!" Lisette cried as she turned and grabbed at the other woman, Alva.

"Leave your hands off the queen!" a voice warned and Lisette was struck from behind.

That was too much for Alain who snapped into action, flicking the blade aside from his throat with one hand while jabbing upwards towards his attacker with the other. He was surprised at how solidly his blow landed — he was expecting to hit a knee but felt the solid flesh of a stomach or something higher and more feminine. A squeak of surprise proved that his blow had been unexpected but suddenly he felt a weight on his knees. He sat up in surprise and glared at the dark figure.

"You're just a girl, a child!" Alain exclaimed.

An arm wrapped around his throat from behind and squeezed tightly as a bass male voice spoke in his ear. "She's no child! She's our queen!"

As the queen rolled off Alain's legs and rose to stand beside him, Alain heard a shriek and a scuffle that indicated that Lisette had been subdued.

"Queen?" Alain repeated through, his voice choked by the arm around his throat. "You must be Queen Alva of the Zwerg!" Alain said. "My father speaks highly of you!"

Queen Alva dusted off her leather trousers and put her hands on her hips, leaning down to stare at him haughtily. "And just who might your father be, boy?"

"Pier Casman," Alain said, throwing his shoulders back with pride, "Grand Duke of the Jasram plains."

A gasp came from all around him.

"Not any more," Queen Alva said as she peered down at Alain.

"Excuse me?"

Alva gestured for the man holding Alain to release him. "Gather your things," she told him, "you will want to come with us."

#

"I'm going to check on back," 'Matthew' told the engineer when they were well underway. It was a cold night and Margaret knew that she'd need her rest — and strength soon enough. There was nothing wrong with the engine, while the engineer and his two stokers were not much in the way of company. The engineer nodded at her silently as 'Matthew' turned and made his way lightly up the side of the coal car, along the catwalk and down into the gap between the coal car and the rest of the train.

It was no problem to jump the gap over the large metal couplings and open the door to the first carriage. Faces looked up in surprise as 'Matthew' entered. 'Matthew' greeted them with a relaxed nod and moved on through to the next car which wasn't as crowded. Pulling up his shirt collar, 'Matthew' stepped past a grizzled soldier and took a place by the window. Shortly after, he closed his eyes.

But 'Matthew' couldn't sleep. A wind blew in his ear. 'Matthew' stretched with a yawn and blushed one arm beside the ear. A moment later, the wind blew in the other ear. With a frown, 'Matthew' turned, stretching his arms again and just — accidentally — punching the 'wind' away from him.

"Kitzis," 'Matthew' growled in a voice barely above a whisper, "if you want to help, use warm air to pillow my head."

The air demon had had no problem recognizing Margaret in her disguise — she'd expected as much — but obeying orders was another matter entirely. It took several more minutes and many irritated looks from fellow passengers before 'Matthew' was able to get comfortable — and Kitzis settled in a warm band behind 'his' head.

#

"My wife — *the Queen* — was murdered while she slept!" King Markel roared at his collected advisors and military men. "And we have proof —" he waved the Sorian rank tab of a colonel in evidence "— that Soria was behind it. Sorian soldiers! *After* they had surrendered!" He glared at all the men arrayed in front of him. "I shall have vengeance!"

"Sire," Minister Mannevy asked. He had arrived from Kingsford only hours before. His mahogany face was lined with exhaustion and they were rings under his eyes. "What would you have us do?"

"Ten thousand!" Markel roared. "Kill ten thousand of their men, now!"

"I — I'm afraid, sire, that they do not have that many men here," General Ambrose replied in a small voice.

"A thousand, then!" Markel said, waving a hand dismissively. "Tonight!"

"Your majesty," Minister Mannevy said in that annoyingly calm tone of his, "I fear that it takes time to kill men. At least to do it in such a way that the killings are respected as just and meaningful."

"Use muskets," Markel snarled.

"I can have a company assembled within the hour, your majesty," General Ambrose offered. "They could kill a hundred men at a time. At… three minutes to reload, the whole lot could be done in half an hour."

Markel frowned in thought. Finally, he nodded and waved a hand at the general. "So to it, then."

First minister Mannevy stepped forward. "Sire," he began, licking his lips as he always did when preparing for a cautious and careful argument, "it might not set the best example to kill so many soldiers out of hand —"

"Out of hand?" Markel bellowed. "They killed *the queen!* They should all rot!"

"But would it not be more effective, sire, to spend some time examining the prisoners, determining the guilty from the innocent?" Mannevy pressed. He gave a slight bow and a wave of his hand. "That way your new people would know firsthand of your justice."

Markel glowered at him. To Ambrose he said, "You have your orders."

"As you wish, your majesty," General Ambrose said, bowing low and moving backwards, away from the royal presence. At a further wave from the king, the rest of the court filed out.

When they were all gone, with only Mannevy remaining, the king darted his eyes around the room to be certain they were alone. Then he smiled. "I think that went rather well, don't you?"

#

"Get up! Get up!" A uniform-clad man bellowed, rattling a metal cup against the metal sides of the seats as the train slowed to a halt. Margaret — 'Matthew' opened her eyes slowly. "Get off the train!" the man shouted, glaring down 'his' way. "Everyone off," the man bellowed, gesturing to the slowly stirring soldiers. "This train leaves for the north in twenty minutes, everybody off!"

She waited for the others to move and inserted herself into the crowd, shuffling off the train and onto the snow-covered station outside. She shivered and banged her arms around herself to warm up. A hot spot under her collar caused her to hiss in anger and brush it away.

Margaret, still very aware of her disguise as Matthew Wayfarer, swaggered through the others with head erect and elbows loose and ready to poke anyone who intersected her path. She spotted the trainmaster's office and altered her path toward it.

A bell above the door clattered when she entered. There was a lamp lit on a table behind the counter and a clock ticking above. Light came from an open door in the back of the office.

"Hello?" Margaret called in 'Matthew's' deep voice. "Is there anyone there?"

A sound from the room in the back came — a chair landing on two of its feet as if its owner had been startled from slumber and let the chair fall back onto all four feet. A moment later a sleepy, grumbling, gray-haired old man came out. "What do you want?"

Margaret didn't bother to reply, instead pulling her orders out of 'his' pocket and unrolling them with studied indifference. "My name is Matthew Wayfarer," Margaret said in that pleasing deep voice she'd 'inherited', "and I have orders here."

Pulling aside the small parchment and the flesh rolled up inside it, she turned the remaining royal paper toward the trainmaster. The man looked down at it, grunted, and pulled the office stool under him, sitting on it.

"Everything's ready," the man said. "I — I've just been waiting for you." 'Matthew' gave him a knowing look and the man added, "No one was certain when you'd arrive, so —"

"When can we go?"

"Well… I'll have to collect the lads, they're nearby but —"

"Twenty minutes," 'Matthew' said imperiously.

"We've got the rails and the timbers," the man said, licking his lips nervously, "but how are you going to set them? There's three feet of snow and more up by Korin's Pass." He shook his head and added, "The betting's that this won't be done until the spring."

"The *king* has ordered it done this week," 'Matthew' replied in a steely voice.

"So you'd be betting against, then?" the man guessed. He pulled a small paper ledger from his pocket. "And how much would you wager?"

"What are the odds?"

"Twenty to one against it being done in a week, that's a given!" the man replied. He put the ledger on the counter and held out his hand. "Jor Gevvin."

Margaret took it and shook it firmly with her young man's hand. "Matthew Wayfarer." Still holding the train master's hand, Margaret reached into the left pocket of her trousers and pulled out a small roll of paper. "Three hundred guineas.'

"That's paper," Jor Gevvin said, shaking his head while taking the bills in his other hand. "Not worth as much as gold."

"King's seal, king's gold," Matthew Wayfarer said.

Gevvin's eyes widened as he took in the printing on the bill. He peeled one off and unrolled it, fingering the lettering on the lower left corner which read: "By my mark and with my hand."

"That's as good as it gets," Gevvin breathed, eyes wide with awe. He counted the bills quickly, rolled them up and disappeared them into his own pocket. "Are you certain, lad? That's a lot of the king's gold to wager?"

"Just be certain you can pay," 'Matthew' replied. "Six thousand guineas, I believe?"

Gevvin's face paled as he considered the number. "Or three hundred to me," he said. He nodded to her. "Your winnings I can cover, if needs be."

"Well, now that's settled, let's get on with it," 'Matthew' said. "And, just so we're clear, if you do anything to wreck this, I'll have your heart beating in my hand."

Gevvin glowered at that, his hand going to his side — toward a hidden weapon, Margaret guessed — but leaving off at the last moment.

"The king has ordered this," 'Matthew' reminded him. He glanced at the large clock at the back of the trainmaster's office. "Twenty minutes."

Jor Gevvin drew in a slow breath, turned to eye the clock behind him and back again to nod to his new acquaintance.

"At the north siding," Gevvin told him. "Nineteen minutes."

"Good," 'Matthew' said. "I'll pay my respects to the Steam Master."

"Good luck with that!" Gevvin told him with a snort. "Steam Master sees no one."

'Matthew' rolled up his parchment and waved it at the trainmaster. "He'll see me."

#

"Minnor! Halston! You know what to do!" Mage Vistos growled as he stomped his feet in the cold snowy night air.

"Sir?" Minnor said. "Which side should I move the sound?"

"From the back!" Vistos snarled. "We don't want the townspeople alarmed." He glanced toward the makeshift prison which housed many of the surrendered Sorian soldiers. "*They* can get the extra noise."

Minnor looked worried and glanced toward Halston who merely nodded in understanding.

"I — I've never done a spell like this, sir," Minnor confessed.

"And now you will," Vistos snapped. "It's simple enough, you make the sound heading toward the town head toward those jails, there." He frowned. "Even a dolt like you should understand that."

Minnor gave him a frightened look but nodded.

"They're shooting a hundred at a time," Vistos said. "After each group, they'll have to move the bodies, reload, bring in another group." He looked to see if his apprentices understood. Halston nodded solemnly. "Ten groups, a thousand shots." He pursed his lips. "Should be done in no more than an hour." He glanced over to a noise coming up the road and spotted the king and his ministers riding up. "The king will be watching so be certain you don't make any mistakes."

Minnor swallowed in a gulp.

Vistos looked at him sharply then said, "Halston, start clapping."

"Sir?" Halston said.

"You clap, and I'll show Minnor here how it's done," Vistos said. He waved an irritated hand toward the confused apprentice. "Go on! Do it!"

Halston began clapping. Vistos drew his wand and turned to Minnor. "You're making the sound go some place, right?" Minnor gave him a tremulous look. Vistos waved his wand toward Halston and his clapping. Then he twirled the wand tightly and muttered something before waving the wand in a new direction. The sound of Halston's clapping faded and it took Minnor some moments to twirl around and find the sound coming from behind him. "There," Vistos said, "easy enough. Now you do it."

"What did you say, sir?" Minnor asked, drawing his wand and pointing it toward Halston.

"Don't point it at him!" Vistos bellowed, taking two quick steps and knocking the apprentice's arm down. "Point it at the sounds! If you point it at him you'll *move* him!" Vistos bit his lip and added academically, "Of course, you don't have the power to do that, yet." With a bitter smile, he added, "You'd probably only move his heart or something fatal like that."

Minnor's eyes bugged out. Vistos allowed himself a smile, grim smile before bellowing at the lad. "Well? What are you waiting for? Have at it!"

Minnor raised his arm again cautiously, glanced over to Halston, turned bright green and bent over to his side, spewing his guts.

"What sort of spell do you think *that* is?" Vistos demanded. "Get up, take a breath — no, get some snow first and clean out your mouth."

Minnor did as instructed, moving away from the steaming mess that had moments before been his last meal.

"Start slowly, then," Vistos said with a quick glance toward the king and his party and another toward the assembling company of musketeers. "Halston, keep clapping."

Halston, who hadn't stopped except to grin when Minnor had thrown up, raised his hands higher and clapped louder.

"The word of the spell is whatever you use to make things quiet," Vistos told Minnor as the lad pointed his wand toward Halston's hands. "You must use your brain, too, and think of what you want to do."

Minnor nodded nervously and began muttering to himself. He twirled the point of his wand in a quick motion and snapped his wrist as though pulling something he'd caught with his wand, dropping down toward the ground where his vomit cooled. His eyes widened as Halston's clapping hands went silent and the air above the vomit pounded with the sound. He glanced over triumphantly to Halston to see the other's startled look.

"Good," Vistos said. "Now you stop your spell and start clapping. Let Halston try."

Halston was much quicker to learn the technique which was a good thing because the prisoners were being trotted out, spurred on with whips laid liberally about their bodies.

"Form ranks!" a captain bellowed as the prisoners looked around them in curiosity. "One row, line up now!"

With some confusion, countered with more blows from the guards, the prisoners formed a ragged line.

King Markel moved toward them, still astride his horse.

"Tonight's perfidy will be punished," Markel bellowed, his face red with anger. "My wife was killed by Sorian soldiers!"

The prisoners exchanged looks of surprise and horror.

"Yes," Markel shouted. "You surrendered, then killed my queen!" He spat toward the ground and waved toward the musketeers standing stiffly at attention. He nodded toward their commander.

"The first company will raise their weapons!" the captain ordered. One hundred men moved to obey, raising their heavy muskets to their shoulders. The Sorians looked back in alarm. One raised his hands, palms out in surrender shouting, "We didn't do it!"

"The first company will prime their weapons and cock," the captain ordered.

Some of the prisoners broke ranks but were herded back by the whips of the guards.

"The first company will choose their targets," the captain continued when the men were ready.

"Please!" One of the Sorians shouted, stepping forward. He looked to be an officer, his uniform torn and ragged. "Your majesty, we beg mercy!"

"I will show you as much mercy as your men showed my wife," Markel bellowed back. He nodded to the captain of the musketeers.

"Get ready!" Vistos shouted to his apprentices.

"The first company will fire at my command," the captain called. He drew his sword from its scabbard, raised it high and lowered it in a swift drop as he shouted, "Fire!"

"Now!" Vistos roared.

One hundred muskets flared brightly in the night sky. The roar of their explosions was muffled, moved over to the barracks and away from the sleeping townsfolk by the magical efforts of Vistos' apprentices.

"The first company will reload," the captain ordered calmly as he moved forward to survey the bodies on the ground in front of them, sword still drawn to administer the *coup de grâce* to any still alive. "Carters! Move up! I want this field cleared in three minutes!"

"That was amazing!" Halston said, eyes beaming. He turned to Vistos. "Please sir, can we do that again?"

"As soon as the next group are assembled, yes," Vistos said agreeably. He turned to glance at his king. Markel saw him and raised a hand in salute. "The king was impressed, lads."

He saw Minnor standing stock still, his arm at his side, his wand drooping in it. He moved toward the young lad, his hands going deep into his robes and pulling out a small paper-wrapped object. "Here lad," Vistos said, his eyes glinting, "try this. It'll help."

"What is it, sir?" Minnor said, taking the offering with his other hand.

"Put your wand away," Vistos said. "You'll need two hands to unwrap it." Minnor looked confused. "Have you never had a sweet before, lad?"

"A sweet, sir?" Minnor said, slowly unrolling the wrapper. It revealed a glassy yellow lozenge. "Like from the apothecary, sir?"

"Better," Vistos told him, gesturing that the lad should try it. "You'll please me by accepting my gift."

Minnor gave the sweet one last dubious look and popped it into his mouth. His eyes brightened and he said, "It's good!"

"Yes," Vistos said. "It is indeed." In a lower voice, he added, "It does the job just right."

#

"Master," a low voice spoke in the darkness of the Steam Master's office. Cautious footsteps moved with a practiced grace on the floor, dodging sharp objects and work benches with ease. The door at the back creaked loudly as it was opened. "Master?"

"Go away!" The Steam Master growled. "Can't you see I'm sleeping?"

"I am here under orders," the voice, a man's, though not much advanced in years, came back.

"If it's not the king, you'll wish you were dead," Torvan Brookes, the Steam Master, swore as he rolled up and out of his cot. "I was dreaming about —"

A burst of cold air suddenly tickled his right ear.

"Who are you?" Brookes demanded.

"I am named Matthew Wayfarer," the man's voice replied. "I am here on orders from the king, you may see my warrant if you like."

Another burst of air tickled Torvan's left ear.

"Oh, it's you!" Torvan called happily. "Make us a light, I want to see...."

'Matthew' raised a finger and blew on it. A spark sped from it toward the nearest lantern which flared and then burned steadily. Torvan Brookes grabbed the light and brought it up between them.

"You make a handsome lad, you do," Brookes said.

"Courtesy of Lord Hewlitt," 'Matthew' replied. "I can't stay long; I just wanted you to know that I am back."

"And leaving again," Brookes said with a frown. He cocked a head at his daughter. "Are you sure you're up for this?"

"Never surer."

"You won't be able to hold the disguise while you're doing it," Brookes warned. "For one thing, you might confuse the gods."

"Or insult them," 'Matthew' agreed. "But I'm under orders —"

"And when has that ever stopped you?" Brookes chuckled. He moved forward and grabbed the young man's shape in a tight embrace. Into 'his' hair, he said, "I picked you a good crew. The timbers and rails are all there." He pushed the 'lad' away. "Go! Do us proud!"

'Matthew' grinned, a grin that looked completely out of place on a man's face. "I will, father!"

Chapter Four

Thomas Walpish stepped back into the cave, his arms full of wood. He glanced toward his prisoner who writhed fitfully in some demon-tortured dream and moved toward the fire, dropping the wood onto the pile beside it. He knelt and grabbed the driest piece of wood, placing it on one side of the fire and grimacing as drops of water sizzled and spluttered in the flames. He stayed there long enough to lay in another log, then turned to examine the woman.

She was still delirious. He pulled off a glove and ran a finger lightly over the right side of her jaw, eyes narrowing as he felt the intense heat radiating from it.

"Skara," he said in a soft voice. He had learned her name through careful questioning her in her fever-induced haze. He made a face, pulled off his other glove, turned back to the fire with his hand outspread long enough to warm his fingers and then turned back again to the fever-ridden woman. With a scowl, he gently moved his hands around her jaw, inserting a thumb into her mouth and forced it open once more.

Even in the dim light, he had no trouble spotting it. But he could look only a moment before he turned his head to one side in revulsion, closing her jaws gently and wiping his hands on his pants.

He sat there a long while, wrestling with his thoughts, his eyes travelling the length of the woman's twitching body from top to bottom and back again.

"I owe her nothing," Walpish argued with himself. "She killed seven of my men, would have killed me, too, except…"

Except that he'd traded the new leather jacket with trooper Tavis. Tavis, who now lay dead in some snow-covered hole far from home. Betrayed by a king. Just as the king had betrayed Walpish to cover his treacherous murder of his own wife, the queen.

And now Skara Ningan — what a strange name! — was dying to keep the king's secret.

The fire is warm, at least, Thomas Walpish thought to himself. He glanced around the dark cavern out to the snow-laden clearing beyond. *There are worse ways to die.*

He took one final breath and closed his eyes. Loudly, he called, "Aron, God of Judgement, I call upon you!"

He opened his eyes. He pulled his knife from its sheath and cut into the flesh of his thumb. He turned to the fire and let drops of his blood fall on it.

"I call on Judgement, for I fear something foul," Walpish said. "God of Judgement, hear me and answer my call." Nothing. A moment later, under his breath, Walpish swore, "Dammit, Aron, I'm just asking you to see for yourself!"

"It's not wise to curse the gods," a small boy's voice spoke up from behind him. Walpish twirled but Aron raised a finger in restraint and turned back to examine Skara Ningan. "Is this why you called me?"

Walpish glared and shook his head. He moved swiftly to the other side of Skara's shivering body, grabbing her jaw and forced her mouth open. Releasing one hand he pointed deep into her mouth. "It's this!"

Aron, the child god of Judgement, followed the finger, peered inside the woman's mouth and rocked back on his heels, eyes wide.

#

The last of the shots rang out, the last of the prisoners fell, the captain ordered his men to stand down, the death carts to roll forward, and turned to salute his king. Markel gave him a half-nod, turned his horse, and trotted into the darkness.

"You can stop now," Vistos said, clapping Minnor on the shoulder to get his attention. Minnor gave him a slack-jawed look, recovered and smiled up at the older mage.

"That was fun," Minnor said cheerily. A snort from beyond distracted him — Halston looked pale and white. "Didn't you enjoy it?"

Halston made no answer.

"Here lad," Vistos said, moving over to the other apprentice and digging into his robes. "You need a sweet."

"I —" Halston glanced at the wrapper in the mage's outstretched hand and shook his head. "I don't feel well."

"This will put you to rights," Vistos said, pressing the wrapped sweet into the lad's hand.

"Try it!" Minnor called. "You'll like it!"

Halston glared at him but he took the sweet. He unwrapped it slowly.

"Go on!" Vistos barked. "We don't have all night!"

Minnor laughed at that, and continued laughing, seeming like it was the funniest thing he'd ever heard.

Halston gave him a sour look.

"Just try it!" Minnor shouted before resuming to his insistent laughter.

Halston raised the lozenge to his nose, sniffed. His nostrils wrinkled at the smell. Vistos gave him a sour look and made ready to turn away. Intimidated, annoyed at the continued laughing of Minnor, Halston put the hard candy in his mouth.

A moment later, he smiled. "I see!" he said, starting to laugh. He pointed toward the bloodied ground where a thousand men had died and started laughing louder. "Haha! And we silenced them!" He turned to beam up at Vistos. "In the name of the king, we made their cries into whispers!"

"There lad," Vistos said, his eyes gleaming, his face hard. "That's the spirit."

#

"We should kill them in their sleep," a voice said urgently. "Kill them now, it would be a blessing." In a lower tone, she added, "And their livers will taste great."

"They are innocent," another voice replied.

"Hah!" the first voice returned. "One has blood on his sword already and the other… she's likely to be the worst." There was a pause. "Kill them now, majesty."

"I will not kill them out of hand."

Alain opened his eyes and saw only darkness. The voices — the first was Maro, the second was Alva, the queen.

"If you must kill, spare my sister," Alain said. He heard the rustle of fabric that told him the two had turned toward him but he couldn't see them in the dark. He closed his eyes and opened them again. The world around him got brighter.

"His eyes are adjusting," Maro said. He caught a gleam from the direction of her voice and realized it was the light from her eyes.

"She is young and innocent," Alain said, staring directly at Maro. "She's done nothing wrong."

"Nothing!" Maro spat. "She's the reason we're in this mess today!"

Alain's brows furrowed.

"If she had just married as she was required, all would be well," Maro explained. In a smaller voice, she added, "Your father would still be alive."

"What?" Alain asked in shock.

"His life was forfeit," Queen Alva spoke in the darkness. "He had sworn her in marriage and when… well, his life was forfeit."

"And Paulus took his lands and title," Maro continued bitterly.

"Paulus?" Alain exclaimed, rising to his feet. His hands were tied behind his back. "Prince Paulus of Jasram Plains?"

"The very same," Maro growled. "Immediately the centaurs revolted, and Paulus crushed them."

"He crushed the centaurs?" Alain said in horror. The Jasram Plains had overflowed with centaurs, half-man, half-horse — not twin souls but something even rarer and more beautiful. The centaurs were artisans, farmers, makers of spices and fragrances, roaming in large herds across the grassy plains, making homes wherever they went and trading with everyone. They were the only ones who could manage the huge six-legged hexin, long-bodied, wide-shouldered, slow beasts of burden whom the centaurs raised from birth and cherished as much as their own kin.

"But what of the food?" Alain said. "Without the centaurs, without the traders, how are the towns getting fed? Who is harvesting the grain, planting the fields?"

"Who indeed?" Maro replied scornfully. "Armed bands are in our hills, murdering our people, looking for gold, for food, for *anything* — and all because of your sister."

"No," Alain said. "Because of me." The two zwerg were silent. "She begged me, said she wasn't ready. And I took her away." He moved toward Maro, pulling open his tunic and exposing his chest. "Kill me."

"No," Queen Alva said. Alain turned to the sound of her voice. He caught see light reflecting from her eyes. "That will solve nothing."

"What can I do?" Alain said.

"He needs to fix this," Maro growled. "Him and his sister. Their blood might be enough."

"The dead never bring back the dead," Queen Alva said.

"My father's blood flows in me," Alain replied turning to the queen. "In that, I am his ghost."

"Ghost!" Maro exclaimed. She said a word and a soft light filled the room. Even as Alain blinked to adjust to it, Maro looked him up and down. She turned to her queen. "There might be a way after all."

#

"So?" Walpish pressed as the boy-sized god continued to stare at the thing growing in the girl's mouth. Aron looked at him wordlessly. "It's wrong, isn't it?"

"I do not judge right and wrong," Aron said. He waved a hand toward the girl's jaw. "But this — this is out of balance!"

"Do me a great favor," Walpish said, pursing his lips tightly, "and tell me, great god, am I wise in asking for help?"

Aron smiled at him and shook his head, grinning. "You're a fool and I've told you already, Thomas Walpish of the Kingsland cavalry."

"And it's not stopped me before," Walpish agreed with a fond smile for the god of Judgement. "My life has been interesting, at the very least," he said to himself before taking a deep breath and calling out, "Gods of Death and Life, I call upon you now!"

Aron shook his head but Walpish waved a hand at him in entreaty so he said, with a sigh, "Avice, Terric, I think you should see this."

"Aron, you add your voice to a mortal's —" a woman's voice replied in surprise. And suddenly she was there. Next to her was a man who eyed the young god, and the man kneeling in obeisance beside him. "Ah, Thomas Walpish!" She smiled fondly. "Do you know how many times —"

"My Lady of the Dawn," Thomas Walpish said, raising her head, "I greet you and your husband with great pleasure."

"You *do* know that Death must always extract price, don't you?" Avice asked him mildly. She turned and saw the shivering woman laid out near the fire. "And what have we here?"

"She's an assassin," Walpish replied. "Goes by the unlikely name of Skara Ningan —" Terric's head snapped around at the name and he stared down at the woman's body with wide eyes. Walpish saw his reaction and said, "Ah! I see you're aware of her."

"Before you do anything, you should see inside her mouth," Aron said in a small voice, pointing to Skara's jaw. "And, yes, she's dying."

"She's not on my —" Terric's deep voice rumbled and he cut himself off with a horrified look in his eyes, glancing in sorrow toward Walpish.

"Once you hear his voice, a life is forfeit," Avice said to the cavalryman in a small voice. She shook her head sadly. "I'm sorry, Colonel but —"

"Perhaps not, my brilliant lady," Thomas Walpish interjected with a raised hand. He bowed his head toward Terric, god of death. "If you would look, first, my lord…"

Terric eyed him doubtfully but nodded silently. Walpish moved forward and gently prised open Skara Ningan's jaws as far as he could. He turned back. "You may need a light, it's all the way in the back on the lower right."

Terric moved forward and, with a nod toward his wife who was happy to provide a glowing spark of life to illuminate the interior of Skara's mouth, peered deeply inside. And, with a hiss of indrawn breath, jerked his head backwards, eyes wide with horror. He turned to Aron who nodded.

"You should see," Terric said to Avice.

"You couldn't stop me for worlds," Avice said, reaching forward to lay a hand on Walpish's thigh as she leaned forward and peered inside. She looked at the horror and leaned back, turning to Walpish and asking, "What is it you propose?"

Walpish's lips twitched upwards and he nodded in gratitude. "A balance of life and death."

"I'm listening," Terric said, glancing toward Avice who lowered her chin in agreement.

"Kill the thing growing in her jaw, take it with you," he said to Terric, god of Death and then turned to his wife, "and leave a new life in its place."

Terric's eyes widened and he looked in surprise at Avice, goddess of Life. Avice laughed and turned to the god of Judgement. "Will that do?"

"It will balance," Aron said after a moment's thought. He jerked his head toward Walpish. "But it does not pay all debts."

Avice pursed her lips and turned to Walpish. "Who is this woman to you?"

"She killed seven of my men and would have killed me," Walpish said. He grimaced. "I would have left her to die until I found that... thing. Now I have to ask what she did of her own and what she did under compulsion."

"If we do this," Aron said, nodding toward the older gods, "what is your price?"

Terric chuckled and shook his head at the young god. "You have something in mind."

"This is wrong," Aron said by way of answer. "Whoever committed this wrong will do others."

"I shall find whoever it is and stop them," Walpish offered. Aron and Terric both shook their heads. "What else do you desire, great gods?"

"She must help you," Terric said. Walpish started to protest but the god of Death raised a hand. "You saved her life when she owed you life-debt. She lives if she agrees to go with you."

"She is feverish and cannot speak," Walpish said, shaking his head. "I'll not force an oath."

"Good," Terric said, reaching a hand into the woman's face. He didn't open her jaw, his fingers just went through her flesh as though it were air. He grimaced as a dark gray light flashed and smiled as he pulled his hand back. In it was the gnarled stump of something with long, twisted roots and a dark crown — like a tooth turned to evil. He nodded toward his wife.

Avice smiled at Walpish. "I believe you deserve this, falsed knight."

"I've never —!" Walpish protested loudly.

"You are betraying your oaths now," Terric corrected him. "And my lady said 'falsed' not 'false' — you have been betrayed into betrayal."

"What — what is going on?" Skara called feebly, trying to rise on her elbows and failing.

"You are in the presence of gods," Walpish warned her. "You were betrayed, there was an evil in your jaw and I asked for mercy."

"My jaw?" Skara repeated in confusion. "It was the mage! He gave me a sweet! It tasted so good and then... I didn't think anything of it for the longest while."

"Did you kill before he gave you this sweet?" Avice asked.

"She did," Aron said. "She's killed many times."

"Did you kill this man's men?" Avice asked, jerking her head toward Walpish.

Skara looked up and over and blinked. "They were wearing the red jackets, the bolts were magically aimed."

"Your life is his, you know," Avice told her softly. "If that is too much, my husband will take you."

"Your husband?" Skara said, blinking and turning her eyes to Terric. She glanced at him, at the boy and then at Avice. With a nervous flutter of her fingers, she begged Thomas, "Help me up, please!"

Thomas grabbed her hands and pulled her forward.

"More, I must kneel!" Skara begged.

"You have not the strength," Terric said at last. He reached forward with a hand. "I could ease your pain, if you wish."

"You are the god of Death?" Skara asked in surprise. She turned to Walpish in shock. "I'm talking with gods?"

"It is never wise to talk with Death," Aron said in a sad warning. "He only talks with those who die."

"There is a way, still, if you wish," Walpish told the assassin. Skara turned toward him, brows raised. "I have taken an oath to avenge my men, to destroy the maker of the evil that grew in your jaw."

"I owe you seven lives," Skara said to him. "What would you have me do?"

"I understand that these great gods are willing to take your oath in return for your life—"

"No!" Terric spoke up and Walpish turned to him. "I can only grant more time. Your death is a given." He nodded toward Walpish. "And so is yours."

"I will take this oath," Skara said. She reached for Walpish's hand and clenched it tightly in hers. "Great gods, may I have your names that I may give you my oath?"

"I am Avice," the goddess of life replied. She gestured toward Aron. "This is Aron, god of Judgment." She smiled as she nodded toward her husband. "And I believe you know my Terric, the god of Death."

"I have served you many times, great god," Skara said with a nod toward him. She turned to Avice and smiled. "What service may I give you, my lady of the dawn?"

"The oath," Avice replied. "The oath to find the creator of this evil and to bring them to Judgement."

"And, child," Terric said in a warning tone, "you have *never* served me. You have always served others."

"Death is quite capable of serving himself," Aron added with a small grin.

Skara leaned forward, bowing as best she could, her hand still holding Walpish's.

"Great gods, I, Skara Ningan, do make this oath to you," Skara said as she raised her head once more. "I swear to find the mage who betrayed me and to bring him to Judgement."

"What's his name, child?" Aron demanded.

"His name, Lord Aron, is Vistos, a mage of King Markel's," Skara replied. "He trained me, taught me magics, and set me to kill in the name of the king."

"Who betrayed us all," Walpish added darkly.

"Falsed Knight," Aron said to him, his eyes flashing with delight.

"Your oath is accepted," Terric said. He leaned forward and placed the blackened stump of a tooth in her hand. "Clench this in your fist when your quest is completed."

Skara took it and grimaced. "It hurts."

"Let me hold it," Walpish said, pulling a glove from his pocket and taking the evil thing from her.

"Is that okay?" Skara said, looking up to ask the gods. But there was no one there. "Where did they go?"

"They have other things to be doing," Walpish told her. He scanned the cave and started to move. "If you're feeling well enough, we should start out."

"Now?"

"Many things get interested when three gods appear," Walpish replied with a shrug. "It's not wise to linger."

Chapter Five

"And you're going to lay the track all by yourself, are you?" Diktor Vincet, a grizzled old tough demanded of the lad in front of him. They had boarded the work train a half an hour ago and Diktor had determined that this Matthew Wayfarer was responsible for their being woken in the middle of the night and rustled out 'on the king's orders.'

"I am," 'Matthew' replied stoutly. He lay his head back down on the seat he'd been resting against. "If you'll let me sleep."

"Sleep!" Diktor snorted. He moved forward, eyes squinting. "And if I don't?"

'Matthew' muttered something and suddenly Diktor felt a chill wind run down his spine and out the front of his trousers.

"What did you do, what did you do?" Diktor squealed, his eyes bulging, hands patting himself in fear.

"I showed you what would happen if you wouldn't let me sleep," 'Matthew' replied. He moved his head against the seat and closed his eyes.

Diktor scowled, saw the smirks on the others and moved forward quietly, hands outstretched — he'd show the bugger.

Only it didn't work out that way.

"Let me go, let me go!" Diktor squealed as invisible icicles raced all over his body. He dropped to the ground, his arms over his head as though afraid of unseen blows. "I won't do it again, I swear!"

One piercing frost settled on his earlobe and he screamed in again. "My ear, my ear!"

"I think that's enough," 'Matthew' said quietly, waving a hand languidly toward the trembling man.

Diktor lay on the ground for a long while before he dared to move his head from the protection of his arms. Slowly, fearfully, he rose to his feet and stepped quietly away, turning only when Matthew Wayfarer called, "Let me know when we're a half an hour from the station."

"Yes, sir," Diktor replied in a small voice. He turned to the other rail crew. "Someone get him a blanket."

The others stared at him until he glowered and one of the smaller men nodded.

'Matthew Wayfarer' slept untroubled for the next five hours.

#

Walpish insisted that they enter South Sea Pass from the west which meant that they had to circle around the hill and come down the far side and then walk — out of sight — around the walls that guarded the southern part of the town until they at least came to the western plains and the open gates.

They were both tired and hungry by the time they entered the gates — hidden amongst the crowds of people entering the same way. Walpish quickly led them off the main thoroughfare and down a side street.

"Where are we going?" Skara demanded.

"A place I know," Walpish replied secretively. Skara glared at him but he offered nothing further until they pulled up in front of a dimly lit three-story building that might — only with a great deal of charity — be called a tavern.

"What is this place?"

"It's a house of comfort," Walpish replied, pushing open the heavy oak door. Inside, heads turned toward him and sour faces dismissed them, all except the innkeep.

"You again!" the woman snarled. "I suppose you want to make more trouble?"

"No, I'm here for the comforts of your establishment," Walpish replied. The woman snorted, eyed Skara and said, "'Seems like you brought your own."

"We need hot water, two tubs in separate rooms and clean clothes," Walpish replied, moving toward the innkeep and slapping some coppers into her hands. The coins quickly disappeared into her apron. "And we'll need a place to sleep —"

"To sleep!" Someone guffawed. "That's extra!"

"Food before that," Walpish said. He glanced around the room and pulled some more coins from his pocket, slipping them to the tavern keeper. "And buy our friends some good drink."

There was a roar of approval. The innkeep signalled a youngster toward her and issued quick instructions. In a lower voice to Walpish, she said, "Are you sure about this?"

"Clean clothes," Walpish reminded her. "And our bath."

"I can bring up some fresh rolls and butter," the woman said.

Walpish nodded. "We'll relish it."

She nodded toward Skara. "Has she got a name?"

Walpish thought for a moment, then said, "What day is this?"

"Thursday," the innkeep replied.

"So she's Thursday," Walpish told her with a grin. He gestured Skara to follow the youngster. "Come on, Thursday, let's go get clean."

Heading up the stairs, Skara turned her head back to hiss to Walpish, "You've got them thinking that we're going to… going to —"

"Bundle?" Walpish asked with a chuckle. "Just as long as they're thinking that, we're safe."

"Do they know you here?"

"They know that I caused trouble when I came here the other night to roust out three of my troopers who'd gotten roaring drunk and had — ahem" — Walpish coughed to cover his hasty change of words — "dallied with the women of the house."

"So this is like the Inn of the Broken Sun back in Kingsford," Skara said. She caught Walpish's surprise and snorted. "I'm not a child, you know."

"I had guessed," Walpish agreed. "It takes a while to create a trained killer."

"Unlike yourself?" Skara retorted.

"No," Walpish said. "Which is how I know."

The youngster in front of them turned to the left at the top of the stairs, opened a door and waved Skara through. When Walpish made to follow, the girl tutted at him and pointed to another door, "That one's for you."

Walpish peered inside, saw the tub and turned to the youngster. "Hot water? Towels, soap?"

"I'm bringing them now," a woman's voice called from the bottom of the stairs. A clatter of feet presaged the arrival of several more youngsters, mostly girls bearing towels and toiletries but a few lads bringing up steaming buckets of water.

"Start hers first," Walpish said, grabbing a lantern from one of the boys and heading into his bathroom. "And the clothes?"

"We'll find something but it won't be pretty," the innkeeper called up the stairs.

"Just as long as it's clean and pest free," Walpish called back. "Have our room and the food ready when we're done."

"As you wish."

Forty glorious minutes later, Walpish was clean, dry, and dressed in a tunic, a pair of trousers, fresh socks and his knee-high boots. He seated himself at the small table and dug into a hearty beef stew while helping himself liberally to the wine set out.

Someone knocked on the door and he looked up, his hand going to the knife hanging at his side from his belt and he called, "Come!"

He was surprised and jumped out of his chair when Skara — the woman could only be she — entered, looking worried, pleased, and alarmed all at once.

"Come in," Walpish said, waving her to the empty seat. "I've just started." He sat back down and resumed his eating without waiting for the assassin. He looked up when she pulled the seat back and sat into it. He poured her some wine. "It's not bad," he told her.

Skara took a sip suspiciously and then a larger gulp.

"I wouldn't trust the water around here for another week or so," Walpish said, his mouth full. "You don't know what might have fallen into the wells."

Skara nodded. Walpish finished eating and leaned back in his chair, eyeing the woman across from him.

Clean, she was nothing to look at. She was skinnier than most, had a gaunt face with dishwater blue eyes and thin straggly brown hair that was pulled back tightly to keep her field of vision clear. Her neck was longer than some and her shoulders thinner than Walpish would have imagined but there was nothing wrong with the muscles of her arms and shoulders. Her ears, though, what he could see of them, were quite dainty. Her skin was weathered and her cheeks red with wind-burn.

Skara glanced down at her food and grabbed a spoon. She took a small bite of the stew at first and then, ravenous, picked up the bowl and emptied it in a few moments.

"Hungry?" Walpish teased. He pushed the rolls and butter toward her. "Have these, too, if you wish." He leaned back again. "I've had my fill."

She slowed her eating long enough to glance at him. He was handsome, she realized with a start. Brown hair, piercing dark brown eyes, a rugged body. "How old are you?"

"Me?" Walpish replied, surprised at the question. He toyed with his glass and raised it to his lips. "How old do you think I am?"

"I don't judge age," Skara said.

"Just distance," Walpish guessed. "Well, in the cavalry we need to think about age."

Skara gave him a questioning look while buttering up another roll. They were going cold and she wanted to finish them while they were still warm.

"If our enemies are old enough," Walpish continued, "we can hope to scare them away."

"Why? If they're still alive, they're a danger," Skara countered, swallowing a roll whole and chewing it awkwardly.

"It's much easier to kill someone running than someone standing ready to fight," Walpish said. He shrugged, amused. "Also, the dead are not much use when it comes to planting crops or mining ore."

Skara's look made it clear she didn't agree with this notion.

"You were trained to think in ones and twos," Walpish told her. "I am trained to think in hundreds and thousands."

"So?"

"It's easier to frighten than to murder," Walpish said. "Convince your enemy that they cannot hope to win and that their best choice is to surrender and your battles are over." He waved his hand around, indicating the city they were in. "That's what we did here."

"I blew up the hinges to the gates," Skara said, chewing on yet another roll. She eyed the basket. There was only one roll left. She offered it to Walpish who raised his hands towards her, gesturing for her to have it.

"I know," Walpish said. "And then me and my men stormed the towers and my cavalry rushed from the west to the east, completing the trap that made the enemy surrender."

"Huh," Skara muttered. Clearly, she had not considered this before.

"We killed maybe a dozen men and took the surrender of thousands," Walpish told her.

"And then the king ordered me to kill you," Skara said, nibbling on the last roll.

"And your mage triggered his trap to kill *you*," Walpish added firmly.

"Will you kill the king?"

"In time, perhaps," Wapish replied. "But our oath now is to destroy your mage." He watched as she finished her roll and took a gulp of the wine. Then he rose and gestured away from the table. "Are you ready?"

Skara gave him a startled look. He moved past her, rummaged in the room's one cabinet and pulled out more clothing: sweaters, coats, and knit caps. He smirked when he saw her look change from worry to comprehension. He pushed open the window and peered out.

"I think this is our best course," he said to her, putting on his sweater, cap, and coat.

"I don't have any weapons," Skara said.

"We'll have to fix that," Walpish agreed. He eyed her thoughtfully. "How good are you with a sword?"

"I'm better with a crossbow," Skara said.

"Bow?" Walpish countered.

"I like my crossbow," Skara said.

"The one given you by the mage who tried to murder you," Walpish reminded her in a tight voice. "I destroyed it," Walpish told her. "It and the quiver." She looked desolate. "Think, please," he snapped at her. "The mage — don't say his name —" he barked when she started to reply "— the mage enspelled your bolts and those jackets to be targets. Why wouldn't he do the same with your possessions?"

The color drained from Skara's face. She rose quickly from her chair, grabbed the sweater from Walpish and put it on. She grabbed the cap and the coat and said to him, "Which way do we go?"

"Out and down," Walpish said, climbing through the open window. "And we should try to be quiet."

"Then let me lead," Skara said, pulling him back from the window. He gave her a look. "I'm trained to climb around quietly."

Walpish accepted this with a nod and stepped back in, waving her to precede him.

#

Peter Hewlitt walked quietly into first minister Mannevy's temporary office in the mansion that King Markel had taken over upon his entrance into the newly acquired Sorian town of South Sea Pass. Mannevy looked up at his cough.

"Yes?"

"I've heard an interesting rumor," Hewlitt said as he closed the door behind him. Mannevy glanced at the door and back to the spymaster.

"Indeed?"

"Someone just reported seeing Colonel Walpish enter a house of ill repute here in the city," Hewlitt said.

"I thought the poor Colonel was among those who died in that unfortunate accident," Mannevy said calmly. He glanced up at Hewlitt. "How certain are your informants?"

"I've left some people to watch the place," Hewlitt said with a shrug. "Apparently he's in company with some woman."

"I'm sure that you'll sort this out quickly," Mannevy said. "Doubtless it is an impostor, the king is already composing a eulogy." He added, with a shrug, "A man can only die once."

"Indeed," Hewlitt replied. "I was wondering, however…?" Mannevy cocked his head in encouragement. "Should I inform the mage?"

"Vistos?" Mannevy said. He thought for a moment and shook his head. "I don't think he should be bothered with such a wild claim."

"As you say," Hewlitt replied. He turned and opened the door. "Until later."

Mannevy grunted in agreement and returned his attention to the notes on his desk.

#

"My name is Jaro and, no, I'm not related to Maro," the large burly zwerg — whose head came up to just under Alain's chin, declared when they met. "I'm to test you and train you." He jerked his head, indicating that Alain should follow him from the bare-walled room he'd occupied for the past two days.

"Where's my sister?"

"I don't know," Jaro replied. He lengthened his stride. "Keep up, we haven't got all day."

To his amazement, Alain soon found himself hard-pressed to keep up with the much shorter zwerg. He started breathing heavily, then panting.

"Sky-touchers!" Jaro muttered to himself. "Too tall to walk properly."

Alain said nothing, using all his breath to keep up with the burly zwerg.

Jaro pushed open a small door that Alain hadn't noticed and a burst of light blinded him.

"Don't tell me you've never seen sunlight, sky-toucher," Jaro grumbled, holding the door open and urging Alain through. As soon as Alain emerged, still blinking, into the sunlight, the zwerg let go the door and it closed silently. Alain turned back but saw only moss-covered rock — and no sign at all of their exit. Jaro noticed his look and grumbled again, "Sky-touchers don't know how to build decent doors."

"Not into the sides of mountains," Alain agreed. He snorted as he recalled memories of his journeys north. "But if you think what we do in Jasram is bad, you should try heading north."

"There are some quite good things up north," Jaro said. In a lower voice he added, "Most of them underground."

"There are zwerg up north?" Alain asked in surprise.

Jaro waved a hand at the mountain rising beside them. "There are zwerg wherever there is an underground."

Alain considered that for a moment then nodded. "What are we doing out here?"

"They tell me that your eyes aren't adjusted to living with the earth," Jaro told him. "And I'm supposed to train you."

"I've been training since I was old enough to hold a sword," Alain replied, drawing himself up proudly.

"Good," Jaro said, drawing his short blade. "Let's see how good you are." And he proceeded to charge toward Alain.

"But I haven't got a blade!" Alain protested as he rushed away from his assailant. "That's not fair!"

"See," Jaro said happily as he whacked Alain's backside with the flat of his blade, "you've learned something new already!"

"What?" Alain demanded, still running.

"Two things, I'd say," Jaro said. He whacked Alain again. "One is that you can run even when you're breathless —"

"I can always run when someone is trying to kill me!"

Jaro drew himself up short and lowered his blade. Alain turned back to him. "Know this, sky-toucher, if I was trying to kill you, you'd be dead."

Alain absorbed this, taking in the small man's stance, the hard look on his face. *Yes,* he realized, *Jaro would kill me.* He collected himself and said, "And what's the other thing?"

"That you don't know a thing about fighting without a sword," Jaro said. He smiled up at the taller lad and sheathed his sword. He moved around Alain, at the trot, turning his head back to call behind him, "Follow me and I'll teach you."

#

"Mr. Wayfarer," a deep voice called gently. A hand nudged his shoulder and pulled away. "Sir, we're here."

'Matthew' opened his eyes and saw an anxious face peering down at him. It was not Diktor Vincet. That one stood further away, watching his lackey dubiously and 'Matthew' himself with worry.

Margaret stirred herself, decided that stretching was something that even 'Wayfarer' would do and allowed herself a long luxurious stretch before rising from her seat.

The train had stopped. Cold entered from the air outside and Margaret could feel it in her bones.

"Good," 'he' said in his deep man's voice. He nodded to the lackey and said to Diktor, "Have the men meet me outside."

The lackey cast a worried glance to Diktor who angrily motioned him away. Diktor said, "As you say."

Margaret walked toward the front of the passenger car, stepped out through the door onto the ledge outside and jumped from there down lightly to the snow-covered ground at the side of the train.

She frowned as she moved forward, past the still steaming engine and beyond to the end of the tracks. There was a pile of timber formed as a barrier to keep the train from running off the end of the tracks. She turned back and saw that the train had taken the turn north toward the pass.

This was the end of the line.

"Driver!" Margaret called in her deep man voice. "I need you to go back to the turn and switch the train around."

"What?" the driver cried in surprise.

"I want the timbers and the rails up here," Margaret said, jabbing her hand down to the ground, "and your engine in the rear."

"That'll take hours," the driver grumbled.

"Then you'd best get started," Margaret told him in Matthew's voice.

"Who are you —?"

"That's Mr. Wayfarer," Diktor shouted angrily, "and he's in charge."

Margaret bit back a grin: it was the way with bullies, once they'd been tamed they took it as their job to bark at anyone who contradicted their new master.

"You have an hour," Margaret called. She turned to Diktor. "Is everyone off?"

"Yes," Diktor replied.

"Have them scour the forest for wood then, and build a fire," Margaret said. "And see if we can set up a warming tent or a shelter."

"I've already got men on it, Mr. Wayfarer," Diktor replied.

Margaret nodded and turned back to the timber piled at the end of the track. "They can have that, too."

"But," Diktor said worriedly, "won't we need it later?"

"When we get to the town, maybe," Margaret allowed with a shrug.

"But that'll take *days*," Diktor replied.

"How fast can you men bolt down track?"

"Bolt down?" Diktor repeated, shaking his head. "They're quick enough but —"

"Don't worry, I'll do the rest," Margaret promised in Matthew's deep voice.

"It'll still take days," Diktor replied dubiously. He glanced back toward the train as it slowly started backing away. "Just to lay in the timbers —"

"Have them ready to bolt the track," Margaret told him firmly. "Once the train gets here." She waved a hand toward it. "You've got an hour."

Diktor grimaced, clearly not satisfied but Margaret waved him away, turning back to the end of the rail line.

She moved behind the timber barricade and crouched down behind it, peering ahead. Ahead of her was the valley of Korin's Pass. It lay straight for three leagues, then twisted east a league, then back west for another league and, finally, straight for the last two leagues. She'd seen the plans.

Four days. That was the time she'd been given. Margaret Waters smiled to herself and patted her hands on her thighs before standing once more.

No problem.

#

Swords and daggers were no problem. There were plenty in the camp. It took only one guard to tell them where Vistos was sleeping. They left that guard sleeping in a corner. Skara raised an eyebrow in surprise when Walpish had used his simple spell on the man.

"I see no reason to kill the innocent," Walpish had explained.

"He's a soldier, how can he be innocent?" Skara replied.

Walpish shrugged in acceptance of this point. "Let us say, then, that I see no reason to waste useful material."

"Huh," Skara said. "More 'strategy'?"

Walpish nodded.

"And what now?"

"Now we deal with the mage," Walpish said.

"And after?"

"I have no idea," Walpish told her honestly. He gestured for her to lead the way and together they vanished once more up to the rooftops of the city.

#

"This idea of yours," Queen Alva said to Maro from her throne, "I don't like it."

"It is a solution to all our problems," Maro replied.

"The girl… you ask a lot of her."

"She is the cause of the problems," Maro said. She shrugged. "I cannot say how much of it was in her rearing and how much is in her manner. But the truth is that without her willfulness, many today would be alive that are dead."

Queen Alva grimaced. "I still do not like this notion."

"And if she accepts it, freely of her own will?" Maro asked. "If she takes it on herself, what then?"

"Then I cannot stop her," Alva said. "But what of her brother?"

"He will avenge his father, protect her honor, and get what he wishes," Maro said.

"What does he wish?"

"Well," Maro said after a moment, "perhaps not what he wishes but what he deserves."

"Before we go further, witch, you will explain your plan," Alva said.

"Your Majesty, my plan is to protect our kingdom and recover from our losses," Maro said simply.

Alva snorted. "We have our gold. Annabelle saw to that."

"But we need more than that for our safety," Maro said. "We need to know that the sky-touchers will stop their efforts to steal it from us, that they'll protect our borders and that they'll *trade* for what they want."

"And you intend this boy to guarantee us all that?"

"Him and his sister," Maro replied. "They are part of the same puzzle, we will need both pieces to finish it."

#

The train backed up slowly and stopped in a swirl of steam. Margaret nodded to herself. "It's time." She turned to Diktor. "Are you men ready?"

"They are," Diktor said. "But —"

"Watch and learn," Margaret said. She motioned him back to his men. "Have them stand well clear of the timber and the rails or they'll get hurt."

"I don't understand —"

"You will," 'Matthew' replied. "Now get back."

Margaret heard Diktor back away and crouched down at the end of the tracks, looking north.

With a sigh, she pulled out the parchment from her coat. She unrolled it enough to find the skin and, touching it, said the word of release. Her body changed around her. She took a breath, tried a sound, and smiled to herself.

Then she turned back to the rail cars behind her. She saw Diktor's eyes narrow as he took in her changed appearance. From his distance he would know that her face looked different and might see that she had longer hair but probably nothing more. Diktor could wait.

Margaret took a deep breath, held it for a moment and let it out. She took another breath and rose to her full height. "Hissia, Hanor, hear my plea!" she shouted to the airs around her. "I call upon the gods of air, I call for your strength, for your power, for your winds."

Behind her a breeze blew her coat against her legs. Margaret smiled.

"I challenge you to aid me," Margaret said. "I call upon you to show these men the power of your magic."

The wind picked up.

"They think the air is only soft," Margaret jeered, pointing to the men in the distance. "Let us show them your true strength. Lend me your power and I will strike such awe into their hearts that they shall sing of this through the ages."

She crouched again, raised her arms above her head and then dropped them straight in front of her. Winds twirled in circles from the ends of her hands. The winds tore through the snow in front of her, raising it in giant whorls that filled the sky. The snow swirled higher and higher and fell away, revealing the bare frozen ground in a long straight line. A line that ran three leagues straight in front of her.

"Thank you!" Margaret shouted. "Thank you great gods of the air!"

Margaret could feel the two gods of air buffeting her. She turned and pointed her arms towards the first stack of timbers. She raised her arms and felt them strain under the weight of her magic.

"Hissia, Hanor, let us make magic," Margaret said. And with a roar, the winds came to her. She could feel Kitzis flicker around her hair, delighted at the attention of the gods that created it.

With a shout of joy, Margaret lifted the timber rail ties high in the air, laying them out in the sky with a precision that caused her to laugh with glee. She turned toward bare ground and lowered her arms, flicking them at the last moment.

The timbers, laid out like a giant fence in the sky, fell with precision on the ground below.

With a triumphant cry, Margaret used her aching arms to raise long lines of rails from the second car and then laid them out on top of the rail ties.

She knelt and bent her head low toward the ground. "Hissia, Hanor, great is your power."

She heard shouts from behind her, shouts of amazement and awe. She rose with a weary sigh then turned toward the approaching men.

"Well?" she shouted to them. "What are you waiting for? You've three leagues of rail to bolt before the sun sets."

The grizzled men stared at her. "Diktor!" Margaret shouted. Diktor Vincet came forward, glancing at her in surprise.

"Who are you?" he asked, glancing back to the others in the crew for support.

"My name is Margaret Waters," Margaret told him. She twitched a smile. "You knew me as Matthew Wayfarer."

"You?"

"And you know my father," Margaret added with a nod.

"Your father?"

"You call him the Steam Master," Margaret said. She pointed to the tracks. "Now get to work."

"As you say, miss," Diktor Vincet replied, glancing down the long gleaming line of rail. "Come on lads, the lady has given us a challenge!"

#

Walpish and Skara found Vistos unguarded, in his bed late the next night. They came silently through his window. At a nod from Walpish, the two drew their dirks. Skara went around the far side of the bed. Once she was in position, Walpish leaned forward with his free hand and covered Vistos' mouth.

The mage started awake, eyes wide as he caught sight of first Walpish and then Skara.

"You left us a present," Walpish told him in a whisper. "We wish to return it."

Skara plunged her knife deep into the old mage's chest. Vistos writhed and groaned as the blood flowed from his wound. Walpish added his blade next to hers, saying, "This is for my men."

Skara came back around the bed, leaned over Vistos' still open eyes and spat. Walpish pulled her away and they vanished through the window into the night.

The blood slowly ceased its flow from the two wounds.

A moment later, the mage's eyes blinked and his aged hand pulled first one and then the other knife from his chest. He turned in his bed, eyed the open window and rose slowly. At the window ledge, he looked out. After a moment he closed the open window. He turned then and went to the basin on the nightstand beside him. He placed the two knives in it, said a *word* and watched with pleasure as the two blades burst into flames. In a moment there was nothing left but ashes.

He ran a hand down his bloody front and brought it to his mouth. With a smile, he licked the blood off his hand.

Cursed Mage

Book 14

Twin Soul series

Chapter One

"So what will you do now?" Thomas Walpish, formerly of King Markel's cavalry, asked Skara Ningan, herself formerly an assassin working for Mage Vistos. The mage they had so recently left with two steel knives stuck in his heart — payment for the evils which he had perpetrated.

The two huddled outside a tavern, fresh from their assault. Snow was falling and it was cold enough that their breath was visible in the night air. The town of South Sea Pass was solemn but the tavern inside was bustling with steady trade — some from the conquering soldiers and some from the townsfolk.

"Shouldn't we call the gods, first?" Skara said. "Before we consider anything else?" She drew the darkened remains of the cursed tooth from her coat pocket.

"You're supposed to clench it in your fist," Walpish reminded her, gesturing toward the tooth.

Skara glared at him — she knew what to do. Slowly and obviously she closed the fist of her right hand around the gnarled, dark remains of the tooth in her hand. She squeezed tight, her face showing signs of strain. She held her grip tight for the longest time before turning her eyes up to Walpish. "Is something supposed to happen?"

Walpish shrugged. "Open your hand."

Skara did, showing that the dark tooth still remained.

"Perhaps —" Walpish began but a sudden sound from behind him caused him to turn in curiosity.

Soldiers burst forth from the King's mansion, moving with speed and deliberation. One squad split off and started toward them.

"Run!" Walpish said, grabbing Skara by the elbow and pushing her along in front of him.

Skara jerked her elbow out of his grip and told him angrily, "I'm better at hiding than you!"

Indeed she was, leading Walpish around the side of the tavern and then up into the dark of the night, climbing from windowsill to rooftop and then quickly away into the slums of the town.

#

"Why, spymaster, have you dispatched soldiers throughout the town at this time of night, if I may ask?" First Minister Mannevy asked as he sat behind the large desk in the room requisitioned for his use in the occupation of South Sea Pass.

"An attempt was made on the life of our mage," Peter Hewlitt replied smoothly. "I thought it best to discourage any future such events, at the very least to ensure his majesty's rest."

"How kind of you," Mannevy replied silkily. "And do we have any idea who might have impugned our good mage?"

"Colonel Walpish, I believe," Hewlitt replied.

"He is dead," Mannevy sat in a flat voice.

"Perhaps he was attempting to express his ire at being killed," Hewlitt said.

"He did not succeed, I presume?"

"No, the mage seems undamaged," Hewlitt replied.

"But?"

"My reports indicate that two people accosted him," Hewlitt said. "I can see perhaps one making an error, but two?"

"Doubly inept," Mannevy agreed. "And most certainly fleeing the mage's revenge."

"I should imagine," Hewlitt said. "But, on the off chance that the two assailants try a different tact, I decided it was wise to send out the guard to discourage them."

"I see," Mannevy said. "And the town?"

"Word of the… retribution for the murder of the queen has not spread," Hewlitt said cautiously.

"Tomorrow Queen Arivik will be buried with all honor," Mannevy said. "That should subdue any protests."

"She's being buried here?"

"Not buried, cremated," Mannevy replied. "A large pyre, suitable for a queen."

"Charming."

"Well, at least visually stunning," Mannevy allowed. He glanced toward the door to his office. "Is there anything else?"

"Not at the moment," Hewlitt allowed. With a half-bow, he took his leave of the first minister.

Mannevy followed him with his eyes out the door and sat for a long while after, staring off into the distance. *He troubles me.*

#

Peter Hewlitt smiled as he entered the small office at the nearby tavern… well, house of repute, the next morning after a leisurely breakfast.

"To what do I owe the pleasure, sir?" the dark-haired woman asked, her eyes glinting. "Are you hoping to avail yourself of the many joys of my house?"

"You know who I am," Hewlitt said in a voice that cut through all courtesies and drove to the heart of the matter. "And I know who you are, Madame Aubrey."

"You work for King Markel, I'm told," Madame Aubrey replied. "Some say that you gather intelligence."

"I'm his spymaster, yes," Hewlitt said with a wave of his hand.

"So how may I help you, sir?" Aubrey said after a moment's thoughtful silence.

"I need intelligence," Hewlitt said. "I have discovered that a lot of lips are loose in the presence of a pretty lady."

Aubrey's lips twitched in humor. "I noticed this myself."

"Recently, I came into possession of the House of the Broken Sun," Hewlitt told her.

"I had heard that Madame Parkes had suffered a mischance."

"I rapier slit her throat," Hewlitt said. He glanced meaningfully at Madame Aubrey's scarf-covered throat.

"I… see," Madame Aubrey said after a moment.

"Apparently Madame Parkes had been willing to provide more than companionship for our late queen," Hewlitt replied. "She paid for it with her life."

"As well she should," Madame Aubrey said firmly. Hewlitt twitched an eyebrow upwards. "There's no profit in playing with princes, they say."

"And yet, I'm sure it's been done."

"Always," Madame Aubrey agreed. She frowned. "I do my best to keep my ears to myself, spymaster. I'm not sure I would be able to help you."

"That would be a pity," Hewlitt told her in a cold voice. He waved a hand around her office and further, to her premises. "Such a pity."

Madame Aubrey licked her lips. "Perhaps I could help but I would need —"

"You'd need to stop lying to me, firstly," Hewlitt said. He pounded his foot on the ground by his chair. Abruptly the door opened at the hand of a large, well-armed man. "Or you will find yourself looking for a new throat."

"I —" she broke off. "What do you know?"

"That is not how this game is played," Hewlitt told her. "You will tell me all you know and, if I consider it enough and true, you will be able to continue breathing." He rose from his chair, nodding to the man. "I'm going to leave you alone for a few moments with my friend here."

"Wait!" Madame Aubrey cried. Hewlitt pulled the door closed behind him. He waited, just as she'd asked, until the door opened again and his man gestured him inside.

"I did as you asked," Hewlitt said in a silky voice. He looked at the crumpled form of the woman, her head resting on her desk, a small pool of blood surrounding it. "Now, are you prepared to talk?"

Madame Aubrey uttered a pitiful whimper and raised her head. Her eyes were blacked, her nose broken, and her lips bleeding.

"What do you want?" she asked, moving her mouth gingerly. Her eyes flared at him in anger.

"Everything, starting with what you've told your King and how," Hewlitt told her. He stomped his foot again, this time his other foot and he stomped twice.

Madame Aubrey cried in terror, raising her hands pleadingly.

"Oh, don't take on so!" Hewlitt growled at her as the door opened and a small, rat-faced man crept through. "It's just my secretary, Rafkin."

Rafkin, keeping his eyes off the ruin of Madame Aubrey's face, gave her a half-bow and pulled up a seat. He pulled out a ledger and set up his quill and inkwell.

"So," Hewlitt began, "what was the last word you got out to King Wendel and how?"

"I sent word that the city had been taken by pigeon the other night," Madame Aubrey began immediately.

"The pigeon we got, I'm certain," Hewlitt muttered. "And since then?"

"Well, I sent another this morning when I hadn't heard back," Madame Aubrey said.

"This morning?" Hewlitt repeated, his eyes going wide. "And how quickly do you hear back?"

"I can't say," Madame Aubrey replied. "The last spymaster was killed as a traitor and I don't know if his replacement knows about me."

"Vitel is no more?" Hewlitt said, his eyes going wide. "Are you certain?"

"Through two sources," Madame Aubrey replied. "He was accused of attacking the Crown Prince."

"Really? And he didn't succeed?" Hewlitt asked.

Madame Aubrey shook her head firmly.

"Two sources, you say?"

"A ship pulled in from the capital port yesterday morning," Madame Aubrey said.

"What ship?"

"The *Marten*," Madame Aubrey replied. "It left before your men took the town."

"Your contact?"

"The first mate," Madame Aubrey said. Her lifts twitched. "He's a regular here, gets a discount for his efforts."

"Well, we shall have to see if we can continue the arrangement," Hewlitt said. He glanced sharply at Madame Aubrey. "His name?"

"Seaforth," she said. She saw his eyes narrow and added, "Gordon Seaforth."

"Who is the new spymaster," Hewlitt asked, "do you know?"

"The last news is three days old," Madame Aubrey replied, shaking her head. "I imagine there *must* be one by now but I don't know who."

Hewlitt frowned. "I need to know what happened to Vitel." He gave Madame Aubrey a thoughtful look. "I can't believe he tried to kill the Crown Prince."

"And failed," Rafkin added.

"Yes, that too," Hewlitt agreed. He glanced toward Madame Aubrey. "Vitel was known to be skilled in such things." He sat back in his seat for a moment, then pounded the desk with a fist and sprang up resolutely. "Rafkin will take down everything you say." Madame Aubrey's eyes widened fractionally but narrowed again as Hewlitt added, "My man will wait outside if your tongue fails you."

To Rafkin he said, "I'm going back to see to the king. Find me when you're done." He turned his attention back to Madame Aubrey. "We'll be seeing each other again, soon."

Madame Aubrey swallowed and nodded nervously.

#

The door to Mannevy's office burst open and banged so hard against the wall that it started back only to be pushed firmly aside as Peter Hewlitt stormed into the room. "We have a problem."

"Two, I'm certain," Mannevy replied looking at the spymaster sourly. "The first would be manners, certainly."

Hewlitt frowned at him, turned to the open door and, moving quickly, shut it firmly. "King Wendel knows."

"What? How?"

"A message was sent this morning," Hewlitt said. "By pigeon."

"Pigeon? But Vistos' man — woman — oh!" Mannevy pulled his silk handkerchief from its pocket and blotted beads of sweat off his forehead. "Yes, that could be a problem, indeed." He lifted the silver bell on his desk and shook it, hard, twice. "I'll get us some tea." He gestured Hewlitt toward a chair. "Sit, sit!"

Mannevy himself stood and moved toward a locked cabinet behind him. Hewlitt recognized it as the same one Mannevy had installed at the castle in Kingsford and was surprised to realize that it had been brought all the way here. He himself tended to work with less clutter, often using Rafkin alone as his 'storage' system. The clerk had a surprisingly good memory and was very diligent.

Mannevy returned with a large roll held by two ribbon ties. He unfastened both and unrolled the bundle out on his table. It was a map of Soria. He beckoned Hewlitt to approach.

"So, what is the timing on our advance?" Mannevy said, pointing to their location in South Sea Pass and moving his fingers to point toward Sarskal, Soria's capital. "And how quickly can they muster their reserves?"

"Georgos is nearly a day's march on the route," Hewlitt said, pointing toward the coastline road. "He's not due to cut inland until they reach Sarskalport —" he moved his finger up along the coast to a point midway in the kingdom of Soria and then to the right — eastwards — along the Sar river to the large knoll that contained the capital.

Sarskal's low hill protected the city from assault. Siege and starvation were possibilities both men knew but had never succeeded in all the years scribes recorded.

"They'll have about two weeks, then," Mannevy muttered to himself. A knock on the door was answered by him with, "Enter!" and a servant brought a tray with piping hot tea and some light rolls. "Put it there and leave us," Mannevy ordered, pointing to a side table. The serving girl did as told and left without a word. Mannevy moved to grab a cup of tea, raising his eyebrows toward Hewlitt in inquiry. When Hewlitt waved him off, Mannevy shrugged and took the tea cup back to his large desk. "So how many troops can they muster in two weeks?"

"In winter?" Hewlitt said, shaking his head. "The household guard, the local troops… not much more."

"So there's no problem," Mannevy said happily.

"There's the sea," Hewlitt said, spreading his hand toward the long curving coastline. "They have ships."

"Are you saying — what are you saying?"

"I don't know this Wendel well," Hewlitt admitted. "But if his seamen are smart enough — and some are I'm certain — they'll harry Gergen's supplies. If they can take his train or burn it…" his voice trailed off and he shrugged.

"Yes, that would be a problem wouldn't it," Mannevy agreed. "And, of course, attacking in winter has its own problems."

"No forage for the horses," Hewlitt guessed immediately. "And the strain on the soldiers slogging away — particularly if there are storms and such like."

"Well, perhaps Margen or Vistos will be able to convince our great goddess —"

"There is more than one god who may have an opinion on this affair," Hewlitt interjected.

"And what of the other route?" Mannevy asked, moving his hand along the map to the south of Korin's Pass. "How fares your talented young friend?"

"I have not yet heard," Hewlitt admitted. "And she must be circumspect in contacting me."

"Because you do not wish to alert mage Vistos to his error," Mannevy murmured, leaning back in his chair and bringing his cup to his lips. He nodded to himself and put the cup down. "And if she proves as capable as you suspect, what then?"

"Then our troops — the second cavalry squadron — will be moving north before Vistos knows anything."

"Our airships are almost complete," Mannevy said. "With them and the trains to provide supplies…"

"We'll see," Hewlitt said. "It all depends on one rather young, newly trained mage."

"Often that is the way of things," Mannevy said. "After all, we've been working with an untrained *King* for quite a while, haven't we?"

Hewlitt's lips twitched. "He is our king."

Mannevy's eyes gleamed. "Ours indeed." He allowed himself a smirk. "And soon to rule two kingdoms."

"Long may he reign," Hewlitt replied in a soft voice. He rose from his seat and moved to the side table. "I believe I'll have that tea after all."

Chapter Two

"Your majesty," Abner Crippens said, dropping to one knee and bowing deeply to the small zwerg queen. In his hands he held a roll of parchment, neatly tied in two places. "The drawings are done."

"Excellent," Queen Diam of the Silver Mountain said, taking the proffered roll and passing it to her armsman, Granno. "Have these delivered to Genni, she'll want to see them."

"As you wish," Granno said with a quick nod, taking the roll and placing it on the table beside him.

Diam frowned at him and turned back to the young human, gesturing for him to rise. "And how are the men faring, lieutenant?"

"I'm just a lowly midshipman, your majesty," Abner said demurely, rising to his feet but keeping his eyes downcast.

"To the humans, perhaps," Diam said. "But you have sworn fealty to me, have you not?"

"I have," Abner replied with fervor.

"Then I shall appoint you lieutenant," Diam said, dismissing the matter. "But you have not answered my question, lieutenant."

At the repeated rank, Abner Crippens drew himself up as straight as his injured knee allowed.

"They're in reasonable spirits, your majesty," Crippens admitted. "They're worried about their fate and their kin."

"And the mages? Have they any luck?"

"They have, your majesty," Crippens replied in a happier tone. "They can fill and raise the balloons as needed." With a nod, he added, "And we've got enough to lift the ship when it's repaired."

Diam waved a hand toward the plans. "Oh, it won't be repaired, lieutenant."

"Your majesty?" Crippens asked in confusion.

"Granno, take our lieutenant with you when you give the plans to Genni," Diam said. "Might as well tell the tale to all at once."

"I —" Granno's expression turned dark. "Is this wise, your majesty?"

"It is," Diam assured him. "We need to ensure our safety and I can think of no better way." Granno continued to hold his truculent look. "With this ship, we'll be able to go where we wish, trade when we wish." She turned to him and smiled. "And we'll have *much* to trade."

"I suppose there's that, your majesty," Granno allowed with a glimmer in his eyes. "In fact, I rather suspect that with our people we'll be able to trade at an advantage."

"Indeed we will," Diam agreed. "Now take the lad to Genni!"

#

"How, by the gods, how?" Skara Ningan demanded as dusk settled two days later on her and Thomas Walpish as they huddled behind a chimney way up high overlooking the mansion King Markel had appropriated. She was referring to the figure moving purposefully away from them.

"I think you have," Walpish said. She glanced toward him and he explained, "By the gods."

"But — but the gods —!" she spluttered.

"Not all are working in accord," Walpish told her. "And, apparently, some are more willing to engage than others."

"We killed him!" Skara said, pointing to the mage moving away from them far on the ground. "I know it."

"I do, too," Walpish agreed. "Apparently we were not as complete as we'd thought."

"His heart had stopped," Skara said. "His blood had ceased flowing."

"Yes," Thomas agreed. "So whatever help he had was proof against such things."

"He likes death," Skara began slowly, "perhaps —"

"You heard our friend," Walpish said with a slight emphasis on the word 'friend.' "He told you that he takes no direct part in such affairs, does nothing to hasten things." He moved a hand toward her as she started to reply. "Again, young assassin, I caution you on the matter of names."

Skara glared at him for a moment, then nodded. Finally, she asked, "If the mage has such help, why can't we ask for some ourselves?"

"First, I think we should rely on our own skills," Walpish replied.

"Didn't we just *do* that?" Skara said. "And weren't we thwarted?"

"You have more than one skill, surely," Walpish replied. "For myself, as a cavalryman, I am the eyes and ears of the army."

"So you want us to be the eyes and ears of the — of our friends?" Skara guessed. She pursed her lips for a moment. "I suppose we can do that."

"We need to know more of his allies," Walpish said.

"And his enemies," Skara added. She frowned. "Why didn't the Sorians have their own mages? Working against ours?"

"Like a spy," Walpish replied, "or an assassin —" he smirked at Skara Ningan's reaction "— such people need to be worthy of trust."

"Or suitably threatened," Skara added. She bared her teeth at Thomas as she added, "'Cowed' as you would say."

"Better a willing accomplice," Thomas said. "In such positions of power, threats are dangerous."

"Yes," Skara agreed. "So, which do you want: friends or enemies?"

"I think I'd best take enemies," Walpish admitted.

"Meet back here in three days," Skara said, diving from her hiding place and disappearing into the night.

"I was going to suggest that we eat first," Walpish muttered to himself in the darkness.

#

"Tilly, my dear, where were you?" Crown Prince Sarsal of Soria asked as his spymaster — and lover — crept back into their court apartments. "I haven't seen you in *hours*."

Matilda Gregory — "Tilly" to some — forced a pleasant smile on her face. "Oh, dearest, I had something important to do and I didn't want to trouble you."

"What, my dear?"

"Well, as you know, we've had some trouble with Vitel's old people and I wanted to make a clean sweep of things," Tilly began as she moved into the room and started to artfully dispose of her outer clothing. She saw his pleasure and continued disrobing as she added, "I was just finishing up the last of that."

"Oh, and how?" Sarsal had flipped the sheets of the bed back invitingly and now patted the place beside him.

"Well, I had forgotten that some of our messages are sent by pigeons and other birds," Tilly said with a frown, before pulling her shift over her head and tossing it aside.

"Birds?"

"They take messages for us," Tilly said. She saw his puzzled look. "We write really small, roll up the parchment and tie it to their legs."

"But how do they know where to go?" Sarsal asked, brows furrowed in confusion.

"They're trained to home to a particular place," Tilly replied. She waved a hand dismissively as she slid into the bed beside him, sliding off the last of her garments. "I don't know how, really, it's all rather tedious."

"And?"

"Darling," Tilly said, leaning over so that her mouth was just inches from his, "is this really what you want to be doing right now?"

Crown Prince Sarsal looked at her lovely lips and shook his head mutely.

#

"Your Majesty, we have not got a message from Kingsland for the past three weeks," Dieter Morgen said as he bowed low before his emperor, ruler of all Vinik. They were in the emperor's receiving room just off the main throne room. The receiving room was only slightly less lavish in style than the throne room. Large rugs adorned the floor, covering a parquet flooring of various hardwoods chosen from among the many found in the mountains of the empire. The walls on either side leading to the throne were covered with tapestries depicting past victories and behind the throne was a huge mural painting of the Emperor himself, mounted majestically on his destrier and holding a pike with the bloody head of his father triumphantly in front of him.

Emperor Maximilian Kurst frowned. "How many men do you have employed there?"

"Three, your imperial majesty," Dieter replied. Morgen was a wiry, tight man who was just beginning to show his age. But his mind was one of the sharpest in the empire and his network vast. "In the past one or two might have had reasons to keep quiet but I've never had this long a silence from all three."

Maximilian Kurst was approaching middle age but still maintained his vigor and strength through constant practice and skirmishes on his borders, particularly these days with Felland to the north but occasionally with the emperor of South Vinik — Jurgen Kurst, his cousin.

He had learned, time and again, the value of a good spy network. "Should we try to recruit someone or send in a new man?"

"That is an excellent notion, your imperial majesty," Dieter agreed, rising from his deep bow to kneel in front of his ruler. "But I am more concerned over the possible reasons for such a silence."

"Markel is a fool but not even he is foolish enough to attack us!'

"Directly, no, your majesty," Dieter agreed. The Emperor motioned for him to explain. "What concerns me is that Markel's men seemed to have created a thrust toward Soria."

"If he takes Soria…" the emperor responded, bringing up one large fist to pick at his teeth as he thought. He finished ruminating and lowered his eyes to his spymaster. "How can we turn this to our advantage?"

"If Markel takes Soria, your highness, we might find ourselves… vulnerable," Dieter warned.

"What?" Emperor Kurst roared, leaping out of his chair. "And how could such a worm as Markel ever consider to threaten us with his mere kingdom?"

"Your highness," Dieter said soothingly but with firm honesty, "if Markel controls two kingdoms, he will control their armies as well."

"So? We have our side of the Pinch guarded with hard walls," Emperor Kurst roared back. The Pinch was the only open ground between the two countries. It had been the traditional route of wars between Soria and Vinik for all time. The current, Sorian King, Wendel, had learned his warcraft there. "Let us see him try to breach those!"

"Indeed, your highness," Dieter agreed. "However… I am concerned."

"Hmm." The Emperor had learned long ago the value of listening to his spymaster. "What do you suggest?"

"Perhaps we should consider moving some of our men to reinforce the border," Dieter suggested. When he saw the emperor's eyes bulging with fury, he added, "That would put us in a position to take advantage of any problems the Sorians might face."

"Hmm," Emperor Kurst responded after a moment. "I'll talk to my generals." He rose from his throne and stomped down the long hall. As he passed by his kneeling spymaster, he patted him on the shoulder and murmured, "Good job."

#

"Again!" Jaro ordered as he loomed over Alain Casman, hand outstretched to help the taller human up to his feet.

Alain, hip sore and throbbing where he'd hit it against the hard cold ground below, groaned but reached for the hand, taking it and rising to his feet. His hands were gloved in zwerg steel and he grinned as the zwerg trainer stepped back, raising his short sword with a shout before thrusting at Alain once more.

"Ha!" Alain shouted, moving back and to the side away from the thrust. He lunged in immediately, moving his hands to grab at the sword and pull it sharply from the zwerg's grip.

"Good!" Jaro smiled at him. He slid his arms and twisted his blade, freeing it from the lad's steel grip. "But not good enough!"

Alain smiled in return and raised one gloved fist challengingly. "Bring it."

With a roar the zwerg charged at him, sword in one arm, swinging down wildly. Alain stepped to the side again, using his mailed hand to swat the blade aside. He swiveled as the zwerg stormed past and planted a hard boot in the zwerg's butt. With a cry of surprise, Jaro went down, sprawling, to the cold ground below.

Alain loomed over him and knelt quickly, putting his knee in the small of the zwerg's back and pinning the zwerg's sword arm with a mailed fist.

"I believe that gives me the win," Alain said, breathing hard over the zwerg fighter.

"Yes, I think so," Jaro admitted breathlessly.

Alain savored his victory.

"Uh, lad," Jaro said nervously as the moment stretched out. "Are you ready to learn more?"

Alain smiled down at the back of the zwerg's head. He raised his knee and slid off the zwerg's back. Jaro turned over slowly. His brows rose in surprise as Alain Casman extended a hand down to him, smiling broadly at their reversed roles. With a groan, Jaro accepted the hand and was raised back to his feet.

Chapter Three

"Do you think the King is trying to send a message?" Josiah Prentice, Kingsland's Exchequer, asked first minister Mannevy as they stood shoulder to shoulder and tried not to shiver in the cold winter air.

"Possibly," Mannevy agreed. "What do you think he's trying to say?"

"Well, he's burning his late wife's body on the pile of Sorian soldiers he had murdered after her assassination," Prentice observed. "So one message would be that she is worth a thousand of them."

"And another?" Mannevy inquired mildly, his lips twitching at the corners.

"That his mages have the fury of fire at their call," Prentice said, choosing his words carefully. He had heard rumors, of course, of the queen's infidelity. He had heard other rumors — mostly discounted — of darker schemes in the kingdom.

Mannevy glanced toward the four gathered mages — two full mages and two apprentices — and nodded solemnly at them. Only mage Margen seemed to take note of the action, jerking his head minutely before returning to the task before them.

The King, mounted on his stallion — the same fractious beast that had *not* been used for his triumphant procession into South Sea Pass — moved forward to stand on the mound of bodies that surrounded his wife's body.

"Today we are gathered to mourn a great loss," King Markel called out. His voice, on mage Vistos' orders, was magically enhanced and filled the air clearly around every soldier and villager gathered in the large circle surrounding the late queen and the dead Sorians. "And, also, to accept into our kingdom the grateful people of South Sea Pass. The first of many towns to defect from King Wendel and join Kingsland in a great war of union."

Mannevy's eyes flicked down to the townsfolk who shifted nervously on the ground below. Clearly they were not happy with the king's choice of words.

"Already my general has marched northwards and soon the upstart Wendel will bend his knee and yield his lands to our greater glory," King Markel continued. As eulogies went, Mannevy thought to himself, it seemed a bit lacking.

"But today," Markel continued, perhaps realizing that his speech was straying from its subject, "we mark the end of Queen Arivik's reign and send her body back to the gods."

Mannevy turned at a snort from chancellor Prentice. He gave the exchequer a frown and returned his attention to the King who was deftly backing his mount away from the circle of bodies.

"Watch and see how Kingsland honors its royalty," Markel shouted. In a lower voice, he added, "And how we punish traitors."

He turned to his mages and nodded firmly.

Vistos and Margen raced each other to complete their spells. A brilliant flash and a roar of heat erupted from the ring of bodies, rising high in the sky and carrying — thankfully — with it the smell of burnt hair and flesh.

In a matter of moments all that was left was a fine pile of ash layering over the burial ground.

King Markel bowed in his saddle, tears rolling down his face. "May the gods grant you grace, my queen."

#

Walpish was wearing the garb of a Sorian burger — neither too rich nor too poor — burrowed for the occasion of watching the King burn his wife's body. He kept his hood pulled low over his head. His beard was coming in and its color disguised with soot to change the color. He didn't know if the mages had special spells to track him. He wasn't sure that, even if they had, Vistos would bother. What threat is a man with a knife to someone who can't be killed?

When the King had retired, followed by his loyal retinue, the assembly of Sorian townsfolk slowly dissolved through the arches of the gates back into the town and, probably, the warmth of their fires. Walpish ensured that he was in the middle of the largest crowd and in the middle of that crowd when it passed its way back into the town. The guards at the gate stopped no one.

Inside, Thomas Walpish pulled the collar of his coat up higher against his neck and slouched, moving slowly toward one of the smaller temples in the town. He was not alone.

He bowed when he entered the darkened hall and moved slowly, grouping himself with a large party that was moving to pay their respects to their gods. He noticed ruefully that while many people seemed to pass by the statue of Ametza — and her offering pile was vast — not many of the ex-Sorians seemed to be inclined to worship her overtly. Thomas nodded warily at her icy form and moved off with the others as soon as he could. He was on a mission.

For every god there was a shaman, a mage, a witch, and even a sorcerer. Walpish knew only a little of mages, and less of witches. He had dealt with the shaman in Kingsford as little as possible but he understood her dedication to communing with her god.

Here, in the temple of the gods, Thomas was looking — looking for a god who might provide Vistos with his mage… and, perhaps, his sorcery.

The god would have to be powerful. It seemed to Thomas that the god was one of the old gods — neither a god of earth, air, fire, or water. Thomas doubted the god that supported Vistos was Ophidian, the trickster god. Ophidian was the oldest god of fire, it was true, but Thomas believed that Ophidian felt more compassion for humans. Dimly, Thomas recalled hearing once that Ophidian had fought a battle against the older gods — a battle in support of humans.

The god that Vistos worshipped, Thomas thought, was no friend of humans. What sort of god would that be?

It was not Terric, the god of death, nor Avice, the goddess of life. And it certainly was not Aron, the god of Judgement. Thomas felt certain of this — else why would they have charged him and Skara with destroying Vistos?

Thomas walked slowly around the temple, looking at each statue, examining the manner and meaning of each god. He walked around twice, once rightward and once widdershins.

Quenkorian. God of conformity, of beliefs, of tradition. A god that would think it good and right that all humans act exactly the same, that they all look toward him as their god and they all accept the rule of one.

Vistos was working with Markel in part to make him the one ruler of all the lands — Soria was just the first. Thomas recalled how Vistos' two apprentices had moved in lockstep, like animated statues, the pleasure on their face mirroring — identical to — Vistos'.

Vistos wanted to bend everyone to his will. He wanted to put a tooth — Thomas gasped at the thought! He wanted to put a magic tooth in every mouth under his control.

Quenkorian. Thomas looked at the stone statue with barely concealed loathing. The god of right was his enemy. Thomas moved quickly to distance himself from the statue's gaze lest the real god felt his thoughts… and decided to take action.

Outside the temple, Thomas darted his eyes to the left and the right, ensuring that no one was watching him. Then he strolled off, in search of the nearest safe tavern.

I need a drink!

#

"The men want to know: could we watch?" Diktor Vincet, hat in hand, asked Margaret Waters early the next morning. Margaret raised an eyebrow. "I mean, it wouldn't be disrespectful to the gods, would it?"

Margaret's mouth twitched. She shook her head.

"Oh," Diktor said, mistaking her. "It's just that — well, it was quite a sight yesterday."

"I didn't say no," Margaret said. "I shook my head to say that the gods would not mind." She nodded toward the white plains before them. "In fact, I think they'd appreciate it."

They were in the warming tent which had been erected at the end of the line of newly laid tracks as incentive for the work crews who were hammering the rails to the wooden timbers they were laid on, securing them. Margaret had flown there on a wind of her own making after she'd laid the steel rails over the thick rail timbers she'd placed on the frozen ground. The railmen had labored through the rest of the day to secure the steel rails to the timbers, reaching Margaret well after dark, trailed by the steam engine backing slowly up the newly-laid line in preparation for the next day's work.

Today's work.

"Have them gather round at the end of the track," Margaret said. "This won't take long, we're only laying out a league today."

"And a league tomorrow, and two the last day," Diktor said. "It's as well the greatest length was done on the first day, it makes it easier to convince the men that they can do the job."

Margaret said nothing, as the man's words were only too obvious. Diktor Vincet was not a smart man but he was strong and able to bully the rest of the railcrew — that was all Margaret needed.

She rose and pushed back the flap to the warming tent. Diktor followed, pulling the flap back down as he exited.

"She's agreed!" Diktor bellowed to the worried men outside. A quick cheer went up from them.

Margaret nodded and walked to the end of the track. "You may watch," she said, turning back to the men, "but you must bow to the gods and remain silent while we work."

The railcrew promptly went to their knees, disregarding the cold ground and thick snow.

Satisfied, Margaret turned back to the task at hand, thought, and turned back again. "Leave a clear path between the train cars and me."

A group of men hastily moved away from the tracks, leaving the railcrew arrayed in a crescent circle facing toward the blank snow of the plains to the east.

Margaret turned back once more and peered down the long expanse of white snowy plain. There was a river there, too, somewhere but it had iced over, Kitzis had scouted the path for her. Of course, the air demon was not so smart as to know whether a river was frozen; Margaret had asked it to look for any warmth — that Kitzis could do.

"What's she doing?" a curious voice asked behind her.

"She's readying herself," Diktor Vincet said knowingly, adding, "Shush!"

Margaret's lips twitched at the notion of dumb Diktor pretending to be knowledgeable. But it was just like a bully to behave so.

She closed her eyes and cleared her mind, calling to Kitzis to settle into her power. She could feel the ache in her muscles from the efforts of the day before, could feel the pain in her head from the magic-burn. She'd never tried to lay so much track in such a short period of time.

Silently, deciding to keep all aspects of her magic hidden from the men behind her, she called on the gods of the air: Hissia and Hanor. She imagined them, imagined them standing behind her, looking down over her and out to the snowy plain beyond.

And then she felt them. Hissia and Hanor were proud of her! She gasped at the notion.

Thank you, she thought to them. *I am honored.*

You are not the only one with these gifts, Hissia warned her. *But you are learning quickly.* Margaret wondered — with a flash of jealousy — who else the gods had so blessed. Then she stepped on her resentment for the unknown mage, determined to prove her worth.

Please, she thought to them, *it is but a short distance this time, though over a frozen river.*

Oh, think of Ametza! Hanor's amused thought came to her.

She will be livid, Hissia agreed. *She thinks to lord the power of water over our air.*

We will be delighted to show her the error of her ways, Hanor agreed.

And Margaret felt it when the two gods of air filled her with their power. Her head seemed to expand and her breathing became labored — as though her lungs were too small to gather the air needed for the magic.

Concentrating on creating a wide swath of cleared ground, Margaret raised both arms, conjured the winds and sent them roaring in twin cyclones, parallel to the ground, whirling and driving the snowfall up high into the sky — and away from the ground in front of her.

Nicely done! Hanor thought to her.

Quiet, dear, now comes the hard part, Hissia cautioned.

With a groan, Margaret flexed her knees and stood up. She turned, opening her eyes as she did to stare at the long line of cut rail ties on the supply car behind her.

Slowly, carefully, she raised each stacked layer — one layer for each length of rail — a total of nineteen ties for every twenty feet of length. She raised the layers above each other until she'd built a lattice of rail ties rising high into the cold morning sky — over ten thousand of them darkened the sky above. Margaret pivoted, her outstretched arms bearing the magic of the air that held the railway ties overhead and turning them with her until they were aligned above the line over bare ground stretching out for more than a league in front of her. She lowered the lattice until the first tie was positioned precisely nineteen inches from the end of the current rail line. And then, with a triumphant shout, she flicked the winds forward and bent the lattice over until the lattice was angled over the ground far off in the distance. Using instincts — and perhaps the understanding of the gods — she flung the ten thousand railway ties forward in a windy arc, releasing her magic and revelling in the long, loud, staccato sound of twelve foot wide rectangular slabs of treated wood thudding onto the ground, one after another in rapid succession. The sound grew until it was a continuous rumble as the ground below was hit with the falling ties — each falling from a slightly greater height — creating a crescendo that echoed throughout the valley.

As the echoes faded and Margaret could *feel* that all the ties had fallen straight, she turned back to the railcars behind her, to the stacks of rail lines and began assembling them in two high, parallel lines of metal rising into the air. Finally, two thin lines of steel floated above her, reaching high into the morning sky. Again, Margaret turned and moved the steel above her to align it with the newly laid timbers. She inclined the steel rails and then let them fall, more gently than the timber of the rail ties so that they kissed the rail ties on the ground in front of them — two straight lines angling down to touch the ground. The steel rails clinked softly as they landed on their ties, the sound fading in the distance as the further ties reached the ground. When all the rail lines were laid, their sound died out.

Thank you! Margaret said, falling to her knees and bowing deeply to the two unseen gods of air.

You're getting better, Hanor thought to her with pride.

And you have created such beauty in the air as I have never seen before, Hissia added in a tone that sounded just short of praise. To Margaret, the god's tone sounded somewhat dangerous, biting like a fierce gale.

I could only do it by your grace, Margaret thought humbly.

Indeed, Hanor agreed.

If it does not disturb you, great gods, I must let this body rest now, Margaret said, forcing herself heaving chest to slow and concentrating on the cold air entering her lungs.

The presence of the gods — and their magic — vanished as if it had never been. With a muffled cry, Margaret fell full length to the ground.

"Help her!" Diktor Vincet's voice rang out. "Carry her — carefully! — to the warming tent."

Strong hands grabbed her, lifted her and Margaret felt the world twist around her as her stomach threatened to get violently ill.

"Carefully, there!" Diktor's voice rang out in command. "She's not a piece of timber, you dolts!"

The hands that carried her did not change their stride but Margaret could feel herself being borne more gently. Moments later, she was laid gently on a soft cot.

"Rest lass," Diktor's voice rumbled near her ear even as rough hands pulled a thick blanket over her legs and chest.

"The lines," Margaret muttered.

"You've set the challenge," a different voice said. "The crew won't let you down."

"Out!" Diktor ordered. "She needs her rest!"

There was a blast of cold air as the tent flap was raised and lowered. And then Margaret felt a small bundle of warmth settle in at her back. *Kitzis*.

Margaret gave a small smile, scooted her backside closer to the warm air demon, closed her eyes and fell into a deep, relaxed sleep.

Chapter Four

Granno would not admit to liking young Abner Crippens, at least never to the lad himself. That would mean saying something nice about a sky-toucher and Granno felt that he'd exceeded his quota on *that* long ago. But the lad was wide-eyed and watching everything as they rolled down the long corridor, switched to a side corridor and continued on in their crank-powered cart. Admittedly, the spacing of the seats and crank were awkward for the sky-toucher but Crippens had adjusted to the difficulty by placing a large package on top of his seat, raising him dangerously toward the ceiling.

"You want to watch lest something takes your head off," Granno had grumbled when they'd first started out.

"Do the ceilings get lower?" Abner had asked, eyeing the beautifully carved ceiling above them which ran straight and true.

"No," Granno admitted, "but there are carvings, you know."

"Carvings?" Crippens sounded surprised.

"What, do you think because we don't live by the light of your burning sun we can't appreciate beauty?" Granno grunted.

"No, no — not at all," Crippens replied hastily. "I — I — well, to be honest, I didn't even know about the zwerg until you captured us."

"And that's how we like it," Granno admitted. He turned the cart onto another side corridor and slowed, indicating that Crippens should do likewise in his pedalling. "Look here, both up and to the side as we pass by."

Abner Crippens turned in his seat and craned his neck up and to the sides. And he gasped. "That's amazing! Can we stop? I'd love to see this properly!"

'This' was a vast array of gold carvings, of colored stones, and intricate work that glowed in the lights raining down from the top of the tunnel.

"This?" Granno snorted. "This is nothing!" He turned to look behind him. "Besides, we can't stop, there's another cart behind us."

"I imagine it's best viewed on foot," Abner guessed, craning his neck and turning around to get a last glimpse of the amazing carvings.

"And shorter, too," Granno remarked. Abner glanced at him. "Well, we don't make our art for sky-touchers, you know!"

"I can well imagine," Abner said with what sounded like a wistful sigh.

"Well, cheer up," Granno said. "We're almost here and then you'll get to see the other set on the return."

"Other set?"

"We travel only the one way on our tracks," Granno explained. "We'll be using a different corridor for the return trip."

"Oh!"

"Lift your leg off the pedals now, lad," Granno barked. "I'm slowing us down." He indicated a side rail. "We'll be stopping there."

"And is it far from our stop to this engineer?" Abner asked.

"Not far at all," Granno replied with a grin. He pointed to the large doors just to their right. "That's Genni's den right there."

#

Lisette was in the stables when Alva found her, brushing her mare fastidiously. The stables were placed a distance from the nearest entrance to the underground zwerg kingdom and well hidden in a cave behind a large tree. Alva watched for a long moment in silence, considering the young girl.

The wind shifted and the mare caught her scent, moving away from Lisette who tsked at her.

"Why? Don't you like —?" Lisette broke off when she saw the zwerg queen. Not quite sure what to do with both brush and curry comb in her hands, Lisette nevertheless gave the queen a deep curtsy, her face flushing at her gawkiness. "Your majesty."

Alva nodded to her and moved further in, entering the stall with the young girl and her mare. She raised a hand to pat the mare's hind leg, as high as she could reach. "She's quite something."

"We traded for her at the mountains between Kingsland and Palu," Lisette said. She smiled at the bay mare. "She's got great action, you should see her when she's in form!"

"I hope to someday soon," Alva said, working to keep her tone light and pleasant.

"Is there something I can do for you, your majesty?" Lisette asked nervously. "Bethkin is the last one for a brushing today —" she waved her hand to indicate the long line of stalls "— I've already done yours and the others."

She did not add that only Alain's gelding was anything like a challenge — the zwerg preferred sturdy hill ponies to full horses, understandably.

"I wanted to talk with you," Alva admitted. "Is there a place we can go?"

"Anywhere you wish, your majesty," Lisette said, bowing her head and gesturing toward the stable door. She gave the queen a curious look. "Is your guard nearby?"

"For the moment, young Lisette, you can be my guard," Alva said, smiling up at the taller human. Lisette straightened to her full height in recognition of the honor and moved in front of the queen, pointedly checking the exits both ways before gesturing for the queen to follow her. Alva laughed. "Young Lisette, we're in the midst of my kingdom! I don't think you have to be *so* cautious."

"Of course, your majesty," Lisette said, her cheeks coloring once more. "It's just that… well —"

"I appreciate your concern, young human," Alva said, realizing that the child was at a loss for words. Alva gestured to the left, away from the entrance to her kingdom. "There's a marvelous spot here where you can look down over all of Jasra, if you're willing to climb a bit."

"Oh, of course your majesty!"

"Say that again when we get there!" Alva told her with a chuckle, setting a brisk pace with her sturdy short legs.

#

It took them nearly forty minutes to get where the queen intended and when they arrived, Lisette let out a gasp of amazement. Below them stretched the vast plains of Jasram. Lisette almost fancied that she could even see the sea in the far distance but that didn't matter: what she could see was *home*.

"I come up here when I want to think," Queen Alva admitted shyly. They had climbed up and around the front of a pinnacle that thrust itself proudly away from the rest of the mountain range — a single finger of rock that stood like a sentinel over away from the rest of the mountains — and still several hundred feet below the highest peaks. "Do you like what you see?"

"I've never seen it this way, from this height," Lisette said, tearing herself away from the beauty laid out in front of her to answer the queen's question.

"Do you know where you are?"

As if in answer, Lisette raised a hand to shade her eyes and peered intently to the left, following the line of the valley far below. Finally, she pointed and asked, "Is that Jasra down there? The town?"

"It is indeed," Alva agreed. "Now, can you find Tinnar?" She cautioned, "It will be harder."

Lisette turned to the right and looked down. After a moment she raised her sights and gave a yelp of pleasure as she pointed to the hill town.

"Yes, that's it," Alva said. "And, out of sight behind us and through the mountains there are Dakrah, Valdosh, and Iishlin," Queen Alva said, turning her back on the valley to point toward the distant sea to the west then midway behind the mountains and finally nearly in parallel with Jasra town. "We are surrounded in our hills, you see."

Lisette didn't know how to respond to that, so she kept a glum silence.

"Do you know the names of all the duchies and the towns, little one?" Alva asked.

Lisette shook her head. "I know the names of the Grand Duchies and the towns."

"And what are they?"

Lisette pointed toward Jasra town. "High Jasra is the capital of the Grand Duchy of Jasram Plains, my father's —" her voice faltered "— old domain." She turned to look at the queen. "Are you sure?"

Alva nodded slowly. "We were friends with many of your father's people, particularly the centaurs."

"I always liked them," Lisette admitted with a sniff.

"And the other towns?" Alva prompted after a moment, hoping to distract the child from her sorrow.

Lisette turned back and pointed. "Riverside Kanash, seaside Yenvah, and mid-plains Torkar." She gave the queen a tentative smile as she added, "That's where I met the centaurs."

Alva's face turned grim. "I'm afraid there are no centaurs in Torkar today."

"What?" Lisette cried in alarm. "But there were thousands! They traded in spice, they herded the hexin, they tilled the oases and plowed the fertile plains!"

"And they are dead," Alva replied implacably. "They were killed by Paulus when they revolted in favor of your father." Before the girl could react, Alva pointed to the east, toward where the high peaks of Cuiyeval mountains joined with the Shredded Hills. "And there?"

Lisette forced herself to follow the queen's hand and answered woodenly, "That's the Grand Duchy of High Jasram. Together Jasram Plains and High Jasram make the middle of the three princedoms."

"And the towns there?"

"At the highest is Hinoma. Yurnam is to the east, nearer us and at the headwaters of the great river Jamar. At the south and the west is the last town, Grand Tor on a great mount splitting the Highwater river into the Kanash river and the Jordu river."

"South and east of Grand Tor is the Grand Duchy of Locktor with its two towns of Tinrok and Jordu which sits on the river of the same name," Lisette continued. "South of Locktor is Inslam with its coastal city of Aluvastah." She turned to her right and pointed into the distance. "Beyond Jasram Plains lies Cunan with four towns: Cunnar the inland capital, Ivash at the river Cunan's fork, Trenan at where the Trenish fork flows to the see, and

Dimlash where the river from the Cunan's left fork flows into the sea. Cunan is known for its fruits, vegetables, tea, and coffee, particularly its bananas.

"West of it lies Kennir with the towns of rough hilled Eijor and coastal Kinrah. Kennir is rich in coffee, tea, and strange animals who look like humans but aren't."

Alva coughed sternly at that and Lisette blushed. "I mean the ones who climb in the trees, your majesty. The ones who have no sense or reason."

"And what are they called?"

"The names for them vary, your majesty," Lisette said, now sounding like someone reciting rote learning. "As do their size. The small ones we call Treeskees for they rarely come down from the treetops. Then there are larger ones who amble on the ground as easily as in the branches and we call them Morags. Finally, the larger ones — well, the names vary but mostly they seem so sad and lost that it's wondered if they aren't humans the gods threw down from reason and so we call them the Castlings."

"And the last Grand Duchy?" Alva prompted.

"That is here, your majesty, the Grand Duchy of Dakram," Lisette answered. "It has four towns: seaside Dakrah, mid-river Valdosh, riverhead Iishlin and, of course, Tinnar, the capital."

"And the princes?" Alva prompted.

"There are three princes, your majesty," Lisette said. "There is the prince of the mountains, over Inslam, Locktor and High Jasram, also known as the Prince of the East.

"And then there is the Prince of the Plains who rules over Jasram Plains but has influence in both High Jasram and Inslam," Lisette said, clenching her jaw as she added, "But, as you tell me, Prince of the Plains has taken direct control of the Grand Duchy of Jasram Plains."

Queen Alva agreed with an unhappy nod. "And the last?"

"The Prince of the West, known also as the Prince of the Hills. He rules over Cunan, Kennir, and Dakram," Lisette said, completing her recitation. She added, "He is almost always the High Prince and ruler of the whole of Jasram."

"But his position is being contested," Alva said now, turning her head in the direction of Tinnar.

"By Paulus?" Lisette guessed.

"Indeed."

Lisette was silent for a long moment. Finally, she said, "You didn't bring me here for the sights." She turned to the queen. "What is it you want of me, your majesty?"

#

"Miss Waters," Diktor's voice came to her softly. Margaret tried to ignore it. "Miss Waters, please!"

"What is it?" Margaret asked in a raspy voice.

"It's just that, well, the men were wondering…"

"What?" Margaret snapped.

"There's the bend, miss," Diktor said. "The lines are straight but we've got to have a bend, you know."

"My father will fix it," Margaret said. "He'll be here soon, wake me when he comes."

"Your father?" Diktor repeated, almost as though the notion was impossible for him to comprehend.

"The Steam Master," Margaret said. "He'll probably bring my brother, too." She rolled over in her cot and opened her eyes to thin slits. "Just make sure your men are done before sundown."

"They — they will be," Diktor promised nervously. "But that's only a few hours —"

"Wake me then," Margaret said, turning her back on him once more. She waited, tense, until she heard the tent flap open and fall back into place. *Idiot.*

#

"Is this the human?" the zwerg asked as Granno brought Abner Crippens through the door.

Granno snorted and the zwerg gave him a sour look. She held out her hand, "Where are the drawings?"

Granno pulled them out from his messenger bag and handed them over. "Oh, by the way, Genni this is Abner Crippens," he said to the zwerg. He waved a hand to Abner, saying, "Lieutenant this is Genni, in case you didn't guess."

"Follow me," Genni said, leading them from the entrance to an alcove off to the right. There was a workbench there and Genni moved most of its clutter out of the way to give her room to spread out the drawings. She used bits of metal and other oddments to weigh the edges down. She poured over the drawings from top left to bottom right, rolled up the first drawing with a grunt, examined the next drawing beneath it, and finally looked at the third and final drawing. When she was done, she turned to look up at Abner. "You drew these?"

"Yes," Abner said. "I had some help from one of the mage apprentices —"

"Terrible!" Genni said. She glared at Granno. "Why'd you bring him here?"

"The queen sent us," Granno said with a slight emphasis on the word 'queen.'

"Look at those drawings, sky-toucher, and tell me what you think," Genni ordered Abner.

Abner frowned and glanced down, wondering if somehow the ink had smeared or something. But he saw nothing wrong. Finally, he guessed, "Did you need the balloon on a separate sheet?"

Genni snorted. "The balloon?" She shook her head. "I've never heard of anything sillier!"

"But it flies," Abner said in confusion.

"Of course it does," Genni growled. "Put enough magic on anything it'll do whatever you want!"

"But —"

"Do you know what our queen wants?" Genni said, turning first to Granno and then to the human.

Abner shrugged.

"She wants to use the dragon steel," Genni said with another snort and a shake of her head. She turned again to Abner. "Can you imagine? Dragon steel?"

Abner turned quizzically to Granno. The zwerg guard merely gave him a sardonic look in response.

"What's the use of sheathing this — this — waste of wood in dragon steel?" Genni barked. She turned to Abner. "Tell me, sky-toucher, what is the use?"

Abner gave her a dumbstruck look.

"The first shot that hit it would buckle the timbers and where's the use in that?" Genni continued, grabbing the plans and throwing them aside in frustration.

"No use," Abner agreed feebly. "But —"

"But what?" Genni growled at him, turning her head to pierce him with her bright eyes. "What, sky-toucher?"

"Well, dragon steel is very strong," Abner said slowly. "Couldn't we just build a new hull out of it? And make it lighter than the timbers in the wooden ship?"

"Couldn't we…?" Genni gaped at him. After a moment she shut her mouth and rubbed her chin. She pulled the drawings back on the table and spread them. She glanced at them for a long while, then said, "And what about that balloon? A shot and it'd fall right out of the sky!"

"The balloon only holds the magic air," Abner said. "If we could build a steel shelter —"

"By the gods, you don't think small do you?" Granno shouted in surprise. He slapped Abner on the back and the young human staggered forward from the blow. Granno turned to Genni, "Can you do that, smith? Or is that too hard for you?"

"How *dare* you —!" Genni roared. But she caught herself off, frowning at the drawings. "Gardant!" she shouted. "Paper and ink, now!"

"Who's Gardant?" Abner muttered down to Granno.

"Her husband, poor sod!" Granno whispered back.

Abner was surprised when the tallest, strongest, widest zwerg he'd ever seen came striding over with a roll of parchment and a pouch at his side.

"Quit your grumbling, woman!" Gardant said, smiling down fondly at his wife. "Keep that up and you'll wake the babies!"

"They're in the nursery," Genni said absently as she relieved him of his roll and snapped fingers at him impatiently for a pen and ink.

"And the way you're going on, your voice will carry all the way there," Gardant rumbled in response. He turned twinkling eyes to Granno, leaned down and whispered, "And don't think I can't hear you."

Granno blushed. Gardant ignored him and turned his attention to Abner. "So you're thinking to replace the balloon with… what?"

"Are you familiar with canoes?" Abner asked. "Usually they're hollowed out of fallen trees —"

"Yes," Gardant said. He frowned. "So you're thinking of making one of dragon steel, turning it upside down and filling it with that magic hot air?"

"It might help to have a balloon inside," Abner suggested. "Just in case. To keep the air in."

"It wouldn't add much weight," Gardant said in agreement. He nodded over to his wife. "What do you think?"

Genni loaded the pen with ink and sketched a series of quick lines. "Like this?"

"With room for the cannon," Abner cautioned. He pointed to the prow. "And, seeing as we're using dragon steel, maybe we can put some teeth on her."

"Teeth?" Gardant repeated. He nodded. "At the front, Genni. Top and bottom."

"And maybe along the keel," Abner suggested. "That way we could fall on any balloon and tear it —"

"Right out of the sky!" Granno roared with delight. He slapped Abner on the back once more. "I like the way you think, sky-toucher!"

Chapter Five

"So, Drake, are you ready?" Torvan Brookes asked the tall gangly lad standing in front of him.

"Of course my father," Drake Fisher replied firmly. Dark hair, dark eyes, mahogany skin, Drake looked nothing like his 'father' — but that was the case with all of the Steam Master's 'children.'

Torvan Brookes had spent much of his later life searching for talented mages among the homeless and destitute of Kingsford. He'd had no want for possibilities, either: King Markel was better at attracting people to his capital than he was at feeding them — it was numbers of desperate people the King wanted, not loyal subjects. The strongest of those numbers were conscripted into his army or his fleet. Others were drafted into his building projects — particularly the plan of building railways to connect all of his kingdom… and the additions he planned by conquest.

That was all well and good for Torvan Brookes who eyes blazed with the thought of building such great lines, so many locomotives, so many railcars — an empire of steel. He'd caught this fever from his acquaintance with Ibb, the mechanical, and the others who were like-minded in building machines of power. People like Rabel Zebala, the steel-maker, and Hector Newman, the mechanic.

While Hector, Rabel, and Ibb had concentrated on building the steam machines that powered the locomotives, Torvan had taken up the problem of creating the railways on which the engines would run. Hector Newman had been seduced by Queen Arivik's wild notion of flying ships, and Rabel Zebala had fled the kingdom in disgrace but Torvan remained — steadfast in his association with steam and rails.

He had recognized, early, that the power of the gods would be necessary to build the long heavy lines of steel to connect city to city. And he — like the rest — had found no help from the King's magicians. He snorted at the recent memory of his interview with his youngest 'daughter' and her ability to fool the old fool mage, Vistos. *Wrinkled prune!*

And, so recognizing, he'd started to build his own academy for mages. With the help — strangely enough — of Ibb, the mechanical, he'd expanded and improved his own skills while also learning how to identify and cultivate the magical abilities of those he found homeless in Kingsford. Rabel Zebala had also help Torvan in his search for those with talent — and, more so, in their education. Zebala, Brookes admitted to himself, had a rare talent to teach. A talent that Torvan Brookes emulated as best he could — although he was not so vain as to consider himself Zebala's equal.

Even so, now, he had four strong 'children' in his family — and was training up another six who would join him. Soon they would have engines, rail, and cars enough to connect all the kingdom — and become sinews of a new, stronger realm. His own strength of will and determination — along with no small amount of success — had caused his true name to be forgotten by most. He was the 'Steam Master' and his name was spoken with awe… and fear.

"And Chandra?" The Steam Master asked, raising an eyebrow in question.

"She… she is ready enough, father," Drake said slowly.

"'Enough?'"

Drake let out a sigh. "Sometimes I think she fears her powers, father. And she's afraid of Granna."

"She should be right to fear the earth goddess," The Steam Master replied with a nod. "But she must not be afraid of her power." He glanced around. "Where is she?"

In another, Drake sent a tendril of bright flame from the end of his fingertip toward the distant door to the Steam Master's workshop.

"Drake," Torvan chided, "how many times have I told you to use your words?"

"I'm sorry, father," Drake said, dropping his gaze. "But Chandra —"

The outside door opened and a blast of chilly air entered the room.

"I am sorry, father," Chandra Evening said rushing in and dropping to one knee, bowing deeply to her 'father.' Chandra's skin was more cinnamon than mahogany, and her hair was as straight as Drake's dark hair was curly. Her features were fine, her bones thin and her carriage graceful. Torvan Brookes had found her shivering in the corner of a warehouse by the docks four years before, nearly buried under an avalanche of crates and barrels which had tumbled from their orderly piling. It had taken Brookes only one more shaking of everything to realize that the cause of the problem was eyeing him fearfully — and one quick lunge to knock the small girl unconscious before she could do more harm.

Oddly of his four grown 'children', Chandra was the one most feared even though she was the kindest and most fearful.

"Come, we go to join your sister," Torvan Brookes said, gesturing for her to rise and nodding toward her 'brother.'

"What, did Margaret mess up again?" Drake asked sourly. Torvan gave him a quelling look. Drake was jealous of Margaret and they all knew it. Torvan had worked hard to ease this feeling from his Fire Master — as he called Drake — but with no success.

While Chandra was afraid of her earth magic, Margaret feared nothing — particularly her older brother's flame magic.

"As far as I know, she's on schedule," Torvan Brookes — the Steam Master — observed mildly. "But, as you know, we had always planned for Fire and Earth to make our lines meet."

Drake snorted but said nothing. Torvan turned to Chandra. "Are your things ready?"

Chandra nodded. "Of course, father."

"Good," Torvan moved toward the exit, not waiting for the two to fall in behind him.

#

"Are we ready, mage?" Commodore Evans, Robin "Robbie" Evans to his friends and intimates — and there were *none* in his entire squadron — demanded of the simply clad pock-faced young man in front of him.

"Aye, sir," Mage Jensin Firth replied. Firth's face was solid under the pock marks — remnants of a disease in his childhood, Evans understood.

"Good," Commodore Evans replied. To himself, he added, "I wish to the gods I knew what we're supposed to do!" He grimaced and turned toward the waiting mechanic. "Mr. Bennet, how stand our propellers?" Evans congratulated himself on saying the strange word as though it were a word he'd been using for all his life — instead of merely for less than two weeks.

"Our engines and propellers are, in all respects, ready, sir!" Percival Bennet, once apprenticed on the famous airship *Spite* — if only for just the one flight — saluted sharply. Apparently something — shame, fear, or the wrath of Mechanic Newman had cured the lad of his worries of being airborne. Although perhaps some of his bravery had to do with the weight and lethargy of their ship, *Victory*.

"Lieutenant Melroy!" Commodore Evans bellowed. The first lieutenant turned from his position amidships and gave his captain and commodore a snappy salute. "Prepare for lift!"

"Aye, sir!" The lieutenant turned about and shouted, "All hands! Prepare for lift!"

Throughout the ship, Evans could hear the order echoed and responses returned to the first lieutenant.

"Fermoy, make signal: *lift ship*," Evans said without turning toward the young ensign assigned to signals.

"*Lift ship*, aye sir!" Young Thomas Fermoy repeated, saluting quickly. He turned to his signals party and bellow the order to him but the grizzled old seaman in charge of the group merely smiled and knuckled his forehead in response.

Evans turned back, raising his glass to peer through the one lens at the others ships in his command. He had six in total. *Vanguard, Surprise, and Eagle* were swift brigs all purloined from the sea navy with vague promises of future replacement — he doubted that himself, just as he doubted that he'd ever command a seaship again. His own *Victory, Conqueror* and *Falcon* were converted frigates. All the airships were of the newer three-balloon configuration. Apparently this was decided upon after reflection on the destruction of two previous airships — *Warrior* and *Vengeance* at the hands of a — if one could believe it — *floating* fortress and a flaming dragon.

As the commander of that small squadron had been none other than the odious Captain Nevins, Commodore Evans was inclined to think that their loss was simply due to incompetence — floating fortresses being a rather fanciful excuse. Given that Nevins' latest command of two new airships was officially 'overdue', Evans' conviction had solidified into near-certainty. *Nevins was insufferable!*

In fact, only one of the first three captains of airships was still alive — and that was the Sorian turncoat, Martel. Evans forced himself to admit that Martel and the first little brig, *Wasp*, seemed to have acquitted themselves well in the battle of the South Sea Pass.

But *Victory* and her consorts were an entirely different matter. Each ship had a separate mage for each balloon and they'd proved sprightly enough in rising to their appropriate stations. The smaller brigs were just as fast as anticipated. Evans frowned, wishing that his frigates could only emulate them. As it was, most of the time, the littler ships would be tied to their slower brethren.

"All ships acknowledge, sir!" Ensign Fermoy reported.

"Very good," Evans said. He watched, his chest swelling with pride as the six ships rose slowly in the morning air.

"Prepare the signal: *Engage Propellers*," Evans ordered. He turned toward the front of the ship and eyed lieutenant Melroy speculatively. The lieutenant must have felt his gaze for he turned back to the commodore at the stern of the ship. Lieutenant Melroy said something to the second lieutenant and rushed back to his commodore. "Sir?"

"Are we ready to engage propellers, Mr. Melroy?"

Lieutenant Melroy glanced around, calculating their height above the city and nodded firmly. "Aye, sir!"

"Very well," Evans said. "Engage propellers." To Fermoy he added, "Make the signal."

"Aye sir, signalling *Engage Propellers*," Fermoy replied smartly.

#

"The little admiral wants us to engage our propellers," First Officer Kitrick said smugly to his captain, Luther Wright.

"Then I suppose we should indulge him," Captain Wright replied mildly.

"He didn't say what speed, sir," Aldous Kitrick noted with a smirk. Kitrick was a short, squat powerful man with sun-worn skin and dark eyes in stark contrast to his thinning blonde hair.

"Aldy, old fellow, stop being an ass," Luther Wright chided his first officer mildly. "The last thing we want is to prick our glorious leader's pride."

"Well sir, it's true enough that our *Eagle* can run rings about that old sow," Mechanic Arde Navin spoke up in support. He turned to his stokers. "Get ready, lads!" He turned back to the captain. "What speed?"

"Just enough to keep ahead of *Victory*, for the moment, if you please," Captain Wright said pleasantly.

"Set for one third power!" Navin called to his men. He grinned at the stokers. "Might as well rest your shovels, lads. You won't be needing them." He turned to his mate. "Lower the propellers and engage, please."

The mate snapped smart salute and began the process of lowering the propellers from their stowed upright position down parallel to *Eagle* and outboard. Slowly the propellers, powered by the steam engine, began to revolve. In short order they were spinning in a blur and *Eagle* leaped forward.

"How are the balloons?" Wright asked his first officer.

"As you see, sir, no problem," Kitrick said. He pointed to the three dark bundles on the deck beneath the fore-, mid- and aft-balloons. He spread his cheeks out to let his broken-toothed smile show. "The wee tykes had no problem once I used my starter on them."

"You didn't hit them!" Wright exclaimed.

"No, sir," Kitrick said, his smile broadening. "But I put the fear of the gods in them, and that was enough."

"Aldous," Wright replied, shaking his head in sorrow. "Are we going to need to have another discussion?"

Aldous Kitrick had started his life below decks and had risen to his present high position without much regard for the backsides of others. Wright had noticed it and had already cautioned his first lieutenant on more than one occasion.

"You get more flies with honey," he'd told Kitrick the first time the issue had arisen.

"Aye," Kitrick had replied, "I suppose you do. 'Cept I'm not looking for honey."

Their working relationship was still developing.

"Signal from the flag, sir!" A midshipman shouted. "*Sail nor-'nor-'east!*"

"Acknowledge," Wright replied. He turned to the helmsman. "Make it so, Simmons."

Argus Simmons nodded and turned the wheel accordingly. "Nor-'nor-'east it is, sir!"

"Where are we going, do you know, captain?" Aldous Kitrick asked.

"At a guess, we're heading to the Sorian town of South Sea Pass," Wright replied. "Send the hands to dinner by watches and then set the first watch." He turned away. "I'll be in my cabin."

"Aye, sir," Kitrick acknowledged. "All hands, all hands," he bellowed as the captain disappeared down the hatchway, "dinner by watches. First watch to stations!"

Mage Margen was enjoying himself. He stood on his balcony at the palace and gazed up at the ships flying north towards the evening. *Pretty.*

He swirled the finely spun glass telescope in his hand and allowed himself another sip of the brandy contained therein. He was glad to be back from what Vistos vainly called "the war" and in the comfort of his rooms at the palace.

As the six royal airships finally disappeared from view, Margen turned and entered his study, placing his telescope on a side table and flicking his wrist to send two simple wisps of magic to pull the double doors closed behind him. He smiled as the two spells met, twisted around each other like friendly cats and spread themselves out through the glass and wood of the doors. No one would be entering from that direction without his being warned — and they being spell-stung.

With a satisfied grunt, he retrieved his brandy snifter and walked back to the huge oak desk that was cluttered with grimoires, books, parchments, paper, pens and all the detritus of his work.

A mage works with his knowledge of the gods, Margen thought, recalling the words spoke by his master ages ago. The muffled noise of a distant steam whistle informed him that Torvan Brookes and his brood were on their way — on time — to complete the first of the northern tracks to Korin's Pass. Profit would follow.

Margen worked more with Chancellor Prentice than with General Georgos; working to provide for the wealth of the kingdom rather than the size of its territory. Vistos might like such things, considering himself to be powerful, but Margen knew from times past that it was wealth that mattered.

A small popping sound diverted his thinking and he saw a puff of smoke as a small faintly pink demon appeared to his right.

"You're late," Margen said to the quivering demon. "I'd expected you earlier." He held out a hand expectantly. "Where's the message?"

The demon shivered and shook, chittering to itself as it tried to summon its courage.

"Must I show you again who is master?" Margen asked frostily. He raised a hand, preparing to throw a simple spell — but the demon relented and slid a small metal container onto the desk from its insides. "It had better not be hot."

The demon chittered again, moving closer to the metal container and blowing on it hastily. Frost formed around it.

"That's enough," Margen said commandingly, reaching for the metal container. It was just cool to the touch. He sniffed it first to ensure against possible poisons. Of course, he had a ring for that which he glanced at just long enough to ensure that his original guess was correct. *There are old magicians, and there bold magicians, but there are never any old bold magicians,* the saying went.

He unscrewed the cap and turned the container upside down, tapping it to unseat the small rolled paper stuffed inside.

The message was in code, of course. Not so much to avoid discovery as to ensure that long messages could be encapsulated in such a small piece of paper. And this was a long message, running from one side to another.

Prentice reported that the town was being subdued, that news of the king's midnight massacre was only slowly spreading ,that the new train line into the town was constructed and working perfectly. News of the advancing cavalry and divisions was not to be had. And two people had tried — unsuccessfully — to kill mage Vistos.

It would take a fool or a very determined person to make such an attempt. Margen frowned, trying to imagine *two* such fools. No word of the perpetrators which meant that they had not been caught, nor seen. That was troubling: inept assassins were one thing but assassins who could escape apprehension — even detection — that was something else entirely. It meant that — at the very least — the assassins were skilled at evasion. And two assassins meant either a very rich patron or a very great deal of passion. *Who would want to kill Vistos that badly?*

Margen shivered. Something very odd was happening. Something he couldn't explain. And Margen very much hated encountering the unexplained.

The little pink demon made a small mewling sound and skittered on the desk for attention. Margen turned his head from the small piece of paper in his hand and looked down at the quivering demon.

"You want release?" Margen asked without sympathy.

The demon twitched in agreement.

"Do you know who attacked mage Vistos?" Margen asked. Demons communicated with each other, knowledge was passed. Of course, what was interesting to a demon was rarely of much use to humans.

In this case, however, the little pink demon flared brilliantly and emitted what could only be described as a shriek of agony before it stilled, shrank, and extinguished. In its place was a small bit of black dust.

Margen stared at it for a very long time. Finally, he opened the top drawer of his desk, pulled out two paper envelopes. Cautiously he used one of the envelopes to brush the dust into the other. He carefully sealed the envelope, casting a holding spell over it before placing it, leaning upright against the side of the writing cabinet. He rose with the other envelope in his hand and carefully placed it in the center of the fire on his hearth, adding a word of *control*. The ashes flared momentarily, a bright blue, and then the fire returned to normal. He stared into the fire thoughtfully before shaking himself out of his reverie and returning to his chair.

Something is very wrong.

Chapter Six

"What do you want of your life, child?" Queen Alva asked Lisette Casman as they sat overlooking the huge plain below that was most of the Jasram. Lisette gave her a puzzled look. "What matters to you most?"

"What matters to you, your majesty?" Lisette asked. "And how do you see my life affecting yours?"

Queen Alva chuckled. "You already have, you know. Whether you like it or not."

Lisette quickly discerned her meaning and nodded. "Because of my father's death."

The zwerg queen nodded in agreement. "Small actions can lead to great changes."

"Are you saying if I'd married Prince Paulus, things would be different?" Lisette asked, thrusting her chin up defiantly.

"They would," Alva agreed, "as you certainly can imagine."

Lisette snorted deep in her throat. "I would be worse off than the centaurs —"

"You'd not be dead!"

"Worse," Lisette said firmly. "I'd heard of him. Of what he did —" she broke off "— did you know what he did with his first wife?"

The short zwerg queen nodded, glancing away from the human girl.

"And his second?" Lisette persisted.

"No one knows —"

"No one has to *know*, your majesty," Lisette interrupted firmly. "They say his dogs ate well that week."

Queen Alva grunted. She'd heard the rumors: that the prince had fed his late wife to their dogs.

"And you would want me wedded to *that?*" Lisette demanded. "How long would I have lasted?"

Queen Alva had the grace to remain silent.

"You ask what I want?" Lisette said after a long fuming silence. "I want a choice of my own. I want to live a happy life —"

"No one is guaranteed that, child," Alva interjected quietly.

"I don't see you complaining!"

"Do you know nothing of my realm?" The zwerg queen demanded. "Do you not know our history?"

"Father did not think I needed to know more than women's work," Lisette said, her lips tightly pursed.

"I am not your father," Alva said after a moment. She raised her eyes. "Nor are you."

Lisette snorted in agreement. Shyly, she added, "I would appreciate any learning you care to impart, your majesty."

Queen Alva nodded absently. She gestured toward the horizon: there were clouds gathering ominously. "Let us return underground," she said, rising to her feet, "there is a storm approaching."

Lisette followed her gaze, rose, dusted off her seat and gestured for the queen to show her the way. "If you please, your majesty."

They met Alain at the nearest entrance to the underground kingdom, accompanied by Jaro.

"I was just going to recount some of our history for your sister," Alva told him. "If you'd like, you can listen in." She smiled at Jaro. "Perhaps my good man will see to providing us with warming tea and some hot biscuits."

Jaro snorted but bowed in acceptance of the task royally assigned him.

Alva led the way, being careful to keep her pace slow so as not to cause the humans any trouble in the dim caverns. Some time later, they turned to the huge wrought doors of the throne room but Alva, shaking her hand and pointing, led them to a smaller room off the side.

Jaro met them moments later with another pair of zwergs and a well-laden trolley with a steaming kettle and plates piled high with pastries.

"Cook says you haven't eaten enough," Jaro said with a bow to his queen and a twinkle in his eyes.

"Tell my good —" Alva began heatedly. She broke off and calmed herself, nodding to the long conference table. In a softer tone, she said, "Tell her thank you."

"I will," Jaro said, turning to direct the placement of the pot of tea in the center of the conference table. Cups and saucers were laid in front of them, and plates and flatware to the side.

"Will you join us?" Queen Alva asked when Jaro turned to follow the trolley out the room.

Jaro shook his head. "If it pleases your majesty, no. I've work to attend."

Alva smiled and waved him on. She turned to the two humans. "Let us eat first, talk later."

Alain, fresh from another bout of training with Jaro, was all too willing to comply.

Lisette found herself examining the plates and flatware thoughtfully. When she saw Alva eyeing her, she jerked and hastily converted the motion to a grab for a pastry.

"What?" Queen Alva demanded.

"I was just…," Lisette began lamely. "It's nothing, your majesty."

"The plates don't match," Alva told her. "Cook is trying to impress me so she uses as many of the great plates as are left." She lifted a fork and shook her head at it. "And such goldware as we have left."

"My father said that gold got too cold," Alain observed gallantly. "Silver is better for food."

"I suppose there's that," Alva allowed. "But we eat with a mix because we don't have as much as we'd like." The two humans looked at her in confusion and then flushed in embarrassment when they caught sight of each other.

"I really don't know much of the zwerg," Alain confessed. "My father spoke highly of you." His lips tightened. "But he also seemed sad."

"He would have known," Alva said, speaking so low that the two children wondered if they were meant to hear. She picked up a pastry from her plate and said to them, "Eat."

When they had finished eating and were taking more tea, Alva began her tale.

"My father was Alanior," Alva began then shook her head. "No, that's not the place to start is it." She turned in her seat, pulling her purse around. She rifled through it and pulled out a gold piece.

"What do you see?" she asked, passing it to Lisette.

The human girl peered at the gold piece and examined it intently.

"It's very pretty," Alain commented from the opposite side of the table.

"There's… there's something more," Lisette said, raising the piece close to her eyes and frowning.

"Humans don't see it, mostly," Alva said in a small voice. "They see only the gold and think riches."

Lisette passed the gold piece over to Alain with a frown, challenging him to discover the puzzle.

Alain brought the piece close to his eyes. "The piece is engraved," he said. "There are — wait! There are…" he lowered the piece. "Is this a history?"

Alva smiled at him and gestured for him to return the gold piece. Reluctantly, Alain relinquished it.

"Did you see the rubble?" Alva asked.

"The rocks piled down on the right?" Alain asked. His eyes widened. "Was there a cave-in?"

"There was," Alva said. She put the gold piece back in her purse. "We mark it on all our coin now."

"That was what made father sad," Lisette guessed.

"Two out of every three zwerg died in the cave-in," Alva said. The two humans gasped in horror.

"Your parents?" Lisette asked.

Alva nodded. "I was only spared because I was out with Annabelle."

"Annabelle?"

"Annabelle, my half-sister," Alva said. "A human."

"A human?" Lisette asked in amazement. "How did a human —?"

"She rescued me," Alva said. She shook her head, "Actually, Annabelle would say that we rescued each other." Quickly queen Alva explained how she'd broken her leg in a cave and had been rescued by a starving human girl. How the two of them had become friends even though theirs were very different worlds.

"Did she die in the cave-in?" Lisette wondered. "She's not here now."

"No, she left," Alva said, her voice husky.

"She ran away?" Alain said in horror. "I'm sorry, your majesty, that's horrible!"

"It would be," Alva agreed, "if that were all."

"All?"

"She came back," Alva said. "Years later."

"What happened?" Alain asked, his tone cold and vengeful.

"She brought us five boatloads of gold," Alva told him with a grin. "She saved our kingdom, saved my people." She sniffed. "And then she left. She said she had to, that there was a compulsion on her. We guessed it was a curse put on the gold. She took the curse with her, of course, and we haven't heard from her since."

"That's said," Lisette said.

"If you ever see her, please send her here," Alva said. "But from this you must know that we in the Shattered Hills value our human friends." She fumbled in her purse once more and pulled out a different coin, handing it to Alain.

"Five ships," Alain said, looking at the engraving on the coin. "And gold coins."

"There is more," Alva said. The two children looked at her. "But to tell you, I would have to have your lives."

"Why?" Alain asked.

"Because to tell you is to give you not only my life but those of all the zwerg," Alva replied.

"What would you do with our lives, your majesty?" Lisette asked.

Queen Alva chuckled. "Nothing you wouldn't want, I imagine."

"I would have to think on this," Alain said solemnly. He rose from his chair and nodded toward her. "If you'll permit, your majesty, I am worn out from my training and need to bathe and rest."

Alva nodded back and gestured with one hand for him to leave. She turned to Lisette and raised an eyebrow questioningly.

"I could stay, if it pleases you," Lisette told her shyly.

Alva smiled and waved her away. "No, I'm sure you'll want to be back in the stables."

Lisette smiled and bobbed up out of her seat. "Thank you for the tea, the pastries, and the company, your majesty."

#

Pierre Juin was well dressed, rising from behind his desk with a hand outstretched as Peter Hewlitt entered the room.

"Sit! Sit!" Juin said, gesturing to a chair opposite him.

Hewlitt frowned and remained standing, forcing the mayor of South Sea Pass into an awkward position — should he sit and be considered rude or stand out of fear? Hewlitt's expression remained blank as he watched the portly mayor fight with his thoughts.

"What can I do for you, good sir?" Juin asked, temporizing.

"Do you know who I am?" Hewlitt asked.

"You are one of King Markel's trusted advisers," Juin replied. "Or so I've been told."

"By whom?"

"I believe it was the king's first minister, monsieur Mannevy, who apprised me of this fact," Juin said. He sat down and glanced up at the thin spymaster. A slight smile crossed his lips. "I hear, also, that you are now the silent partner at Madame Aubrey's establishment."

Hewlitt said nothing.

"I imagine that having connections in the houses of pleasure is one of the better ways of gaining intelligence," Juin continued. He spread his hands. "How may I be of service?"

"Chancellor Prentice will be by presently," Hewlitt said. "I'm sure you've already had a chance to speak with first minister Mannevy."

"Indeed, I have," Juin replied volubly. "Quite a marvelous chap. I look forward to working with him."

"I'll want to know how your citizens are feeling, which ones are unhappy, which ones might bear watching," Hewlitt said.

"Well, you know, they so rarely tell me anything," Juin temporized. Hewlitt's expression grew colder. "Everyone is still in a lather, to be sure. It's not every week that one loses a battle and bends knee to a new king. It will take some time for things to settle down. After all, it's only been two days."

"I'm particularly interested in any 'untoward' rumors you might have heard," Hewlitt said.

"Well, spymaster, as you just said they're just *rumors*," Juin said. "Nothing to get upset about."

"Which is why you'll have no problem preparing a list of the top ten complaints, with the names of the complainers," Hewlitt replied.

Juin pulled a kerchief from his pocket and dabbed his face suddenly. "I, uh, I... well that will take time, sir!"

"I'll pick it up this evening," Hewlitt said, spinning on his heels and slamming the door as he left.

Juin took a deep breath to calm himself and wiped the sweat off his brow.

#

"Major, what happened to Colonel Walpish?" General Gergen asked when the cavalry officer reported to him that evening. His troops had made poor time marching the first day, and only slightly better the second day.

"He's dead, sir," Major Sam Lewis said as he saluted the commander of the Kingsland army. Lewis' face twisted as he added, "Shot in the back, actually."

"Well, I'm quite sorry to hear that!" Gergen said. "He was a good man, I knew him a long time." He cocked his head at the major. "Shot in the back, eh?" He returned the major's salute. "Well, I suppose you can never be safe enough, can you?"

Sam Lewis drew a quick breath and nodded jerkily. "Yes, sir."

"And what have you to report, major?" Gergen asked, hastily changing the subject and snapping at his subaltern to take notes.

"We're about ten miles ahead of you sir, following the coastline," Lewis reported. "So far we've seen no sign of the enemy."

"Civilians, surely?"

"Not so much," Lewis said. With a shake of his head, he added, "It's winter so they're all pretty much tucked inside their houses."

"And the villages?"

"We scouted one but went around it," Lewis said, "as per orders."

"Orders," Gergen repeated thoughtfully. He frowned and raised his eyebrows. "We'll probably have to march through that village, major."

"I had considered that, sir," Lewis said. "The village was small, only a few buildings and a rough road. I do not expect your men will have any trouble there."

"Indeed," Gergen allowed. "And I suppose we can just go around if we need to."

"I would recommend against it, sir," Lewis said. The general raised an eyebrow. "There's a small port and a pier there. It would be a good place to land supplies."

"Oh?" Gergen said. "Well, if you say so, major."

"It's just a suggestion," Major Lewis said diffidently. "But, considering the state of the roads, I thought perhaps they might get muddy with repeated passage —"

"We're only going one way, Major!" Gergen barked.

"Indeed sir, but your supplies wagons..."

"Ah, I see your point!" Gergen said. "Well, said, then."

"Thank you sir," Lewis said. He paused then added, "Do we know when we can expect more supplies?"

"Huh?" Gergen said, surprised.

"It's winter, sir," Lewis said. "Our horses —"

"Oh! Say no more, major, say no more!" Gergen barked, raising a hand. He turned to his subaltern. "Make a note — we need hay for the cavalry."

"Yes sir," the young subaltern replied, scribbling frantically.

"Anything else?"

"The men are making do with what we can find as we pass through," Lewis said. "But I fear we'll have picked the larder bare and... well, we're here to stay, aren't we sir?"

"Indeed we are," Gergen said in a bright booming voice.

"Well, sir, I was just thinking that the more supplies we carried ourselves, the less we'd have to demand of the people here," Lewis said. Gergen grew pensive. "If our foraging leaves them hungry —"

"You haven't been doing that, have you?" Gergen cried in alarm.

"No, sir," Lewis said hastily. "We've taken no more than we need. But your troops are following us, sir, and...."

"Oh, I see," Gergen said with a curt nod. He glanced up to Lewis. "Good thinking, major. I'll send word back to minister Mannevy, I'm sure he'll see your point."

"And the hay, sir?"

"I'll make it our first priority," Gergen said. He frowned. "How soon do you need it?"

"Tomorrow, sir," Lewis replied. He saw the Gergen flush in anger and added, "My orders were to move out as quickly as we could and only report when we had need, sir."

"And just who was it, major, who wrote those orders?" Gergen demanded frostily.

Lewis reached into his tunic and pulled out a crumpled parchment. "It was you, sir," he said, handing it over. "Of course, the orders were to Colonel Walpish but you stressed that time was of the essence and he ordered me to continue our mission, sir."

"Oh," Gergen said with a huff. "Very well, then."

#

"We're running out of coal, sir," Lieutenant Fawcett reported to Captain Martel as he came on deck that crisp, cold morning.

"How much do we have?" Martel asked, glancing toward the soot-face stokers and the coal bin in front of them.

"Two hours at most, sir," Fawcett said grimly. "I hadn't quite expected we'd get through it so quickly."

"And how far are we from South Sea Pass?" Martel asked.

"If we go straight over the sea, we'll just make it," Fawcett replied.

"Very well, turn about and set course for the town," Martel replied. He frowned, cast a thoughtful eye across the snow-covered deck and turned back to the hatchway. "I'll be below."

"Aye, sir," Fawcett said, saluting. He turned back as soon as the captain was out of sight and said to the helmsman, "Turn us about."

"Aye sir, coming to heading one nine zero," the helmsman replied, turning the wheel steadily. Slowly, little *Wasp* turned just west of due south and began beating back over the sea toward the town they'd left just a few days before.

#

That night, Thomas Walpish broke into the temple of the gods. He came over the roof — he was getting surprisingly good at that, he thought — and through an unlocked window. The window that he'd thoughtfully propped open with a small piece of wood earlier that afternoon.

His head was clear, no longer fogged with drink, nor blaring with hangover. He had even eaten though he hadn't bathed.

The window creaked loudly as he pushed it open, although it made no noise at all when he swung it closed again. He dropped down lightly on shoes that he'd bought for their suppleness — cavalry boots were not known for their silence, that not being a requirement when on horseback.

He paused a moment, listening. When he was satisfied, he stepped out slowly and carefully following the path he'd reconnoitered that afternoon. He walked down the corridor back toward the double doors that were now shut and turned to his right, seeking a wooden door which opened with another annoying creak and led him down the corridor toward the library. For Thomas Walpish had much to learn, and not enough time.

He made it to the end of the corridor and paused at the door to the library. He squinted — was that a light under the doorway? He paused, letting his eyes adjust and decided that he'd been wrong. Carefully he swung in the door which — thankfully — made no noise. He swung it shut again and waited for a moment, confirming the silence. Satisfied, he moved toward the far end of the library before lighting his storm lantern and raising it to glance around at the titles on the shelves.

He had just turned a corner when he felt someone push something sharp up against his ear. He raised his free hand in surrender.

"What are you doing here?" Skara Ningan hissed from behind him.

"Probably the same thing you are," Walpish said, turning slowly around to face her. "Looking for ways to defeat gods."

"Which god?" Skara demanded.

"Quenkorian," Walpish replied with a heavy heart.

"What can mere humans do against a god?" Skara grumbled. "Why not ask —" she struggled for a moment to speak, realized she couldn't say the names she wanted "— your friends for help?"

"Because they are not equipped to give us the aid we need," Walpish said. He lowered his hand and gestured to the shelves. "I was hoping to find which god might be better equipped and more inclined to our aid."

"And then what?"

"Well, at that point I had planned to think of what to do next," Walpish admitted. Ruefully he added, "I am quite out of my death when it comes to killing someone who *won't stay dead.*"

"As am I," Skara agreed with a sigh. She pointed her index finger at him and made a thrusting motion with it, revealing the source of the sharp pointed object that Thomas had felt against his ear. She smiled at him in triumph. Thomas merely shrugged — a threat was a threat and had to be respected accordingly. "And I don't know how I can defeat such magic."

"Which is why I'm here," Walpish said. He frowned. "I did some thinking yesterday and decided that there are two gods who might help us."

"*Two?*" Skara asked. "I couldn't think of one."

"Lukorva who looks after those who live a solitary life," Thomas said, raising a finger on his free hand, "but I think we are moving out of her protection."

"We?" Skara repeated challengingly.

"You more so than I," Thomas allowed. Skara gave him a look. With a sigh, he explained, "Neither of us is particularly fond of the company of others, we take our own guidance, and prefer solitude."

"And the other?" Skara said without admitting his point.

"We are looking for hope, we each have a renewed purpose, we need to change the way we are, and we need faith that we can succeed," Walpish said.

Skara's eyes widened. "Aravantis? The star goddess?"

Thomas nodded slowly.

"How…? What…?"

Thomas pointed to the books on the shelves. "I do not know," he admitted. "But I'm hoping to find out."

Skara grabbed for his storm lantern and put it on a nail that was stuck in the outside wall. "Let's get started, then."

Chapter Seven

"Well, *there's* a sight!" King Markel bellowed, pointing up to the six ships slowly coming into view over the town of South Sea Pass. He turned to his first minister, "Never expected them to ever get here, to be honest."

"As I assured your majesty previously, the concept was sound," first minister Mannevy said with just the hint of a sniff of pain in his voice. He waved to the airships above them. "I do believe, your majesty, that this proves the point."

"Indeed it does!" Markel bellowed once more, his booming voice echoing around the market courtyard below his appropriated mansion. He turned to the far city walls and pointed. "And how soon before we break that down?"

"As you know, sire, we've promised most of the masonry to the citizens," Mannevy reminded him. "But our first priority —"

"Is laying the rail line through here and beyond," Markel finished. He turned to glower at his first minister. "You've reminded me of the importance of that more than once this week. Don't think I've forgotten."

"Of course not, your majesty," Mannevy replied with a slight bow. "Although I must ask is it possible that you might have confused me with Chancellor Prentice, perhaps?"

"Just because the voice is different, don't think I can't determine who is pulling the strings," King Markel told him testily. He lowered his voice and moved closer to his first minister. "Anyway, we should rid ourselves of this town as soon as we can." His eyes twinkled and he elbowed the minister affably. "And take our favorite mage with us, not so?"

"I'm sure we'll be able to use mage Vistos' many talents better elsewhere," Mannevy agreed.

"Particularly as that will keep his temper in check over the rail lines," Markel added slyly.

"Indeed so, sire," Mannevy allowed. But the king was no longer paying attention, turning his gaze to the skies and northwards.

"What's that?" King Markel snapped suddenly, pointing to a smug on the northern horizon. With wild eyes he turned back to Mannevy. "Soria hasn't got an airship of its own, does it?"

Mannevy followed the royal gaze to the point of interest and pursed his lips thoughtfully. After a moment, he said, "I believe that perhaps it our own *Wasp*."

"Well, it's not getting any closer, what's it doing out there?" King Markel growled.

"I believe it may be out of fuel, sire," Mannevy said in a small voice. Hastily, he added, "We were never quite certain how much coal it would need, after all."

Indeed, a red flare burst over the smug on the horizon. Moments later it was answered by a green flare from one of the arriving airships.

"Well, that's settled then," the king said. "Whoever is running that ship is an idiot."

"Or just unlucky," Mannevy allowed.

"I've no use for unlucky captains in my employ," Markel said. "Make sure he's replaced."

"As you wish, sire," Mannevy said, nodding obediently. "However, it seems that it will take some time before the captain is available for dismissal."

The king waved the issue aside. "That'll give what's-his-name, Evans, right? Plenty of time for him to pick a replacement."

"Indeed sire," Mannevy said. He pursed his lips before adding, "However, perhaps we should wait until we get a full report from the captain of the *Wasp* before we make a decision —"

"Why?" Markel demanded. "He's either a fool or an unlucky fool and I'll have *neither* in charge of one of my airships!"

"I believe, sire, that he is Jacques Martel, our friend and spy who provided us with valuable information on Soria," Mannevy said, trying to choose his words carefully.

"So?"

"Well, sire, we promised him a command in return for his loyalty to us," Mannevy reminded him dutifully.

"Well, he's had it — wait! Didn't he have another ship already?" King Markel demanded.

"Indeed, sire, just as Captain Nevins," Mannevy replied. "They lost their ship in the valuable encounter — and destruction — of the East Pass Fort."

"And we've heard nothing from Nevins since," Markel muttered. "There's *another* unlucky captain!"

"It's possible he ran into difficulties," Mannevy agreed. "But I think it might not serve us to rush to judgement in either case." He paused. "Especially as Captain Martel was the gallant captain who helped us capture this very town just days ago."

"He had help!" King Markel said. "Walpish of the cavalry, for one." The king frowned. "And that's all the more reason to rid ourselves of him. He might ask questions."

"We could easily keep him occupied in the execution of his duties, sire," Mannevy suggested.

"Bah!" Markel snorted. "Get rid of him! Tell Vistos. He'll have some fun, no doubt."

"Is that wise, sire?" Mannevy asked delicately.

"I'm the king, first minister," King Markel replied in slow, icy tones. "Are you questioning my wisdom?"

Mannevy suppressed a shudder and shook his head quickly. "No, of course not, your majesty." He paused again. "And what of the mage, Tirpin?"

"What of him?"

"He is the mage on *Wasp*, sire," Mannevy reminded him. "He was in on our plans from the first."

"Get rid of him, too," Markel said. "Make a clean sweep of it. That will make Vistos happier, too."

Mannevy bowed. It occurred to him that the king's list was getting rather long. He did not want himself added to it. "As you wish, sire."

#

"Poor sod!" Commodore Evans said as he viewed the crippled brig far off on the horizon. "Mr. Melroy!"

"Sir!" the first lieutenant called back, moving briskly toward his captain and saluting sharply when he arrived.

"How are our stores?"

"You mean, coal, sir?" Lieutenant Melroy guessed. He nodded toward the mechanic near the engines who held up a hand in an "okay" gesture. "We're well, sir."

"And you'll check on the rest when we get to our station over the port," Commodore Evans ordered. His lips tightened in thought. "Signal *Eagle* to render aid."

"Aye, sir," Lieutenant Melroy replied, saluting and turning away.

Besides, Evans thought to himself, *it will give Captain Wright something to consider*. He shouted after his first lieutenant, "And signal the rest of the squadron to make anchor at the port."

"Aye sir!"

#

"Well, at least we get to stretch our legs," Captain Wright observed as his *Eagle* went to full power, the huge propellers beating loudly on either side of the ship.

"She flies, sir," Arde Navin, the ship's mechanic, said with a huge grin. "I never thought she'd do so well."

"She's a bit lighter so she'll move faster," Luther Wright agreed with an answering grin. His expression faded as he pointed to the fast approaching *Wasp*, motionless, before them. "But we'll want to watch our supplies, particularly coal and water." He turned to his mage. "Miss Eden, perhaps you can conjure up a way to move our ship as well as lift it?"

Julia Eden was a slim slip of a person but she had a ready wit, a sharp tongue and no willingness to betray either. She flashed the captain a quick grin. "I've already been working on it, sir."

"And?" Wright demanded. "I would have imagined that such a problem would have surrendered its solution to you immediately upon your inquiries."

Julia snorted and shook her head. "It's a bit more than that, sir," she told him. "We —" she pointed to the other two air mages, a girl younger than herself and a thin, emaciated lad just barely in his teens "— have been talking about it among ourselves. Hissia and Hanor — blessed be their names — would be first choice but we fear that they might get overly eager."

The other two mages nodded in support. Of course, as Wright knew but wouldn't say, the two others were far more *apprentice* than mage — Miss Eden having been stalwart in vouching for them.

The new ship arrangement of three balloons — and three mages — had put an unbearable strain on the supply of working mages, let alone *talented* working mages. Wright had not bothered to question Miss Eden's word; he was too desperate to get his ship airborne. He had since seen that both mages had been *capable* but still understrength in their ability to fill their balloons and create lift. On the other hand, they'd had only a few days to practice while, Captain Wright admitted to himself, he'd had years to practice the skills of navigating a ship. *Of course, I've never commanded an* airship.

#

"That ship has *three* balloons!" Mage Tirpin exclaimed as they spied their approaching rescuer.

"So it would seem," Captain Martel agreed mildly. The mage, Martel had noted, was furious with the engineer at their helplessness. It had taken all of Captain Martel's tact — and not a few low-voiced orders — to keep the two from blows. Tirpin, as Captain Martel had come to know all too well, was convinced that only *he* had the true knowledge of all things. In short, he was an insufferable toad. However, he was a talented magician when it came to lifting airships. Perhaps not as talented as others and certainly unwilling to quell his arrogance for one instant but, as Captain Martel reminded himself with an inward sigh, he was Martel's *only* mage.

"Make signal: *Identity*," Captain Martel said to his signals officer.

"What good will that do?" Tirpin growled. "No one else has airships, it has to be one of Markel's!"

"It is always good manners to use a proper name in conversation," Captain Martel explained.

"Hmph!"

Martel saw flags rise from the airship approaching and realized, thankfully, that the name was being spelled out. Whoever was captain on that ship at least thought things through. Martel grimaced as he realized that, if the ship *was* an enemy there was little he could do about it — an enemy could rake him with impunity as *Wasp* could not turn. Although… it could change altitude. *Something to consider for the future.*

"The ship is the *Eagle*, sir," the signals midshipman reported.

"Very good, Ives," Captain Martel said, using the midshipman's first name absently. Ives Bastien swelled with pride. "Please signal that we are out of coal and request —" he glanced toward his mechanic "— one hundredweight if possible." The mechanic nodded agreement. "That should give us enough to get back to port."

"We'll be able to sail for an hour on that, sir," James Sawyer, the mechanic reported.

"And that will be enough, I'm sure," Jacques Martel said with a firm nod. He turned to the midshipman. "Make the signal, please."

"Aye, sir!"

#

"You're here!" Margaret's cry came from a knot of hard-looking men clustered near a small fire at the end of the line. She burst forth and ran towards them, grabbing her father first, then hugging Chandra and turning to face Drake. Her smile disappeared and she held out a hand to him. He frowned at her but did not take the hand. Margaret's lips tightened but she turned to her father and said, "All is ready, sir."

"We'll need to have the engine moved off the line," Torvan Brookes said.

A well-muscled man came striding from the crowd of rail rowdies. "Who are you to be ordering our Margaret —?"

"It's okay, Diktor," Margaret told him. She nodded toward her father. "He's my father, the Steam Master."

Diktor Vincet stopped dead in his tracks, his eyes huge. He recovered quickly, bobbing his head, and stammering, "D-d-didn't m-m-mean n-n-no h-h-harm, sir! It's just our Margaret —"

"No harm," Torvan replied, raising a hand to forestall further comments. He smiled at the burly man. "I see you've done well, here, Diktor."

"Diktor Vincet, sir - uh, your worship, uh, your —"

"I call him father," Margaret added unhelpfully.

"You may call me the Steam Master," Torvan Brookes instructed Diktor. "'Master', if you would."

Diktor Vincet licked his lips. "Uh, yes, sir. I mean Master, sir!"

"Have the engineer back the train off the track, please," the Steam Master ordered. "It's Reg, isn't it? Reginald Storvish."

"It is," Diktor said in ill-concealed awe. He leaned closer to the Steam Master and added in a lower voice, "A bit of a Felland name, if you ask me."

"Vinik, I believe," Torvan Brookes corrected absently. He turned back down the track and shouted, "Reg! Move the train off the track! We're going to make curves!" In response, the steam whistle tooted twice in warning and the railcars started forward as Storvish released the brakes. To Vincet, he said, "Move that fire and get your men well out of the way."

"How far, sir?"

"Half a mile at the least," the Steam Master replied. He nodded toward Margaret. "You can stay with us."

"Maybe you'll learn something," Drake added sourly.

Margaret glowered at him. Chandra moved between the two with a pleading look. Margaret gave her a small smile: Chandra was always the peacemaker.

#

Thomas Walpish jerked awake with a start. Light was streaming into the room. A book lay open in his lap. He lifted his head from the shelf he'd fallen asleep against. Skara Ningan nudged his foot again and he turned to see her raise a finger to his lips. She pushed an open book toward him, saying in a whisper, "It's dawn. You fell asleep. I found something."

Voices came from outside in the corridor. Walpish jerked to his feet, the book on his lap falling unregarded to the floor with a loud sound. Skara shook her head at him and rose beside him.

"Do you suppose we'll get in trouble if we take this?" Walpish whispered to her, raising the book she'd handed him.

"I don't know," a small boy's voice chirped up from beside him. "Are you planning to return the book?"

Walpish jerked at the voice and glared when he spotted its owner — a small boy of about nine years.

"Oh! It's you!" Walpish said in relief. Skara's expression made it clear that *she, at* least, was not relieved. "What are you doing here?"

"Sometimes," the boy returned with a flash of his eyes, "it's because people ask for me."

"I'm sorry," Walpish said, abashed. "It's just —"

"Do you need a Judgement?" Aron, the god of judgement offered.

"Are we on the right path?" Walpish asked.

"That's not even *slightly* a worthy question," Aron said with a snort of humor.

Walpish snorted and rubbed his face with one hand. "I'm sorry, great god, but I've had very little sleep and am desperately in need of counsel."

"You'll have to make do with me," Aron told him with a grin. He nodded toward Skara. "Miss Ningan, how's your teeth?"

"Oh!" Skara said, moving her hand to her jaw. "*You're* —"

"Shh!" Walpish said. "Here it is not a good idea to say his name."

"Unless you want something you might not like," Aron said in cheerful agreement.

"I didn't recognize you," Sakra apologized to the youthful god.

"I prefer it that way," Aron explained. He nodded toward Walpish. "Except for some special cases."

"We still need to talk about that," Walpish said. "But —"

"Yes," Aron agreed, "you have a more pressing problem."

"You knew, didn't you?" Walpish demanded.

"No," Aron said, shaking his head. "Which is why we took your oath."

Skara's eyes widened in surprise. Aron must have sensed it for he turned toward her, saying, "We can only see what we look for, you understand." He caught her incomprehension and explained, "Like you with your bow, we can only hit what we can see."

"Oh!" Skara said, as understanding came to her. Aron smiled.

"My great god and strange friend," Walpish said, catching the god of Judgement's eyes and unabashedly holding them, "would you care to…?"

"I can't," Aron said. As Walpish started to protest, the young god cut him off with a raised hand, saying, "It's not that I don't want to, it's that I don't know yet." He turned to add Skara to his gaze. "Whatever is happening is hidden from me. Events are still unfolding."

"What can we do to help?" Skara asked, impulsively laying a comforting hand on the boy's arm.

"Fulfill your oath," Aron told her, turning to smile up to her and remove her hand from her arm. "Renew your purpose, find your faith, have hope, and —"

"I believe I understand, your greatness," Walpish interrupted. Aron's eyes flashed as he grinned at the taller human. "I suppose my —" he glanced at Skara and corrected himself "— *our* question is: how?"

"And how do you get my attention?" Aron asked with a grin.

"Honestly," Walpish replied, "I'm still trying to figure that out." But the god had vanished.

"Best be quick," his voice came from the empty air.

"Faith, purpose, hope?" Skara Ningan repeated to Thomas with a look of confusion.

"Are you ready to change your life forever?" Thomas asked her solemnly.

Skara frowned. "I gave my oath," she said. "I was betrayed and I want —"

"Don't say it!" Walpish said, covering her mouth before she could speak.

Skara was well-trained, she bit him.

"Some words require a great deal of care in their use," Walpish said as he pushed his hand tighter against her mouth, ignoring the pain of her teeth in his flesh. He caught her eyes in a question. Skara nodded and he released his grip. "And the one you want is not that one."

"Who is it?"

"Do you trust me?"

"Why should I?" Skara asked instantly. She saw his look and dropped her eyes in shame. "What would you have us do?"

Thomas Walpish stepped back from her, scanned the bookshelves for the empty slot and gingerly slotted the book in his hand back in its place. He turned his bloody hand, palm up, toward her. "Follow me."

Skara eyed the bleeding hand sourly. She raised her hand, telling him to wait while she fumbled at her belt for her dirk. Thomas blinked as she pulled it from its sheath. She smiled at him and shook her head as she drew the blade quickly across her palm. Instantly a red line appeared. She sheathed her knife and grabbed his bleeding hand with hers. She saw his look of surprise and explained, "My oath to you."

Walpish smiled at her and tightened his grip, sealing the blood bond. "And mine to you."

"Until this is finished," Skara said.

"That might be a long time," Thomas warned.

Skara Ningan smiled at him. "I wouldn't mind."

Chapter Eight

"They're far enough away," Torvan Brookes announced as he gazed toward the distant pack of railway men. He turned to Chandra and Drake. "You may begin."

"Father?" Chandra asked nervously.

"We need to bend the tracks, move the timbers underneath and make a long gentle curve," the Steam Master told his earth-mage daughter. He gave her a reassuring look, "It's nothing you haven't done before."

"You'll do fine," Margaret added encouragingly. Drake scowled at her but as Drake always scowled at her, Margaret took no offense.

Chandra nodded and lowered herself to the ground. She pulled off her gloves and pushed her hands through the thin layer of snow to touch the earth.

"Drake." The Steam Master said to his fire-mage. Drake nodded, drew himself up to his full height and closed his eyes, clenching his bare hands tightly together. When he opened his eyes again, Margaret could see red flaring in the pupils. *Typical.*

Drake did not notice her. He turned toward the metal rails and moved his hands apart, pointing one hand to each of the two lines of rail. Margaret could feel the magic flowing from him. It was different from hers, alien, tangible but unfathomable. She watched in interest as the cold blue steel of the railways started to glow and turn red.

"Now, Chandra," the Steam Master told his other daughter in a quiet, commanding tone.

Chandra nodded to indicate that she'd heard but outwardly made no other sign.

Around them, the earth started to rumble. It groaned. Flecks of snow, disturbed by the ground beneath, began to float upwards into the sky as though seeking safety.

Chandra rose and made a gesture with her eyes, telling the others to follow her. She pulled back from the tracks, moving toward the knotted group of railway men but kept her distance. She knelt down again, touching the bare earth and pushed her hands tight against it.

The rumbling increased. Chandra raised her head, eyed the tracks and grinned.

"Mother earth, goddess Granna, I beg your indulgence," Chandra called in a low, sing-song voice. "Hear my plea. I ask you to move the ground, slide the tracks, make a curve of beauty. *Show your power!*" And with those last words, Chandra rose, shouting with all her lungs, spreading her hands wide and twisting them.

And the earth heard her. Groaning, heaving, twisting, turning, the earth beneath and around the railroad tracks twisted and turned. The timbers under the tracks, and the molten metal that was the tracks, curved, slowly, steadily. The tracks nearest them, pointing northwards, twisted to the east. The eastward track, once at right angles to the northbound rails, curved southwards and twisted.

Margaret couldn't help herself, she clapped her hands together and shouted with joy. "You're doing it, Chandra! You're moving the earth!" She turned to Drake who was lost in concentration. "Drake, the lines are red with your power!"

In the distance, the railway men cried in fear but Margaret paid them no attention, jumping up and down with excitement and joy to see the two sets of tracks twist and writhe across the ground to bend toward each other. The slow dance of earth and molten metal seemed to take no time but also to last forever. The gods were doing magic and Margaret cried with pure joy.

Finally, the two lines met. Drake waved his hands and the two ends joined, fused metal into one piece. He lowered his hands and the rest of the body followed, slowly descending to the ground, he fell to his knees and stayed there, lungs heavy, body swaying with each breath.

Chandra rose from the ground, wiped her hands, saw the bent rail line and bowed deeply. "Thank you, earth gods." She allowed her lips to curve upwards. "You have made beautiful magic. You have shown us poor humans your immense power and great skill." She bowed once more and straightened, turning inquiringly toward the Steam Master — looking for any sign of praise.

"Not bad," Torvan Brookes allowed.

"Not bad?" Margaret bellowed in outrage. She ran forward and grabbed her sister in a huge hug, lifting her off her feet and twirling her around. "You did great! You and the gods… amazing!" She put the startled Chandra back down on the ground and turned to her brother. "And the fire! Drake, that was the best yet!"

Drake grunted and scowled at her.

"It was well done," Torvan Brookes, the Steam Master admitted after a moment. He gave Margaret a stern look but she shook it off, standing straight and defiant. "I am proud of you all, my children."

The three mages cheered at those words. Margaret practically preened while Chandra allowed her lips to twitch upwards, her expression happy. Drake… seemed less unhappy.

"Come!" he shouted, motioning them toward the newly curved tracks. He raised his voice and gestured to the work crew. "Come! This is just the beginning! We've more work to do." He turned to Margaret. "You've another league to lay today and two more tomorrow."

"We'll do it, father," Margaret said. "And Drake and Chandra will put in the curves." Her lips twitched. "Two days — three days for the curve — and our engine will steam into Korin's Pass."

"We'll have a rest then, while we bring up more supplies," Torvan promised. He turned toward his steam children. "But after, we'll have more work to do."

"What about Dysack, Moira, and Gander?" Drake muttered. "What are they going to be doing?"

"Your younger brothers and sisters will be dealing with the line to South Sea Pass and beyond," the Steam Master said. "They are still young and coming into their skills."

Drake grunted and turned to Margaret. "Well, what are you waiting for?"

"I'm waiting for the track to cool, hot-head," Margaret told him frostily, waving a hand toward the still-red tracks. "We can't do anything until we can bring the train up with the supplies."

"What? Can't you just lift them a mere league?" Drake taunted.

Margaret's hands flew but she stopped herself and clenched them tight against her side. She would save her strength — and her anger — for the work to come. She turned away from her fire-mage brother.

"It's best that you all conserve your strength," the Steam Master told his brood, his eyes resting on Drake. "We have a long way to go and a short time in which to do it."

#

"Very well, Tirpin, let's make this look good," Captain Martel said to his mage as they neared the port of South Sea Pass. They had received their hundredweight of coal, lowered to them by *Eagle* and were now just in range of the piers of the port. It was the first time, as far as Captain Martel knew, that an airship was to engage in such a venture — docking at a seaside port. Such a maneuver was one of the better reasons why airships were built from seagoing hulls — the other, of course, being cost.

"I will have no problem with that, captain," Tirpin replied testily. "Just see to your men."

Martel gave the mage a respectful nod and turned back to his crew. "Lieutenant Fawcett!"

"Sir!"

"Prepare the anchor party, all crew make ready to dock," Martel called. Fawcett paused in surprise then gave him a hurried salute and started issuing orders in rapid fire.

"Mechanic, prepare to disengage propellers," Martel called.

"Aye sir."

"You may begin lowering us now, please, mage," Martel said to Tirpin. "Can you arrange it that we hit the water just as we reach the dock?"

Tirpin glanced about, looking ahead to the pier and the port, gauging their altitude and rewarded the captain with a sniff. "Of course."

"Prepare to descend!" Martel shouted, waving a hand toward the mage. They were about a mile from the dock and still several thousand feet up. He gauged their speed at four knots. Good.

Wasp jerked as though hit by a wind and then began, slowly, to descend toward the sea below.

It's a pity we didn't put the propellers higher, Martel thought to himself, *then we could sail on the sea as easily as in the sky.*

Wasp dropped steadily and, just as they came up to the pier, Martel called, "Disengage propellers! Hoist them up!"

"Disengaging, aye, sir," the mechanic returned steadily. A moment later he added, "Propellers disengaged and inboard, sir."

Martel nodded in acknowledgement although the shadows cast by the raised beams that held the propellers was sufficient evidence on its own.

Wasp continued forward on momentum alone.

The ship splashed into the water and lurched as it found its keel. The helmsman squawked in surprise but soon regained control.

"Stand by, port side!" Lieutenant Fawcett shouted. "Bumpers on the side, there! Lively now!"

A small spattering of airmen cast bundles of fabric over the side of the ship to prevent it bumping too hard against the pier.

"Lines ashore, prepare to tie up!" Fawcett added. Four airmen in two groups leaped over the side and onto the pier, carrying thick ropes behind them. They wrapped them around the huge wrought iron bollards that studded the pier and began to pull against them, slowly and steadily restraining *Wasp's* motion by sheer force. The stern line drew taught, held, and pulled *Wasp* gently backwards.

"Forrard line!" Fawcett bellowed. The two men on the forward line drew their rope taught. "Fore and aft, tie off!"

The two groups tied their lines securely.

Lieutenant Fawcett turned to salute Captain Martel. "Ship docked, sir!"

"Well done, lieutenant," Martel replied, returning his salute. He raised his voice. "Well done, all of you!" He brightened as he turned toward the town and saw a party of horsemen riding towards them. "I'm sure the King will have thanks for every one aboard, I don't doubt!"

#

Captain Martel felt certain of his thanks when one of the riders dismounted and jumped aboard *Wasp*.

"Is Captain Martel here?" the man asked.

"Yes," Martel said, immediately moving forward. His eyes narrowed as he noted that the young man was a mage and not one Martel had met.

"I've been ordered to get you and mage Tirpin to come with me," the man replied.

"By whose orders?"

"By King Markel's," the man replied. He gave the captain a slight bow, adding, "Mage Minnor, at your service." He looked around and spotted Tirpin by his robes. "You must be mage Tirpin," he said, nodding. "I've heard my master speak of you."

"And who is your master?" Tirpin asked archly.

"Mage Vistos," Minnor replied. "Surely you've heard of him?"

"He is one of the king's mages," Tirpin said. "I heard that he has not much regard for mages like myself."

"I know nothing of that," Minnor lied, badly. "But I am requested to bring you along. Your attention is needed immediately."

"Mustn't keep his majesty waiting, I imagine," Martel said, moving up to clap Tirpin on the shoulder. Tirpin eyed Martel's hand distastefully but Martel ignored the look. "I'm sure we'll learn all that we want when we get to the king."

Minnor said nothing, merely gesturing toward the waiting party and two empty saddles. "If you'll follow me, sirs?"

#

Thomas led Skara to an inn. This early in the morning they were offered tea, hot biscuits, and bacon. The inn was mostly empty and the innkeeper none too friendly. She identified herself as Madame Aubrey and made it quite clear that hoped they'd either take a room or leave soon.

"She looks like she lost a fight," Skara murmured when the good lady of the house had wandered off, sending them an ill-disguised look and gesturing for one of the young maids to tend to them.

"More than that," Thomas said. "Her expression changed the minute she heard us speak."

"She doesn't like our accents," Skara guessed. Thomas nodded. Skara shrugged the innkeeper's mood away from her, taking a piece of bacon and consuming it greedily in three bites. "At least she's not trying to poison us."

Thomas nodded, buttering a warm biscuit. He waved a hand toward the now-vanished innkeeper. "I had dealings with her before."

"Did she recognize you?" Skara asked anxiously.

Thomas shook his head. "She's too bruised, battered, and bothered to pay much attention to me." He ate his biscuit with relish, following it with a slice of bacon. "But I wouldn't say that she looks on us with much favor."

"As long as our money's good, she can't complain," Skara said, grabbing a biscuit and buttering it in turn.

"Where are we going?" Mage Tirpin asked Minnor irritably as their ride seemed to go on interminably.

"We have to return the horses to the stables," Minnor said, turning down a side street. "Then my master will want to meet with you —"

"Your master?" Martel cut in. "I thought the king —"

"Oh!" Minnor said, chuckling. "Surely, later."

Tirpin cast a look toward Martel who shrugged in response.

"Why not go directly to mage Vistos and have a stablehand take the horses?" Tirpin demanded.

"I've my orders," Minnor said.

"And who did you get your orders from?" Tirpin asked.

They reached an opening in the street and saw a stableyard in front of them. Minnor waved a hand toward it, trotted forward and dismounted. He called for a stable boy. A lad came out, glanced nervously at the mage, and jerked into motion when he heard Minnor's orders.

"The boy's terrified," Martel muttered to Tirpin. Tirpin shrugged: stable boys were only to be used and were beneath his consideration. Martel dismounted and passed his reins over to another waiting stable lad who took them and rushed off with the horse, anxious to be out of sight.

Minnor turned around at that point and stumbled closer to Martel. He raised an arm. "This way."

Martel turned away from the lad — his breath was foul. Tirpin raised an eyebrow but said nothing, handing over his mount and falling in beside Martel.

He moved quickly, an arm at Martel's elbow urging him forward until they built a gap between themselves and Minnor. "I don't like this," Tirpin muttered to the airship captain.

"That boy," Martel said. "His breath!"

"What about it?" Tirpin demanded, glancing back over his shoulder at Minnor who smiled affably.

"It was foul," Martel said. "Like something had curled up and died inside him."

Tirpin stopped abruptly, causing Martel to twist in his grip and turn to face him.

"Is everything all right?" Minnor asked, moving up to them.

"I don't know the way," Tirpin said, moving closer to the other mage. He waved Minnor in front of them.

"I'll show you," Minnor said as he passed forward. Tirpin grabbed at him, pulling him to a halt. Minnor turned back to him, eyes questioning.

"Are we going to get a chance to freshen ourselves?" Tirpin demanded, moving his face close to the other's.

"I'm sure refreshments will be made available by my master," Minnor replied, his eyes shining brightly. He gently tugged his arm out of Tirpin's grip and motioned them forward. "If you take a right here, you'll see the entrance."

Tirpin nodded and gestured for the lad to precede them. As Minnor moved off, Tirpin turned to Martel and gave him a slow, wary nod.

"You're right," he muttered to the airship captain, bringing his lips close to the other's ears. "He's spoiled. There's something rotten inside him."

Chapter Nine

Mage Margen paced his large study, lost in thought. All he had were clues, scant rumors. He needed more.

"Something is wrong," he muttered to himself. He took another turn. "Who to trust?"

A chittering noise came from a large blue vase covered in gold filigree patterns placed on a side table at the far end of his room, near the tall shelves of books.

"Not you!" Margen muttered, shaking his head. "I wasn't talking to you." He turned his head toward the vase. "And you'd best not be *eating* in there or it'll be the last thing you do."

The chittering changed tone and Margen's lips twitched. *Of course it had been eating, what else did it do?* Margen flicked a hand toward the vase and a burst of air expelled its contents. What appeared to be chicken bones — or perhaps rat — emerged and fell in various clumps on the carpet. Another form had flown out before them, higher and faster — it disappeared behind the curtains.

"Just stay out of the books," Margen warned. "I will *not* be putting out another fire." He turned away and paced once more, muttering, "Vistos, what are you doing?"

Who would want to kill the mage? Margen snorted. That was certainly the wrong question, the right one was who did *not* want to kill the mage?

The king probably didn't, Margen guessed. King Markel would be stupid to kill Vistos without a foolproof plan. Of course, King Markel *was* stupid so perhaps he should not be removed so readily from the list of suspects.

But two people tried to assassinate Vistos. Did they have different employers? Or *any* employers?

One needs an assassin to assassinate, Margen thought. *Or, at least, an assassin is likely to be more successful, at least.*

Vistos has several paid assassins... Margen stopped short and raised his head. He snorted and a smile slowly grew on his lips.

"The King is a fool," Margen said out loud. "And Vistos..." he clapped his mouth shut. *Vistos is playing a dangerous game.*

Well, we both are, Margen admitted to himself. He turned toward the curtains, flicked his fingers and said a *word*. A frightened squawk erupted but the owner did not try to evade his spell.

A moment later, a small set of wings and glowing eyes looked up at the mage.

"I have a use for you," Margen said. "And I don't care if your father knows."

The winged creature chirped.

"Take a message to Hewlitt, the spymaster."

The creature chirped again, its meaning plain. *What's in it for me?*

"I'll feed you when you return," Margen promised.

The eyes glowed brighter and the creature chirped in satisfaction. Then it cocked its head in question.

"Tell him: danger." He threw the creature up to the air. It circled once, chirped at him, and vanished. Margen stared after it for a moment, then sighed. "At least it won't be soiling the place."

#

Thomas and Skara had finished their meal and were just rising from the table when two soldiers entered the front door. They paused, scanning the small morning crowd.

"This way!" Skara hissed, lowering her head and wrapping an arm around Thomas, leading him toward the kitchen.

"There they are!" a soldier shouted, charging after them.

Thomas elbowed her aside, grabbed her hand and pulled her after him, into the kitchen and past the startled cooks and helpers.

"Let go!" Skara said, shaking off his hand. Thomas didn't fight her — which was just as well, as she reached into her jacket and pulled out her dirk.

Thomas' had appeared in his hand as if by magic. He kicked the rear door open and bounded through only to stop dead — a sword was raised in front of his throat.

"Did you enjoy your breakfast?" Peter Hewlitt asked casually from the side of the door, gesturing for Walpish to hand over his dirk. Walpish scowled at him, turned his head back to the kitchen but saw the soldiers rapidly bearing down on them from that direction

"It was quite nice," Walpish said mildly, flipping his dirk in his hand and handing it, hilt first, to the spymaster. "Thank you for waiting."

A chittering noise — like a rat laughing — came from the spymaster's shoulder.

"Yes, yes," Hewlitt spoke absently, turning his head to the right. "You've done your job, you may go."

There was a flash — like a spit of flame — and a burning smell as a small winged thing vanished.

Hewlitt looked at the soldier who held his sword to Walpish's throat and gestured for him to lower it. "You'll give us no trouble?"

"We don't have much choice," Walpish said, raising his hands, palm up.

Hewlitt's lips twitched in agreement. He turned to his soldiers. "Bring them back inside and upstairs. You know the drill."

#

The room the soldiers led Thomas Walpish and Skara Ningan to was one of the better-appointed suites on the third floor of the establishment. There was a bed in the other room, one which looked both well-stuffed and well-used. They were placed in seats around a large table — possibly a gaming table from the size of it.

Spymaster Hewlitt entered last. He shouted some garbled orders down the stairs, heard a satisfactory reply, and moved to seat himself opposite the two. A hand gesture put the soldiers on guard behind Skara and Thomas.

"I've sent for some food," Hewlitt told them in a mild voice.

"We ate already," Skara replied stiffly.

"Well," Hewlitt gave her a small smile, "I haven't."

"What do you want?" Walpish demanded.

"I'm a spymaster, what do you guess?" Hewlitt returned. A drudge stomped up the stairs and through the door, overladen with a tray of warm biscuits, a pot of tea, and three cups. Hewlitt nodded to her and waited until she had unloaded the tray before seeing her to the door and closing it firmly. He sat back down, reached into his tunic and grabbed something.

Skara felt a wave of *something* — magic.

"We can talk freely now," Hewlitt told them, raising the teapot and gesturing inquiringly toward the two prisoners. Thomas nodded and Skara joined him a moment later.

Several moments passed in silence as tea was served, honey added, sniffed and sipped cautiously by the two prisoners only after Hewlitt had conspicuously drunk from his.

Hewlitt waited a moment until they were settled, placed his tea cup precisely back in its saucer and looked up at them.

"So, loyal subjects to the king?"

Walpish shook his head. "He killed seven of my men."

"Yet here you are," Hewlitt said.

Walpish snorted. "Only because my color bearer liked my 'reward' better than I."

Hewlitt pursed his lips at that and turned to Skara Ningan. "And you? Lately in the employ of mage Vistos, were you not?"

"Until he tried to murder me," Skara said. She fumbled through her pockets and pulled out an object wrapped in felt. With a grimace, she passed it over to Hewlitt.

Hewlitt took it with all caution and unwrapped it carefully. The minute the darkened tooth was exposed he gasped and folded the felt back up over it, shoving it toward Skara. "How did you survive?"

Skara nodded toward Walpish. "He called on the —"

"Some things are not yours to learn," Thomas interrupted harshly.

"I see," he turned to Skara and said, "Would you — actually, both of you — do me the courtesy of opening your jaws wide enough that I may see inside?" He nodded to the guards standing behind the two prisoners.

Skara shrugged and complied. Hewlitt leaned forward and eyed her teeth carefully. "You have all your teeth." He turned to Walpish. The ex-cavalry officer fumed but opened his mouth, glaring at the spy. "As do you."

He nodded toward the felt bundle that held the darkened tooth. "How is it that you have this, then?"

"We told you," Skara replied heatedly, "we had help —"

"And that is enough for you to know," Walpish finished for her. He met Hewlitt's eyes. "Some things must remain secret."

Hewlitt leaned back in his chair, took his cup and drank a sip. He put the cup back down and nodded to himself. "Great help, indeed," Hewlitt said at last. "And because of this help…?"

"We swore an oath to see the evil-doer destroyed," Skara said. She made a face. "He gave me a sweet, wrapped in wax paper. Told me I deserved it."

"I think you are wise in not using his name," Hewlitt said. He patted his tunic. "Even my protections may not be enough if he is searching." He took another sip of his tea. "So you tried to remove this evil-doer…"

"And did not succeed, as you know," Walpish said. "We were examining alternatives when we… met you."

"What are you going to do to us?" Skara asked, not glancing at the guard behind her.

Peter Hewlitt eyed them and took another sip of his tea before putting the cup back in its saucer. He made a face and said, "This tea is really too bitter." He rose, dusted the front of his trousers, and waved at his guards. They were startled and Hewlitt, with a hint of pique, waved at them more urgently. "I've learned what I needed." He turned his eyes down to Skara. "Sweets, you say?"

Skara nodded.

"I have heard that two apprentice mages were given sweets just recently," Hewlitt said, holding the eyes of each of his prisoners in turn. "Afterwards, the two became much more… bloodthirsty. Relentless. Remorseless, even."

"Where are you going?" Thomas Walpish asked as Hewlitt reached the door.

"I'm going to ask about a friend's health," Hewlitt said. He turned back once more and met their eyes. "I wish you luck in your endeavors." A thin smile flashed across his face. "But, as I suspect the gods will be looking out for you, perhaps you don't need it."

#

Captain Martel knew this mansion well, it had belonged to rich people of the city and he'd been a guest on several occasions.

"Is this where the king is staying?" he asked as they entered one of the side entrances.

"Of course," Minnor replied with a wave of his hand. "But first, you must see my master."

"Lead on," Martel said. He glanced at Tirpin in warning as they started forward once more. The mage gave him a puzzled look which Martel returned angrily. They had not gone more than a few steps when Martel groaned realistically and lunged toward Tirpin, tripping him and sending him sprawling.

"Argh!" Martel cried, rolling over in agony and grabbing at his leg.

"Ow!" Tirpin cried in genuine pain. "You tripped me, you idiot!"

Guards rushed from all over and surrounded them.

Martel looked up at them and said feebly, "I had a cramp." He rose gently and hobbled. "We are here to see the king."

Beyond them, apprentice mage Minnor made a strangled sound. Tirpin glared at Martel but nodded and added his voice in agreement. "We have news."

One of the guards, surprised, jerked a thumb behind him. "He's in the throne room, back there."

#

"Captain Martel and mage Tirpin of the brig *Wasp*," King Markel's major domo announced as the two came hobbling into the throne room, Minnor following miserably behind them.

"What?" King Markel demanded. He turned Mannevy and speared him with a glare. "Why wasn't I told?"

"Captain Martel's ship had some trouble earlier, sire," Mannevy replied suavely. "I believe Commodore Evans sent a ship to their aid." He nodded toward the freshly-attired naval officer who turned in surprise as he spotted Martel and moved swiftly toward him, hands outstretched in greeting.

"Captain Martel!" he said enthusiastically. "Such an honor!"

Behind him, King Markel gave first minister Mannevy a wide-eyed look of rage. First minister Mannevy responded by raising his hands and waving them aside, cautioning for patience.

"And you are?" Captain Martel said.

"Commodore Robin Evans, sir, at your service," Commodore Evans replied. He turned back toward the king, started as he realized his position and bowed in recompense, before moving to stand beside Martel and put his front toward his monarch. "I'm given to hear that you and your gallant crew are the reason we are meeting *here* at this time."

"We had help," Captain Martel allowed. "A colonel of the cavalry and his hand-picked squad stormed the tower. Aided by a crossbowman of unprecedented skill." He glanced around. "Where are they?"

"They are presently attending their duties," first minister Mannevy replied smoothly. He allowed a smile to cross his face. "I'm sure you'll be meeting them presently."

Minnor found his voice. "I was bringing these gentlemen to my master when they found you, sire."

"Your master?" Commodore Evans regarded the apprentice with a frown. He turned to Mannevy. "Surely Captain Martel should be reporting to me, shouldn't he?"

"I understand that mage Vistos wanted to thank the captain and the mage personally, sir," Mannevy told him.

Evans raised an eyebrow in worry but let go of Captain Martel's arm. "Well, Captain, I suppose I shall see you later."

Captain Martel braced to attention and saluted the commodore.

"Please," Minnor almost-begged, "if you'll follow me."

With a final bow to the king who waved a hand in languid acknowledgement, Martel turned and followed the apprentice. Tirpin, after a penetrating glance toward the king — who avoided it — turned to follow.

"Your master," Captain Martel asked as they followed reluctantly after mage Minnor, "how long have you served him?"

"How long?" Minnor asked with a chuckle. "It seems like all my life."

"And do you like your master?" Tirpin asked, casting a glance toward Martel.

"He is great," Minnor said, chuckling once more. "The other night he taught me how to move sound."

"Move sound?" Tirpin asked, brows raised. "And why did you do that?"

"Oh," Minnor said, his chuckles growing louder, "so that no one would hear when they killed the prisoners."

"Killed the prisoners?" Martel asked. "Why did they kill prisoners?"

"The King ordered it," Minnor said with another raspy chuckle. He wheezed a bit, then added, "It was to avenge his wife." Another laugh. "Of course, he *killed* his wife but he blamed the Sorians, so he killed a thousand prisoners." Minnor laughed, a stuttering sound like a donkey's bray. "I like killing Sorians. They didn't make a sound."

#

"*Nous sommes trahis*," Jacques Martel muttered in the language of Soria: we are betrayed. Mage Tirpin twisted his head to meet the captain's eyes and nodded slowly. Martel added, "What do you suggest?"

Tirpin smiled, turned to the apprentice mage in front of them and said a word of power. With an evil grin he watched as the apprentice mage rose swiftly to the ceiling, banged his head hard against the ornamental moldings and went limp in unconsciousness.

"How long will that last?" Martel asked as they turned down a different corridor. One that led back toward the stables.

"All day, at least," Tirpin said, his eyes twinkling. "I use the same spell to raise ships."

#

Peter Hewlitt dispensed with his guards as soon as he entered the king's mansion. He moved with speed and grace, as was his custom. His mind raced as he walked. He turned down a corridor and stopped as in shock as he came face to face with Captain Martel and mage Tirpin. His eyes lifted and he spied the unconscious form of one Vistos' apprentice mages bobbing up against the roof as though desperate to float higher. His hand went instinctively to the weapon at his side but then he removed it. He walked forward and nodded politely at the two. "Gentlemen," he told them pleasantly, "so good to see you whole and hearty."

Tirpin made a magical gesture — the same one he'd used on the apprentice — and threw it at Hewlitt.

Hewlitt rocked back on his heels but did not rise up to the ceiling. Instead, he smiled at the mage, and said, "Thank you, I hadn't had a chance to collect that particular spell."

Tirpin's eyes widened and he moved to cast another spell but Captain Martel grabbed his arms and pulled them down.

"By your action, I can guess that you've learned that the king has decided to terminate your services," Hewlitt said.

"We were supposed to see mage Vistos," Martel said.

"Yes, the king recently has come to respect that mage's abilities in that regard," Hewlitt said. "I doubt you've caught all the news."

"Magic leaves traces," Tirpin said. He jerked a thumb up toward the floating mage. "What was done with him?"

"I do not know," Hewlitt admitted with a frown. "And that troubles me."

"It is dark magic," Tirpin said. "Foul."

Hewlitt nodded. "I believe it has something to do with poisoned sweets and corrupt teeth."

Tirpin's eyes widened and he looked back toward the floating apprentice, an expression of horror on his face. He nudged Martel. "We should leave, *now*." He turned his gaze to Hewlitt. "You would be wise to do so."

"I serve my king," Hewlitt replied levelly.

"Even when he serves another?" Tirpin demanded.

Hewlitt considered that but gave no answer.

"We are leaving," Martel said. "Stop us if you must. We mean you no harm."

Peter Hewlitt drew a knife so fast that neither could detect his motion. He raised his other hand in a warding gesture, a ring glowing visibly on his index finger. "I'm afraid —"

A blow from behind knocked him out and he toppled to the floor. Martel and Tirpin looked beyond the fallen body to see a slim shape emerge from the shadows of the corridor. Skara Ningan reached down and retrieved the bludgeon she'd thrown to knock out the spymaster. Another shadow emerged from the shadows.

"Colonel Walpish!" Captain Martel said in surprise. He glanced down to Skara. "And, unless I'm mistaken, our lady of the crossbow." He frowned. "Though you seem unarmed in that regard."

"What do you want?" Tirpin asked directly.

"The spymaster had caught us and released us," Walpish said. He pointed to the still form on the ground. "We wanted to know why." He glanced upwards to the apprentice floating in the distance. "And we heard about him." He motioned to Skara who frowned but turned back to Tirpin, withdrawing a felt-wrapped bundle.

"This was pulled from my mouth," Skara said, unwrapping the tooth and extending it toward Tirpin.

Tirpin glanced at it and then jerked back in alarm. "That tooth is evil!"

"So we were told," Walpish assured him dryly. He looked toward captain Martel. "Perhaps you haven't heard all the news: Skara here was set up to assassinate me. Set up by King Markel. Apparently he didn't want anyone to know about some of his… more recent dealings."

"I think we were intended to be dealt with similarly," Captain Martel replied with a frown. He pointed at the dark, gnarled shape that Skara held. "What has that to do with this?"

"Apparently it was to ensure that Skara did not live to tell tales," Walpish said. He nodded to the assassin who folded the tooth back up and put it carefully in a pocket in her jacket. "We were told —"

"By whom?" Tirpin interjected.

"We find that we cannot say their names," Skara told him. "They are gods."

"Must be," Tirpin said, "if you are still alive after having *that* in your mouth." He nodded toward her pocket and its hidden contents.

"We swore to destroy the originator," Walpish said.

"That won't work," Tirpin said with a frown.

"So we discovered," Skara said. "We were trying to learn how to deal with the mage —"

"Don't say his name," Tirpin warned with an upraised hand. He took a deep breath, glanced back toward the floating apprentice and waved his hand in a magic spell. The lad fell — hard — to the ground below. Tirpin moved toward the fallen, winded, apprentice, gesturing for the others to follow him. He knelt and glanced up to Skara and Walpish. "Do you have a glove?"

Skara nodded, pulling gloves out of her belt.

"Open his mouth — but carefully," Tirpin ordered. He moved to one side to allow her closer. Skara, with a frown toward Walpish, knelt, put on her gloves and pulled the slack jaw open.

Tirpin nodded and extended a finger near the opening, lighting one fingertip for more light.

"That's a useful skill," Walpish muttered in appreciation.

"I'll teach it to you," Tirpin said affably. He peered in and pointed with his lit fingertip. "There."

"Yes," Skara said, looking ill. "That's it."

"It is quite grown," Tirpin said. Captain Martel moved close to get a look for himself and back away hastily, swearing in horror. "As long as there are those teeth in people, your mage cannot be killed."

"What can we do?" Skara asked.

"What do you plan to do?" Tirpin demanded. He glanced toward Martel. "Our lives are not safe, here." The captain nodded. "I think we should leave."

"I have an idea," Martel said in agreement.

"The stables are back the way we came," Skara volunteered. She gestured to the unconscious apprentice. "What do we do about him?"

"If you can remove the tooth, he might recover," Tirpin said, frowning. "But he might die."

"Skara didn't," Thomas Walpish said.

"Only because she had help," Tirpin said. "I doubt you will get such aid twice." He pointed toward the still unconscious form of Hewlitt. "He has a magic ring. I suggest you relieve him of it."

"A ring by itself won't do much good," Walpish said as he moved back to Hewlitt and removed his ring. Quickly he searched the spymaster for other objects and put them in his pockets. He found a thin stiletto at the top of the spymaster's boot, a dirk at his side, and took them both, along with his belt which had a magical buckle, according to Tirpin.

Tirpin smiled at him and nodded. "Don't think I can't spot magic, colonel," Tirpin warned, pointing to the colonel's pockets. "You know enough already. Learning the ring's power will take training but you are well on your way." He stood up, dusting off his knees and frowning down at the apprentice. "Your best bet is to kill him."

"It didn't work with his master," Thomas said.

"Because he is the master," Tirpin replied. "As long as there are those with these teeth, he cannot be killed."

"But this one…?"

"He cannot be killed by regular means," Tirpin said. "His body will recover. Removing his head from his body may work."

"But?" Skara prompted.

"Fire is better," Tirpin said. He nodded toward Walpish and gestured for him to return to the apprentice. "Are you willing to do this?"

"In the name of the gods," Walpish said.

"You will attract attention the moment you do," Tirpin warned. He rose and put out a hand to Thomas, gesturing for the colonel to grab it. With a quick grimace, Thomas Walpish grabbed mage Tirpin's hand.

"Close your eyes, breath steady," Tirpin told him. "Now, think of fire. Let go my hand and think of fire at your fingertip."

Thomas Walpish frowned in concentration and opened his eyes, ready to admit defeat only to find mage Tirpin smiling at him and nodding to his finger. There was a small, bright light at the end of it. It didn't burn.

"If you want to destroy this body, you will have to will the fire large enough to encompass him," Tirpin said. He gestured to Martel. "But my price for teaching you is that you wait until you hear horses leaving the stables."

"You're going to escape?" Skara guessed.

"Trust me," Tirpin said with a smile, "when your friend releases his spell, that will be the *only* thing anyone will notice." He motioned for Skara to back up. "If he does it right, the whole wing will catch fire."

"And what of you?" Walpish said, glancing from Tirpin to Martel.

"I have a plan," Martel said. He made a face. "One which you do not want to know."

Walpish considered the air-captain's words and nodded slowly. He glanced toward Skara who gave him a worried look.

"You will be a murderer," she warned him.

"I have been for many years," Walpish said. He nodded toward the apprentice on the ground. "And you know what the tooth will do to him."

"Has done," Tirpin corrected. He nudged Martel on the shoulder and nodded toward the assassin and the cavalryman. "I wish you the luck of the gods."

"And you," Walpish replied. A moment later, Skara echoed his words.

"Be prepared to run," Tirpin warned as he turned and trotted briskly away, Martel on his heels.

As their footsteps faded down the corridor and then grew louder on the cobblestones outside, Skara turned to Walpish. "There will be others."

Walpish nodded.

"You will teach me these spells," she told him. "We will do this together."

Far outside, they heard the distant whinny of horses eager for work and then the sound of two horses galloping away over the cobblestones.

Thomas Walpish glanced at his fingertip, at the young lad with the poisoned tooth, and gestured for the fire to grow from his hand, engulfing the apprentice mage beneath him. The fire roared to his command and in an instant, the living mage was nothing more than a pile of ash. The flames spread to the walls, to the draperies and tapestries all along the corridor.

Walpish shoved into Skara, turned, grabbed her hand and started into a sprint. Together, the two of them fled the flames.

Wyvern's Creed

Book 15

Twin Soul series

Chapter One

"Settle down, settle down!" Mage Margen ordered the students in his classroom with mock ferocity. The students continued on chatting, waving hands, scribbling on books — hopefully theirs — and generally being young snots. "Really, I must say, settle down!"

Silence fell. Mage Margen's students had learned that a sign of his impending explosion was whenever he used the phrase "I must say." After that might come one more warning and then… well, one demonstration of the mage's anger had been enough. Fortunately, Frederick "Freddie" Fenniman was a good sort — and Margen had removed the horns almost immediately.

"Is everyone here?" Margen asked as he scanned the faces gazing at him expectantly.

"Everyone is here, sir," Barbara Garrett reported efficiently. Early on, Margen had decided against a formal roll-call, leaving the issue to the students. Barbara "Babs" Garrett had officiously elected herself class spokeswoman. She had also appointed Matthew "Matt" Evans as her second — in the improbable case that she might fall ill. Margen privately suspected that the "appointment" had more to do with Miss Garrett's affection for the lad, clearly she had arranged that she would be the center of his attention, much to the sorrow of Miss Bree Emer.

Mage Margen was officially immune to class politics. Secretly, he found them a source of fascination and amazement — that humans, even those this young, could consider their affections and desires to be *so* important! Margen was interested in knowledge, in learning, in — well, acquiring a lot of wealth by teaching youngsters the magical arts was attractive, his more avaricious self admitted — but there was a great deal of satisfaction in not just promulgating the arts but in seeing their study *grow*. So while he mostly didn't concern himself with attendance, he knew full well that his class held twenty students, as did the other class he taught on alternate days — with both classes combined for practical work on Fridays.

"Today is the first day of the week," Mage Margen declared. "So we start the week by —" he glanced at all the eyes turned toward him "— what?"

"We praise our gods, sir," Freddie Fennimore piped up quickly. Babs Garrett glared at him as she'd raised her hand and he hadn't.

"Ametza, goddess of the sea, the rivers, the waters from the skies, we praise you," Bree Emer chimed up. Her hands were clasped in front of her and her expression worshipful.

"Geros, god of the earth, I praise you," Freddie Fennimore declared loudly — more loudly than the worshipful Bree.

"You can't praise *him*," Bree said with a disgusted look. "This land is Ametza's and we are her subjects."

"What about fire, then?" Babs Garrett snapped back, cupping a respectable ball of flame in her hands.

Bree gave a snort and shot a fistful of damp air at Babs, extinguishing the flame and causing the other girl to shriek in anger.

"Students!" Mage Margen said. His heart wasn't in it, though, and they could tell, he knew. Bree's water ball had been noticeably larger than her first attempt at the beginning of this new semester, and Babs' fireball had been quite respectable. Freddie hadn't — fortunately

— tried any earth magic which was just as well, as it had taken a good three days to restore all the books to the shelves after his rumblings. Matt Evans was enjoying the show and not tempted to add air to the excitement. But others in the class were considering their options and that could get —

"Why aren't you worshipping me?" A voice bellowed suddenly outside the classroom door. There was a loud splash and the door burst open, propelled by a tall wave of water. Goddess Ametza followed on the waters, her eyes glaring at Mage Margen. The children shrieked and raced to the far side of the room, eyes wide with terror — all except Bree Emer who jumped on top of her desk and hailed the sea goddess.

"I worship you, great goddess!" Bree cried, dropping with a splash onto the water spreading on the floor and kneeling without a thought to what the water would do to her expensive garb.

Ametza jerked her head towards the girl, saw her obeisance and nodded curtly. She turned immediately toward Mage Margen. "Aren't you a mage of this court?"

"Indeed, great goddess, I have that pleasure," Margen replied. "I have studied your ways for many a year." He waved a hand and produced a fine wine-red ball of liquid in front of him. "If I may offer you a libation?"

Ametza waved her hands irritably and the ball of wine splashed all over the mage, dripping down his fine clothes.

Mage Margen bowed his head and swept his hands in another spell, wiping the liquid off his outfit and making it disappear.

"I am the goddess here!" Ametza snapped, turning back to the students. "How come they are not being taught to fear me? How come they learn other arts than those of —" She broke off, her eyes going wide. In an instant she was frozen, encased in a thin sheet of solid ice.

The temperature of the room plummeted and the water on the ground froze solid. Mist appeared, as through the doors a tall, dark god stomped into view. He spied Ametza and called out, "Darling, I'm home!"

"Did you miss me?" the god asked the frozen goddess, his expression clouded with anger. He snapped his fingers and the ice around Ametza disappeared. He waved a hand and she could move again. "Dear, why don't you introduce me?"

Ametza's expression flashed through a range of emotions. Finally, she turned to him with a look of delight. "Arolan! It's so good to see you again! You know how much I've missed —" Arolan waved his finger and she froze once more.

"I know exactly how much you've missed me," Arolan told her icily. "Two hundred years. For two hundred years I was imprisoned —" he broke off, turning to the students and then to Margen. "How much do you know?"

"I would — and I'm sure my students would — be delighted to hear all that you would like to tell us, great god," Margen said with a low bow. Not being turned to ice, he raised his head and continued, "I must confess that for all my life I've wondered about you." He made a face. "I decided as a youth that you had more important things on your mind than this kingdom and its people."

"I do, and I did," Arolan admitted. He made a rueful grimace. "But I might have attended to you more —" he turned a frosty gaze to the sea goddess "— had my wife not arranged my internment in the bitter north!"

He waved a hand and let his goddess wife thaw long enough to change expression until, finding it not to his liking, he froze her again with her mouth open, words unspoken. He turned to glare at Bree Emer and started to wave his hand but Margen interrupted him.

"If it pleases you, great god, you might want to know that your existence was kept a secret from those in this kingdom," Margen spoke hastily, moving to interpose himself between the sea god and the young girl. "Miss Emer has not heard one single word of your existence."

Arolan's expression changed and he nodded thanks to the mage. He said to the girl, "You are a mage of water?"

"I am, great god," Bree said stoutly. "And if you are a god of water and the sea, I should like to make your acquaintance."

Margen hissed with an indrawn breath. "Great god Arolan, please take her words with some salt. She is young and means no more than that of a youth by them."

Arolan shot the mage an amused look and turned back to Bree. "I should be glad to have your respect and kindness, small water one."

Bree beamed at him and curtsied. Arolan turned to the other children in the room and identified three more water mages. They bowed to him and approached at his request. He nodded to other students genially but without the same warmth.

"Take your seats and I will tell you a tale," Arolan said, gesturing to the chairs. He flicked a finger and the floor was dry once more. The student mages rushed to take their seats.

"Arolan, it might be best if they arranged them in a circle, so that all could see and hear your words," Margen suggested diffidently.

"Make it so," Arolan said with an indulgent nod.

"Actually, if you don't object, great god, our Frederick Fennimore has skill with earth and our Master Evans with air," Margen said. "If it pleases you, they can do the honors."

Freddie and Matt looked at their master goggle-eyed. When Arolan nodded acceptance, Margen gestured them to action.

The floor groaned and the air whistled but in short order the desks and chairs were re-arranged in a loose — very loose, Margen noted — circle.

"We shall practice this at a later time," Margen told the two boys in a dry tone.

"It suffices," Arolan said, gesturing and sending his frozen bride to the side of the room. He made another gesture and a chair — it looked like diamond but was probably ice — appeared. He sat and smiled in a big circle to the students.

"This tale begins two hundred years ago," Arolan said. "Perhaps more." His lips quirked and he nodded. "Yes, certainly more. But that is not a matter for your ears." He took a breath. "As you may not know, I am the god of the sea, the rivers, the waters, of clouds, of snow, and I hold affinity for all that flows." He glanced at Margen. "A glass of wine would not be amiss, mage."

Margen smiled and sketched a spell in the air, sending a silver goblet filled with red liquid toward the sea god. Arolan caught it and sniffed. He looked to the mage. "It is quite good."

"From my cellar," Margen admitted with a certain amount of pleasure.

Arolan took another sip and placed the goblet on the arm of his throne chair.

"My kingdom is everywhere," Arolan said. "I rule over the denizens of the deep most of all." He nodded toward the frozen goddess. "My mate, Ametza, sometimes prefers the coastline and the land — particularly wet land." He sighed. "It is in the nature of all thinking creatures to think. And oftentimes, they think differently."

"Did you fight?" Babs asked, her eyes sidling toward Bree Emer and back quickly.

The sea god gave the young girl a sharp look. He nodded. "We did." His lips twitched. "Often and loudly."

"The great gales and hurricanes are often taken of signs of strife amongst the water gods," Margen instructed.

"And sometimes we make them because they're pretty," Arolan added drolly. He returned to his tale. "Under my care are many great creatures. Some are good, some bad, some just are." He paused. "What do you know of the twin souls?"

Matt Evans' hand shot up just before Babs Garrett's. She looked at him in surprise but he waved his hand determinedly.

"When they raise their hands, great god, they are begging your attention," Margen explained.

Arolan laughed. A deep, rumbling laugh that was both joyful and threatening. "I know children, mage, and learning." He pointed to Evans. "Yes, young master?"

"Matthew Evans, great god," Matt said by way of introduction. "Just recently there was a wyvern here."

"And a dragon!" Babs interjected.

"There was?" Arolan said. He nodded toward Freddie Fennimore. "Tell me more."

"S-she was an albino girl," Freddie said, awed to be talking with a god. "Her lover pierced her heart and she fell over the cliffs and then —"

"She turned into a beautiful wyvern!" Babs exclaimed. "White and gold, and just beautiful."

"She flew off north," Freddie finished, glaring at Babs in objection to her interruption.

"Ah, yes," Arolan said. "I met her."

"You did?" Margen said, unable to contain himself. "The girl was the daughter of Rabel —"

"I know," Arolan said. Margen shut his mouth with a snap. The sea god turned his blue-green eyes on his goddess wife for a moment then turned back to the class. "A twin soul is magic. A twin soul has two halves — magical and mortal."

"Human," Babs guessed.

"Couldn't they be zwerg, too, couldn't they?" Freddie Fennimore asked.

"Are there others, great god, besides —" Babs started to ask.

"Mer-people, you ninny!" Bree Emer snapped. She turned to Arolan imploringly. The god smiled at her. Bree turned to Babs with a victorious look.

"Many of the twin souls," Arolan continued in a tone that made it clear he was not used to — nor respectful of — interruptions, "are associated with one god in particular." He glanced around at the faces staring at him. "Can you guess who?"

"You?" Bree said breathlessly.

"No," Arolan said. "My people are, as you say, the people of the waters and of the sea. The mer-people." He took another sip from his glass and waved it toward mage Margen in acknowledgement of its superior heritage. He returned the glass to its place and raised an eyebrow to the students. "Do you know who is the god of the dragons, wyverns, and drakes?"

A nervous chirp came from somewhere in the room and Margen glared toward it but the others paid no attention, rapt at the sea god's words.

A small child's hand raised slowly. All the others turned toward her in annoyance.

"Put your hand down, Thane!" Babs growled.

"It's Bethany," the little girl said with a lisp.

"It's Thane, unless —" Babs said threateningly.

"Miss Bethany, please tell us what you have to say," Arolan cut across the other girl. Babs shut her mouth with a frightened squeak.

"Ophidian," Bethany 'Thane' Murray said stoutly. She shot a glance toward Babs. "*Some* of us know our gods."

Arolan gave the little girl — she couldn't have been more than seven — a nod and a smile.

"Indeed," Aroland said. "Ophidian is the god of change, of chances, of trickery."

"He was betrayed," Bethany said. She glared at Arolan and then at Ametza. "I was told that the gods betrayed him and there was a great battle."

"Not all gods betrayed him," Arolan said. "And some came to his aid when they realized the virtue of his cause."

"What cause?" Matt Evans asked. Hastily, he added, "If it pleases you, great god."

"Ophidian believed that humans and other thinking creatures deserved more than the gods were giving them," Arolan said with a distant look in his eyes. He raised his head and smiled at the children. "Along with the gift of fire, and of learning, he believed that humans, zwerg, and the others should be able to do magic."

"*Ophidian* did that?" Freddie Fennimore cried in surprise.

"He did," Arolan said. "And I came to agree with him." He waved a hand, dismissing the issue. "And when the gods fought, when he was injured, or when he cried…" he nodded toward Bethany expectantly.

"He created the dragons and the wyverns and the drakes," Bethany said in a small voice. She raised her head and met the sea god's eyes, adding conspiratorially, "But it's supposed to be a secret."

"And we —" Arolan waved his hand around the room, including everyone, "— will honor that." He smiled at Bethany who accepted this pronouncement with a nod. "All of his creatures are very powerful —"

"As powerful as a storm, great god?" Bree asked without fear.

"Some are," Arolan admitted. He raised a hand in entreaty. "But I will not be able to tell my tale, children, if you keep asking questions."

"Mage Margen says that questions are how we learn," Babs replied, nodding toward the mage. Margen ducked his head in rueful acknowledgement, saying, "But I've also said that you can't learn anything if you don't keep quiet."

Babs nodded reluctantly.

"One of Ophidian's get fell into the sea and became a sea serpent," Arolan explained. "She was a gentle creature and found a twin soul early. For many thousands of years —" he ignored the gasps of astonishment from the children "— they lived in harmony. When her first twin soul died, she found another and they lived for many thousands of years more.

"But one day that twin soul died," Arolan said. "Why, we do not know. But I suspect treachery." He frowned at the frozen form of Ametza. He turned back to the students. "Pallas — the serpent — lost her senses and attacked everything." He frowned for a moment, adding, "She had great power. She attacked many things before I became aware —"

"How, great god?" little Bethany asked in a small, respectful voice.

"A seaman — a group of seamen — called to me and begged me upon their lives to aid them," Arolan replied. "And so I took Pallas. Her power was so great in the sea so I had to take her from it lest… well, lest terrible things happen.

"The only safe place was far inland," Arolan said. "I took her to the frozen north and there I held her." He made a face. "But her magic was such that I could not let her go." He shook his head in memory. "And together we froze, solid."

The children gasped.

"But your wife!" Bree cried, pointing to Ametza. "Didn't she help?"

Arolan shook his head. "Remember, little Bree, sometimes my wife and I quarrel." The room grew very quiet. Bree eyed the frozen sea goddess thoughtfully.

"How did you get free?" Matt Evans asked.

Arolan smiled. "Those seamen?" He asked. The others nodded in recollection. "One of them became captain of an airship —"

"The *Spite?*" Matt asked breathlessly.

Arolan smiled. "The very same," he agreed. "And Captain Ford and his crew showered me with treasure and bowed to me and… I was freed."

"But what about the serpent?" Bethany asked. "Was she freed, too?"

"She was," Arolan admitted. "And still insane. Captain Ford and the others went after her —"

"But what about you, great god?" Bree asked. "Couldn't you —?"

"I could help but no more," Arolan said. "Such things are affairs of the gods and, in the case of twin souls, fall under the protection of Ophidian or the other twin soul gods."

"There are more?" Matt Evans asked.

"There are," Arolan said.

"What happened to the *Spite* and Captain Ford?" Matt asked.

"*Spite* was destroyed by the wyvern it first attacked," Arolan said, sounding pleased.

"And Captain Ford?" Bree asked in a small voice.

"He fulfilled his oath to me," Arolan said. He made a face, remembering. "He died valiantly in my name."

"And the serpent?"

"The serpent found a twin soul," Arolan said. His lips twitched. "They are… adjusting to each other."

"Can a mage become a twin soul?" Bree asked wistfully. The others all nodded their eagerness to know the answer.

"Yes, of course," Arolan said. "But now, children, you know what has become of me." He pointed toward Ametza. "She had a great hand in it." He turned back to the class. "So I ask you, what should I do with the sea goddess?"

"Do you love her?" Babs asked immediately. Arolan turned to her in surprise. She persisted. "Do you?"

Slowly, Arolan nodded.

"So, if you love her, you can forgive her," Babs said as if this were obvious. She glanced meaningfully to Matt Evans who turned pink.

"And if she betrays me again?" Arolan asked.

"She has in the past," Mage Margen spoke up. Arolan twisted his gaze to the mage. Margen shrugged. "Unless the histories are wrong, that is."

"They are not wrong," Arolan admitted ruefully.

"Perhaps you might keep her frozen for a while," Bethany suggested. Arolan turned toward her, with a raised brow. "Just to let her understand what it was like for you."

"Or you could just thaw her out and kiss her," Bree said. The rest of the class twittered with delight.

Arolan turned to wag a finger at Bethany. "You have chosen your god wisely, little one."

Bethany beamed at the godly praise.

"Kiss her, kiss her!" the class began chanting.

"Students!" Mage Margen barked but they knew his heart wasn't in it. "It's not wise to —"

Arolan waved his worry away, stood up from his ice throne, grabbing the cup as the throne vanished and turned toward the frozen form of his wife.

Arolan stepped toward Ametza and broke the spell. She had just time to open her mouth in startlement before the sea god kissed her. She wrapped her arms around him in joy.

The class cheered. Arolan waved a hand behind his back in thanks — and then the two gods were gone.

There was a long moment of silence. Finally, Margen cleared his throat. "Well, I think we can safely say that we have learned a lot," he said to his students. "Freddie, Matt, please rearrange the classroom and then I think we can call it a day."

#

Peter Hewlitt woke up on a bed of straw. And it was not clean straw. With an irritated sigh, he rolled off a pile of manure that had plastered itself to his head. The movement nearly caused him to vomit. His head was in agony.

He remembered, dimly, talking with Captain Martel and Mage Tirpin. And then someone had hit him from behind. That explained the headache.

He rolled to one side and — gingerly — raised himself into a squat. His head protested every movement. He was also sore in far too many places. He looked down at his boots and saw that the backs and heels were scuffed. Someone had dragged him here.

There was a smell of smoke and ash in the air. He dimly heard voices talking in the distance — they were not anxious.

Hewlitt felt around for his things. His stiletto was in its sheath. His rings were — he frowned. Someone had used his spell ring. Used and returned it to him.

Hewlitt's lips twitched. That someone had been smart enough to guess that Hewlitt — the king's spymaster — would be able to track any item stolen from him. He had a good guess as to who had 'borrowed' his magic ring.

He tensed his muscles and rose to his full height. Immediately his stomach clenched in protest and he had to fight to keep himself upright. After a moment, he regained his composure and — slowly — started from the stables.

Whoever had assaulted him — and he had a good guess — had decided to let him live. *Well, turnabout is fair play.*

#

Mage Margen knew that he had visitors the minute he approached the door to his rooms. And he knew that at least one of the visitors could do magic, so he was prepared when he entered.

He was not prepared to find the room empty. The windows were open from the inside and a light breeze filled the room. Margen grunted and closed the windows with a simple puff of magic.

"Are they really gone?" Margen asked the room. A soft chitter agreed with him. A shape darted from the ceiling, alighted briefly on his table, and flew off again, *through* not out of the window. Margen raised an eyebrow in calculation and decided against recalling his messenger. For the messenger had alighted next to a velvet covered item.

Margen moved cautiously to his desk, eyeing the velvet covered item with ill-disguised unease. He traced a spell over it and frowned when the air turned dark around the velvet.

"What do you know of this?" Margen called *through* the window. A distant chirp came back to him. "Come here, I haven't got all day." Margen sent a spell along encouragingly.

Margen said a rude word and made another spell over the object. The air turned darker but glowed purple: poison.

"Well, I'd guessed as much," Margen said to himself. He glanced toward the window once more. "Really, if I have to ask you again —"

The small creature flew *through* the window and landed at the edge of his desk, tilting its head up to him and chirping in inquiry.

"Better," Margen said. He frowned at the velvet object. "Do you know what this is?"

The small creature gave a frightened squawk and soared upwards, into the molding on the ceiling, peering back down toward the object with wide eyes, chittering nervously to itself.

Margen eyed the creature thoughtfully then moved around to sit at his desk. The creature chirped in warning.

"It would be much better if you could talk, you know," Margen muttered as he opened one of his drawers and pulled out a set of instruments. He picked up a light silver probe and gently used it to lift up the flaps of the velvet and reveal the object inside. When he saw it he dropped back into his chair in a giant huff, his eyes troubled. "By all the gods!"

The creature in the ceiling chirped in agreement.

"Where did you get this?" Margen demanded. The flying creature chirped in denial: he didn't get it. Margen nodded to himself. "Did you see who left it?"

The creature chirped: it had.

"Can you find them again?" Margen asked.

The creature chirped, dropped from the ceiling and butted the double doors with its tail.

"What, they're outside?" Margen said, rising from his chair and preparing a spell with his hands.

"May we come in?" a muffled voice — a woman's — came through the door.

"You've been in once already," Margen said with a sniff.

The door opened and two people entered, closing the door behind them as quickly as they'd entered. One — a man — stood with his back to the door. The other — the woman — pulled back her hood to expose her face.

"You're the one Vistos trained," Margen said immediately. "The archer."

"Crossbow," Skara Ningan corrected quickly. She glanced up to the ceiling and frowned when she spotted the creature hiding against the molding. "Is that yours?"

"He's auditioning for the role," Margen replied dryly. The creature chirped.

"I've never seen a —" the man spoke up from where he stood.

"It's best not to speak the name," Margen interrupted quickly. "While I have no ill will toward their master, there are many who find them… troubling."

"And there are some who say that they're a delicacy," the man said.

Margen turned to him, brows drawn down. "I've heard your voice before."

"I once served the king," the man admitted.

"What changed?" Margen asked in surprise. He could imagine many reasons why someone might stop supporting King Markel but he was certain there were many more beyond his consideration.

"I did," the woman replied with a frown.

"You saw what we left," the man said, nodding to the desk.

"It is a work of evil," Margen said with a hard tone.

"We know who made it," the man told him.

"It was in a jaw, it controlled the person… how did they die?" Margen asked.

"I didn't," the woman said. She waved a hand toward the man. "He saved me."

"I had help," the man admitted. "Help I cannot call upon again."

Margen gave him a probing look and nodded. "You called on the gods, and they answered." He saw the man's reaction and smiled to himself. "You were both very foolish and very brave." He waved a hand and two chairs appeared at his desk. He waved another and the lock in the double doors clicked shut. With another gesture, the curtains flew on their rails, covering the windows. He gestured to the lamps and they burst into light.

"Come, sit," he said. "It has been an eventful day already; I suppose I should have expected more." When the two stayed where they were, he changed his tone. "I am not the sort to repeat his requests twice."

The woman glanced at the man. With an unspoken agreement, the two moved and took the seats.

A silver tray and a steaming pot of tea appeared on the desk, cups and saucers slid opposite the chairs. Margen raised the steaming pot and hovered it over the woman's cup. "Some tea?"

#

"There was a fire," First minister Mannevy explained to Peter Hewlitt when the two met in Mannevy's office some time later. "I'm surprised you weren't there."

"I may have been," Hewlitt replied, "but I was dragged to safety." He raised an eyebrow. "No one hurt, I hope?"

"We're not sure," Mannevy said. "Usually such questions are answered by you, not asked."

Hewlitt grimaced as the barb hit home. "Was it bad?"

"One of the corridors was destroyed but the guards got the blaze under control soon enough," Mannevy told him. "Mage Vistos was most upset."

"The mage? Why?"

"Apparently the fire was set by magic, can you imagine?" Mannevy said his eyes bright as he rested them on the spymaster. "Vistos said the magic was ring-born and he would find the culprit." Mannevy sniffed. "He changed his tune, of course."

"He did?"

"When they poked through the ashes, later," Mannevy said, delighted to be trolling information to the man who was supposed to know all.

"And what did they find in the ashes?"

"Nothing at all," Mannevy said, his lips twitching. "Nothing, except one blackened tooth. A molar, I believe."

Peter Hewlitt's shivered as a memory came back to him. He rose to his feet in one quick move, drew his stiletto and darted around Mannevy's desk to press the tip against the first minister's throat. "I hate to importune, my lord, but would you please open your mouth? Wide?"

Mannevy, eyes bulging, found himself doing so instinctively. Hewlitt pressed the tip of his stiletto against Mannevy's tongue, lowering it to his jaw. He grabbed the lamp on the minister's desk with his other hand and brought it up close. He stood there for a long while, staring intently into the first minister's mouth before he released his hold on the stiletto and stood back.

"What — why — how dare you!" Mannevy spluttered in shock and anger.

"I had to know," Hewlitt said. He pulled his ring from his pocket, slipped it on quickly and made a warding gesture. The ring flared. "We are safe now," he told Mannevy.

"From what?" Mannevy gasped.

Hewlitt smiled. "You haven't been offered any sweets recently, have you, my lord?"

Mannevy's eyes widened. He reached into his pocket and pulled forth a paper-wrapped object. He put it on the desk, eyeing the spymaster fearfully.

"Mage Vistos gave it to you, didn't he?"

Mannevy grew very pale. Slowly, he nodded.

#

"I'm to take command?" Lieutenant Walter Fawcett said with a gasp of surprise. "Really?"

"My orders come direct from the King," the messenger told him. He had come aboard and asked Fawcett to accompany him to the captain's quarters. Inside, he gave the startled officer his news. He pulled out a notebook and hastily charged his quill. "Captain Martel and Mage Tirpin have been found guilty of treason." He passed the notebook over to the startled lieutenant. "Sign here, please."

Fawcett signed. The messenger handed him another roll of parchment and indicated another entry in his ledger. "And here."

"What's this?" Fawcett asked.

"That's your orders, sir," the messenger said. "I'm told you're to open them as soon as you're provisioned."

"But… I'm not sure my mages —" Fawcett cut himself off. He had a chance at *command!* He was not going to lose it with prevarications. He signed.

"I'll take my leave, sir," the messenger said. He gave Facwett a quick nod and added, "Good luck to you, sir!"

"Thank you!" Fawcett said heartily. The messenger headed back down the corridor and up the stairway. Fawcett barely heard his footsteps. He turned to read the parchment. It was signed by King Markel's first minister. Fawcett frowned: that was odd. He'd never got orders from the first minister before. *Well, perhaps it was different with ships' captains.*

He scanned the orders quickly and re-read them immediately. He took a deep breath, as if expecting the words to change. Then he went to the captain's cabinet. It was locked.

"Officer of the watch!" Fawcett bellowed.

"Sir?" the voice came back dimly. He recognized Midshipman Bastien.

"Send the carpenter to the captain's cabin with his tools!" Fawcett shouted.

"Aye, sir!"

Chapter Two

"This bloody snow!" General Georgos Gergen swore as he stomped on the thick white layer beneath him to warm up his feet. "How long until we have the tent up?"

"Not long, sir," Ensign Fetter replied, glancing over to the boiling group of soldiers who were working as fast as they could to erect the general's quarters for the evening. "Another ten minutes, I'd say."

"It's deuced cold out," General Ivar Gideon agreed with a frown. He glanced toward his commander. "I'm not quite sure we expected this when we laid our plans."

"We're still moving just fine," Gergen told him in a voice that carried a hint of steel in it.

"Oh, I didn't say that, sir!" Gideon said. "It's just that the men need more food for this weather."

"To say nothing of the horses and fodder," Gergen agreed glumly. He glanced up at the dark sky, filled with steadily falling white flakes. "I don't see how any ship — particularly an *airship* can find us in this weather."

"We're good for another two days at least, aren't we?" General Gideon asked.

"Provided Lewis' horses don't eat up all their hay," Gergen grumbled.

"If worse comes to worst, we could eat the horses," Gideon said in a low voice

General Gergen turned to eye him. Slowly, he nodded. "There is that."

#

Acting-Captain Fawcett adjusted his uniform as best he could and proceeded up the gangplank to the *Victory*. His carpenter had provided him with a complete set of keys for all locked rooms on the ship and he'd taken the opportunity to explore the ship from bottom to top. He'd just completed his inspection when a messenger arrived with his invitation to the commodore's ship, *Victory*. The side party had already been mustered and Fawcett kept his expression stern as he was piped aboard.

"*Wasp*, boarding!" the officer of the watch called. The side party came to attention and Fawcett returned their salutes sharply.

"Lieutenant Melroy," the officer introduced himself. "The commodore is below, expecting you, sir." He nodded toward an ensign who was waiting expectantly. "Fermoy will take you."

"Thank you," Fawcett replied, nodding to the ensign to lead off.

They made their way down the wide stairway and turned toward the stern. A moment later told the marine sentry, "Captain Fawcett to see the commodore."

"He's been expecting you, sir," the marine replied, knocking on the door and announcing his presence.

"Come in, come in!' Commodore Evans called cheerfully. Fawcett entered and paused in surprise. The room was full. Several captains were already seated at the long table. Commodore Evans was standing at the far end and waved Fawcett to the last seat, the one at the other end of the table. "We were just waiting for you!"

"I understand that you were instrumental in capturing this city," another captain said, "you must tell us all!"

"Actually, sir —"

"That's Captain Wright of the *Eagle*, the lout," Commodore Evans boomed with mock ferociousness. He went around the table introducing all the captains of the *Vanguard, Surprise, Conqueror,* and *Falcon*. "But he's quite right, you *must* tell us all!"

"Sir, as you know, I have just this day come to command," Fawcett replied diffidently.

"But you were *there*, surely!" Captain Wright replied. Fawcett nodded. "So… enlighten us!"

Fawcett took a deep breath and began, "Our first problem was getting over the Silver Mountains…"

#

"So, captain, you have your orders," Commodore Evans said as he and Fawcett remained behind after the other captains returned to their ships. "How soon can you depart?"

"My mate was seeing to the loading of the forage when I left, sir," Fawcett replied. "I should hope that all is ready now."

"Very well," Evans said. "I'll expect you to take 'air' upon your return. If you run into any difficulties, please alert me."

"Of course, sir," Fawcett replied, saluting. Evans smiled and clapped him on the shoulder. "I'm sure you'll do fine, captain."

#

"*Where* are the mages?" Captain Fawcett asked his distraught first mate when he received the news.

"We don't know, sir," Midshipman Bastien replied miserably. "I was too busy getting the forage aboard. When I sent the mechanic to find them… they were gone."

"I see," Fawcett said, more to give him more time to think than anything else. "Well, we can't lift ship without mages." His insides turned to ice. "I'll have to tell the Commodore —"

"Ahoy the ship!" a voice called from the shore. Fawcett turned to see the two apprentice mages leaning against each other and laughing hysterically. The voice belonged to another person, an older man. "Are these two yours?"

"Yes, they are, thank you!" Fawcett called back in relief.

"Well, they'll cost you two pounds six shillings," the man said. "They said you'd pay."

It took Fawcett a few moments to discover that the man was an innkeeper and the two mages had taken themselves off to get roaring drunk — a task at which they had succeeded amazingly well.

"Mr. Sedgewick," Fawcett said to the ship's Master-at-Arms after the purser had handed over the money, "these two need to be fit for duty."

Sedgewick gave him a piratical smile.

"Don't kill them or render them useless," Fawcett warned the man.

"Aye sir," Sedgewick said. "How soon will you need them?"

"James," Fawcett said, turning to the stern of the ship to catch the attention of the ship's mechanic, "how soon can you raise steam?"

"The stokers are on it now, sir," James Sawyer returned amiably. He paused, considering the matter. "Five minutes, ten at the most."

Fawcett turned back to Sedgewick. "You have five minutes."

Sedgewick gave him an evil grin and bounded down the gangplank. He told the innkeeper, "Here I'll take those two!"

"Mister-mister Sedgewick, sir," the taller of the two apprentice mages said, "I'm glad to see you."

"W-we're drunk!" the other mage announced unnecessarily.

"Not for long," Sedgewick promised, grabbing the two by the scruffs of their necks and propelling them toward the edge of the pier. "Do you know how to swim?"

"No," the first mage, Marsters, said with a sickly grin.

"You'll learn," Sedgewick said, pushing the two drunk mages off the pier and into the freezing harbor water below.

He was right. In moments the two mages, much worse for the wear but remarkably sober, were bobbing in the water and spluttering in astonishment.

"Lower a rope," Sedgewick called. "Heave them up."

Three minutes later, two very wet, very bedraggled, and very miserable mages reported to their captain.

"What happened to Martel?" Marsters asked groggily.

"And Tirpin?" Horace Warren asked, casting an eye about the deck nervously. "He's not gone, is he?"

"He is," Fawcett said. "He and Captain Martel were charged with treason." He let that sink in. "I am now in command of this ship and you are my mages."

"Oh, thank the gods!" Horace Warren said fervently. He nudged Marsters on the shoulder, "Did you hear that? Our prayers have been answered!"

"That's why we got drunk, sir," Marsters admitted. "We were trying to steal up our courage to —"

"It doesn't matter," Warren interjected, glowering at his fellow mage. He turned to the captain. "What do you need us to do?"

"We're going to find the cavalry and drop them fodder," Fawcett told them. "It's deep winter where they are —" it was deep winter here, too, Fawcett noted, seeing the blue lips on the two mages "— and the horses have no food." He tightened his lips and then jerked his head toward the steaming boiler near the stern. "Can you do your spells from there? You could warm up."

The two mages nodded gratefully and sprinted toward that source of warmth.

"Mr. Bastien!" Fawcett roared. "Get some towels and blankets for the mages, we can't have them freezing to death."

"Aye, sir," Bastien replied, quickly issuing orders to a small knot of airmen.

"Bosun!" Fawcett shouted.

"Sir!"

"Stand men by the moorings, prepare to cast off," Fawcett ordered.

"Aye sir."

Fawcett walked back toward the mages who were hovering, hands outstretched by the warmth of the boiler. "We're going to need to turn her nose around and head out of the harbor," Fawcett said to them.

"I can do that sir," Warren offered. "My magic's more wind than fire."

"I'll need you to turn the ship about then," Fawcett said.

"Say the word, sir," Warren replied, sounding much more sober, warmer, and far more cheerful than Fawcett had ever seen him. Come to think of it, both apprentice mages had seemed more nervous than mice in the presence of mage Tirpin. Fawcett could understand: the mage had been rude and almost insolent to *him* on a number of occasions, and he'd often heard him abuse his two apprentices.

Fawcett nodded in response to Warren and turned to the bosun. "Cast off forward lines!"

"Forrard lines, aye sir!" the bosun called back. A moment later, he called, "Forrard lines free."

"Can you start turning our bow?" Fawcett said.

"It'll be slow at first, sir," Warren warned. Fawcett nodded and then turned as the men at the bow of the ship started gabbling to themselves. He could see the rigging shake as if in a wind and saw that the bow was turning away from the dock.

"Stand by stern lines!" Fawcett ordered. He gauged the speed of their yawing turn from the pier and called, "Release stern lines!" A moment later he added, "Dip our colours to the harbormaster." It was a courtesy only: as a military ship *Wasp* had precedence over all traffic in the harbor; but it was not a bad idea to warn the harbormaster of their actions. Fawcett had no idea where the harbormaster's office was or if, indeed, there even *was* one. "Dip our colors to the flag," Fawcett ordered a moment later, turning his gaze toward Commodore Evans' *Victory*. He was pleased to see the frigate's colors dip in acknowledgement.

"Signal from the flag, sir!" Ensign Bastien called.

"I see it," Fawcett said. He read the colors and shapes of the flags: *Carry on*. "Bosun, log that the flag has ordered us to carry on." The bosun grunted in the distance, turned a gimlet eye turned his appointed scribe and then turned back to his duties.

Wasp had now turned one hundred and eighty degrees and was facing toward the harbor entrance.

"I can't give us much speed, sir, but I give us enough to steer by at least," Warren said, waving toward the stern of the ship and uttering some spell. A moment later, Fawcett had to grab at his hat as the wind rushed against them.

"I understand that lifting a ship from the water is harder than just lifting a ship," Fawcett said.

Marsters nodded and smiled at him. "Horace and I can manage, sir."

Fawcett nodded at him and turned to bellow the length of the ship, "All hands, all hands, prepare to lift ship!" He turned back to the two mages. "Ready?"

"Aye sir," Marsters said. Warren nodded, his face showing signs of the strain he was under in blowing the ship forward.

"Mr. Sawyer, prepare to deploy propellers on my command!"

"Aye, sir, propellers at your command," James Sawyer replied crisply.

Fawcett turned to examine his crew, the helmsman on the wheel, the crews at their stations: all were ready. "Mages, lift ship!"

There was a moment's hesitation and then Fawcett felt the pull from the center of the ship. He glanced over the side to the sea below but couldn't detect any change. He turned back to examine the shoreline. *Wasp* was already ten feet in the air. He waited until she was thirty feet up.

"Deploy propellers!" he ordered. The two furled propellers on their large wooden beams were ponderously lowered from straight up and perpendicular to straight out and parallel to the deck of the ship. A moment later the propellers themselves started turning, first unfanning their four blades out one blade at a time until all four were spread at right angles. Slowly, they began rotating, their speed increasing faster and faster until they were a blur and Fawcett could feel the wind on the front of his chest.

"Propellers deployed, what speed, sir?" Mr. Sawyer reported.

"Set for six knots," Fawcett replied. He glanced to the two mages. "Can you get us to three thousand feet?"

Warren and Marsters exchanged worried looks. "We'll try," Warren told him. Together the two turned toward the single balloon lifting them upwards, closed their eyes, spread their arms and cast their spell.

Wasp lurched upwards, climbing steadily. Warren collapsed to the deck with a groan. "Mr. Bastien! Have some hands escort the mages below."

Marsters gave him a grateful look and managed to croak, "We'll be up if you need us, captain."

Fawcett nodded and turned back to the handling of his ship.

Wasp was underway.

#

Tea had given way to a meal as their conversation continued. Finally, Margen sat back from his empty bowl of stew and eyed his two visitors critically.

"You are traitors to King Markel, he has ordered your death," Margen said. "In fact, you are believed to be dead."

"And it is much easier to kill a dead man," Thomas Walpish observed dryly.

"By your admission, spymaster Hewlitt knows you are alive and let you free," Margen continued, looking as if he were sucking on something very sour. "You have sworn an oath to gods and they accepted it." He made a face. Then, with quirked lips, "How could you have been so stupid?"

"It was that or her life," Walpish said. "And, for myself, I must say that I think this is something we should stop."

"If gods are helping you," Margen said slowly, "at least one other god is opposing you."

"Do you have a set of figures?" Walpish asked, rising from his chair and glancing around the mage's comfortable study. Margen pointed to a special shelf which was covered by two wooden doors. Walpish looked at him for permission and when the mage nodded, he went to the shelf and opened the doors. Inside were row upon row of finely carved figurines of gods.

"Just point," Margen warned. "It's safer." He rose from his chair and came to stand behind the cavalryman. Skara Ningan followed, standing on Walpish's right side.

Thomas Walpish looked at all the figures of the gods, his expression intent. He looked for a long moment and then turned to Margen in surprise. "It's not here."

Margen looked at the figurines for a moment, then turned to look at Walpish with pity.

"It is best not to speak his name," Margen said after a moment. He moved in front of Walpish and closed the wooden doors. Heavily, he returned to his chair and motioned for them to do the same. He bowed his head to his chest and closed his eyes. When he opened them again he gave each of them a fierce look and said, "Do you know what you have got yourselves into?" Reading their replies in their expressions, he shook his head in irritation. "No, of course you don't. And it's better that you don't know." He frowned. "What do you want of me?"

"Teach us magic," Walpish said. Margen jerked in his chair and started to protest but Walpish held up a hand. "Teach us enough that we may fulfill our oaths."

"Magic?" the mage barked. "You?" He turned to Skara and corrected himself, "You two?"

The two gave him sad looks. "We know some already," Skara said. "And we can learn."

"Learn?" Margen spluttered. "I take children and spend ten *years* trying to get them to *learn!*"

"We're not children," Walpish said. "And we don't have ten years," Skara added.

Margen turned his gaze on her. "No," he said a moment later in a sad, hoarse voice, "no you don't."

#

"I must rest, your majesty," Mage Vistos told his king later that night. "Losing poor Minnor was quite a fright. And then there was the other night."

"I could have Margen replace you, I suppose," King Markel replied with his lips pursed.

"No!" Vistos shouted. "I mean, Mage Margen is more useful at your capital training new mages." He shook his head. "I shall only need a few days — four at most — to recover and then I'll be back at your side, ready to smite your enemies."

King Markel's expression brightened at the thought.

"I think that Mage Vistos' suggestion has merit, your majesty," First minister Mannevy said as he entered the chamber and bowed to his king. "It will take some time yet before we encounter any further opposition from the Sorians and it would be best if he were then at his fullest potential."

Vistos turned to the first minister with a thoughtful look.

"Well, if Mannevy says so, I suppose that's what we should do," King Markel said with a twisted smile. He waved to his magician. "Go! I understand the train is about ready to leave. You can escort me back to the capital. Rest up, you've done well!"

Vistos pursed his lips to speak but thought better of it and bowed deeply to his king. He backed away, casting a wary glance toward Mannevy before leaving the room. Mannevy smiled cheerily at the mage as he closed the doors on him and turned back to his king.

Markel smiled. "Excellent! Now we won't have him moaning when we set the steam mages on their duties."

Mannevy answered his smile with one of his own. "The Steam Master is here, sire, and requests an audience."

"I'm tired, just give me his report and I'll see him when this new track gets laid through the town," Markel replied testily.

"All goes well at Korin's Pass, sire," Mannevy said. "The Steam Master has left his three best-trained mages to continue there. They are just about ready to build the station in the town itself. When they're done with that, they'll start laying track to join us here."

"And what about the track to Sarskar?" Markel asked. "Won't we need that, too?"

"Indeed, sire," Mannevy agreed with a polite wave of acknowledgement, "but we have to wait for our supply of rail and timber to catch up. It makes more sense to build the line back here to South Sea Pass so that we'll be able to move cargo on both lines."

Markel spent a moment absorbing this notion before nodding. "Then we can go twice as fast to the capital!"

"That is the plan, sire," Mannevy agreed.

"And Gergen is going to keep them busy with his assault up the coastline," Markel said, rubbing his hands together in glee. "When the real assault comes straight up their heartland, the Sorians won't know what to do!"

"As you say, sire."

"And well I should, first minister," Markel snapped back. "It was my plan, after all."

"Indeed it was," Mannevy agreed suavely. In fact, it had been Mannevy's plan. But part of being first minister meant learning when to let credit go where it would do the most good. "I thought it was stunning brilliance, myself."

Chapter Three

"So, what needs doing?" Torvan Brookes, the Steam Master, asked the three young mages standing in front of him with expressions ranging from eager to alarmed.

"We need to tear down a section of the wall," Gander Norit, the earth mage, said, eyeing the wall surrounding the town of South Sea Pass thoughtfully. "It shouldn't be hard."

"We need a bridge over the river," Dysack Mercer, the fire mage, added with a warning look to the younger Norit.

"Do we know where we want to put the station?" Moira Ayles, the air mage asked.

"Just on the other side of the wall," the Steam Master replied. He nodded to Dysack, adding, "And you're right, we're going to need to build a bridge." He glanced at Gander. "A sturdy bridge."

"Do we have a design?" Moira asked. "For the bridge?"

"We do," the Steam Master replied.

"We've never built a bridge before," Dysack said.

"Your siblings have," Torvan Brookes told them. "I think you're ready now." He reached into his bag and pulled out a rolled up parchment. He unfolded it and gestured for the three mages to gather around him. "First, we'll need to wait until mage Vistos has departed."

"The King's mage?" Moira said. "I thought he'd want to watch."

Torvan Brooke's lips quirked upwards. "Which is why we'll wait until he leaves."

"Oh," Gander said, "you don't want him to see."

"Margaret spent time convincing him that she was no good as a mage," Torvan said, his lips twitching now.

"Margaret?" Gander repeated in surprise. "And he believed that?"

"It's not hard when you do everything wrong or pretend that you can't because of your gender," the Steam Master replied.

"And he believed that?" Moira said, rolling her eyes.

"Some will believe what they want, no matter what the evidence," Dysack said.

"And he's lost one of his apprentices," Torvan added. He nodded toward Dysack, "He was lost in a fire."

"I hadn't heard," Dysack said, sounding subdued.

Behind them the steam engine tooted a loud whistle, warning of its imminent departure.

"Now, we'll be needing the stones from the wall," Torvan said, pointing to the drawing and nodding toward a portion of the great stone wall surrounding South Sea Pass. "Gander, you'll pull them and place them along the path…"

#

"I bet you'll be glad to get back to your rooms!" King Markel exclaimed as he thumped mage Vistos' bony back with a sturdy hand. The mage gave him a long-suffering look and nodded.

"I'll have to find a replacement as well," Vistos allowed sourly. "It's not a task I enjoy."

"Well, you're going to find it harder, no doubt, because I'm looking for new mages, too!" Markel boomed jovially. He pointed upwards through the ceiling to the unseen fleet of airships floating overhead. "Mannevy tells me we'll have another half dozen or so before the end of the month."

"Indeed," Vistos said dryly, "I look forward to it."

"Well, we're going to need them," Markel said, glancing with pursed lips over toward first minister Mannevy. "Although we still need to find out how to make dragon steel."

"Spymaster Hewlitt and I are keenly aware of this, sire," Mannevy replied. He waved a hand to the spymaster. "In fact, I believe Lord Hewlitt has some ideas in that direction."

"Have you?" Markel boomed. "And what are they?"

"I would prefer not to say at the moment, sire," Hewlitt replied, casting a sideways glance at mage Vistos. "My plans are still too new to speak of with certainty."

"And you don't want Vistos to poach your prospects," Markel chuckled. He glanced around. "Well, I certainly will be glad to get back to the capital and away from all this." He waved a hand around the luxurious appointments of the mansion he had commandeered for his stay in the town of South Sea Pass. He looked at Mannevy and Hewlitt. "Are we ready to depart?"

"Indeed sire," Mannevy allowed, waving for his king to precede him. Picked guards gathered around and bustled the group out of the mansion and down to waiting horses.

It was a short ride to the train which had waited patiently. The King and his party boarded but it was another ten minutes before the train pulled out of the station.

"We had to load your horses and the last of your things, sire," Mannevy explained when the king complained of the matter.

"Well, let's be gone from here!" King Markel replied with a wave.

A short moment later, the train started puffing its way back to Kingsford.

#

It was nearing sunset when the cart stopped in the city of Kingsford. The two carters hopped down and moved to the back of their cart. The lead carter pulled back the canvas covering their cargo and motioned for his lad to help him pull it down.

"Cripes, this thing is heavy!" the lad said as he and the carter hauled it down. "What's it made of, it's not wood!"

"Metal," the carter said. "Not iron but some sort of copper or the like."

"Worth a pretty penny, I'd bet," the lad said with an avaricious look.

"We're being paid well enough," the carter said in a repressive tone. "And besides, you know where we are, don't you?"

"Where?" the lad said as they puffed their way to a door.

"This is the back of Ibb's," the carter said.

"Ibb?" the lad said, eyes widening. "Ibb the mechanical?"

"Pay's good," the carter said again, to forestall the lad's growing panic. "And all we've got to do —" he puffed a deep breath and signalled for the lad to lower his side of the heavy barrel to the ground "— is put this thing here. Then we return to the docks for the rest of our money."

"Oh," the lad said, "in that case, that's all right." He eyed the darkened alley suspiciously. "We just go?" He glanced around. "And do they know that we've delivered our cargo?"

"They'll know if we *don't*," the carter growled. "You don't mess with mechanicals."

"How would they know?" the lad challenged. "What if we said we delivered the barrel and someone stole it?"

The carter swore and cuffed the lad on the side of his head. "Get back in the cart!" When the chagrined lad moved off, the carter added, "We'll have a pint when we get the rest of our cash."

The carter flicked the reins to the carthorse and turned the cart around. Moments later they were clopping down the cobblestoned streets back to the docks.

The sun fell, the last of its light dying on the distant horizon. Shadows deepened until they were black. A cat howled in the distance.

Silence stretched for hours. The evening crowd had gone to bed, the streets were deserted.

The metal barrel stood where it was placed, not far from Ibb's back door. A moment later the top of the barrel bulged upwards slightly. No one could see it in the darkness, of course. The bulge grew then split into a distinct shape — a cylinder, smaller than the barrel that had contained it. As it extended upwards it revealed two blue lights, glowing dimly. The cylinder rotated quickly and then back again, slowly, the dim lights examining every nook and cranny, stopping to rest on a few darker areas.

A moment later, the cylinder and the bulge disappeared back into the barrel. Silence. A groan and a drunkard rolled on by toward the main street, completely ignoring the barrel hidden in the shadows. Minutes after the silence returned, the cylinder extruded from the barrel once more.

The cylinder moved upwards and the barrel's shape changed. The cylinder resolved itself into a metal head, a nose sliding out of the cylinder in between the two blue lights while on the side two ear-like projections emerged. An opening below the dim blue eyes functioned for a mouth. The metal mouth twisted for a moment... either in disgust or thought, it was not clear. The head twisted around completely, scanning its surroundings.

Satisfied, the barrel seemed to contract and change shape; the head rose on what became two distinct sections connected by a thinner cylinder — almost like a human's chest and pelvis connected by a stringy spine. Cylinders extended noiselessly from the upper chest part and became arms with three metal clamp-like fingers. The change continued until the barrel was no more. In its place stood a sturdy but spindly human shape.

The head bent and examined each part of the body it was attached to with meticulous attention. Satisfied, the head turned to the darkness and the back door to Ibb's workshop.

Time to work.

#

"What is it you want of me, your majesty?" Lisette Casman asked Queen Alva of the Shredded Hills. Lisette was only eleven but her father had been the Grand Duke of the Jasram Plain — until Lisette and her brother, Alain, had fled to keep Lisette from a forced marriage. Unknown to Lisette, her flight had sealed her father's doom — he'd been forced to repay his broken promise with his life.

They were looking down over the vast expanse that was the High Princedom of Jasram with its three Princedoms and seven Grand Duchies. They were perched on a high peak of the Shredded Hills overlooking the plain below. The sun had moved in the past hours and was now nearing the western horizon.

"When you humans fight, when there is lack or starvation, many of you climb our hills," Queen Alva replied slowly. "Some are just looking for food." She frowned. "Others are looking for gold." She waved a hand at the plains below. "When they come, my people are in peril."

"And you have few people," Lisette said.

Alva nodded grimly. "When the caves collapsed, two out of every three zwerg were killed," the queen said. "My mother, my father, all my siblings…"

"I am sorry," Lisette said. "That was a long time ago, though, wasn't it?"

"Time flows differently for the zwerg than it does for humans," Alva told her. "Your life will be near its end in another sixty years while mine will only be beginning."

"Is it a good thing to live so long?" Lisette wondered.

"Ask me again when I'm a hundred," Alva told her with a short chuckle.

"And will you be old, then?"

"No!" Alva replied with a laugh. "A zwerg can hope to live for three hundred years. More, with luck."

"I couldn't imagine that."

"There are some creatures who live for much longer," Alva said with a dismissive wave of her hand.

"What do you want of me?" Lisette said again. She pointed to herself. "I'm just a girl and I'm not all that good at *that*."

"The lands of your fathers are in peril," Alva said, pointing to the plains below. "That peril will spill over on my people." She made a face. "And we are not strong enough to survive it."

"What can I do?" Lisette cried. "I'm just a girl!"

"You can do whatever you decide to do," Alva said. She shrugged. "I was just a girl when I became queen."

"But… you always knew you were going to be queen!" Lisette protested.

"And didn't you always know you were going to be a girl?" Alva teased, shaking her head to take the sting out of her remarks. She turned to Lisette. "I can't help but think that you were — however unwittingly — the cause of this woe. Why can't you be the cure?"

#

Ophidian said this wouldn't work, Annabelle remarked to Ellen as they burst forth above the Shredded Hills with the sun setting on the horizon.

Ophidian doesn't know everything, Ellen replied. Annabelle caught a hint of the young girl's amazement as they spiralled down toward the tops of the mountains that housed the underground realm of Queen Alva. *I thought it was worth the try*, Ellen continued. *After all, if it didn't work, what would have happened?*

We would have died, Annabelle replied tartly. But, with the evidence of their own eyes, Ellen's wild assertion that they could jump from one place in the world to another simply by imagining their location had proven correct. *And,* Annabelle thought to herself, *Ophidian never told us.*

The two were still coming to grips with their new existence. Forged in grief, love, and desperation, Ellen Annabelle was the newest wyvern in existence — and the dragon-god Ophidian's greatest secret. She was also, perhaps, his most difficult offspring.

If father gets mad, I'll blame you, Ellen said with giggle in her voice. *You're older, after all.*

Annabelle accepted her other half's teasing with humor. *I'm going to land.*

We're going to land, Ellen corrected. The wyvern was nearing the ground at an alarming rate and Ellen felt a thrill of fear run through her. It wasn't like she and Annabelle were well-versed in such efforts. This was perhaps their *sixth* landing, after all. And there was that rather sharp cliff to their right falling down to the valley below.

As it was, Ellen was right to be worried. As Ellen Annabelle dropped toward a level landing, they misjudged their distance and their legs snagged on a treetop. With an anguish cry, the twin-souled wyvern crashed to the ground below. *Ow!*

Worse, they had company. A human girl came running at the sound of their crash and put her arms out protectively in front of another, smaller person who rushed up behind her.

Ellen Annabelle, startled and shaken, reacted instinctively and lashed out her long neck and open-fanged mouth to defend herself. At the edge of panic, Ellen urged Annabelle not to send poison darts toward the girl… but the girl reacted as if she were going to be attacked and, using one arm behind her to pull the other person down to the ground, rolled away — and over the cliff.

No! And in an instant Ellen Annabelle was a small girl once more, eyes wide with horror as she took in the nature of the disaster she'd caused. She turned her eyes toward the surviving girl only to say, to her shock, "Alva?"

But the zwerg queen did not recognize the girl and lunged at her, knife drawn and deadly. "Who are you and why did you kill that child?"

"Kill?" Ellen asked in a small voice. She moved to the cliff and looked over. There was no sign of the other girl.

"You can join her!" Alva shouted, lunging forward and pushing the girl over the edge.

"No!" Annabelle shrieked through Ellen's mouth as they fell. "Alva, you don't understand!"

Enough of that, FLY! Ellen told her. In a moment they were a wyvern once more and spiralling down to the valley far below.

#

They found the girl's bent, broken, and lifeless body on the plain far below. Dark had settled in the valley and it was only with their superior wyvern vision that they were able to find her at all. With a cry of anguish, Ellen Annabelle gently grabbed the girl's body in her claws and bore her aloft, back toward the high mountains above and the waiting queen.

The queen was not alone. There were three zwerg with her and a taller person, a human.

As Ellen Annabelle gently lowered the still form of the girl to the ground, the human — no more than a youth — rushed forward with a cry. "Lisette!"

Alarmed, Ellen Annabelle transformed into her seven year-old self. Ellen rushed forward, crying, "I'm sorry, I'm sorry!"

Strong hands grappled her and held her. "Who are you?"

"What are you?" another zwerg asked.

"She's Lisette, she was at the Inn of the Broken Sun," Ellen said, ignoring the questions. She glanced at the lad and realized that she recognized him also. "You're her brother."

"Who are you?" Alain Casman challenged, his hand going to his side and his sword.

"She is magic," Maro the zwerg mage said, moving forward and gesturing for the zwerg man holding Ellen to let her go. The zwerg mage turned back to the others. "You saw her change."

"She knocked Lisette down," Alva said.

"My queen, I did nothing of the sort," Annabelle said through Ellen's voice. "I was startled, I mislanded, and I reacted with instincts I did not know I had."

"And now she's dead," Alain replied grimly, pulling his sword. "And your life is forfeit."

"Lord Casman, she's *magic*," Maro said in a warning tone. "Put away your sword, it will do nothing."

"You speak like you know me," Alva said, glaring at the small child. She gestured toward Lisette's body. "And you say you knew her, too."

"One of us did," Annabelle spoke. "Ellen knew the girl. She saw her sometimes when she was trying to survive on the streets of Kingsford."

"'One of us?'" Maro quoted with a quizzical look.

Annabelle forced Ellen into as elegant a courtly bow as the small girl's body could provide. "Queen Diam told me that you'd made me a Duchess, your highness."

"What?" Alva demanded in shock. "The only person I ever made a Duchess was — Annabelle?"

"Annabelle died," Ellen said, taking back her voice and rising from the bow to meet Alva's eyes directly. "She died saving me from a poisoned arrow and I —"

"— she saved me with her tears, Alva," Annabelle finished with a lump of pain in her voice. "We became one, a twin-souled —"

"Wyvern?" Alva asked in bewilderment. She moved forward, nudging aside Ellen's captor and put her hands on the smaller girl's shoulders. "Annabelle, is this true?"

"I swear upon my name, your majesty," Annabelle replied firmly. "I — we — came as soon as we could." She glanced toward Alain and then Lisette's body. "I am so sorry, we did not mean any harm!"

"Harm!" the word barked out of Alain's throat like a gunshot. "You killed my sister!"

"Annabelle, can we… can I…" Ellen asked in sorrow. "Could we trade my life for hers?"

"No!" Annabelle cried immediately.

"Alain's mare is lame," Maro spoke up suddenly. The others stared at her. She nodded toward Alain. "We'd come looking for you, Alva, because we wanted your advice."

"It was my fault," Alain said. "I didn't realize the ground was so rocky here and I wanted to practice jumping."

"Both forelegs," Maro said. She glanced at Ellen. "You saved Annabelle with your tears, can you do it again?"

"She's dead," Alain said, turning to the zwerg mage in frustration. "No one can —"

"I can," Ellen said. *You don't know if that's true*, Annabelle warned her. *We won't know until we try*, Ellen responded.

"It might be possible," Maro said, turning first to Alva and then to Alain. "What do you know of centaurs?"

"Centaurs?" Alain repeated blankly, overwhelmed.

"Do you remember your mother, Lord Alain?" Alva asked, as she turned to look first at her mage and then the lad.

"Father said she died," Alain said sadly. "She died when Lisette was born."

"So you know nothing of centaurs," Maro pronounced firmly. She smiled sadly. "You know nothing of your heritage."

"He's half centaur?" Annabelle asked through Ellen's lips.

Alva turned and smiled at her. "Prove that you're Annabelle. What do you know of centaurs —" she cocked a finger toward Alain "— and him."

"Your father said that some of the Jasram princes were strange," Annabelle recalled even as she felt Ellen's rapt attention and eager interest. "He said that too many of them had forgotten the gods and their gifts."

"And what gift in particular?" Maro prompted.

"You know, I liked you better when you were smaller," Annabelle snapped to the zwerg mage. She turned toward Alain. "The centaurs are a joining, like wyverns but not quite."

"A joining?" Alain repeated. He glanced down at his sister's still form.

"What has this to do with Lisette?"

"And you," Annabelle said. "From what Maro is saying, you have centaur blood."

"My father was no — you're not saying that my *mother* was a centaur!" Alain cried in anger.

"There's one way to find out," Annabelle said, glancing toward Maro. "That's what you're thinking, aren't you?"

"She's Annabelle," Maro declared to her queen. With a twisted grin, she added, "No one else could be *that* slow."

"Alain, we would need your consent," Alva said to the lad, nodding toward the body of his sister. "And we cannot guarantee the result."

"What?"

"I cannot bring your sister back to life on my own," Ellen said, looking over to the taller youth. "But with your blessing, I can *try* to unite her with your mare. I could save two lives making by them one."

"You can make my sister into a centaur?" Alain asked in astonishment.

"It's easier that she already half is," Maro murmured, moving forward and gesturing for the other zwerg guard to accompany her. She looked up to Alain. "The only question is: will you let us try — or will you have us bury her and put your mare down at the same time?"

Alain didn't hesitate. He waved a hand toward his sister, saying, "Save her."

Chapter Four

"Honestly, I'd say I was annoyed but I'd be lying," the god of Death said to Ophidian as they mused over the proceedings. "It's not the girl's time, you know."

"So she can bring back the dead?" Ophidian asked.

"She's done it once already," Terric said with a huff. "*Your* doing, as I recall."

"I didn't know I could," Ophidian said half in apology and half in awe. He gave the god of Death a solemn nod. "I shall use this gift sparingly."

"It's no skin off my nose either way," Terric replied. "What bothers me much more is this issue with that Walpish and Ningan. I must say, I don't like any of what... well, I won't mention his name."

Ophidian nodded. "I was surprised at that, too."

"Not everyone has forgiven you for your *disagreement* with the rest of us, you know," Terric said.

"The humans — those that record such things and remember — call it *The God's War*," Ophidian said.

"Hmph!" Terric snorted. "More like *Ophidian's War*."

"I like the sound of that," Ophidian said smugly.

"Which is why we've encouraged the humans *not* to use it," Sybil, goddess of Strength, piped up from where she stood at the high counter that marked the edge of her kitchen and the start of the dining hall. They were in the House of Life and Death at the far end of the bitter north.

"Don't want you to get a big head," Avice, goddess of Life piped up.

"And," Terric said, "now that you've won our blessing on this latest experiment by your offspring, I've got vegetables to prune." He vanished.

"Thank you," Ophidian said, certain that his words would carry to the death god wherever he was. He nodded toward Sybil. "Excellent food, as always."

"You're welcome."

"And a good day to you, Avice," Ophidian said before himself disappearing into nothingness.

In the silence, Sybil said to her mother, Avice, "Do you suppose Ophidian knew that Ellen Annabelle could just *go* wherever she imagined?"

"No," Avice said with a chuckle, "I think she — they — rather surprised him." She smiled. "You could tell that he was quite pleased with their initiative."

"Oh, of course!" Sybil snorted. "What else would the god of change expect from his offspring?"

#

Thomas Walpish cast a sideways look full of despair toward Skara Ningan: he feared that mage Margen would not agree to their wishes. *What now?* His expression asked. Skara shrugged in response.

Margen paid no attention at all to the byplay, rather glancing to the door. He frowned and turned to his guests, raising a finger to his lips in warning before waving a hand toward the locked double doors with an expression of mild amusement mixed with irritation.

Thomas and Skara jerked in their seats as a small, shiny object suddenly materialized by the door and flew through the air to land in the mage's outstretched hand. Margen and his astonished guests examined the object uncomprehendingly for a moment — and then Margen snorted in amusement.

"Hmph! A glass," the mage said, turning it in his hand and waving it toward his guests. "Suitable for drinking water or carrying other liquids." His eyes narrowed as he turned once more to the locked double doors. In a more thoughtful tone, he added, "Also useful as a listening device." He smiled as Skara and Thomas reacted. "Let's see who is using such a limited device, shall we?"

Thomas started to rise from his chair, clearly ready to open the doors and nab their spy but Margen stopped him with a raised hand.

"I've a better way," the mage said. He stood, turned to the door, raised both arms, and *pulled* them back toward him. In his hands he held the small form of a very startled, rather frightened young girl. "Margiss, how many times do I have to tell you: *don't get caught!*"

The little girl gave him a sorrowful look and dropped her head. "I tried."

"You were listening in," Margen said. "And what did you hear?"

"All of it," Margiss replied firmly. "I heard about —"

"She's lying," Skara said suddenly. She reached for the glass and examined it. "The glass is too thick and misshaped for good listening." She turned to the girl, a small thing of no more than eleven years, blond-haired, blue-eyed, and thin-boned. She turned back to mage Margen with a thoughtful frown. "She's your... grandchild?"

"And protector," Margen agreed with a smile and a nod. He turned toward Margiss who had turned pink. "At least she tries to be."

"They want to learn magic," Margiss said. She gave him a mulish look. "You said you'd teach *me* magic."

"I *am* teaching you magic," Margen reminded her firmly. He gestured toward the still-locked double doors. "I just taught you teleportation, firsthand, at no expense to you." He eyed the glass in Skara's hand. "Although perhaps I should give you more instruction on *listening*." Margiss clenched her jaw. "Or might it be that you forgot my orders for you to *stop spying* on me."

"I just wanted to make sure you were safe," Margiss said apologetically. She cast a hard glance toward Walpish and Ningan. "They look like thieves or assassins."

"I'm an assassin," Skara told her, showing the young child lots of teeth and no smile.

"So you're half-right," Margen said.

"Who are you?" Margiss demanded of Walpish. Her brows furrowed. "I've seen you before, haven't I?"

Walpish gave Margen an alarmed look.

"Do you remember what else I said about *listening*, Margiss?" Margen asked, waving down Walpish's worry.

"I can't tell anyone — not even mother or father," Margiss said worriedly. She raised her eyes toward Margen. "But what if someone hurts you?"

"Then I shall be *very* glad that you heard," Margen replied, adding heavily, "*and* that you were not caught." Margiss' eyes widened. Margen wagged a finger at her. "Anything powerful enough to hurt me is not something you can survive, little one." He turned to Skara and Thomas with a thoughtful look. "I might add," he said to them, "the same to you."

"We need to know how to fulfill our oath," Thomas said.

"Or you will die trying," Margen finished. He nodded toward Margiss. "Young lady, are you ready for your punishment?"

Margiss gave him a glum nod.

Mage Margen pointed to the far end of the room and walls of books. "Your task is to go through the L's and find a better way to listen in," he told her, pointing at the section on the shelves marked 'L'. Margiss beamed with joy. "And *not* get caught when you do." Margiss started to dash to the other side of the room, only to be halted by Margen's voice. "*And*, when you're done, you're to teach your spells to these two!"

"*Teach* them?" Margiss asked, her hurried race halted, her head turned back in surprise to her grandfather.

"The only way to really show you know something is to teach it," Margen told her. He waved her off to the books.

"Does that mean…?" Thomas Walpish asked.

"You'll teach us?" Skara Ningan added at the same time.

Margen looked at the two of them and nodded, slowly. He pointed to the small girl at the far end of the room who was busily pulling down dozens of books and spreading them around her like a rainbow. "I have *her* future to consider."

#

The train was out of sight when Moira, Dysack, and Gander emerged from the tent where they and Torvan Brookes — the Steam Master — had been waiting. They were just a dozen yards from the train track.

"See?" Torvan said, waving at a cleared spot just beside the track. "Right there is where we want it."

"The station?" Moira asked.

"Yes," the Steam Master agreed.

"Shouldn't we build the bridge first?" Gander asked.

"I don't know, Master Norit, should we?" Torvan teased.

"Don't be stupid," Dysack said, scowling at Gander. "You'll need the stones, so why not pull them down for the bridge and use the rest for the station?"

Gander Norit frowned in thought. He turned to Moira. "Are you ready?"

Moira, in answer, waved her hands in a twist in front of her and sent a gust of air at him.

"The timbers and window frames are over there," Torvan said, pointing to a pile of wood that had been off-loaded beside the train tracks. "I've men ready to lay the floors and do the finishing work." He waved his hand toward a surly bunch of men who scowled at him then jerked in fright as they recognized him. Torvan merely smiled and waved in their direction.

"Margaret and the others think they're the best of my children," Torvan told his three adopted mages with a bitter smile.

Gander Norit needed no further urging, turning to the distant wall surrounding South Sea Pass and extending his hands outwards, palms down, as though pressing on the ground.

Moira smiled at him and sent a swath of roiling air in the same direction.

At first, nothing happened. And then the guards at the top of the wall started shouting in alarm.

"Shouldn't someone warn them?" Dysack Mercer wondered.

"We just did," Moira said with a wicked grin. She flicked one hand and several guards found themselves being pushed further along the wall.

Gander grunted in amusement even as the wall rumbled in imminent collapse.

"Be ready, Dysack," Torvan Brookes warned.

Dysack nodded, moving to stand beside the other two, raising his hands in preparation.

The wall shook, stones started tumbling and Moira cried out with glee as the stones rose in the air and curved back toward the stream that ran outside the town. Dysack Mercer let his magic fly and the stones turned bright red in the air even as Moira dropped them into the river in a neat line. The river hissed with steam that rose higher and higher even as the magical pair continued building the first pylon to support the bridging span.

Gander Norit shouted happily as the rumbling continued and more and more stones fell free only to be lifted by Moira's air magic.

A steady stream of red-hot stones flew side-by-side to land next to the first batch and the support pylon grew thicker.

"Next," Torvan called over the noise in reminder.

"Ready," Moira and Dysack replied in unison, Moira gesturing with a flick of her hands and the next pile of rocks landed closer to the town, building the second pylon. The river steamed and hissed continuously but Moira blew the steam away from their view even as she rained the stones down perfectly aligned.

"Now comes the hard part, Dysack," Torvan Brookes warned. "Gander, get a bunch!"

"Got them!" Gander cried as a whole section of wall crumbled and fell as separate stones — only to rise into the air under Moira's air magic.

Moira sank to her knees under the strain and Torvan moved to stand behind her, ready to add his aid to her if needed. The stones collected into a wall which was glazed into one continuous mass by Dysack's fire magic, glowing red-hot, and hovering in the sky.

"Gander, stop," Torvan said and the earth mage nodded, dropping his hands and halting the tottering remnants of the town walls.

"Ready," Dysack said to Moira through grit teeth.

"Rolling," Moira said, pushing up with one outstretched arm while pulling back with the other.

"That looks good," Torvan said critically. "Now lower it slowly, dear."

Sweat streamed down her forehead as Moira fought to lower the stones, now only a dull red, level to the pylons and then, finally, dropping them in place.

"Yes," Torvan said, gazing at the newly finished bridge. "That should suffice." He smiled at his three mage children and said, "Now, a bit of a break and we'll get the tracks laid."

#

Crown Prince Sarsal was annoyed. "Tilly, what are you doing?" he asked as his spymaster hastily dressed. "We've got the whole night still —"

"I need to check on something," Matilda "Tilly" Gregory said as she found and put on her leather jacket. She turned back to smile at the crown prince in the dim light. "Won't be long, I promise."

"Hmph!" Sarsal snorted. Since making her the King's spymaster, he'd seen less and less of her, *much* to his annoyance.

Tilly blew him a kiss and sped away silently. Out of the room, she turned right and sprinted toward her office. She met her man at the entrance and gestured for him to enter first. Inside, she moved briskly past him and flounced into the comfortable leather chair that was hers by dint of arranging the last spymaster's death… *at the hands of the crown prince, no small piece of blackmail, that.*

"Well?" Tilly asked, a brow raised imperiously. "You said this was urgent."

"South Sea Pass has fallen," the man said, dropping two small rolls of paper on her desk. "I've got it two ways."

Tilly picked up the first paper and unwound it, reading the message with a growing frown.

"This couldn't wait until morning?" Tilly asked sharply, dropping the paper back to her desk and reaching for the second.

"It could have, I suppose," the spy said with a flick of his wrist. "But read it again."

Tilly scowled as she picked up the first message again and re-read it carefully. Her expression changed to surprise. "This says that South Sea Pass was taken nearly a *week* ago!"

"It does," the spy confirmed.

"So how come we didn't hear about it sooner?" Tilly demanded.

"Uh," the spy said uncomfortably, "it could be that some of our normal sources were compromised."

"You mean, I killed them," Tilly said sourly. "But I thought we had replacements in place."

"We do," the spy agreed, pointing to the note. "It's just that —"

"How could they take the town?" Tilly interjected. "And how come we don't know about it? What are they doing now?"

The spy shrugged helplessly.

"They could be on their way to the capital even now!"

"And we'd have no way of knowing," the spy agreed grimly.

"Send for the mage —"

"The King's —?"

"No, you idiot, ours!"

#

"Stand clear!" Colonel Samuel Lewis called once again to his troops who were looking up, wide-eyed as another bale of hay dropped from the heavens. Their meeting with the airship *Wasp* had been most fortuitous — they had less than two days' rations for the horses. They had quickly acquired — *stolen* — several local carts to haul all their supplies which caused some grumbling among the Sorian farmers. It also caused not a little bit of grumbling from the troops who were reduced from cavalrymen to carters but that was the way of things. Lewis was pleased to find among the dispatches dropped from the airship his appointment as colonel. He regretted what had happened to Colonel Walpish but *one man's loss is another man's gain*, as they say.

"Sergeant Major!" Lewis called. The sergeant major trotted his horse forward. "Have the horses fed, watered, and ready to ride by first light."

"Yes sir!" the sergeant major replied with a swift salute.

"Marless!" Lewis called to the nearest lieutenant. The lieutenant saluted him and spurred his mount closer.

"See to the men," Lewis said. "We're going to split the troops — one troop back to the general and the rest, with me, to move forward."

"Sir?"

"You'll take your troop and provide a screening force for General Gergen," Lewis expanded. He waved the rolled parchment in his hand. "I'm to press forward with all haste." He pointed to the airship lost somewhere in the white sky above them. "The airship will provide me with cover and form a liaison back with you and the general."

"I see," Lieutenant Marless said with a grim look. "I wish I was coming with you, sir —"

"Your job is to be the eyes and ears for the army," Lewis told him.

"And yours is to get all the fame, sir!" Marless told him with a grin.

"Such is my fate," Lewis replied with an ill-feigned sorrow. He waved at the lieutenant. "Now get going." He gestured upwards. "I've been invited aboard the ship."

"You have?" Marless' brows shot up. He glanced around. "How —"

His words were cut off as a rope fell to the ground close by. Lewis jumped off his horse and passed the reins to the lieutenant. "See to my horse."

Marless nodded silently as he took the reins. He glanced at the rope going up into the white snowy night. "How — you're not expected to climb all the way up, are you sir?"

"Nothing so crude," Lewis said with a grin, finding the end of the rope. It was knotted into a loop and there was another large loop tied further up. He crawled inside the large loop, anchored one foot firmly in the smaller loop and tugged. He smiled at his lieutenant as he slowly ascended into the sky above. "I shall be raised up just like an anchor."

#

The rope ascent was slow. Colonel Lewis had time to look below and see his horse and his lieutenant grow smaller and smaller until finally obscured by the layers of snow swirling down below him. Then he looked up. Presently a dark shape loomed above him. He had a moment's fear that he was going bang his head on the bottom of the boat — ship, rather — but apparently that had been considered and his line was well clear of the ship's side. He had just enough time to compose himself before his head drew even with the deck and the bustling airmen on it.

"A moment, sir," an airman called to him as Lewis made to board. "We'll haul you in, no worries."

Sam Lewis affected to look *not worried* even as the evolution was completed and he was pulled in — dangling — over the deck by a well-caught boat hook. A moment later, he was lowered and his feet touched solid… well, not ground… wood.

"Captain Fawcett, your servant, sir," a young man said, moving forward and saluting.

"Colonel Samuel Lewis, Second Cavalry squadron," Lewis replied, returning the salute.

"Please, come below!" the airship captain offered, gesturing toward a dark hatchway. "We've got all your supplies lowered."

Lewis accepted the offer with a nod and followed the captain below, through the narrow corridor and back into a stern cabin — the captain's quarters.

Steam was rising from a pot held in the hands of an airman who smiled upon seeing the captain and gladly filled two cups with the hot liquid. Captain Fawcett gestured for Colonel Lewis to take the nearest seat and moved around to take the one opposite. He raised his cup. "Your good health, sir." He frowned as Lewis sat but did not touch his cup. "Or we could provide something stronger, if that's your wish, sir."

Colonel Lewis shook himself and raised his cup. "No, no, tea will be fine, captain," Lewis said. "It's just that… it's rather a shock to be offered tea at three thousand feet."

Captain Fawcett gave him a blank look then brightened. "Oh! Oh, I suppose it would be at that!"

"Nothing *you* don't do every day," Lewis said, taking a long sip — it was good tea. "But not something a simple cavalryman as myself often does. Especially after being raised up on a rope."

"Hmm," Fawcett said. "I hadn't considered that." He raised his eyes to the colonel's. "Must be rather a bit much, come to think."

"I'm used to it now," Lewis allowed. He glanced around the cabin. "I didn't realize that the King had made so many airships. Last one I saw was the *Wasp*."

Fawcett blushed. "This *is* the *Wasp*, sir."

"But the captain —?"

"Captain Martel and mage Tirpin have been detained by order of the King, sir," Fawcett replied quickly. He saw Lewis' surprise and continued quickly, in a lower voice, "I don't know what they did, sir, but the king has ordered their death."

"And so their loss was your gain," Lewis murmured.

"It was all quite sudden," Fawcett agreed. "We were ordered out of the harbor almost immediately. "And you, sir? Did you perhaps know Colonel Walpish? He was aboard this very ship when we took the east gates of South Sea Pass."

"He was my commander," Lewis said, his expression darkening. "Until he was killed by an assassin."

"Oh!" Fawcett said. "Oh, I'm very sorry to hear that."

"As am I, even though it was to my gain," Lewis agreed, reconsidering his earlier reaction to Fawcett's tale. He cocked his head. "I suppose we are both benefactors of bad luck."

"Yes," Fawcett agreed feebly. "And now?"

"The orders you dropped to me say that we — you and my men — are to continue toward the Sorian capital on reconnaissance."

"We are?"

"And there to take stock of the situation," Lewis said. He smiled and leaned forward. "If we can, I mean us to take the capital."

Fawcett's eyes bulged. "Can we do that, sir?"

"We won't know until we try, will we captain?" Lewis told him with a grin.

Chapter Five

"Your Majesty, I have news," Matilda Gregory announced as she entered the Great Hall. In one corner near the door was a large table at which King Wendel was holding court with his staff, including his leading generals.

King Wendel looked up at her entrance and eyed her thoughtfully. He struggled with his mind to identify her — his confusion was apparent on his face. Tilly decided to take pity on him, this once.

"Matilda Gregory, Your Majesty," Tilly said, dropping to a respectful curtsy. "I am your new spymaster."

Wendel's brows furrowed. "What happened to the old one?"

"He was a traitor, he attacked the Crown Prince," Tilly replied quickly. "I am here because I have grave news."

"Someone else died?" Wendel guessed, trying to parse the meaning of 'grave.'

"We are being attacked, sire!" Tilly replied. She threw two strips of parchment on the large table, nearest General Armand. Quickly, she added, "The reason we haven't heard from South Sea Pass and Korin's Pass is because they've been taken by the Kingsland army!"

A tumult of voices erupted around the table as generals jumped to their feet and rushed to read the messages Tilly had dropped. She turned to the king. "Sire, I do not know how close the enemy is to our capital."

"The enemy? Kingsland?" Wendel said, trying to grapple with the notion. He turned to his generals. "General Armand, is this true?"

General Armand, by dint of superior rank, reached in through the sea of hands and grabbed the nearest message. He pulled his hand back, unrolled it and read it carefully. He threw it back on the table when he was done. "We should assemble the troops, sire," Armand said. "Close the gates and stand to the guard."

"Close the gates?" Wendel repeated in puzzlement. "But it's… we're far from the border, aren't we?"

"At least a week's hard ride," Armand agreed. "But that message is over a week old."

"Two weeks for an army," one of the other generals objected.

"More, in this weather," a second added with pursed lips.

"We've got the cavalry," the first general suggested. "It'll take a month or more to assemble the reserves."

"So the reserves are out," the second general said. He turned to Tilly. "What size is their force?"

Tilly frowned, trying to remember the general's name. She hadn't concentrated on generals when she'd laid her plans.

"I am still waiting for that information," Tilly said, buying herself time.

"General Trim, surely their forces must be greater than ours or else they could not have taken a fortified, *walled* town," the first general said, helpfully providing the second general's name.

"If they had mages —"

"*We* have mages," the first general interjected. *What was his name?* Tilly wondered. *Something to do with fire, like coal or — Smoke!*

"They have more," General Trim replied. "Their king spent a lot of time and effort promoting the education of mages." General Trim carefully kept from glancing at Wendel. After all, it wasn't his fault — the fault, if any, lay with the late King Sorgal who had little interest in such things. "Soria is a land of farmers, what do we need of mages?" Sorgal had asked not too long before Wendel had removed his head.

"Who's in charge of the cavalry?" King Wendel asked, his voice carrying over the rabble.

"That would be Colonel Pratchett," General Armand said. Prudently, he added, "He works closely with Captain Peters of the guard." He gestured for a subaltern who trotted up. Quickly he scribbled two notes. "With your permission, sire," General Armand said, passing the notes to his aide, "I'll have them alerted."

"Yes, do that," Wendel agreed with an absent wave of his hand. He glanced around and spotted Tilly. "What are you doing here?"

"I was conferring about the invasion, sire," Tilly reminded him gently.

"Invasion? What do you know of the invasion?"

"I'm your spymaster," Tilly said. She gestured toward the table. "I brought the news."

"Oh! Oh, very good!" Wendel replied. He glanced around, his expression distant. "Well, General Armand, what's on our schedule?"

General Armand glanced at his generals quellingly. Wisely, they made no response. He glanced toward Tilly who returned his look blandly. "I think, sire, that in view of this troubling news, we should put the capital on alert. Our generals will see how quickly we can recall our troops and build up the defense."

"Oh," Wendel said. "Oh, very good." He glanced around nervously. "So, it seems you've got everything in hand." He frowned. "You don't need me anymore, do you? I think the queen… " he brightened as his voice trailed off.

"Sire, I think it is your duty to inform the queen immediately," General Armand agreed with alacrity. "The generals and I here will continue to protect the kingdom and, always, will await your orders."

"So I can leave?" Wendel asked. General Armand nodded. "Good," he said, nodding to himself, "good." A moment later he said, "We're done, right?"

"Shall I have someone find the queen?" one of the lesser ranks asked.

"The King is quite capable of finding his queen," General Armand replied in a cold tone.

"The queen!" Wendel brightened. "Yes, I think I shall go see to her." He nodded brightly at the assembly and hastily left the room.

There was a moment of silence.

"We need to make plans," General Armand said, glancing around the room. His eyes fell on Tilly. His expression was not welcoming. "See what you can learn, please, spymaster."

"The King… " one of the junior officers began.

"King Wendel fought brilliantly at the Pinch for many years," General Armand said. "He was wounded a number of times, with many blows to the head." Sadly, he added, "It makes thinking rather… *difficult*… for him."

"I see," the subaltern added with feeling.

"He is better with the queen," General Peters observed.

Armand gestured to Tilly. "Spymaster, you have duties…"

Tilly nodded. "I'll send a messenger when I learn more."

"In the meantime, I shall see that patrols are sent to the coast and south to Korin's Pass," General Armand replied. He nodded gravely to the new spymaster.

After she had left, General Armand, turned to one of his aides. "Send for Oliver."

The aide swallowed, hard, but saluted and strode resolutely from the room.

"Do you think that's wise?" General Trim asked in the silence that fell.

"I don't think we have any choice," General Armand replied.

#

"Now you understand that mages don't necessarily *worship* a particular god," Margen said, wagging his eyebrows at Skara and Thomas as he spoke, "but we *request* their aid in the creation of our magic."

"And that's because the gods are the source of all magic," Skara piped up.

"Well… all the magic that we know of comes from gods," Margen temporized.

"There could be magic from somewhere else?" Thomas Walpish asked.

"Perhaps," Margen said. "Or perhaps there are gods unknown."

The former assassin and the former cavalry officer exchanged looks.

"Magic comes from knowledge," Thomas said, repeating one of the mage's maxims.

"Knowledge is constantly changing because we learn more every day," Margen said. He took on a bemused expression as he added, "Which explains why so many spells don't work."

"I thought it was a lack of faith," Skara muttered.

Margen shrugged. "Could be that, too." He collected himself and nodded toward the third member of his special class who had remained dutifully silent. "What do you think, Margiss?"

"I think you're right," Margiss said quickly. She caught his look and grinned as she added, "It could be either."

"So it could," Thomas agreed. "But what has this to do with today's lesson, sir?"

"What is today's lesson on?" Margen asked pedantically.

"Listening," Margiss said in a low voice pitched for Thomas Walpish's ears.

"Yes, listening," Margen said with a dry look for his granddaughter. "And why do we listen?"

Skara opened her mouth to respond but was cut off by a loud whistle, blowing twice.

"That's the train from Soria," Thomas said. He glanced around and gave a different sort of whistle. A small figure appeared before him, chittering with pleasure. "I've a job for you." The winged figure chirped inquisitively. "I want you to see who comes off the train —"

"And where they go," Skara added, although she was speaking to her winged creature.

Three, Margen thought to himself grimly. *There had been* three *of the dratted things*. He glanced toward Margiss who gave him a hopeful look. With a sigh, he nodded permission.

The third winged creature appeared in front of her and she issued her own quick orders.

"Go on, now!" Walpish urged his chittering friend. The creature squeaked in acknowledgement and disappeared. Moments later, the other two followed it.

"They can be useful," Margen allowed after the creatures had left. "But it is important to remember the god that made them."

"Ophidian," Skara said.

"The god of change," Walpish added.

"Of chaos," Margiss said with a gleam in her eyes.

"He is not the god that we seek," Skara said. "I'm certain."

"It is never wise to assume you know the thoughts of the gods," Margen told her quellingly. Skara met his eyes frankly, challengingly. Margen sighed. "Though, in this instance, I suspect your evaluation is correct."

Skara's lips twitched briefly in triumph.

"Mage Vistos is on that train," Thomas Walpish said, sitting straight up in his chair. He glanced around nervously. "We must hide."

"How did you —?" Margen began but broke off as his nose twitched. "Yes, I can smell him." He gave Walpish a thoughtful look. "I believe you are correct, sir." He grinned. "And I know just the place!"

#

A young lad appeared at the door anxiously holding the elbow of a wizened, bent figure who tottered through the door with an undisguised look of triumph on his face.

"You sent for me?" Mage Ingam Oliver asked in an old, dry voice ending in a cackle of glee.

"Yes sir," General Armand said, rising from his chair. The others rose after a bare moment of surprise, the younger ones exchanging surprised looks.

"Too late, of course," the old mage said as he tottered toward a chair. His aide pulled it out hastily and gingerly helped the old man seat himself. "Everything is lost."

"Sir?" General Trim asked.

"You've seen this?" General Armand challenged.

Mage Oliver snorted which turned into a long hacking wheeze before he recovered. "Do you mean, did the gods show me a vision?"

"Yes sir," Trim replied meekly.

Mage Oliver swiveled his head to turn to the general. "You always were an ass, weren't you?"

General Trim stiffened but said nothing.

"Don't you people read your intelligence reports?" Oliver asked, his aged voice growing stronger.

"Our intelligence has been rather spotty of late," General Armand admitted.

"And didn't I tell you to fix *that* when old Sorgal got his?" Oliver said. "Now you're dependent on this new toy of Sarsal's and her best qualities seem to involve being horizontal and appreciative." Oliver chuckled at his wit which turned into another dry cough before he recovered.

"We knew that Markel was toying with steam," Oliver said. "Knew that years back. And then there was the locomotive. Faster than a horse, more powerful, too."

"But it has to travel on a line," General Trim muttered.

"A line straight to our borders and you didn't wonder?" Oliver said. Under his breath, he added, "Idiot."

"We fortified the borders, strengthened the garrison at South Sea Pass," General Armand replied. "But it's the middle of winter —!"

"And since when do your enemies have to accept your worries?" Oliver demanded. He shook his head. "When they started building toward Korin's Pass, I warned you."

"Spymaster Vitel —" Armand began in his defense.

"And where is he, I wonder?" Oliver asked. "His expertise is 'intelligence', is it not?"

"Crown Prince Sarsal says that the spymaster attacked him, tried to murder him," one of the aides spoke up.

"He says that, does he?" Oliver replied with a mocking look. He turned to Armand, adding, "In my day, juniors knew to keep their mouths shut."

The aide closed his mouth with a snap, his face going bright red.

"In *my* day, I ask them to speak up," General Armand returned mildly. "So what do we do now?"

"What do you want of me?" Oliver replied.

"Suggestions, advice, as always," Armand said. He pointed toward the wall and the hanging map of Soria. "How should we react?"

"You're going to lose," Oliver said.

"That's treason!" the same red-faced aide swore. Oliver gave him a hard look and waved a hand. The aide stiffened in his chair, going rigid everywhere except for his eyes.

"Let him breathe at least," Armand said. "After all, he only said what the rest of us thought."

"Thinking is not something you do well," Oliver said. He waved a hand toward the aide, relenting enough to allow him to breathe. The aide gasped in deep, heavy breaths. Oliver frowned. "I told you back before I retired that there are changes coming."

"And you said that you didn't know what," General Trim said with a frown. "It makes it most difficult to plan, you know."

"If it was easy, we could have peasants do the planning," Oliver returned with a sneer.

"Enough, Ingam," General Armand said in a tired voice. "We didn't listen to you: we were wrong. Can you take that as enough and move on?"

"Oh, I have, I have," Ingam Oliver, formerly general of the Sorian Army, replied with a wave of his hand. "But that doesn't mean that you aren't doomed."

"What can we do, then?" Armand asked.

"You should look to the skies, you should prepare for the worst, and you should be ready to bend knee to the victor," Oliver said.

"Look to the skies?" Trim repeated in surprise. "What, ask the gods for auguries?"

"If that's what you want to call them," Oliver agreed with a cackle.

"And what of you?" Armand asked. "What will you be doing?"

"I'll be waiting," Oliver said. "I've still got a few good years in me and I believe they'll be most exciting."

"Ingam… please," Armand begged.

Ingam Oliver sighed. "I don't know everything," he said in a low voice. "What I know, I don't necessarily believe."

"You've been working with the immortals," General Trim said.

"Yes," Ingam agreed. "And I've learned humility."

General Armand snorted.

"You'd think," Oliver said in agreement, "that those who turned their backs on the gods and made themselves into metal immortals would have no humility." He cocked his head to one side for a moment, thoughtfully. "But they do. They do." He met General Armand's eyes. "You should do what you have always done: uphold your honor, your vows. But don't sell your men's lives for nothing. Or to no purpose."

Oliver tilted his head back to catch his aide's eyes. "I'm ready."

The aide knelt at his side and helped pry the old man back to his feet. The officers rose in reverence as the old man tottered back out of the room. He paused at the door and turned back to Armand. "I don't envy you."

And then he left.

"Well —" General Trim began but was cut short by a high-pitched shriek from the rigid aide who suddenly collapsed in tears, his head in his hands. "Ah, yes, it's never wise to upset an old mage, you know," Trim observed dryly.

"I want the first cavalry alerted immediately," General Armand said, rising from his chair. He glanced toward the ill-fated aide. "You're to go with them. Tell them to split into two groups — one to head to the coast and south, the other mid-country, heading toward Korin's Pass."

"Sir?" the aide asked, trying to recover from his shame and fear.

"Ingam is right," Trim said. "They're coming and they're coming one of two ways —"

"Or both ways at once," General Armand said grimly.

"Sir, but the horses!" the aide protested. "It's the middle of winter."

"Which hasn't stopped the enemy," Armand replied frostily. "Get moving, we haven't a moment to lose."

Chapter Six

Alain was the largest and the strongest, no one argued when he insisted on carrying his sister to the stables by himself.

Alva found herself walking beside the young girl, Ellen. She eyed the youngster dubiously, "So you're Annabelle?"

"Half," the girl replied. She smiled. "And we're both now a child of Ophidian and bound to keep his secrets."

"That's unlike you," Alva said. "You were always —"

"It's a secret that must be kept," Ellen said. "Your friend Annabelle would love to tell you but… there are gods listening."

"Maro could make a spell to keep them from hearing," Alva said.

"And then you would know the secret," Ellen replied. She made a face. "Father was ready to kill us all to keep this secret."

Alva's eyes grew wide in surprise.

"Ellen managed to talk him out of it," Annabelle said. "She told him that he was going to have a hard time keeping allies and children if he always went around killing them."

"But this has to do with the girl now, doesn't it?" Alva said. She was silent for a few paces, thinking hard.

"I know that look!" Annabelle said with Ellen's voice. "And you're right. For everyone else, the story must be that she was always a centaur and that she never fell."

"She stumbled," Ellen continued with the same voice in a different tone and cadence. Younger. "She fell and when she tried to recover —"

"She changed form," Alva finished. "That will work. Of course…"

"We have to succeed," Annabelle said. "And, to be honest, we haven't tried all that often."

"How many times?"

"Um, this will be the first," Annabelle admitted. There was a long silence as the two glanced at the young lad carrying his dead sister towards the stables.

"Why didn't you come back?" Alva asked to break the silence. "I missed you."

"I missed you, too, sister," Annabelle replied. Her expression twisted. "But remember that gold?" Alva nodded. "I told you it was cursed."

"I thought you were making that up!" Alva said with a snort.

"*I* thought so, too," Annabelle said. "But I was wrong."

"And?"

"The curse was that I couldn't stop thinking of him," Annabelle said in a small voice. "I went after him."

"And?"

"And I found him," Annabelle said, her voice going small.

"*And?*" Alva demanded.

"He died," Annabelle said with a sniff.

Ellen stopped their body moving. "Wait a minute! You were in *love* with Captain Ford?"

Alva glanced at the girl's form, surprised at the great difference not just in tone but body language.

"Yes, I was," Annabelle said. Sounding surprised, she added, "And all this time I thought it was the curse."

Alain turned left just in front of the stables and led them down a well-worn path to the exercise ring.

Ellen uttered a cry and ran forward as she caught sight of the mare lying on the ground, pawing and whimpering in agony. "There, there," she said. "We're here to help."

Alva, who had been taken off guard, was surprised at the girl's worried tone. Alain stopped before the girl. Peremptorily, Ellen said, "Put her in front of her, facing away but close enough that the horse can smell her."

Alain, glanced at Maro before complying.

"I'm going to need you all to leave," Ellen said as gently stroked the wide-eyed mare's neck.

"I'm staying!" Alain and Alva declared in unison.

"No," Ellen said forcibly, "you're not." When the two gave her mulish looks she added, "I can't do this if anyone is here."

"Annabelle?" Alva asked trying to find her friend in the small girl in front of her.

"Remember what Ellen said," the woman replied. "We cannot do this if we are seen."

"Very well," Alva said. She gestured for Alain to precede her. "I'll have Maro set up wards."

"No," Annabelle said firmly. "I'm quite capable of protecting myself."

Alva smiled and nodded. "Yes, I recall." She put a hand on Alain's back and urged the taller human forward. "You'll tell us when you're done?"

"You'll know when we're done," Ellen said. Annabelle took over, saying, "You should go into your realm, your majesty."

"Protection from the spell," Maro muttered from in front of the departing group. "Good thinking."

"I'm pleased you agree," Annabelle replied with a chuckle.

#

"This is Ibb's place!" Walpish cried in surprise. "The mechanical's!"

"It is," Margen agreed. "I'm sure he won't mind your staying here, as he's fled the city a while back now." His lips pursed into a thin line. "Just after the King arrested him, in fact."

"But — he's a metal man!" Walpish protested. "What are we to eat?"

"I think you'll find he has a kitchen," Margen replied. "I'm sure he's entertained humans, he would have supplies for them." Margen jerked his head toward a door and stalked through it. The two followed warily. "Yes, yes! See! And a stove and a sink, all the best conveniences!"

"There's a cold box here," Skara said, bending down to peer into a small dark object. She put her hand in. "It's still cold!"

"Probably one of that man Reedis' workings," Margen said with a loud sniff. "Fancied himself a mage."

"The one who made the first airship fly?" Walpish said with a shrug. "I'd say he most certainly was!"

"Well, perhaps in some respects," Margen allowed dubiously. He raised a finger and wagged it at the cavalryman. "I expect *you* to do better, you know."

Walpish said nothing. Glancing around the kitchen and moving toward the cupboards. He searched quickly and grunted in satisfaction. "Dried beans, oats… not much variety but we could survive for several days."

"I'll arrange for more supplies as needed," Margen said. He turned to the front door and they followed. He glanced around the room, his lips tight in a puzzled look.

"What?" Skara asked.

"Nothing," Margen said, shaking his head. "Just… well, I've not been here in recent years."

"You were a friend of Ibb's?"

"I knew of him, spoke with him," Margen said. "He made some small things for me…"

Thomas and Skara exchanged looks: it was clear there was more to the story than the mage was willing to admit.

Margen pointed to a metal barrel near the front door, frowning. "I don't recall seeing *that* before." He glanced around again, worriedly, then shrugged. "Well, I must leave you. Vistos will be at the castle shortly and he'll wonder where I am."

"Can't he track you here?" Skara asked.

"Never in his best days could mage Vistos track *me!*" Margen said with an angry snort.

"But his god —"

"That," Margen said, raising a hand in agreement, "is why I should leave immediately." He went out the door without a backward glance.

"Well," Thomas said after a moment, "I suppose we should get settled."

"I'll set the wards," Skara said, moving toward the door and gathering the magic she'd learned. She had, as an assassin, learned many tricks from mage Vistos. Those tricks she'd explained to mage Margen, worried that they might alert Vistos to her presence. Margen had agreed that some of them could do just that but had instructed her on the spells that were untraceable and generic. To her magic, Skara added her own physical protections, including pushing a doorstop under the door and placing a bell as an alarm if anyone tried to enter.

Thomas Walpish, meantime, applied the same skills to the windows and the back door. When they met again, Walpish said to her, "How about we make some tea?"

There were two bedrooms but the two, by unspoken agreement, decided to share just the one — and the one bed.

"This means nothing more than protection," Skara warned Thomas as they settled in.

"Of course," Thomas replied genially. "Two sets of ears, two sets of eyes, adds more protection."

They turned their backs to each other and closed their eyes.

#

Thomas woke when a hand touched his mouth, covering it tightly until he nodded, then releasing it. He strained his ears.

Something was moving, very quietly *inside* the front room. He reached a hand around to touch Skara's exposed arm. He tapped on it: one, two, three. She moved her hand to tap acceptance: one, two, three. Thomas clenched her arm in acknowledgement and the two took two deep steadying breaths. Skara tapped his arm: one, two —

"What are you doing here?" a voice demanded loudly from just inside the open door as lights flared to life. The two jumped to their feet, knives in their outstretched hands and

— stopped as a pair of dim blue lights met their eyes. In the doorway stood a metal immortal. *Not, however,* Thomas thought to himself in surprise, *a man.*

"Where is Ibb?" the metal... woman demanded. "And how did you get past his wards?"

#

When they had left, when Annabelle was certain that there was no one within earshot, she called out, "Terric, Avice, Aron, I call upon your guidance."

"Your father has already spoken with us," a woman's voice came from nowhere.

"He knew?" Annabelle asked in surprise.

"Well, you disappeared," Aron spoke up, chuckling.

"And, being your daughter, he guessed what you were going to do," Avice said. "*And* guessing that, he could guess the consequences."

"Besides, it's your gift," the god of Judgement added in his young boy's voice. "You are expected to use it."

"Very well," Annabelle said, bowing. "I shall try."

"No," Aron said, "you're going to *do*." Ellen Annabelle smiled at the young god's firmness. "Also, when you're done here, go north, to Ibb's. There's work you must do." And with that final word, the gods were gone.

Ellen Annabelle nodded once in acceptance and then reached out a hand toward the quivering mare.

"I can mend you," she said. "I can fix your legs and you'll roam many a year." She reached with her other hand to touch the back of Lisette's head, touching her hair and stroking it gently. "But she will be dead." She turned back to mare, catching her eyes. "Does this human mean anything to you?"

The mare whimpered and quivered.

"I have learned," Ellen Annabelle said. "I am the daughter of Ophidian and the first of my kind." Little Ellen smiled at that, adding to Annabelle: *the first of many.* Annabelle was surprised and pleased, adding in a humorous admonishment: *Let yourself grow up, first!*

"I have learned about the twin souled," Ellen continued for the mare's benefit. "There are many different ones. Most are magical and human." She stroked Lisette's hair and the mare's neck. "But some are even more amazing." She met the mare's eyes. "If you consent, I can join you. I can let you walk again and her live with you. You would be twin-souled. Would you like that?"

In answer, the mare twisted her neck and nuzzled Ellen Annabelle's hand with her lips.

"Very well," Annabelle said. "But now I must ask more of you. Lisette is dead. She cannot consent." Ellen whimpered. "You knew her, I'm told. You must choose for her, too."

The mare nickered, sounding peeved, like she was saying, *Didn't I think of that already?*

Ellen Annabelle smiled. "Sorry," Annabelle said, "I just wanted to be sure."

Ellen smiled and then her expression slipped and she twisted Lisette's still head so that it was cocked on one side. She stroked the dead girl's throat and stood. She moved so that she was standing just at the feet of the mare and the girl, halfway between the two.

"This is going to hurt," Ellen said to herself. She pulled out a small folding blade, one that she had stolen from Ophidian's horde, and ran the sharp edge hard down the base of her left thumb. It bled profusely. Ellen whimpered with pain even as she gently licked the blood off the blade and folded the blade back down. She pocketed it, still grimacing in pain and looking at the blood flowing down her fingers.

She stepped forward, daubing Lisette's neck with the fresh blood. She moved to the mare and wiped her bleeding hand against the mare's neck. And then she moved her hand toward the mare's mouth.

"Drink."

The mare's eyes were wide with the smell of the blood and her pain but she opened her mouth and her thick tongue touched Ellen's hand. Ellen nodded to her and stepped back to her original position.

She rubbed the bloody palm of her left hand on her right, raised the left hand to her mouth and sucked on the wound, gathering blood in her mouth.

Then she stretched out her hands, one toward the dead girl and the other toward the maimed mare.

"Join," she said, "and know a new life!"

Magic surged through her, shocking her. Her head snapped back even as she felt the purple flare of her magic flow from each hand, seeking her blood, joining it, making two halves into one whole.

Ellen Annabelle screamed at the top of her lungs. She fell to her knees, weak, battered by the magic backlash. She fell forward on her bloody hands and slowly found the strength to raise her head.

Lisette was lying on the ground, naked. Ellen cried out in fear and frustration.

Lisette's eyes flashed open. She moved her hands and turned her head. She was lying on the ground.

Ellen pushed herself up, trying to understand what had happened, to grapple with what her eyes were showing her.

"What happened?" Lisette asked.

"You're alive!" Ellen cried joyfully. She glanced away from Lisette's exposed skin and down... and saw where the girl's body joined the horse, fused at the waist. "You're both alive!"

"Both?"

Acknowledgements

No book gets done without a lot of outside help.

We are so grateful to Jeff Winner for his marvelous cover art work.

We'd like to thank all our first readers for their support, encouragement, and valuable feedback.

Any mistakes or omissions are, of course, all our own.

About the Authors

Award-winning authors The Winner Twins, Brit and Brianna, have been writing for over ten years, with their first novel (*The Strand*) published when they were twelve years old.

New York Times bestselling author Todd McCaffrey has written over a dozen books, including eight in the Dragonriders of Pern® universe.

http://www.twinsoulseries.com

Printed in Great Britain
by Amazon